Caroline

pay the stake • roll the dice • do the dare

#FORFEIT

with love to
Leanne

Caroline xxx

ISBN-13: 978-0-9932611-2-1

Published by Batten Publishing

Cover design by designforwriters.com

www.carolinebatten.co.uk
twitter: @daisy_fitz

for Stu
x

About the Author

Caroline lives in the Lake District with her husband, small child and two Kune Kune pigs.

She daydreams of one day owning a pair of Louboutin's and having somewhere fabulous to wear them. Until then, she'll be found plodding up a mountain in her trusty hiking boots.

#Forfeit is Caroline's debut novel. Her follow-up, *Nearly Almost Somebody* is available from Amazon.

Chapter One

#fail

It was the hashtag of her twenty-five year-old life, but from the safety of her sunglasses, Daisy Fitzgerald studied the guys warming up to bat in the village cricket finals and her smile grew. Hiking boots, cagoules and ruddy faced farmers who were overly familiar with their sheep – that's what she expected when she moved to the Lake District, not eleven pieces of calendar-worthy eye candy. Well, ten – she couldn't include Clara's fiancé, Scott, in her mental pin-up.

'Where did Scott find these blokes?' Daisy asked. 'There can't be a guy in the Miller's Arms' team who I'd rate less than a seven.'

'Check out the opposition, hot or what?' Clara replied, nodding to their left.

The nearest fielder bent down to tighten his laces and flashed more hairy bum crack than Daisy ever needed to see.

Repressing a shudder, she turned back to the batsmen. They were in a circle, attentively listening as Scott, their captain, discussed team tactics. 'What I want, is some ego boost flirting.'

'And the rest. What you need is a shag. It's been a while.'

'Six months hardly makes me a born-again virgin.'

'You sure?' Clara grinned for a second, but her face soon turned serious. 'How did it go?'

'I need a drink.'

'That good?'

As they headed towards the beer tent, Daisy shed her bank-manager appeasing jacket. 'He laughed at me, actually laughed at me. The idea of a business loan raised a smirk, but when I mentioned a mortgage, he nearly choked on his tea.'

'Did he offer you *any* money?'

'Not even an overdraft, so that's a deposit on the bakery cottage out of the window.'

'Then I have good news. Scott's found you a house share. It's with the brother of his best–'

1

'Like I want to live with some skanky bloke.' Daisy swore as she nearly turned her ankle avoiding a cowpat. Her enormous wedge heels were as utterly out of place as her skinny black trousers and vest top. All the other girls wore flip flops and chiffon blouses, the absolute only thing to wear with denim shorts that summer. 'He'll expect me to do all the cleaning while he sits around playing on his Xbox.'

'Beggars, choosers?'

An excellent point, perfectly delivered. Without the twelve hundred pounds she needed for a deposit and first month's rent, even a dingy flat in the worst part of Haverton looked beyond Daisy's means. Surely coexisting with some bloke, even a Neanderthal who watched TV with his hands down his pants, had to be better than moving back in with her parents, effectively admitting defeat at her attempt to be a self-sufficient adult.

'Anyway, he's—' Clara held up a hand, shielding the sun from her eyes as the Millers' Arms huddle broke up. 'The game's starting. Go and take some pics of Scott.'

'He's your fiancé; you take them.'

'It's your camera and I'm crap at taking photos. Please? I'll buy you a drink. Cheap white wine in a plastic glass?'

Daisy nodded, already taking off the lens cap. Of course, she'd take the photos – the last thing Scott deserved was to be photographically decapitated by his future wife. And like she'd turn down a free drink from Clara.

The Lake District hills and Gosthwaite Hall provided a picturesque backdrop as locals milled around the beer tent and tourists cooed over the homemade craft stalls. Undoubtedly, a fight or three would kick off in the village later – the young farmers already hitting the Famous Grouse in the straw-carpeted beer tent guaranteed that, but until then, this was the rural dream.

Although, why did the rural dream always seem to include cricket? It had to be the most baffling of sports. Daisy valiantly tried to keep track as she photographed Scott, but the commentator offered bugger all help as he struggled with the microphone, a can of Boddingtons and the names of the Flintoff wannabes.

A raucous cheer went up and Daisy, who hadn't a clue what was going on, zoomed in, desperately snapping Scott as he high-fived his teammate. Surely they weren't out already? The other batsman saluted the cheering crowd, raising his bat and Daisy's smile returned.

Even in the ubiquitous white trousers and polo shirt, the guy stood out – tall, rangy with a truly fabulous arse. Annoyingly, a helmet hid half his face, but what Daisy could see looked yummy. Okay, his hair was a bit blonder and longer than she preferred – an eight, maybe a nine at a push?

The commentator congratulated him on scoring the maximum thirty-six runs in just six balls bowled and a semi-jovial yell from the crowd proclaimed blondie a ringer who'd played for Lancashire. As the batsman jogged off the field, Daisy tracked him with her camera lens, relishing the challenge of keeping his bum in focus. What were the odds on him having washboard abs? Two to one? Fingers crossed for a Diet Coke break to find out.

Over by the picnic rugs where yummy mummies clutched glasses of pink fizz and kids sat munching organic burgers, he perched on the tailgate of a four-wheel drive and took off the helmet, tossing it into the boot.

Oh hello.

The guy was off the scale eye-candy. Daisy zoomed in as he languidly yawned and dragged a hand through his hair. It had to be seven levels of tragic to be perving through a camera lens, but she couldn't tear herself away, not when he stared back at her like that.

Bugger. He really was staring at her.

'Heads up!'

Daisy's rugby-obsessed big brother had shouted those two words with reliable consistency as she grew up – instinct kicked in and she scanned the sky. The cricket ball headed straight for her, as did a fifteen-stone fielder. Oh God, should she run left or right? Rooted to the spot, she watched transfixed as the fielder leapt into the air, arm outstretched to catch the ball. He missed by at least two feet.

Duck! Duck, you stupid cow and the ball will miss you.

But the fielder wouldn't. He flailed backwards and Daisy closed her eyes, preparing for the impact. Oddly, it came from her right as someone knocked her sideways. Her eyes opened in time to see a male hand pluck the ball from the air as his other arm wrapped around her waist, pulling her to him. They fell, her head bashing the baked ground and she lay gasping for the breath he'd knocked out of her, all too aware of cricket pads and some divine aftershave. Was it the fit batsman?

The fielder stood where she had moments ago, grinning. 'Nice catch.'

The batsman sat up, laughing, and tossed the ball to the fielder. 'She certainly is.' He leant over, his hair flopping into his eyes, and gave Daisy a curious smile. 'Hello.'

Thank God for sunglasses because it was the fit batsman and his smile, one that had to be sponsored by Colgate, had Daisy staring like a loon.

'Are you okay?' he asked.

Daisy nodded, but the movement made her forehead sting and she winced.

'You're bleeding,' he said, helping her to her feet. 'Come on.'

Crikey, he was well spoken. And very tall. She gazed up at him as he placed a gentle hand on her back and led her to the Land Rover where he'd sat earlier. Even in the enormous wedge heels, she had to be six inches shorter than him. What was he, six-one?

'Sit,' he said, rummaging in the boot.

Obediently, she sat on the tailgate and he joined her, placing a first aid kit between them as he peered at her forehead. Perhaps he was some delusion caused by blunt-force trauma.

'What brings you to Gosthwaite?' he asked. 'Holiday?'

She shook her head.

'But you don't live here?'

She nodded.

'In Gosthwaite, really?' His brow creased with doubt as he ripped open a sterile wipe and she gave a tiny nod. 'Oh.'

Oh what? But Daisy didn't ask out loud as he leaned in, gently cleaning her forehead. Who cared if each stroke felt like a razorblade across her forehead when his eyes appeared to be made of Cadbury's chocolate?

When he leaned closer still, applying a Steri-strip over the cut, his aftershave wafted over her, all citrus and spice, mingling with his cricket-playing pheromones. Why did she have to get knocked off her feet by someone like him? For months, the only two men she'd had any physical contact with were her dad and Scott; there was a fair chance she might drool.

'There's no bump,' he explained. 'I think you'll survive.'

Or maybe not if she didn't breathe soon. To her horror, he lifted her sunglasses, placing them on her head. Daisy barely managed to restrain her squeak, but he held her chin, looking in her left eye, then her right. A smile twitched at the corners of his mouth. Oh God, had he clocked that she'd been struck dumb, and not by his exemplary Saint John's skills?

'What are you doing?' she asked, leaning away.

'Ah, you can talk.' His smile grew. 'I'm checking your pupils.'

'Because...'

'You might have a concussion.'

'I don't.' She pushed her sunglasses back down, desperate to be back behind her comfort blanket. 'I'm fine.'

'And your camera?'

Stupidly, she turned it on, checking it wasn't broken, but the screen showed the last shot she'd taken – one of him high-fiving Scott. Could she look more like a stalker? Time to run away.

'I should let you get back to the game,' she said, 'but thanks for patching me up.'

'You're welcome.' Amusement twinkled in his eyes. 'It's not every day I get to rescue a damsel in distress.'

Taking the piss? Her embarrassment waned. 'That's right, sunshine, because you're a regular Knight-in-Shining-Cricket-Pads.'

He laughed, his cheeks taking on a definite pink tinge and he ripped the pads off. 'I'm Xander, by the way.'

'Daisy,' she said, shaking his proffered hand.

'I guessed.'

'You *guessed*?'

'Not many girls move here, so you must be Clara's friend, the soon-to-be homeless Daisy.'

Her name sounded so good when he said it. Hang on; surely he wasn't Scott's mate's brother? Her question was answered by Clara sauntering up, who wasn't bothering to hide her grin.

'I see you two have met,' Clara said. 'You okay, Xander?'

He nodded, still smiling at Daisy. 'How about you buy me a drink to say thank you for saving your ass and we can discuss the house?'

Before Daisy had chance to respond, he walked away, leaving her staring blankly at his departing arse. '*He* needs a flatmate?'

'Thought you'd like him.' Clara offered her one of the plastic cups of wine. 'Dutch courage?'

Grateful, Daisy sank half of it. 'I can't move in with him. It'd take me three wardrobe changes just to leave my bedroom. Does he have a revoltingly beautiful girlfriend?'

'Single from what I hear.'

'Good, because I could do without listening to him shagging. Do you know him?'

'Not really, but his brother, Robbie, is without doubt the sexiest man I've ever met—'

'I'm not interested in him or his brother. Sexy or otherwise.'

'I would be.' Clara sighed wistfully up at the sky. 'Sadly, Robbie's married and Scott's best mate, but his eldest daughter is in my class next term and he does the school run sometimes, so I'm hoping he'll be up for some playground flirting.'

Undoubtedly. Clara was a five-nine, leggy, Scarlet Johansson lookalike and her pencil skirts had the ratio of dads collecting their kids from Gosthwaite Primary triple the national average.

'You'll love Xander's house.' Clara hauled Daisy to her feet. 'It's the cutest cottage in the village.'

'Are you coming?' Xander called back.

Cutest cottage in the village? Daisy downed the rest of her wine. He'd rescued her from almost certain and very public humiliation, the least she could do was buy him a drink. Pity he was heading towards the Oscar's Bar and Bistro marquee where girls in high-end sunglasses were knocking back icy mojitos. The twenty quid in Daisy's purse would only cover about two drinks in that place. Hopefully, he wouldn't expect a second round.

'Jen,' Xander said to the girl behind the bar, 'please, can I have a bottle of the prosecco Marcus raves about?'

Then, to Daisy's astonishment, he reached over the bar, grabbing a bottle of vodka and two glasses. The barmaid set about opening the wine without giving Xander so much as a disapproving tut.

'Do you work here or something?' Daisy asked him.

'Better than that,' he said, pouring two shots. 'Oscar's my dad. Free booze. I wasn't really going to make you buy me a drink.'

Hurrah for small miracles. She chinked her glass against his and as the prosecco cork popped, they downed the shots.

'Shall we take the vodka too?' Xander whispered conspiratorially. 'Say yes. I've had an awful day.'

Daisy certainly hadn't anticipated afternoon binge drinking when she left the bank manager's office – hoped maybe – but who was she to argue with her potential new landlord?

Outside, once they'd settled at a picnic table, Daisy kicked off her shoes and let down her blonde curls from their bank-manager-couldn't-be-less-appeased bun. Okay, the morning had been nothing short of pointless, but sharing a bottle of prosecco with a hot piece of eye-candy totally made up for it. God, Xander was pretty, the smidgen of dark stubble just managing to take the edge of his stupidly perfect face. What was he, twenty-two or three?

'Where are you from?' he asked.

'Cheshire originally, but I've lived in Brighton for the last few years.'

'Bit of a culture shock coming here.'

'I love it here.' She smiled up at the fells. 'It's like my spiritual home.'

That induced another Colgate smile. 'Scott said Clara's selling her house and moving in with him?'

'Yes, selfish cow.' But Daisy grinned, glancing over to where Clara cheered on her man. Really, Daisy couldn't be happier for the loved up pair. 'How come you're looking for someone to share your cottage?'

'My mate, James, was staying with me, but he's moved into his own place. Are you working around here?'

She nodded. 'Teaching textiles and design to over-confident, twatty posh kids at St. Nicks. It's a private school near—'

'I know it,' Xander said, stifling his smile.

'Oh God, is that where you went?'

He saluted her. 'Twatty posh kid, at your service.'

Despite her mortification, Daisy laughed. 'It's hardly my dream job and it's only part-time, but they're actually paying me *not* to work over the summer. Mental or what?'

'That's St. Nick's for you,' he said. 'It's easily the best school I went to, and there can't be many schools who'd let you get away with having your nose pierced.'

'True.' Daisy touched her tiny diamond.

'What is your dream job?'

Shrugging, she lit a cigarette. 'I did a fashion degree because I always wanted to be a handbag designer, to work for Mulberry. I like making things.'

'Why don't you do it? Be the next Mulberry?'

Daisy laughed. 'Nice dream. What do you do?'

'Glorified rep for a six-star holiday company. We pander to the whims of rich people who want to do... well, whatever-the-hell they want to do. Last week, the clients staying at our place in Grasmere wanted to play *polo*.'

'In the Lakes? Are there any fields flat enough?'

'That...' He high-fived her. 'Is exactly what I said.'

'Sounds an awesome job though.'

'It's not. This morning, I got back from a two-week cruise around the Med. I'd been in the house ten minutes and Richard, my boss, rings me to say they want me to go back out there tonight.' He sighed, running a hand through his hair. 'I told him to piss off.'

To another two weeks cruising around the Med, why? 'Are there any jobs going?'

'You wouldn't want one. Can you imagine smiling nicely for a week on a yacht full of accountants just after tax season?'

'Actually, yes. And surely the travel makes up for it?'

'Five days in Wales with ten Premier League WAGs on a hen weekend?' He shuddered. 'The wives are always a nightmare.'

'Yes, I could see it being hell, all those rich women throwing themselves at you.'

'Novelty wore off a long time ago,' he said, flicking a beer mat at her.

'Why don't you quit and do something else instead?'

'That'd mean working for my dad. I'd rather put up with chavvy accountants.'

'You don't get on with your dad?'

'Nope.'

'What would you do if you didn't have to work? Rescue damsels-in-distress full time?'

Okay, she was taking the piss, but to her relief, the corners of his mouth flickered with a smile and he plucked a daisy from the grass.

'I'll keep that,' he said, tucking the flower into her hair, 'as a weekend treat.'

How adorable was this guy? She could so share a house with him – even if it did mean putting on mascara to make tea in the morning.

'And what do you do when you're not teaching over confident twatty posh kids?'

'Mostly, I go walking–'

'What? Like hiking?'

She nodded. 'But this week, I'm tiling Clara's bathroom.'

He mouthed, *whatever.*

'Honestly, I'm quite good.'

Slowly, he looked her over. 'It's easier to believe you're a teacher.'

Trying not to grin, Daisy leaned forwards, holding out her hands to show off her disgraceful nails. This was suspiciously close to flirting. 'Grout. Piss off.'

But he leaned closer too. 'I have another question.'

'Fire away.' Dangerously close to flirting.

'What were you doing with the camera?'

'Taking photos of Scott,' she replied, innocently.

Xander raised his eyebrows.

'Okay, okay, so I was familiarising myself with the village eye-candy.'

Xander's grin said enough, but this time when he picked a daisy and tucked it into her hair, the twinkle in his eyes had her crossing her legs. Utter, blatant flirting. And dear God, did her ego need it.

At four o'clock, while the Miller's Arms lifted the Gosthwaite Ashes, Daisy and Xander snuck off to the village. The afternoon had been a blast, but due to the prosecco and a stupid amount of vodka, he'd failed to bowl out any of the opposition, so they ran away in case Scott gave him an ear-bashing for letting the side down.

Burgers, binge-drinking and more eyelash batting were on cards, but before they headed to the pub, they popped by Xander's house so Daisy could look around. The three bed, leaded-windowed cottage dripped with English charm and she wandered in, her mouth gaping. Xander even suggested that the third bedroom could be for handbag making.

'Make yourself at home,' Xander said, kicking off his shoes. 'I need a shower. There's booze in the kitchen.'

Like she needed inviting twice. Merrily, Daisy staggered down the hall, but a photo of Xander on a mountain bike distracted her. Hurtling down a hill, his t-shirt had ridden up, revealing a snippet of trim abdomen. What must that boy look like with his kit off? Utterly beautiful she suspected.

No, no, no.

Okay, the odd bit of arm touching, hair raking and little whispered comments might've turned her cheeks pink, but the last thing she ought to be thinking about was seeing Xander with his kit off. Somewhere to live – that's what she needed, not a random shag.

She had to think of a politician... Winston Churchill could dampen a nympho's lust. As Xander ran down the stairs, she hastily grabbed the vodka. They'd do a couple of cheeky shots then go to the pub – it'd be fine.

But it wasn't fine.

Perched on a windowsill, Xander was talking on his phone. Disappointingly, he'd changed out of the rather sexy cricket gear and into jeans, but less disappointingly, his t-shirt remained in his hand. Poor Winston was beaten into submission. Daisy fell onto the ancient leather sofa, determined not to stare. She should've had a tenner on the washboard abs.

'Get off the phone, Sofia. If Richard hears you, he'll kill me.' Xander covered the mouthpiece and smiled apologetically at Daisy. 'I won't be a minute... No, I'm still here... No, you can't. I'm busy.'

Clearly, reception was as appalling in his house as it was in Clara's because Xander remained glued to the window. Daisy checked her nails, pretending not to eavesdrop, but when Sofia screamed obscenities, she couldn't hold back her giggles. The girl was bonkers.

'She's a friend of a friend...' Xander sighed, rubbing his forehead. 'She might be moving in... Yes, she is.'

Another screeched tirade poured from the phone and he closed his eyes. The guy was a superhero; he didn't deserve that crap. Impetuously, and with booze-fuelled bravado, Daisy dashed over and grabbed the phone.

'Oh, piss off, Sofia,' she said, then ended the call.

She couldn't believe she'd done it and, by the look on his face, neither could Xander. He stared at her, his brow creasing in a deep frown.

'Oh God, I'm sorry,' she said. 'It's just you've been so nice to me and she was being—'

But then he laughed. 'Christ, I could kiss you.'

After a couple more drinks, I'd probably let you.

His eyebrows shot up.

'Did I say that out loud?' she whispered.

'No, but it's written all over your face.'

'T-shirt on, please.' Ignoring his growing smile, she moved away to sit on the coffee table. Things would go somewhere they shouldn't and common sense tutted at her, telling her to leave. She didn't. Instead, she poured two shots. 'Who's Sofia?'

'She's the boss.' Xander sat on the sofa, facing her with their knees almost touching. He'd put the t-shirt on, but she couldn't miss the cheeky glint in those fabulous brown eyes. 'Well, the boss's wife.'

'You're shagging your boss's wife?'

He glanced at his feet but didn't actually blush. 'Not anymore, thanks to you.'

They downed the shots.

With a slow, deliberate finger, and without touching her skin, Xander lifted the hem of her top a few inches. What the... Daisy held her breath, but he tilted his head to peek at her navel where a couple of cherries dangled from a silver belly-bar.

'You were playing with it earlier. Pacha?' he asked and she nodded. 'You are full of surprises. What did you think you might've said out loud?'

She looked up at the ceiling, determined not to blush as she told him.

'A couple more drinks?' Grinning, he refilled their glasses.

Oh God, was she actually going to kiss him? Her heart thumped in her chest as he handed her a shot, but without dropping eye contact, they chinked their glasses together and downed the shots.

'Why are you doing this?' she asked. 'To piss off your boss's wife?'

'Maybe. Or maybe I think you're... something else.' He smiled, looking her over. 'But the real question is, why are *you* doing this, Daisy?'

Me?

To her horror, he took hold of her left hand, his thumb gently brushing over the white tan-mark on her ring finger. 'What happened?'

She lost herself in his fabulous brown eyes, her head reeling from the booze, her heart racing with the anticipation of kissing him. And just for one night, that's all she wanted to think about.

'Does it matter?'

Chapter Two

He kissed her.

Slow, assured and utterly confident, his lips moved against Daisy's and it was all she could do not to whimper. She was being kissed by the best-looking bloke in the world and dear God, did he know what he was doing. One of his hands held her face, his fingers in her hair, a thumb brushing down her neck. How did a twenty-two year-old get that good at kissing?

And how the hell could a ten second kiss, one that hadn't even strayed towards French, have her pressing her thighs together? A shiver ran through her body and she pulled back, desperate for air and a few seconds to regain control of her senses.

Clearly Clara was right; clearly, it had been a while.

But surprisingly, Xander's breathing was as ragged as her own.

'I've wanted to do that since...' A small smile played on his perfect lips. 'Well, since I knocked you over on the cricket pitch. Christ, you're hot.'

Hot? He thought she was hot? Daisy couldn't help a ridiculously pleased grin. This amazing piece of eye candy actually fancied her. Sensibly, she should leave; sensibly, she should suggest they go on a date. But when Xander kissed her again, any hint of sensible flew out of the window. A date? Bugger that. What she needed was a shag.

They clung to one another, fingers raking, tongues exploring and Daisy's hands delved under his t-shirt, wanting to feel the perfection she'd witnessed earlier. Smooth, hard and to her amusement, flinching under her touch.

'Careful,' he said, grinning between kisses.

He was ticklish? Well, that was almost too tempting, but Daisy's giggles settled into a pleased grin as Xander pulled her to her feet, his hand on her arse, pressing her against him. Was there anything about him that wasn't rock hard?

They shed his t-shirt first, but her vest top quickly followed, and Daisy dropped her head back, adoring the sensations Xander's lips created as he kissed and nibbled her neck. How long had it been since anything, anyone had made her feel so beautiful? Maybe she should've stuck to the date idea.

But his fingers tugged down the zip on her trousers and her eyes flew open. That was a side zip. He'd already clocked how to undress her. The boy wasn't date material; he was a player. Daisy suppressed her grin. Like it mattered.

His lips worked their way down her body, lingering over her stupidly responsive nipples. Seriously, how long had it been? Her head said six months, but her body screamed, *FOREVER*.

'You have,' he whispered, gently slipping her trousers down, 'the sexiest arse I've ever seen.'

She sincerely doubted it, but with his tongue flicking the Pacha cherries, she was incapable of arguing. How would it feel if he did that six inches lower?

He'd ventured a mere inch by the time her trousers were gone; a teasing three when her shoes were tossed aside. She needed more. Arching towards him, she dragged her fingers through his hair and finally, as his hands drifted back up her legs, thumbs on the insides of her thighs, he kissed her through the black lace of her knickers. Why the hell was she still wearing knickers?

Her mental complaints escalated when he stood up, but any sulkiness vanished as he brushed her hair back, his brown eyes twinkling.

'You've shrunk,' he said. 'Shortarse.'

Daisy laughed. It was a fair point. Barefoot, she was a head shorter than him. 'You'd better come down to my level then.'

She pushed him back onto the sofa, grinning as she knelt over him. The advantage of not being twenty-two like him was she had three years' more experience. Three years' experience she didn't plan to fritter by playing coy. And if he thought he could tease her, to leave her with one, over-the-pants kiss, then she had the perfect trick for him – one Clara had taught her the week they'd met at uni.

Teasingly, Daisy kissed her way down Xander's happy trail, her fingers popping open the buttons on his jeans. Tactically, she avoided touching his cock and never dropped eye contact with him as she discarded his jeans and shorts. Okay, she sneaked a peek and dear God, the boy was put together well.

Xander's eyes were dark, laced with undisguised lust as she reached for the vodka bottle, but when she knocked back a mouthful and took a second, he raised his eyebrows. Trying not to grin, she shot him a wink before moving her head lower.

'Don't you dare,' he said. 'That'll—'

Her hand closed around him and she swallowed before giving him the full effect of *Absolut* fumes and her warm mouth.

'Jesus Christ.' He sank back groaning, his hands in her hair. 'Always full of surprises...'

At eight o'clock the next morning, Daisy knelt on the floor, valiantly trying not to throw up as she fished a wedge heel from under the sofa. There were three golden rules for successful one night stands: be clear about what you like, use condoms and leave before the morning. Not exactly rocket science.

Okay, so she might've obeyed rules one and two, but she still had to get out of there before Xander woke. The last thing she needed was one of those awkward goodbyes where he politely said he'd be in touch about the room. They'd not discussed her moving in all night – clearly that was off the cards. Stupid, stupid, stupid cow. Daisy bashed her forehead against the carpet. She'd blown her last chance at living in Gosthwaite.

Quite literally.

Why hadn't she stuck to getting to know her potential housemate? Well, maybe because of a bottle of prosecco and way too many vodka shots? Her stomach churned, but she couldn't blame the booze. It was all Xander's fault. If only he'd been an arrogant arse, like every other good-looking bloke, then she'd never have shagged him. Sadly, he wasn't an arrogant arse – far from it.

The previous evening, she'd sat on the kitchen worktop while he knocked up some pasta dish and they'd chatted about everything and nothing. Why had it been so easy to play house, just for a few hours, when the last two years had been hell? And why, instead of being paranoid about her podgy stomach in the company of such physical perfection, had she let him feed her pasta?

And the shagging... Daisy's fingers half-heartedly reached for an ankle strap. Shagging Xander certainly couldn't be notched up as a sloppy, drunken fumble. Okay, it had been a while, but the final time, her favourite of the three, was nothing short of... intense. They'd held hands, fingers linked, her forehead resting against his. Totally intense. And at the end of everything, as they lay face to face, she fell asleep to the soothing rhythm of him stroking her hair.

No.

At the end of everything, it was a one night stand and Alexander Golding was suspiciously adept at unzipping a girl's pants. She yanked the strap and sat up, triumphantly brandishing the freed shoe.

'Morning.'

Oh dear God, no.

Wearing jeans and bugger all else, Xander leaned against the wall looking tired, hung-over and possibly sexier than the day before. Her gaze lingered on his perfectly taut abs. Around midnight, they'd done tequila body shots and she'd licked salt from the line going down to his navel.

'Running away?' he asked.

'Fast as I can in these shoes.'

'Ouch.'

A few years ago, she would've tottered away wearing yesterday's clothes as a badge of honour for pulling someone like Xander, but those were the days before she'd stood in a white Vera Wang frock and vowed to forsake all others.

'Look,' she said, fiddling with her shoe strap, 'you're sweet–'

'Sweet?' He folded his arms, tipping his head to one side.

'But I'm not sure what the hell I was thinking yesterday. I mean, I don't make a habit of shagging twenty-two year-old playboys I just met.'

'Rewind. I'm a twenty-two year-old *what*?' An angry scowl darkened his perfect face, and he wandered off to the kitchen, shaking his head. 'Close the door on your way out.'

Well, she'd made a pig's ear out of a Hermès scarf there. Time to run away. Daisy glanced out of the window. Sadly, Lynda from the Post Office stood down the lane, chatting with Beryl who lived opposite Clara.

As lovely as it was to live in a village where everyone knew your name, the downside was they'd also know you were married and that you'd drunkenly staggered home with the village eye candy. And if they didn't know, Lynda from the Post Office would merrily fill them in. It wasn't quite the time to run away.

Besides, she couldn't leave with him still cross; how mortifying would it be to bump into him at the grocer's?

In the kitchen, she hovered by the doorway as he filled the kettle. Mercifully, he'd put on a t-shirt, because that boy's body could undermine any girls' desire to flee the scene of a crime. After he'd switched on the kettle, he glanced at her, shaking his head again. At least his scowl had eased.

'I'm not sure which I'm more offended by, playboy or sweet.'

'Sorry, sorry, sorry.'

He dropped two teabags into an ancient yellow teapot, a smile twitching at the corners of his mouth. 'So, in the cold light of sober, you're legging it because...'

'I shouldn't have done this. I'm... married, Xander.'

'I'd worked that out.'

'To Finn Rousseau.'

Xander's eyebrows shot up and for a moment, he simply stared at her. 'The actor?'

Wearily, she nodded.

'Didn't see that coming.' Xander let out an astonished laugh. 'He went to St. Nick's too. Before my time though.'

'I may have name-dropped to get an interview.' She took a deep breath. 'Xander, you won't...'

'Kiss and tell?' He shook his head. 'Promise. Why aren't you wearing any rings?'

'We split up.'

'Getting divorced kind of split up? That's why you ran away to Clara's?'

She nodded. But until Finn signed the papers, they were still married. Hell, until a judge declared the decree absolute, they were still married. 'I feel like I've committed adultery. I suppose, technically I have.'

'You shouldn't beat yourself up.' He leant against the worktop, his hands in his pockets. 'Would you like a cup of tea before you run away as fast as you can in those shoes?'

She glanced back towards the door.

'We can discuss when you want to move in.'

'But I'm not going to. Not now.'

He stared at her as if she were perfectly bonkers. 'Why?'

'Because...' *I gave you vodka head.* 'It'd be complicated.'

'You should've thought of that before you started flirting yesterday.'

'Me? I didn't start anything, mister oh-let-me-tuck-a-flower-in-your-hair. This is *your* fault for wandering around without a t-shirt on.'

He pressed his lips together, obviously fighting a smile.

'Oh my God, you so did that on purpose, didn't you?'

He let loose the Colgate grin. 'Only because you're a shameless flirt.'

'I am not,' she argued, swatting his arm.

'See,' he said. 'Flirting.'

'I just hit you, that's not flirting.'

'Yes, it is,' he tugged her hair. 'Like pigtail pulling in the school playground.'

Trying not to laugh, Daisy mouthed, *whatever*. And hit him again.

'We can be friends, you know,' he said. 'Or are you scared you won't be able to keep your hands off me?'

A grin spread over his face and Daisy gave him the finger he so richly deserved. 'I don't have my beer goggles on now, sunshine.'

His grin grew. 'Tea?'

Oh, what the hell. It would make the grocer's situation a lot less mortifying. 'Milk, no sugar, please.'

'Breakfast?'

'If you even mention bacon and eggs, there's every chance I'll hurl.'

He laughed up at the ceiling. 'My grandad taught me it was the height of bad manners to let an overnight guest leave without feeding them. How about toast?'

She nodded and since his mood had improved a thousand fold, she couldn't resist a little piss-taking of her own. 'Do you make toast for overnight guests a lot?'

'Well, the playboy in me doesn't usually want them to stay over, but you know what a *sweet* guy I am.'

Okay, she deserved that, but instead of cringing with embarrassment, she sat on the kitchen table, swinging her feet while he pottered around, slicing doorstops of bread, grabbing jars of jam and a tub of butter.

'What'll happen with your job?' she asked. 'You won't get sacked will you?'

He shrugged. 'It won't be the first time, but they always take me back.'

'And what about Sofia. Will you apologise to her?'

Xander stopped, frowning down at her. 'The table's for food, not your arse.'

'Ohmigod, you sound like my mother...' Daisy gave her best teenager-worthy groan as she plonked herself into a chair. 'How long have you been seeing her?'

'Your mother?'

'Don't be gross. Sofia.'

'Being a bit nosy, aren't you?'

'You want to be friends; friends are allowed to be nosey.'

'Well, when you're done being nosey, it'll be my turn.'

Daisy shrugged her shoulders with a nonchalance she didn't feel. 'Whatever.'

'I've been seeing her a while.' He poured the tea, glancing at Daisy. 'But I'd say I've spent fifty percent of that time trying to get out of it. You did me a huge favour, seriously.'

'What's she like?'

'Why do you want to know?'

'I'm intrigued.' Daisy said. 'You look like you fell out of a boy band and must have girls queuing up, so why are you shagging someone else's wife when you don't really like her?'

Notably, he didn't respond. He handed her a mug of tea, and ran a hand through his hair, but his mouth remained resolutely closed.

Daisy caved, the silence too much. 'You need a haircut.'

'Christ, so now I'm a *sweet* playboy with bad hair?'

'It's not bad-bad, just... it'd look better shorter. Come on... Sofia, what does she look like?'

'She's tall, dark and incredibly beautiful.'

The antithesis of me. Daisy sipped her tea. 'Sounds awful, but there must be *something* about her you like?'

He gave a little laugh. 'Well, as you heard, she is a bit of a psycho. That's always a treat.'

'How old is she?'

'Thirty-six.'

'Ooh, a cougar.'

He grinned as he liberally buttered one of the inch-thick slices of toast. 'My turn, Mrs Rousseau?'

Bugger. 'I always thought that sounded a bit grand for me so I stuck with Fitzgerald, but fire away.'

He sat back. 'Who were Finn's text messages from?'

Daisy forced a smile. 'Which text messages?' But she knew fine well.

A month after they'd split up, Finn stupidly lost his phone and within a day, half the world had tweeted some... *wholly* inappropriate texts. She knew Xander's careful tone meant he assumed they were from another woman, and that was why Daisy was getting divorced. It's what the media had insinuated, but the truth was way more humiliating.

'They were from me,' she admitted, burying her burning cheeks in her hands.

'Seriously?' Xander said, clearly struggling not to laugh. 'From what I remember, you write a hot sext, Ms Fitzgerald.'

'Oh, bugger off,' she said, once again hiding her face in her hands. 'The entire episode was mortifying. My parents read them and everything.'

'How long have you been married?' he asked.

'Three years in November.'

'How did you meet him?'

'Guess.' He never would and she couldn't resist a smug grin. Or reaching for a slice of toast. The fantastically *bread*-like smell had her stomach grumbling.

'Pacha?'

'Cold.' She poked at the yellow block of butter. 'No Flora?'

'Butter's more natural and you're already too skinny. You did costume design on one of his films?'

'Ice cold,' Daisy said, wincing as she spread a week's supply of fat and calories onto the toast. 'Need a clue? I met him the summer I lived in Gosthwaite.'

'He was in one of those Shakespeare plays by the lake?'

'No. Doing something most people do when they come here.'

'Buying Kendal mint cake they'll never eat?'

'We were wearing boots.'

'Hiking boots?'

She nodded.

'Are you telling me, you pulled an A-list actor out *fell walking*?'

'I'd put him at B-list, but yep, I was walking up Catbells. Rock'n'roll or what?'

'What was he doing up here?'

'Visiting friends.'

Xander shook his head. 'You're wearing Prada shoes. Can't see you in boots and a cagoule.'

'I own three pairs of high-end shoes – all remnants from my previous existence as the B-list movie star's wife. I have these, a pair of Louboutin pumps and the most amazing black python Gucci knee boots, but I have four pairs of walking boots and my waterproof jacket cost more than these jeans. So there.'

Xander laughed. 'You really are something else.'

'Well, we can't all be tall, dark and incredibly beautiful, so we make up for it with character.' Daisy sat back, taking a mouthful of toast, mostly to hide her smile.

'You're also very weird.' Xander leaned forwards, resting both elbows on the table. 'Seriously, you pulled Finn Rousseau walking up a mountain?'

She couldn't talk; her taste buds were exploding. How did bread and butter taste so good? She looked from Xander to the toast, blinking in disbelief.

'What's wrong?' he asked.

'I don't know if it's the butter or the bread, but it might be the best thing I've eaten.'

And the full-on Colgate smile returned. 'I can't take credit for the butter, but the bread's mine.'

'You made it?' she mumbled through a second, divine mouthful.

'Not many *playboys* can say that, can they?'

She stuck her tongue out at him and for a minute, they simply sat, grinning at each other. Maybe she could move in. Maybe they could be friends.

'So why are you getting divorced?' he asked carefully.

Flippant. Flippant was the best response. 'Well, I was twenty-two, he was twenty-six and we got married two months after we met. You know the old saying, marry in haste...'

'Seriously, two months?'

'It seemed a good idea at the time.' Daisy's smile came more naturally than she'd expected. She usually hated talking about Finn, but Xander's easy-going manner somehow made it okay.

'And why are you really getting divorced?' his tone turned as soothing as his tea and toast. 'Did he have an affair or something?'

Before her lip wobbled, she jabbed her nails into her palms. 'I'm divorcing him for unreasonable behaviour, but can we leave it there?'

'Of course,' he said, nursing his cup. 'Sorry.'

Daisy picked at her leftover crust. 'Where did you learn to make bread?'

'My granddad.' Xander glanced around the kitchen. 'This was his house. He left it to me when he died.'

God, the boy lived a charmed life: drop-dead good looks, mummy and daddy have a chain of bars and Grandpa leaves him the quaintest cottage in the village.

'Was he a baker?' she asked.

'No, a chef.'

'So he taught you to cook?'

'The basics. I trained as a chef and worked for Anthony Errington after I left school.'

'Isn't he on TV, that chef versus chef thing?'

Xander nodded. 'And he has the Boathouse at Grasmere.'

'The Michelin-starred place? Clara went there. Scott was still starving when they left.' Daisy sipped her tea. 'But you said you were a holiday rep taking people on high end sporting adventures.'

'I am.'

'But if you hate your job and you're a chef, why don't you do that instead?'

His easy-going manner evaporated as he sat back in his chair. 'Long story.'

'I have half a mug of tea left.'

'I should've let you run away.'

'Tough. Once upon a time…'

Xander leant forwards, seemingly finding his tea fascinating. 'I can't because there's not a head chef in the county who'd give me a job.'

'Why? Can you only cook bread?'

A sheepish smile took over his face. 'Anthony's wife.'

'OMG.' Daisy stared at him. Another married cougar? 'But okay, so Anthony Errington's hardly going to want you back, but the Lakes is littered with restaurants.'

'After I left Anthony's, I spent most of my time wasted. I got sacked from four jobs in six months.'

'Why? Because you liked her?'

'I can't believe I'm telling you this.' He shook his head, a smile threatening. 'Yes, I liked Lucy Errington far more than I should have.'

'And what's *she* like?'

'Doesn't matter,' he said, hastily. 'It was ages ago.'

She'd have to Google Mrs Errington.

'Anyway, I realised I wasn't cut out to be a chef at a Michelin-starred restaurant and I couldn't face working for my dad so my brother got me a job with the holiday company. He's a director there. Will that do you?'

Quite frankly, no. Why was he shagging older women instead of supermodels his own age? Why did he work a job he hated when he'd trained as a chef? Actually, Daisy had a million other questions, but her mug was empty and her toast nothing but crumbs.

'I should go,' she said, squeezing her reluctant toes into the wedge heels. 'It's going to take a very long walk up a bloody big hill to get rid of this hangover.'

While she gathered her phone and bag, he perched on the same windowsill he had the night before, but this time Winston would win the war. There was no way she was letting herself get involved with Xander – too young, too good-looking, too much like heartbreak waiting to happen.

'Well, thanks for everything,' she said, flashing a cheery smile. But Xander didn't look up. He stared at his feet, the little muscle in his jaw twitching away. 'Your Grandad would be proud.'

He gave a half-laugh but still didn't look up. Was he cross with her again?

'I really needed yesterday,' she went on, 'and...'

His frown deepened.

'And well... that was the best... *toast* I've had in a long time.'

Finally, he raised his head, his eyes twinkling with amusement. 'Come with me to a party?'

'What?'

'It's my friend's birthday in a couple of weeks and he has a huge party. DJs, dancing... like Pacha in a Windermere mansion. You can wear one of your three pairs of high-end shoes.'

Oh good God, no. Was he expecting more of the same? This was worse than the awkward phone number conversation. 'Xander, I don't want... I'm in the middle of a hideous divorce and okay, I totally needed a...but I don't—'

'It's okay,' he said, flashing an affable smile. 'I get it, but I was thinking we could go as friends. We'll hang out, have fun and you'll see it'll be okay for you to move in.'

'Are you desperate for someone to do the cleaning while you play on your Xbox?'

'Mrs Oxford down the road does the cleaning and I don't have an Xbox.'

'Then why?'

'Because you're fun.'

'*Fun?*'

'I don't mean shagging. Friends, I promise.'

This was not the usual post-one night stand conversation. He wanted to hang out with her but not shag her... Well, that was okay. It was, wasn't it? Besides, she had to give him a chance; his cottage was a dream come true.

Oh who was she kidding? Dancing, music and a new friend to play with – that was better than a dream come true. Not quite the life she'd planned when she moved to the middle of nowhere, but her smile grew. This would be okay, absolutely okay.

'Is that a yes, Fitzgerald?'

'Yes.'

As that Colgate smile took over his face, she shot him her cheekiest wink and left.

Punishing her legs, relishing the burn, Daisy marched up the final incline, anticipating the solitary bliss she'd find on Lum Crag, her favourite mini-mountain. Aside from clubbing, fell walking was the only exercise Daisy had ever tolerated and when she'd arrived in Gosthwaite with nothing to do but obsess about Finn, she'd dug out her hiking boots. Clara said she was mental, but there was nothing better for the soul, or a hangover, than sitting on the crag after a character-building ascent.

With Café del Mar in her ears, a mug of tea by her side, Daisy lit a cigarette and smiled at the village below. Gosthwaite nestled in the Lum Valley – a less well known corner of the Lakes. It had no Peter Rabbit or lonely poet wandering around, but every day she stayed, Daisy felt a little more at home.

From up high, it looked like a daddy-long-legs – the village green providing the fat body, the little lanes and roads making long, spindly legs. The shops ran along Market Street, on one of the northern legs, while to the west, on Chapel Street, stood the terrace of little workers' cottages where Clara lived. And to the south, two hundred metres away on Mill Lane, was Xander's cottage.

Oh God, she'd had cheap and meaningless sex with an utter stranger. Daisy took a long drag on her cigarette, closing her eyes. And what level of crazy was it to say yes to the party? Pacha in a Windermere mansion with a twenty-two year-old who made his own bread. Who would buy into that bull?

Me.

Lulled into a faux sense of security by comfort blanket tea and toast, she'd totally bought into it.

Stupid girl.

And what if Finn found out? He could launch a counter attack, suing her for adultery. No way was she giving him that satisfaction. Her phone sat in her hand, a message drafted, but before she had chance to hit send, the mobile buzzed into life. Xander.

Having second thoughts yet? Don't. I'll see you a week on Sat.

X

Oh, he was good. How many girls had read what they wanted into that x? Was it a kiss or his initial?

With her soul invigorated, her hangover cured, Daisy strode down the mountain with a smile she couldn't temper. And for over twenty-four hours, she hadn't even considered Facebook-stalking Finn. It had to be a record.

Thank you. X.

Chapter Three

I'm ignoring that and picking you up at 7.

Daisy laughed at the latest text from Xander. For two weeks, they'd swapped endless messages all instigated by her daily decisions that going to the party was a really bad idea because Finn might find out. But each evening, she'd receive a text from her new friend as he sailed around the Med on a super yacht and be reassured the party would be okay, more than okay.

Besides, school had closed for the summer and she'd finished Clara's bathroom – didn't Daisy deserve a treat for all that hard work?

Absolutely.

She also deserved a kick-ass outfit.

One day, she'd be able to shop at *Net-a-Porter* again, but in the meantime, she'd settle for its second-to-none, dressmaking inspiration. After a lengthy online window shop left her with a strapless playsuit in mind, she splashed out on one and a half metres of black silk, dug out her sewing machine and put her fashion degree to good use.

The *Net-a-Porter* version had Swarovski crystals dotted around the hem of the shorts, but Daisy made do with clear glass beads – no one would know – and teamed with her black Louboutin heels, the effect was perfectly VIP clubbing.

'Xander's here– Jesus Christ.' Clara stared at her. 'You look fabulous. You two will so end up in bed again.'

'No, we won't,' Daisy replied, adding yet another layer of mascara. 'We're just friends.'

'Whatever. He said you've got the sexiest arse he's ever seen, right?'

'He was drunk, that doesn't count.' Daisy paused in front of the mirror. Why would Xander fancy her, really? Okay, she was no horse, but there were way hotter girls out there, girls who'd fall over their endless legs to get to him. Daisy stood at five foot four if asked but five foot two with her curls flattened. And her face could hardly be described as *incredibly beautiful.*

'Why else would he invite you to the party? Twenty-two year-old boys answer to the beck and call of their dicks.' Clara's eyes widened. 'Think he's after your divorce settlement fortune?'

'Ha, ha. And as if he'd need it. His cottage must be worth half a million and he's got a six month-old, top of the range Golf GTI – do you reckon his parents pay his insurance? Lucky bugger. I mean, how loaded must they be? The Oscar's Bar & Bistro empire has eleven bars around the country now.'

'I still think he fancies you.'

'Well, he knows I'd say no.'

'No, you'll get drunk and screw him again. It's better to regret something you've done...'

'...than something you haven't.' It had been their mantra throughout university, but as Daisy teased her curls, making them more enormous than usual, she met Clara's eye through the mirror. 'We're just friends. It won't happen.'

'Bet you twenty quid, you shag him tonight.'

'Bet you twenty quid, I won't. He's promised no shagging.'

'Just don't fret about HMS Rousseau if he breaks that promise.'

Daisy held up a three-finger salute. 'Brownie's honour.'

But what did the kick-ass little black playsuit get from Mr Golding? He leaned against the doorframe and shrugged.

'You'll do,' he said.

There wasn't even a cheeky wink, but mercifully he was too busy peering back at the roadside to see her disappointed pout.

'Whose is that?'

'The Mazda MX5?' Daisy glanced distractedly at her twelve year-old little black convertible with affection. Xander had gotten a haircut. 'It's mine.'

'Not exactly practical for driving around here.'

'No, and it's a bit of a step-down from the Audi TT I did have, but it's cute as, right?' Oh God, she'd told him to cut his hair and he'd cut his hair off. He'd listened to her. Was he that desperate for her to move in? Or was it... he couldn't *like* her, could he?

'Always full of surprises, Fitzgerald.' A smile flickered at the corners of his mouth as he pushed his hands into the pockets. 'Ready?'

She was right though; his hair did look better shorter. In fact, somehow everything about him looked better – a peacock blue t-shirt showed off his perfect torso, while his tan made those deep brown eyes even richer. Clearly, sailing around the Mediterranean for a week hadn't done the boy any harm.

Not that it mattered; she'd so be winning the twenty quid.

'How did the end of term party go?' Xander asked, accelerating as they left the village. 'I take it the punch got spiked?'

'Apparently, it's so customary the bursar provides the booze these days.'

For ten minutes, she regaled him with tales from the St Nick's disco, choosing to concentrate on Xander's perfect face rather than the oncoming corners. Clearly the boy could drive, but he'd overtake too close to the bends and his foot seldom met the brake.

'I got hit on by three sixth formers.' She closed her eyes as they reached eighty down a straight. 'Oh God... we're so going to die.'

Xander grinned. 'You don't trust me?'

'Not in the slightest.'

'So, these sixth formers... did you pull?'

'Ha ha.' Despite her abject terror, she swatted his arm. She'd forgotten just how much how he made her smile. 'How was the cruise?'

'Actually, good,' he said, relaxing back into his seat as he pootled behind a Volvo. 'No annoying fuckwits. They could bore you to death about golf, but they all said please, thank you and tipped very nicely. I loved your messages by the way. I'd spend the day guessing what that evening's excuse would be. *My body's a temple and I shall not succumb to the temptations of liquor*, was my particular favourite.'

'I'm so glad I provided you with some entertainment.'

'Well, the odd sext wouldn't have gone amiss.'

Sext? Had he actually said that? Daisy's cheeks flared into life, but when she glanced at him, he was trying very hard not to grin – taking the piss, yet again.

'You're too easy to wind up,' he explained.

Before Daisy had chance to chastise him, they drove over the crest of a hill, and she knew exactly how Elizabeth felt when she first saw Pemberley. A vast mansion sat in immaculate parkland, taking up a chunk of lake frontage. Pacha in a Windermere mansion... Daisy struggled to restrain her smile as they drove past a queue of eager guests waiting for burly security guys to check their tickets.

'*This* is a birthday party? Whose?' she asked.

'James Dowson-Jones.'

Daisy squealed. 'India Dowson-Jones' brother?'

'He's my best mate. Well, him and his brother, Marcus.'

'Will India be there?' *Please say, yes.*

'No idea. She's doesn't always get on with James.'

'Bugger. I'd love to meet her.'

India Dowson-Jones... expelled from Cheltenham Ladies for drugs, photographed arriving at V festival with the headline band after escaping St Nick's in a helicopter and getting pregnant at fifteen to some rock star she refused to name. Magazines regularly covered India's private school antics and Daisy had devoured every word, wishing she didn't have to go to a beyond boring state school.

It wasn't something she mentioned in her St Nick's interview, but it being India Dowson-Jones' alma mater was half the reason Daisy applied. And India's daughter, Freya, being a pupil there didn't hurt either.

After he parked in a reserved space near the house, Xander quickly glanced in the mirror, running his fingers through his inch-long hair.

'Looks good,' she said. 'I was right.'

'Feels weird.'

'Then why'd you get it done?' And why did she ask that?

But Xander pushed open his door, grinning. 'Well, it wasn't to get into your pants again, Fitzgerald.'

Oh.

Daisy pasted on a faux-smile and climbed out of the car.

'Not that I'd say no,' he added, giving her a good coat of looking at. 'You look fucking amazing.'

She didn't bother to stifle her grin. 'That's better than, you'll do.'

Giving an embarrassed laugh, he kissed the top of her head and they wandered up the steps to the main doors, ignoring the queue.

'Are we VIP?' she asked, trying to act utterly nonchalant.

'No, we're V-VIP.' He took hold of her hand and nodded to the doormen who let them in without even checking a guest list, let alone a ticket.

Inside, a Radio One DJ stood behind decks stationed halfway up the main staircase, while a couple of hundred twenty-somethings danced with their arms raised in adoration. Daisy itched to join them, her head already bobbing to the beat, her smile growing as a shirtless guy turned to her, his grin enormous. Oh God, it wasn't just him, everyone she passed looked E'ed up to their dilated eyeballs.

Daisy buried her desire to dance and dutifully followed Xander to the other side of the ridiculously large house. Even burlier security guys opened French doors and Daisy stepped out onto a terrace where waitresses circulated with trays of cocktails in the evening sunshine.

'You're in luck.' Xander pointed to their right.

India Dowson-Jones, in a slip of white silk, leant against a life-size granite lion as she chatted with a guy who had to be her brother, James. The offspring of a Greek supermodel and an English furniture billionaire, they looked like twins with their coal black curls, regal roman noses and black olive eyes, but where she radiated a relaxed, ethereal glow, he came across as demonic and thoroughly bored.

'OMG,' Daisy whispered.

'Do you have to look so awed?' Xander said, trying not to laugh. 'Why on earth are you star stuck by India Dowson-Jones?'

'Because she's the coolest person ever.'

When Xander introduced her, James barely acknowledged Daisy's existence as he started cutting lines of coke on a low glass table but, to her absolute delight, India kissed her cheeks, cooing over Daisy's playsuit and asking if she'd got it at London Fashion Week. Daisy's mouth opened, but her brain couldn't muster a single sentence über-cool enough to utter to India Dowson-Jones.

'Hello, Daisy-chain,' purred a female voice purred behind them and Daisy turned to see the only person she'd ever truly hated.

Tabitha bloody Doyle.

Daisy never held grudges, but for this posh, second-rate actress, she made an exception. The previous year, Tabitha had tried it on with Finn yet here she was, her arms open waiting for a hug, her freckled face and emerald eyes a picture of concern. Daisy remained rooted to the spot, but Tabitha, the melodramatic tart, didn't give up. She strode over and clasped her arms around Daisy.

'Oh Daisy, I thought you two were like a rock.' Her upper-class vowels were sharper than a diamond on glass. 'How can you be getting divorced?'

'Acting lessons are coming along well. You should get an Oscar for that little performance.' Daisy almost smiled as Tabitha's face fell and her eyes flickered away.

'I deserve that,' she said, taking Daisy's arm and leading her away from the others. 'I'm sorry about last year. I know it's no excuse, but my marriage to Dex was a shambles. I feel awful.'

And? What did she want, forgiving?

Tabitha glanced nervously at her hands. 'I was pretty messed up. Can you forgive me?'

Was she for real? Daisy shook her head. '*My* marriage is a shambles and *I'm* pretty messed up. For God's sake, you tried to cop off with my husband on our *wedding* anniversary. You've got some bloody nerve.'

'I know.' She gnawed the edge of her thumbnail. 'But can we do lunch, to talk?'

Do bloody lunch? 'Why? It's not like we were ever friends.'

'Please give me a chance. I always thought you seemed pretty terrific, sweetie. To be honest, you make me green with envy.'

Tabitha Doyle was jealous of *her*? Daisy blinked. Actually, the Hervé Léger dress might show off Tabitha's fabulous figure, but her usually glossy auburn hair could've done with a wash three days ago and Daisy had seen better skin on a teenager. The girl needed a bloody good scrub with a wire brush.

Mollified by the crumbling pedestal at Tabitha's feet, Daisy wavered. She wavered for two whole seconds until Tabitha obliterated any sympathy by tilting her head to one side, clearly calculating the situation as Xander wandered over, cocktails in hand.

'At least you have him to cheer you up.'

'Xander's a friend, that's all,' Daisy replied, tempted to slap the silly cow.

Tabitha gave a tinkly laugh, shaking off any suspicion with a warm smile. 'Sorry. I'm teasing. Xander's one of the loveliest people I know. Please, let's do lunch.'

And she kissed Daisy's cheek. Still reeling, Daisy stared at Tabitha's departing back, too stunned to verbalise the expletives forming in her head.

'Here you go, Fitzgerald,' Xander said, handing her a glass.

'Martini.'

Daisy gulped the drink. 'Why the hell does that silly bitch have to be here?'

'She's not that bad.'

'Oh, she is. There was this bar Finn and I used to go to in Brighton. She'd pop her evil little head in every so often and try really bloody hard to cop off with my husband.' The last time, on their anniversary, he'd looked sorely tempted. 'Have you known her long?'

'She's related to the Dowson-Jones' so she's always been around. Seriously, I know she'd stab herself in the back if it would help her career, but other than that, she's harmless.'

'Xand,' James said, sitting back and rubbing his nose. 'Rails?'

'Fitzgerald?' Xander raised his eyebrows. 'It's up to you.'

Daisy hesitated, her mouth open to say no. She shouldn't; she really, really shouldn't, but the pretty white lines lay on the table, whispering promises of chatting to India with ease, and that Tabitha wouldn't be intimidating, or annoying. Slowly, Daisy nodded and seconds later, she sat with a rolled up twenty. What the hell was she doing? As it always did in the moment just before, her heart raced, her head panicking at the idea of doing Class-A drugs, of dying, of addiction, but before she over-thought it, the two skinny lines were gone.

'You sharing, miss?' said a female voice.

Oh God, no. Daisy sat up, her hand instinctively shielding her nose. This couldn't be happening, but when she blinked, Freya Dowson-Jones stood smirking down at her. To make matters worse, she had the school bad boy, Travis McKillican, in tow. There was no way this could actually be happening.

'Freya, Travis,' James said, waving a dismissive hand, 'fuck off back to the underage playpen.'

But the insolent pair were already heading away, Freya's fingers a blur over her phone.

'Oh God,' Daisy said. 'She'll have tweeted the whole bloody school by Monday.'

'Your new friend's a *teacher*,' James asked Xander, his voice dripping with disdain, 'at St Nicks?'

Xander merely grinned and pulled Daisy to her feet. 'Come on, Fitzgerald. Let's dance.'

'*Tonight...*' With her arms raised in honour of the zeitgeist classic remixed to a one-twenty bpm bass, Daisy couldn't stop her grin. Okay, maybe it was the coke, maybe it was the cocktails, but dancing with Xander had become her new favourite thing in the whole world.

'*Than the sun...*' Xander sang back, his forehead resting against hers.

They were sweaty, grinning, loved up idiots. He was the best date – her glass never empty, be it vodka shots, cocktails or water, whatever she needed, he provided. Better still, he didn't look at another girl the whole time – which was quite extraordinary considering the number of girls stalking him.

They were legion and would gaze longingly or pout angrily, causing Daisy to mentally divide them into Has-Beens, Maybes and Never-Will-Bes. Only the coke prevented her from wilting under the animosity each and every one exuded as they looked her over with the same disdain James had.

'Alexander, who is this?' A pair of arms wrapped around her waist, pulling her back towards a tall male – another Saint Nick's old boy by the sound of him. 'Can I play with her?'

Xander shook his head, smiling and the arms dropped away. Aside from James, it was the only time that evening Xander appeared genuinely pleased to see someone. 'This is Marcus, James' brother. Daisy's my new best friend.'

'She can be mine.' Marcus blatantly eyed her up.

Laughing, Daisy returned the favour. Clearly, he'd fallen out of the same Abercrombie and Fitch advert as Xander – his snug white shirt contrasted perfectly with his mocha-brown skin and Disaronno-brown eyes. He was every bit as beautiful as his siblings, but they were Greek; he was black. How was he James and India's brother?

Marcus laughed. 'I'm their half-brother, different mothers. Don't ask.'

Daisy's cheeks burned, but Marcus' attention had already switched to a pair of matching blondes in red dresses.

'*Ciao, bella,*' he said, before putting a hand on Xander's shoulder. 'James is asking where you are. He's gone to the boathouse, bored.'

As Marcus bee-lined for the girls in red, Xander tipped his head, signalling an abrupt end to Daisy's dancing.

'It's his party. We'd better go.'

Daisy tried valiantly not to sulk as they dawdled across the lawn, holding hands and sharing a cigarette. 'How can James be bored? The music is beyond fabulous.'

'He hates parties.'

It was looking ever-more likely that she and James wouldn't be terribly good friends.

The boathouse, overhanging the edge of the lake, had been converted into a des-res – open plan with acres of glass, smooth oak and shiny steel, its impeccable, contemporary styling screamed of overpriced architects and interior designers.

'Bit of a step up from your cottage,' Daisy said, trailing her hand along the smooth slate handrail running around the edge of the deck.

'Just a bit.' Xander smiled. 'He has an Xbox.'

There was a smaller, more exclusive party going on with dozens of people milling around, most out on the floating deck. Daisy spotted several actors from Coronation Street, two footballers and the lead singer of a boy band but, sadly, no India.

On an ancient leather chesterfield, James and Tabitha sat shoulder to shoulder as he cut up yet more coke. Smiling like a pussy cat, Tabitha patted the sofa, inviting Daisy to join her. One day, she might give Tabitha a second chance, but it wouldn't be that night. Instead, Daisy offered a half-hearted smile and glanced around, looking for a distraction. Next to them was a huge pile of still wrapped gifts.

'James, why haven't you opened your birthday presents?' she asked.

'It's not really his birthday,' Xander explained, dropping onto the sofa opposite James. 'That's on New Year's Day.'

'But who needs a party on New Year's Day?' James glanced around as Marcus arrived with the matching blondes. 'There'll be nothing of any interest. You open them, Daisy.'

He managed to make it sound like an order, but whatever, because that whole *better to give than receive* concept always struck Daisy as nonsense, and she strongly suspected opening someone else's gifts would still rate higher than giving.

Sitting cross-legged on the floor, she merrily tore open the gifts. The first was a rather foul painting, but the booty contained concert tickets, DVDs, books, cufflinks and, rather oddly, a glass vase. Okay, it was pretty, but why would a man want a vase?

'This one has a letter.' She held up a page of barely legible scrawl.

James, glaring at Marcus' blondes, told her to read it out as it could be from some love sick bitch. Marcus jerked his head and the girls went out onto the floating deck.

'Happy?' Marcus sighed.

'They're fawning tarts,' James said. 'You can do so much better.'

'They're fun.' Marcus shrugged. 'You should try them.'

Did James hate women? How was he Xander's best friend and since he was, what did that say about Xander? He met her gaze and his face broke into that Colgate smile. Reassured he was nothing like James, Daisy shot him a wink then read the letter.

'*Dear Jim. What do I give a spoiled, misogynistic bastard for his birthday?* This isn't a very nice letter.' She looked at James, but he smiled, for the first time she'd seen. '*I've decided it's time to part with an old favourite of mine. If you don't like it, the Teetotum gambling ball should fetch a few grand. The game is something my gaggle of bored young things invented back in the Eighties. We had bugger all sense and too much money, but I'm sure your crowd would put us to shame.* Charming. *We all made it to Stage Three, so don't let the side down. Yours etc. Uncle Seb.*'

James leant forwards. 'Uncle Sebastian? Christ, no one's heard of him in years.'

He took the shoe box sized package and put it on the table between the two sofas. Carefully removing the paper, he revealed a heavy wooden box. The only decoration was a small silver plaque inscribed with one word: *FORFEIT.*

Intrigued to know what kind of game their counterparts had dreamed up a few decades ago, Daisy perched on the corner of the table as James took out the Teetotum gambling ball, a handmade, peach-sized, many-sided dice; so worn, so battered, it seemed ancient. Still inside the box were a handwritten card and three smaller boxes, all wooden and each with a silver label.

Stage One: £50

Stage Two: £500

Stage Three: £5,000

'I'm surprised they ever got past Stage Two,' James said, an intrigued smile taking over his face as he opened the card. '*Those who play must pay. Each player rolls the dice and takes the appropriately numbered dare card. The dares are based on the Seven Deadly Sins and*

Heavenly Virtues, testing the players' mental, physical and moral mettle. There are three stages of increasing challenges and appropriate timeframes.

Stage One: One Hour
Stage Two: One Month
Stage Three: One Year

At the end of each stage, the players vote for the winner, the person they believe completed the best dare. The winner takes the stage pot.'

'It sounds fun,' Tabitha said, draping herself over James' shoulder and kissing his ear lobe. 'Let's play, sweetie.'

'It sounds insane.' Marcus lit a cigarette, earning another scowl from his brother. 'Oh, come on, five grand to do a dare?'

Xander snuck an arm around Daisy's waist, resting his chin on her shoulder. 'And seriously, dares? We're not thirteen.'

James rolled the Teetotum ball around in his hand. 'Who's playing?'

To her utter surprise, Daisy was the first to speak. 'I'm in.'

Xander frowned at her, but she merely shrugged. She'd been paid by the school, the money was in her purse so for one night only, she wasn't Daisy Fitzgerald, crappy teacher from Cheshire – she was Daisy Fitzgerald, friend of the rich and the fabulous. Tonight, she was India Dowson-Jones.

'Okay, me too.' Xander kissed her head.

Besides, she could so do with two hundred quid; how hard could it be to win a silly dare?

Marcus dropped his money on the table. Daisy and Xander's followed.

Tabitha sulked. 'I don't have a bean on me. James, loan me?' He obliged and she picked up the Teetotum ball. 'Bagsy first go.'

She rolled a twelve. James handed her a dare card which she read and grinned. Okay, they couldn't be too bad then. Daisy rolled the Teetotum ball, praying for a pleasant dare, and when it landed on twenty-five, she smiled. Her age, surely that was fortuitous? She took the card out of the *Forfeit* box and read the dare.

Lust: Kiss another player for five minutes. Don't tell anyone what you're doing, or why.

Oh bugger.

'This is nuts,' Xander said, shaking his head as he rolled the ball.

Totally nuts, Daisy mentally replied. The dare was doable, absolutely doable, but who the hell was she going to kiss? The obvious answer was Xander.

He laughed as he read his dare card. The obvious answer, but *should* she? He'd stuck by his *no shagging* promise and hadn't been even slightly flirtatious all night, but what if he got the wrong idea? Or got pissed off because he thought she had? She couldn't ruin their *new best friend relationship*, or her chance to live in the dream cottage.

'Mine's a piece of piss,' James said, grinning.

Maybe she could kiss James. She could walk right over and just kiss him. As if he'd read her mind, he glanced at her, his face crumpling with disdain as he checked out her chest. What the hell? They might not be enormous, but her boobs were one of her better features. Clearly, she couldn't kiss him. He might tell her to piss off. That would be horrific. Not James.

'Twenty-to-one,' James said. 'One hour. Let's do it. Tab, give me your bra.'

'Not wearing one. I need a bottle of Jack and a shot glass,' Tabitha purred to James, showing him her card.

'Unlucky.' He laughed, already heading for an open cabinet crammed with spirits. 'It says *whisky*, spelled without an *e*. How about a sixteen year-old single malt?'

Tabitha's smug smile faded. 'But you know I can't stand scotch fucking whisky.'

'Aren't you doing your dare then?' Daisy asked sweetly. Wasn't payback a bitch?

Tabitha snatched a bottle of Jura from James. Game on. Daisy grinned, appreciating Tabitha manning up, but she couldn't help wishing that knocking back ten shots of top-quality whisky were her dare. It'd be a lot easier than kissing one of the other players for five minutes.

What about Marcus? He grabbed a guitar that stood propped beside the piano – because what respectable bachelor pad didn't have a Steinway to hand? Casually, he sauntered up to a pretty girl with a dark, elfin cut. Any conversation she was having with her friends dried up as Marcus took her hand, kissing it briefly, before bursting into song. And not just any song. He'd chosen One Direction's *Little Things*.

Daisy would've giggled at the cheesiness, but Marcus knew the words and he could play the chords. Better still, despite being off-key and horrifically flat, he delivered the song as if he were Harry Styles himself. The pixie girl never dropped eye contact with him.

He'd so pulled. Daisy wouldn't be kissing him.

Which left Xander.

He'd settled back on the sofa with his eyes closed. Was his dare to go to sleep?

'If I die, I leave everything to my cat,' Tabitha said, lifting the first of the ten shot glasses James had lined up on the table.

It had to be Xander, but what if it all went wrong? God, she was acting like a twelve year-old over a stupid kiss-dare. Wasn't that the point of a dare, to do something humiliating? And she had to do it – no way would she flake out in front of Tabitha bloody Doyle. Then Daisy had a brilliant idea; how to make it a lot less messy – she'd cheat.

Buoyed up on cocktails, coke and escapism, she sat astride a somewhat stunned Xander.

'Help me?' she whispered, surreptitiously showing him the card.

Tabitha groaned as she sank number four. She was so going to be sick, but Daisy's stomach churned too. What if he said no?

He didn't.

Clearly fighting a smile, he gave a slow nod and Daisy stared at him, her nerves building. Oh God, she was about to kiss Xander. He raised his eyebrows, his eyes twinkling as he waited. She'd have to start this – it was her dare, not his. Tentatively, she brushed her lips against his, testing the water before she set the timer on her phone.

Five minutes, easy-peasy.

It all started harmlessly – even a little mechanical, but after the first minute, Xander's hands moved up her back, his thumbs caressing her skin through the thin silk and shivers surged over her. He'd done the same on the one night stand, just before he'd undone her bra.

And I want him to do it again.

What the hell was that drumming noise inside her head? Was that her heartbeat? She wanted to pull away, desperate to breathe, to take control of her head, but her hands still held his face and his Bulgari aftershave still sent her senses reeling.

Slow, sweet, teasing, this was no teenage kiss-dare. Xander's hands had moved up her bare shoulders, his fingers doing wicked things to her neck. How long had they been kissing for, three minutes, maybe four? Why wasn't it thirty seconds? Then she'd have four and half minutes still to go.

Tequila body shots. Oh to lick salt off his abs again.

'Supposed to be just friends,' Tabitha slurred behind her. 'That doesn't look like friends.'

Daisy's phone beeped. The five minutes were up, but no way was she stopping.

I want more.

'I bet it's her dare,' James replied.

A dare.

She dragged her lips from Xander's, looking down, watching his chest rising and falling. It was just a stupid dare. How had she got so carried away? How had they got so carried away? Oh God, what if he wasn't carried away? What if he thought she were some desperate cow, throwing herself at him? Mortified, she closed her eyes, her head dropping. How could she laugh it off, put on her bravest of brave faces when she'd made such a fool of herself?

Xander dropped a kiss on her neck.

Chapter Four

His lips were still on her neck, his thumb brushing over her collarbone.

Warily, Daisy looked up, but Xander's eyes twinkled back at her. OMG, it wasn't just a stupid dare. Her smile grew. As did Xander's. He liked her.

Before she lost her nerve, she kissed him again and to her relief, he pulled her closer, teasingly biting at her bottom lip. She was so going to owe Clara twenty quid.

'I guess this proves my point,' she said between kisses. 'It really would be complicated.'

With his lips still against hers, he smiled and gave the tiniest nod. Oh why were they in James' house, why couldn't they be somewhere more private? Like her bed. There was no doubt that Xander was as up for it as her.

'Can we get out of here?' she whispered. 'Back to the party... or something?'

He opened his mouth, but quickly closed it again, scowling.

'What?' Had she pissed him off? 'I'm sorry, I just—'

He shook his head, smiling before glancing around as if he were looking for the right words. Instead, he picked up her phone and typed a message.

Can't leave. Not yet. Still playing game.

Okay, but why... She laughed, getting it. 'You can't talk?'

He shook his head.

'Your dare?'

He nodded.

'But if you talk, you lose and we can get out of here.'

No, he typed. *Want to win.*

'More than party with me?'

He nodded, but Daisy had other ideas. Mischievously, she wriggled closer, pressing against him, adoring how he stifled a groan and looked up at the ceiling.

Stop it.

'No. If you talk, you lose and I have more chance of winning the pot.'

Do a deal? If I win, or you win, we share and get money back.

Her smile grew more coquettish. 'I'm in, but what on earth will we do in the meantime?'

Xander flashed that Colgate smile and with his hands holding her face, he kissed her, making her truly grateful she wasn't standing up. How could she when her entire body appeared to be made of spaghetti?

Tequila slammers, top-up rails, and long, indulgent kisses filled the remaining minutes of the game. They watched with increasing amusement as Marcus' serenading not only had his little elfin-cut pixie enraptured, but his tuneless rendition of Christina Aguilera's *Beautiful* raised an emotional tear from at least two of the misty-eyed fangirls crowded around him.

'I'm going to be sick.' Tabitha ran off towards the toilet, her hand clasped over her mouth.

'Marcus' singing isn't that bad,' Daisy said, desperately trying not to laugh.

Xander playfully slapped her arse.

'One-forty-one,' James said, walking back in from the deck. 'Time's up.'

'Thank Christ for that.' Xander sat on the dining table, his arms raised in a victory salute. 'No talking for an hour. Job done, but Jesus it was hard.'

Daisy plucked the card from his pocket. *Kindness. If you don't have anything nice to say, don't say anything at all. For an hour, no talking.*

'Ten bras, given up.' James dropped his booty on the table, giving it a disparaging sneer. 'Though most were more willing to drop their knickers.'

He really didn't like women.

'I'm done.' Marcus headed for the door, guitar in one hand, elfin girl like putty in the other. He didn't even bother to leave his card.

'Well, I did my dare,' Daisy said, tossing her card on top of the bras, 'about four times, so I should totally win.'

'You'd totally get my vote too.' Xander's arms circled around her, pulling her to stand between his legs.

James sighed, glancing from Xander to the bathroom door

hiding Tabitha. 'Fuck, I'd better go check on her. *Mi casa...*'

The boys bumped fists, but James didn't offer Daisy even the most fleeting of smiles. What a guy. But still, this was a three-bed des-res... She edged a little closer to Xander.

'What did he mean, *mi casa?*' she asked. 'Can you, like... stay here?'

Xander pushed her hair back. 'I can, like stay here. *We* can like stay here.'

So owing Clara twenty quid in the morning.

'But there's a rule. No shagging, Fitzgerald.'

What?

'I promised you there wouldn't be any.'

He was sticking to that?

'Now,' he said, 'how do you fancy getting absolutely wasted instead?'

She dropped her head back, laughing. 'Wasted works for me, sunshine.'

Thank you, *Forfeit*.

The night disappeared in a blur of unrestrained snogging and dancing until the rising sun ruined the club atmosphere. In the soft morning light, Daisy pulled on her denim jacket and gazed up at her Knight-In-Shining-Cricket-Pads. They'd been inseparable the whole night. He'd rubbed her aching toes; she'd massaged his head. They'd shared joints and talked utter crap. He'd proclaimed her the most awesome new best friend he'd ever had and oddly, she'd started to believe him.

'What now?' Daisy asked. 'It's only eight o'clock. What do we do until we're fit to drive home?'

He held the latest joint to her lips. 'We chill out in the lap of luxury.'

'Boat house?'

'Boat house.'

They wandered across the manicured lawns, Daisy barefoot, her fingers firmly linked with Xander's. The arrogance of the coke had long since worn off, leaving her with an emptiness, a comedown she only wanted to share with one person: Xander.

The floating deck surrounding three quarters of James' house stood deserted, with no evidence of a party having ever taken place – all Henry, the butler's, handiwork apparently. But of course

James would have a butler. What self-respecting twenty-two year-old, billionaire's son wouldn't? Oh how the other half lived.

Daisy curled up into a wicker armchair and despite the morning sun shining down from a cloudless sky, she shivered. Within a minute, Henry appeared with a blanket over one arm and a tray laden with two cups of espresso, Xander's favourite apparently.

'Breakfast?' Henry offered.

Xander ordered bacon and scrambled egg, but the thought turned Daisy's stomach.

'Bloody Mary?' she asked hopefully.

Xander shook his head, smiling at her. 'Could you get Daisy some toast and fresh fruit, please, Henry?'

She scowled as Henry walked away. 'I don't feel like eating.'

'If there's one thing I'd change about you, it's that you'd stop fretting over what you eat. You look like one of those size zero idiots.' Xander's smile never faltered. 'Sexy as fuck, but please eat something.'

'Charming.' Yet instead of sulking, she found herself smiling back. 'Really, there's just the one thing you'd change about me?'

'I'm sure I'll come up with more, given time.'

Given time? She lit a cigarette, desperate not to grin. He wanted more? Oh, she was under no illusion she was on the rebound, pinging from the guy who broke her heart, but if you had to ping to someone, could there be a better someone than the Knight-In-Shining-Cricket-Pads?

Stupidly content, she settled back, snuggled under her blanket. 'It's fair to say I haven't come down anywhere like this before.'

'Class A drugs a habit, Little Miss Pacha?'

'At uni, Clara and I used to work summers at whatever super-club would have us. Gatecrasher, Ministry of Sound, Cream. She was a podium dancer at Pacha Ibiza one summer.'

'Clara, the primary school teacher, really?' Xander's eyebrows headed towards the clear blue sky. 'I hear she's moving in with Scott next week.'

'I'll miss her.'

'But she hasn't accepted an offer on the cottage?'

Daisy shook her head. 'Not homeless yet.'

'You know the answer.'

What did he really want with her? Because as perfect as he was for her emotionally battered ego, she'd seen those girls, the Has-beens, they were devastated and he could barely remember their names. The last thing she needed was to end up like them.

'What are you going to do?' he asked, twirling his coffee cup.

'When someone's mental enough to give me a mortgage, I'll buy somewhere, but I'll find something to rent for now. There's nothing in Gosthwaite I can afford though.'

'There's always something. What would you buy, one of the fancy Georgian townhouses around the green?'

'In an ideal world?' She rested her chin on her hand, elbow on the table. 'Something away from prying eyes. Something that needs a ton of work. Clara's cottage was a mess when she bought it. I came for the summer and did most of the work, organised the builders. I loved it.'

'You're insane.'

'Yes, well,' she said, smiling. 'I like tiling bathrooms.'

He mouthed, *whatever*, earning himself a playful kick to the shin. 'What else?'

'I'd love a little garden.'

'To grow your own mint for mojitos?'

And a second swift kick. 'And a dog.'

'One of those stupid yappy things you carry around in a Chanel handbag?'

'You and I could fall out, sunshine.'

He laughed. 'How about a Lab or a collie?'

'No, a mongrel, something from the RSPCA, something that needs rescuing.'

'What, like you?'

Is that how he saw her? Daisy nodded. 'Yeah, like me.'

Still smiling, Xander leaned forwards, brushing a wayward curl off her face. 'You're going to be fine, Fitzgerald.'

The best rebound buddy in the world.

By the time the sun perched high in the sky, they'd devoured breakfast and the Sunday papers, but when fatigue crept in, they moved onto a vast rattan sun lounger, stretching out their aching muscles. Almost instantly, they'd fallen asleep, side by side, but when she woke, Daisy lay on top of Xander, their legs inappropriately tangled. How the hell had they ended up like that? Trying not to giggle, she moved to sit up, but Xander held her a little tighter.

'No, you don't,' he whispered. 'I was enjoying that.'

'That's what I was afraid of.' The last thing she wanted was to break the comfort of her body against his, but her parched mouth demanded otherwise. As if he'd read her mind, Xander handed her a bottle of ice-cold water and while she drank, he propped himself up on one elbow, smiling at her.

'What?' she asked.

'This has been the best night of my life.'

'It *has* been amazing. Thank you for bringing me.'

'Thank you for coming.'

'Why are you so nice to me?'

'Because you've got the sexiest arse I've ever seen.'

'Ha, ha, but if it were just that, you'd have shagged me senseless last night.'

He laughed. 'I like being nice to you.'

'Because you like rescuing the damsel in distress?'

'Maybe.' He twirled one of her curls around his finger. 'Daze... do you still love him?'

If only she had had sunglasses to hide behind. 'Does it matter?'

He dropped a brief kiss on top of her head before smiling amiably as Marcus arrived with Lexi, the girl he'd serenaded. Wearing nothing more than red lace pants and a t-shirt of Marcus' she casually sat at the table, asking Daisy if the silk playsuit had come from the Manchester Harvey Nicks'. Sadly, any hope of pleasant conversation died when James demanded everyone's attention by slamming shut the French doors.

'You can smell the fags upstairs,' he said, sinking into the chair beside Xander.

Daisy's apologetic smile faded when James' coke-glazed, black eyes fixed on her; he clearly didn't like her. But after he spent ten minutes giving a hideously disparaging account of the two hours he'd spent with Anna and Hannah, the matching blondes Marcus had brought to the boathouse, Daisy couldn't care less; she really didn't like James.

'In the end,' James said, running his fingers through his curls, 'I left them to it and jumped in Tab's bed.'

'Anna, Hannah *and* Tabitha?' Xander asked, flashing a grin. 'Happy not-Birthday.'

They were all utter playboys – Xander included. She'd run away to the Lakes for a quiet life, a little soul searching amongst the peaks and tarns, so how the hell had she ended up coming down surrounded by a bunch of overconfident, twatty rich kids?

James gave Xander the finger. 'I watched TV in Tabitha's bed. She's been throwing up for hours.'

Daisy couldn't help a smug giggle, but when Marcus gave her a curious frown, she stifled her amusement. The last thing she wanted to do was piss off Marcus. Aside from India, he was the only one of Xander's friends who'd made Daisy feel remotely welcome.

'Beer?' James asked Xander.

'No, thanks,' he replied. 'I'm driving Daisy back later.'

James treated her to yet another disdainful once-over. 'Can't *Miss Daisy* drive herself?'

Oh, like she'd never heard that one.

'Pack it in, James,' Xander said, his voice low.

James' return mumble was inaudible, but from his petulant arm folding, he may as well have spat, *she started it*. Daisy lit a cigarette, clicking her heels together three times.

'How is it,' Tabitha asked, her crystal-tipped voice ringing out as she stepped onto the deck, 'that everyone else managed to score thanks to doing their dares...' She raised her eyebrows to Daisy. 'While I've been through hell?'

'Tell you what, Tab,' Marcus said. 'I vote you keep the Forfeit pot. You deserve it.'

'Too bloody right,' she replied. 'I've never felt so ill.' She gave Daisy a perfectly pleasant smile, but her meaning was clear – *just friends, really?*

Okay, enough. Daisy stubbed out her barely smoked cigarette and looked up at Xander. *I want to go home*, she mouthed. Letting out an enormous sigh, he nodded, clearly disappointed.

The drive home felt interminable, all the loved up connection of earlier sucked away. Daisy needed him to hug her, to kiss her, to make her feel like a beautiful princess again. She needed to see him smile. She needed *him*.

But what if he wasn't interested? What if now the drugs had worn off–

No.

She jammed her nails into her palms, shocking her brain into a reboot. This was the coke. Drugs did horrible, negative things to her head. Why didn't she ever learn? Oh God, but it'd be a zillion times worse if Xander dumped her at Clara's with a polite kiss on the cheek.

As they drove into the village, she willed herself to speak up, to make this better.

'Xand...' But what the hell could she say?

'Sorry,' he said, quietly.

'Sorry?' *Because you're about to give me the elbow.*

'James is an arse at times. And Tabitha...' He glanced at her. 'I'd understand if you want me to drop you–'

'No.' She barely restrained her relief. 'I don't want that.'

His shoulders relaxed. 'Will Clara be in?'

She nodded.

'My place?'

She nodded again.

'We can close the curtains and hide from the world,' he said.

'Watch crappy films?'

'Hang out all day on the sofa.'

Oh, that sofa. She crossed her legs, her cheeks burning. Hang on, did he mean... The muscle in his jaw twitched as he stared resolutely at the road ahead and her heart rate rose with every passing second. They were going to have comedown sex. They could kiss, hug, get naked. The sensations would be incredible; the comfort all-encompassing.

'Let me grab some clothes,' she said as he pulled up two doors down from Clara's. 'I don't fancy tottering away from your house in this get-up.'

'Be quick,' he said.

As a bloody flash. Struggling not to grin, she unclipped her seatbelt, but from the car in front of them, a pair of azure blue eyes stared back.

'Oh God, no.' No comedown ever made her feel quite so sick.

'Daze?'

She nodded towards the black Mercedes. 'It's Finn.'

'Why's he here?'

'I don't know.'

She wasn't entirely sure the words had come out. She wasn't entirely sure she was still breathing, or if her heart were still beating. Oh, she may have told herself she wanted a fresh start, a clean break, but how many times had she day-dreamed of this moment, the moment he'd turn up, apologising, begging her to come home?

At least once, but often several times a day.

Yet, she'd never imagined her hair would look ten levels of *just shagged* and she'd be sitting in her rebound buddy's car.

'Don't get out,' Xander said. 'We'll go straight to mine.'

'I have to see him.' Squeezing her aching feet back into the Louboutin's, she turned to Xander. 'Thank you for—'

'If you think I'm leaving you here on your own—'

'I'm fine.'

'You're coming down. You don't need this.'

Daisy kissed his cheek, then as elegantly as she could manage with less energy than a non-Duracell bunny, she climbed out of the car and strode towards Clara's cottage. Finn met her on the pavement while Clara appeared in the doorway to the cottage.

High noon on Chapel Street.

Finn's dark hair was shorter than she'd last seen it, still messy on top though – just as she loved it. His *Nirvana* t-shirt was new. Sleeveless, it showed off his tattoos, most notably, the one winding around his right bicep, a daisy-chain, a dedication to her. Sadly, he'd hidden his mesmerising blue eyes behind aviator sunglasses, but that was probably for the best. The day they'd met, he'd lifted his sunglasses and she knew she'd love him forever.

'What are you doing here?' she asked, her voice wavering.

'I was in the area, walking with some friends.'

Which friends? But she wouldn't ask out loud. Instead, she lit a cigarette, giving her hands something to do. Her nose itched, but she daren't rub it. He'd know.

'Who's the pretty boy?' Finn glanced to Xander's car.

'He lives in the village. A friend.'

'A staggering home in yesterday's heels kind of friend?'

Daisy caved, rubbing her nose.

'Old habits?' he said.

'It's got bugger all to do with you, Finn.'

He found the cobbles under his shoes suddenly fascinating. 'No, you're right. I came to say...'

Sorry? You've made a mistake. You love me. You want me back.

It was what she wanted, what she'd always wanted. That still true, wasn't it? She glanced behind her. Did she want a fresh start or a second chance? Xander still sat in the car, leaning on the steering wheel, his perfect face marred by a scowl.

'You came to say what?' she asked Finn.

'I thought maybe we could talk, but...' He frowned at Xander. 'Is he why?'

'No,' Daisy snapped. 'I met him two weeks ago.'

After apologising with a tip of his head, Finn took a large manila envelope from his car. The street blurred around her. Xander or no Xander, Finn wasn't there to get her back. He couldn't give a damn even if she were shagging Xander. He was returning the divorce papers.

No, no, no.

'I'm sorry, Dee,' he said, giving a rueful smile. 'I should've returned these ages ago. I was being selfish, childish.'

She took the paperwork, her knees shaking, barely holding her up, but then Xander was standing beside her, propping up her shattered self-esteem. Finn wanted a divorce.

But I don't. I never did. I want you back. I just want you to say sorry.

'...you know she'd be here?' Xander was asking.

'...Facebook,' Finn replied. '...supposed to be at that party. Small world.'

Facebook? Daisy took a long drag on her cigarette. 'And who posted the photos? Let me guess, Tabitha?'

She expected Finn to drag a hand over his head, clutching at his hair – his standard *are you bringing up that again reaction* – but he sat on his car bonnet, his face relaxing into an easy-going smile. He really didn't give a crap.

'Look, Dee, the other thing I wanted to tell you... I'm moving to New York.'

Daisy suppressed her desire to scream. They'd daydreamed endlessly about moving there. 'Broadway?'

'Romeo.' His pride-filled grin only amplified her desolation. His dreams were falling into place, but he was leaving her at the roadside. In a vain effort to hide her pain, she stepped forwards and wrapped her arms around his neck.

'Break a leg,' she said, closing her eyes as she struggled not to cry.

'Thank you,' he whispered into her hair. 'You were right. We need to end this, Dee.'

No, I wasn't right. I was wrong. Please don't do this. 'Thank you for signing the papers, but can you go now?'

He kissed her cheek and as he shook Xander's hand, Daisy stared at her feet, teetering at the edge of a hole threatening to engulf her. The love of her stupid life was moving on. There'd be no more daydreaming, what was the point? He simply didn't want her any more. As tears welled up, she dug her nails into her palms, forcing a pleasant smile.

He'd left her.

'Get some orange juice,' Finn called as he climbed back into his car. 'You look like hell, Dee.'

As his car disappeared down the lane, Daisy flicked her cigarette butt into the road, wanting to kick something, hit something, but she barely had the energy left to stand. Xander pulled her to him, wrapping his arms around her, kissing the top of her head. So warm, so safe, why couldn't she stay there forever? Despite jamming her nails into her palms, tears welled up and she reluctantly pulled away. This was over.

'Xander... I can't see you anymore.'

'Why?' The muscle twitching in his jaw undermined his nonchalant tone.

'Because half of me wants to drag you inside and lock you in my bedroom for two days.'

'Sounds like a fucking good reason to keep seeing me. Let's go.'

'No.'

'Why?'

'Because the other half of me... I do love him and you're not him.'

Silence hung between them until eventually, he sighed. 'I take it you don't want a divorce?'

Daisy shook her head. 'He's the love of my life.'

'Don't do this to yourself. Or us. We can still be friends.'

'I don't think we can.'

'You need friends.'

'I'm not ready for a friend like you.'

'Daisy–'

'Look, you're–'

'If you pull that *sweet* crap on me again, I'll drag *you* into the house and lock you in your bedroom for two days.'

'No, you fucking won't.' She backed off, wrapping her arms around herself.

Xander blinked, clearly shocked. 'It was a joke, Daze.'

'Not a funny one.'

'Sorry.' He glanced towards where Finn's car had disappeared. 'What did he–'

'You should go.'

But he made no effort to leave. 'I'm going to Italy for a week or so, climbing in the Dolomites. I'll come round when I get back.'

'No.'

'I'll worry.'

'I'll be fine.'

'You're not pushing me away, Fitzgerald.'

'Yes, I am.' After a final kiss on his fabulous lips, she darted into the cottage and stood with Clara, watching as he reluctantly climbed into his Golf.

'I tried ringing you,' Clara said, 'to warn you the HMS was here.'

'Phone died hours ago.' Daisy tossed the envelope onto the windowsill. 'He finally signed the papers. No contest.'

'Hoo-bloody-rah. But why have you sent Xander away?'

He drove off, his face as desolate as her heart and Daisy went to the kitchen, in desperate need of a drink. She cracked open a bottle of Stella and drained half of it in one hit.

'What are you doing?' Clara asked.

'What I do best.' Daisy sighed. 'Substituting booze for him.'

'Which him?'

'Finn of course.'

Clara raised her eyebrows. 'And Xander?'

'What about him? He's a bloody playboy for God's sake, and you should meet his mates. I've told him I don't want to see him anymore.'

'Why? He's fit as and a massive step up from that twat you're finally divorcing.'

'Not today, Clar.' *I love Finn.* 'By the way, you owe me twenty quid.'

'I'll give you forty if you get your arse to Xander's.'

As much as she needed the cash, Daisy shook her head. 'I'm not ready to rebound.'

Chapter Five

Finn smiled at her from the magazine she'd propped on the worktop. Despite her raging hangover and midday being over two hours away, Daisy poured a hefty vodka and tonic. August 2nd was not a day she planned to get through sober.

'Happy birthday, baby. I miss you.'

The first of the day's tears fell down her cheeks as she toasted him, but they wouldn't be the last and she knocked back several gulps of VAT, relaxing into the familiar buzz.

In the days after Finn's visit, Daisy drowned in misery. To begin with, she drank most nights, but steadily it became every night and most afternoons. Then, after *Heat* magazine showed Finn hand-in-hand with Brittany Carle, the Hollywood starlet playing his *Juliet*, the wine gave way to vodka.

The manila envelope still sat on the kitchen worktop, still waiting to be posted to her solicitor. But posting it meant ending her marriage, like it wasn't already over. Move on, Clara kept badgering her, and talk to Xander.

The Knight-in-Shining-Cricket-Pads called a few times from Italy and sent several texts, but of course, Daisy ignored his calls and deleted any messages without reading them. Maybe if she hadn't gone out with Xander, Finn would've returned the paperwork unsigned, begging for a second chance. Maybe that's why he'd come to see her, but instead, he'd witnessed her staggering home in yesterday clothes.

Xander might be fabulous, but he wasn't Finn; he never could be, so she only spoke to Clara and her parents, the latter begging her to stay with them, or let them stay with her. Daisy refused, saying she was fine.

She was anything but.

The previous week, a worried Clara moved out. She called twice a day and came round when she could, but Daisy missed her. They were supposed to be meeting at one o'clock to see some flats for rent, but it'd never happen. Daisy fully intended to be in a booze-induced coma before then.

By lunchtime, she sat perched in the window, sipping her third vodka as she watched the world shuffle by. If she moved her head, the room swayed so she tried to stay absolutely still, only moving to drop cigarette butts into an empty wine bottle. She'd been like that for over an hour when she noticed the car outside and Xander stood beside it. She blinked and he'd gone, but after she'd knocked back her drink, he was crouching beside her.

'Daisy?' He took her empty glass, sniffing it.

'He's twenty-nine today and that cow is his present,' she said, showing him the photo of Finn and Brittany caught on the Kiss Cam at a New York Mets game.

Xander pushed her hair off her face, swearing, and not under his breath. 'This is stopping, right now. Stand up.'

She tried, but the world shifted sideways and she grabbed Xander's shoulders, the window frame, anything, to stay upright. The world shifted more as he picked her up, carrying her upstairs. Did he think he could take her to bed? He had some nerve.

'Christ, Daisy, he's not worth killing yourself over. No one is.'

Her mouth didn't work. She was in the bath, but there wasn't any water? She opened her mouth to point out his schoolboy error, but ice-cold water came raining down, hitting her skin like hailstones. Daisy screamed, trying to get out, but she fell back, or maybe Xander pushed her, and she stayed, crumpled in the bath with the freezing water dowsing her soul.

'Stop it.' The words were barely audible above the shower, but finally she could think, she could focus, she could talk. 'Xander, stop it.'

He turned the water off. 'Better?'

'You bastard.' She stared at her soaking jeans.

'Obviously better. Time for a real shower?'

He helped her stand, but the room swirled and her stomach churned. Daisy staggered out of the bath, barely making it to the toilet before she threw up. She threw up until there wasn't anything left in the world to throw up and as fresh tears flowed, Xander wrapped her in a towel, wiping her face as he cradled her. Oh God, her life was a disaster, but she didn't have the energy to make it better. She let Xander rock her like a baby until her sobs calmed to shuddering breaths.

'Why are you letting him do this to you?' he asked quietly.

'Because I love him.' She was pathetic. 'I've loved him since the day I met him and I don't know how to stop.' Horrifically pathetic.

But the Knight-in-Shining-Cricket Pads held her a little tighter and kissed her head. 'We've all been there, Daze.'

Utterly, tragically pathetic.

'I still don't believe you tiled this bathroom,' he whispered, looking at the white brick-effect tiles. She could understand why. She'd done a bloody professional job. 'You okay?'

She nodded, clambering to her feet – a little unsteady but just about clear headed.

'Shower,' he said, heading for the door. 'Hair washed, face scrubbed and come out pink, or so help me God, I'll do it for you.'

She believed him.

In the shower, Daisy longed for the scalding hot water to wash more than her bird's nest hair. She scoured her skin until it turned cerise and the shame eased – she even bothered to shave her legs.

Finally, dressed in denim shorts and a university-old Arran sweater her mum knit, Daisy stared in the mirror, repulsed by the gaunt girl who stared back. When had she eaten last? As utter panic took over, she ran from her reflection, looking for reassurance, comfort, something, anything from her Knight-in-Shining-Cricket-Pads. He was in the living room, staring at the ceiling, looking as bewildered as she felt.

'I can't remember last week,' she whispered as she sat on the sofa, not daring to look him in the eye in case she saw pity or loathing.

'I can imagine. I've seen the bottles.' He dragged his hands through his hair, sighing.

Too weary to fight the shame, Daisy curled up and her yawn prompted Xander to cover her in a throw. Gently, he tucked the blanket around her and feeling safer than she ever remembered, Daisy bravely looked up. There was no pity or loathing in those brown eyes, just concern. Why did he care?

'I need to go out.' He crouched beside her. 'Why don't you sleep? There's no alcohol left in the house, but... will you be okay till I get back?'

She nodded, closing her eyes as he kissed her head.

But please, come back soon.

A banging headache and the smell of food had Daisy debating

throwing up again or hunting out the source of the aroma. Surprisingly for her, the food won. In the kitchen, Xander leant against the breakfast bar watching TV.

'You look better,' he said, as she sat at the table.

'I feel hideous.' She needed paracetamol. Did she have any left? 'Headache.'

'To be expected.' He handed her a glass of water and two pre-prepared pills.

'What are you cooking, chef?'

'Soup, and you're having some even if I have to force-feed you.'

He filled two bowls and sliced a loaf of bread, which Daisy had a sneaking suspicion he'd made – it was still warm. The first spoonful of his lentil and vegetable soup felt like a hug.

'It's like having Jamie Oliver in the house,' she said. 'Soup's yummy.'

He smiled briefly. 'Clara's cancelled the viewings you had on the flats in Haverton.'

Daisy nodded, not really caring. All feelings appeared to have been surgically removed while she slept.

'When do you have to move out of here?'

'Four weeks. Need somewhere quick.'

'So move in with me.'

'I think we've proved that wouldn't be a good idea but thanks.' Thanks, thanks, thanks – she'd said that such a lot to him. 'Why are you here?'

'You know why. I like playing the hero, rescuing the damsel in distress.'

'But why today? Why not yesterday or tomorrow?'

He frowned, scratching his neck. 'Clara rang. She said she was fighting a losing battle and you'd find today hell. She doesn't know what to do to help you anymore so needed a change of tack. It was me or Scott.'

Was she that bad? So bad Clara had asked a man for help? Not like her.

Defeated, Daisy put down her spoon, sighing at her half- full bowl. 'I'm done.'

Xander's frown worsened, clearly unimpressed with her efforts, but she couldn't swallow another spoonful. 'How bad is this, Daze?'

Well, you held my hair back while I threw up. 'It's a bad day.'

'A bad day?' He dropped his spoon in his bowl. 'Clara said–'

'What the hell has Clara been saying?' Daisy glanced around, desperate for a cigarette. 'What, so she gets engaged and suddenly she forgets the wine she drank when Scott wouldn't talk to her for two months? Like she never got wasted. God, look at the time she screwed–'

'Don't you dare,' Xander said, his voice steady, but dangerously low. 'Clara's the only reason you're still here. Apparently, your parents wanted to send you to rehab.'

'My parents... what?' Fresh tears rolled down her cheeks, but a tiny smile flittered over Xander's face as though he were somehow pleased.

'She might be terrifying,' he said, 'but Clara's got you nailed. She said you're not that far gone. I think she's right.'

Daisy's heart raced. Why was everything so bloody hard? Couldn't she just have a glass of wine to put the fuzzy edges back? *Wine?* She'd just thrown up in front of Xander and she still wanted wine? Oh God, should she be in rehab?

'Do you want Clara here? I'll ring her.'

No, I want you here.

They stared at each other for a moment and Daisy's head reeled. Really, she wanted some playboy rebound shag with her instead of her best-friend? Xander's deep brown eyes still held hers. No. He wasn't a rebound shag. He was her friend.

'Will you come with me to the post office?' she asked, her voice wavering. 'I need to post the divorce papers to my solicitor.'

Xander nodded as he buttered a slice of bread. 'After that, how about we go for a walk?'

A genuine smile took over and Daisy picked up her spoon again. 'I'd like that.'

She finished her soup. And the bread he offered her.

The glossy red door of the village post office stood between her becoming a divorcee at twenty-five. Actually, a narrow road and the red door stood between Daisy becoming a divorcee at twenty-five. She just had to cross the road, to open the door.

'You know Lynda will have some bitchy comment to make,' Daisy said, just able to make out Lynda on the other side of the glass. Did she really want to go through with this? 'She thinks the sun shines out of Finn's arse.'

'To be fair, so do you.'

She had no answer for that.

'You have to remember why you left him, why you're divorcing him.'

'The unreasonable behaviour.' She glanced down at the envelope in her hands. She had to focus on the negatives. 'I'm divorcing him because he kept me tied to a bed for two days.'

Xander was still blinking, his mouth still gaping when she strode across the street.

Taking a deep breath, she pushed open the door and pasted on a faux-smile. An ancient man leaning on a walking stick was chatting away as his shaking hands tried to fish his bank card out of his wallet.

'He tied you to a bed for *two* days?' Xander whispered.

'Not a conversation for the post office,' she hissed back.

'But seriously, two days?'

Daisy's cheeks burned and she refused to look up at him.

'That's why you freaked out when I made that joke. What happened, did he turn all Fifty Shades on your ass?'

Daisy folded her arms. Mercifully, Lynda was too busy helping the octogenarian with his bank card to be paying attention. 'No. He didn't hurt me. Now, please shut up.'

He did – for about twenty seconds. 'But surely he let you get up. You know, to... go to the toilet.'

Mortified, she stared resolutely at the man slowly tapping out his PIN number. 'Are you getting the *unreasonable* aspect of his behaviour now?' She held up the envelope. '*This* is a legal agreement that says he'll offer no contest to my *allegations* and in return I won't ask for any money. I just want out.'

'Next?' Lynda smiled cheerily as Daisy popped the envelope on the scales. 'Ruth Harcourt? She's who I used when I got divorced.'

Oh, here we go. Daisy let a long sigh. Well, soon enough, the petition would be signed and the world would know Finn Rousseau was getting divorced. They may as well find out from Lynda first.

'Oh don't look so fed up,' Lynda said, patting Daisy's hand. 'It's difficult when these things happen, but he's a look in his eye, that Finn. He came in here a few weeks back, asking if Clara still lived at the cottage. I told him yes, but that I'd seen you go off out for the night. Oh the face on him. Reminded me of my Jim. A wrong 'un.

And that Moll Flanders thing he's in... well, it's nothing short of a mucky film. You're better off with the friends you've got here. Two pounds seventy-three, please. Now, did you hear that Nicola from number four has thrown her eldest daughter out? She was at the doctors last week so you can imagine what people are saying about the poor girl...'

Five minutes later, Daisy walked out of the post office, nibbling the polish off her thumbnail.

'Lynda's changed her tune,' she said. 'It seems the sun shines out of *your* arse now.'

'Then there's hope for you too.'

Xander nudged her, playfully bumping her into the wall and in retaliation, Daisy went to slap his arm, but he grasped her hand, their fingers instantly linking. She couldn't deny having Xander with her was better therapy than a glass of champagne on a summer's day, but he wasn't Finn and she didn't want to give him the wrong idea. She shook off his hand.

Xander's jaw twitched, but to his credit, he made no comment.

'It's too soon,' she lied.

'You will get over this, Daze. It might not feel like it now, but you will. Believe me, I know.'

As they headed down the lane out of the village, Daisy frowned up at him. 'What happened with the Michelin-starred cougar?'

Xander glanced away. 'I was young and stupid. I thought... I asked her to leave Anthony. She said no.'

'That must've hurt.'

Xander gave a half laugh. 'Anthony's a wanker to his staff and she uses that. She let me believe that's what he was like to her, but there was no way she was giving up her celebrity life, not for me, not for anyone. A few months after I left, I found out she'd also been shagging the new *commis* chef. She likes them young.'

OMG. 'When did you know you were over her? How long did it take?'

'Oh, it was a fairly recent thing. But your turn,' he said. 'After the unreasonable behaviour, why are you still in love with Finn?'

It was a really good question, but Daisy's focus drifted as they passed the village recycling centre. The council bins, though subtly designed to fit in amongst the stone walls and bracken, couldn't be more noticeable now they were surrounded by plastic bags of trash.

'For crying out loud,' she said, shaking her head. 'Why would you go to the bother of bringing your rubbish here and not putting it in the actual bin?' Cans, bottles, papers... all in the same bag. 'This is just fly tipping. God, some people...'

'Every time I think I know you, you do this.' Xander stood staring at her.

'What?' She grabbed the nearest black bin bag.

'You wear three hundred quid jeans and Prada shoes. You fangirl India Dowson-Jones and yet here you are, giving a shit about recycling.'

'If you met my parents, you'd understand.' She grabbed a second bag. 'Don't you care?'

'Of course I do.' He tossed two wine bottles into the green bin. 'But you're always full of surprises.'

For the first time that day, Daisy grinned. 'I told you. We can't all be unbel–'

The bin bag in her left hand squirmed.

Squealing, Daisy dropped it, her heart hammering in her chest.

'It moved,' she whispered.

'What moved?'

'The bag. There's something in there.'

'Rat?' Xander picked up a stick and poked tentatively at the bag. It whimpered.

That was no rat. Daisy fell to her knees, ripping open the black plastic.

'Christ, Daisy, watch it doesn't–'

It was a dog – a filthy, terrified, emaciated dog. Its eyes were white, its whole body shaking, but it was alive. Tears blurred her vision as Xander knelt beside her, speaking words she didn't listen to. Who would dump a dog in a rubbish bag, leaving it to starve to death, to just die?

'Why, Xand?' she sobbed. 'Why would anyone treat a poor little dog like this?'

The muscle in Xander's jaw twitched as he lay his fleece jacket on the ground and gently transferred the dog from the plastic bag to relative luxury. 'Let's get him to the vet's.'

'You really are a KSCP. First you save me, now this dog–'

'Whoa, you're doing the saving here.'

What? 'But I can't–'

'Yes, you can.'

Gingerly, she stroked the matted fur between the dog's ears. He looked like something from an RSPCA leaflet – one showing the animal that didn't make it. Every bone in its body jutted out, its legs marred by open, weeping sores. Daisy didn't have a home for herself, let alone a pet, but the little dog looked up at her, begging for help, and without hesitation, she kissed its head. She'd make everything okay.

The vet gave the little dog a quick but thorough examination, proclaiming him to be a collie-spaniel cross, around twelve months old. Happily, aside from two infected sores on his back legs and severe malnutrition, he appeared to have no other ailments, though time would tell.

While the vet got to work, Daisy and Xander settled themselves in the deserted waiting room and she started to fill in the forms she'd been given by the nurse. 'Patient's name. Any ideas?'

'He's your dog now. Call him what you like.'

He's my dog. Daisy couldn't stop her grin. 'It's ridiculous. I have nowhere to live–'

'I keep telling you...'

She pointedly ignored him. 'I can barely afford to look after me, but now I'm facing call out fees for the vet on a Saturday afternoon. This dog will be the most costly but utterly gorgeous accessory a girl could–' She clamped her hand over her mouth, suppressing a squeal. 'Birkin. I want to call him Birkin.'

Xander stared at her. 'Are you still drunk?'

'The Hermes Birkin is my dream handbag, the best accessory a girl could have, but stupidly expensive. Seventy grand for a white crocodile number.'

'Insane.' He settled back in his chair, stretching out his long legs. 'What's a KSCP?'

Bugger. Daisy focussed on the form, hoping to hide her flaming cheeks. 'Clara's a dreadful gossip so we make up acronyms for people, that way no-one knows who we're talking about. Finn's the HMS, the Hollywood Movie Star. You're the KSCP.'

'Which stands for?'

With wide-eyed innocence, she looked up. 'Kinda Sexy Cumbrian Playboy.'

'*Kinda* sexy? Thanks. And I'm *not* a playboy.'

'And I'm joking.' She nudged him with her shoulder, smiling

down at the clipboard. 'You're my Knight-in-Shining-Cricket-Pads.'

'Okay, *that* I can live with.' Xander hooked his arm around her neck, kissing the top of her head.

For several minutes, she concentrated on filling the forms, Xander's head still resting against hers. She couldn't see, but she just knew his smile would be as big as hers.

'Daze, will you tell me about him?'

Her smile faded. 'Who?'

'Finn. Tell me about the day you met.'

'Why?'

'I just want to... understand.' He glanced down at her, his frown growing. 'You were walking up Catbells?'

Daisy took a deep breath, putting her clipboard down. 'He passed me, just before the top, and said hi.'

'Did you know who he was?'

Daisy nodded. Finn might've been hiding under a baseball cap, but once she'd clocked him, she upped her pace, desperate to catch up with his cute bum. 'Turned out he was pretty much waiting for me at the top. He smiled, I smiled; he laughed, I laughed.'

'Flirting on Catbells. Only you, Fitzgerald.'

'The rain clouds rolled in and he could've been a psycho rapist, but I had no desire to leave.' Okay, telling Xander about copping off with Finn was beyond weird, but they settled against each other as she explained how she'd offered to share her flask of tea and they'd sat overlooking Derwent Water on an otherwise unremarkable, grey September day. 'We stayed there for two hours, talking. It's like, we just got on. Do you know what I mean?'

'Yeah, I know exactly what you mean.'

'The Michelin-starred Cougar?'

'No. You really are an idiot at times. Then what happened?'

'He asked me out, I said yes, and then...well, he kissed me.' That had been a moment and a half. 'We never made it out to dinner.'

'Spare me the details.'

'We barely spent a day apart after that. I couldn't believe this utterly amazing film star fancied me. *Me*. I'm this totally ordinary girl from Cheshire and he'd snogged Dakota Fanning in a movie.' And that was the burden of being married to Finn Rousseau: trying to live up to his exes and co-stars. 'God, I totally thought he was the best-looking bloke I'd ever met.'

'He has seven visible tattoos and an eye-brow scar. I can't believe you buy into that bad boy bullshit.'

Daisy stared determinedly at the floor. 'It might be obvious, and I know you won't want to hear it, but he's incredibly sexy. I used to joke that all he needed to do was smile to get me in bed.'

'And there's me thinking it takes a bottle of vodka.'

That earned him a swift kick to the shins, but when he flashed his Colgate smile, she relaxed against him once again.

'For twelve months, we had the most perfect life. Lolling around his beach house in Brighton... Christmas at his parents' *manoir* in Provence.'

'He's actually French?'

'His dad is. Fabien Rousseau. He's a movie director. His mum, Vicky, is an actress. They're lovely, if a little bonkers. Last year, they got remarried for the *third* time.'

'They must really like wedding cake.'

Daisy laughed. 'They live in Ibiza these days. *That* explains my Pacha cherries.'

'What happened after twelve months?'

'On our first anniversary.' Daisy picked at her nail polish. 'He announced he wanted kids.'

'You don't?'

'Well, maybe when I'm like thirty.' Her head swam with well-worn arguments, but she jammed her fingernails into her palms. 'Eventually, I stopped taking the pill but nothing happened. I'd try to look disappointed, but Finn saw through it and each month it ripped us a little more apart. He even accused me of secretly taking the pill. A few things happened...'

'The unreasonable behaviour?'

Daisy's cheeks burned. 'I'll spare you the details. But on January the fifth...'

The arm around her shoulders tightened, Xander's head resting on hers. 'You left?'

'No.' She shook her head, anger building. 'After the unreasonable behaviour, I was left stranded at Claridge's with bugger all but the clothes I was wearing and a credit card in Finn's name.'

'You maxed out his card?'

'Oh, it meant more than spending his money. Finn knew I was pissed off, because no matter how much I obsess over handbags, I *hate* shopping. By the time I got home, I was so angry and so pissed off after a day traipsing around London, I was ready to give him holy hell. But when I got home, he'd changed the locks and packed my bags.'

'He kicked *you* out? Why?'

'I didn't stop to ask. I came up here and talked to a divorce lawyer. Before I know it, our joint account's frozen and I've less money than I started with. All I could do was sell my car to pay off credit cards and start all over again.'

'Good for you.'

'Really?' She let out a long, slow breath. 'I'd started to think I'd made the right decision, but when he turned up, I realised... I still love him.'

The surgery door opened and the vet came out, the little dog cowering, his back legs bandaged up. Quietly, Daisy crouched down, to say hello to the dog and despite a nervous glance in the vet's direction, he skittered across the tiled floor, his tail wagging.

'Hi, hi, hi,' she said, stroking his matted head. 'I thought I might call you Birkin. What do you think?'

From his zillion doggy kisses he seemed to approve.

The vet generously waved his fees, donated a collar, lead and food to get her started, and after she'd attentively listened to his advice on meds, wounds and when to tackle bath time, Daisy finally headed home with Birkin snuggled in her arms.

'Xand, why are you doing this?' she asked as they walked down Chapel Street.

'Doing what?'

'Looking after my pathetic arse. Surely you have better things to do on a Saturday afternoon.' She tipped her head to look up at him. 'Did Clara really ring you? It's just she hasn't asked a man for help, even Scott, since the day she saw her dad punch her mum.'

'No, I rang her.' Xander shoved his hands in his pockets, focussing on the pavement. 'She explained what was going on. I offered.'

'Why?'

For a minute, he tucked his bottom lip between his teeth, but finally he glanced at her, his brow furrowed. 'I would've thought it were obvious.'

Nervously, she tucked a wayward curl behind her ear. 'It's not.'

'I think I love you.'

'Oh.'

Shaking his head, he gave a half-laugh. 'Yeah, oh.'

'You think you love me?' She looked up at him, blinking. 'I don't even know which bit of that to put the stress on. *Think. Love. Me.*'

'I'm a bit surprised myself.'

'And be sensible. You've only known me ten minutes. You can't *love* me.'

'It's hardly a secret I think you're sexiest thing I've ever seen, but when I saw you today, I thought... well I realised maybe it was more, but you were trying to kill yourself over someone else. Not a great situation to be in.' He sighed, taking Birkin from her. 'My head's fucked, so I talked to Rob while you were asleep. I wasn't sure if I should hang around, wait 'til you're divorced then make you fall in love with me, or run the fuck away and never come back.'

'Please don't go anywhere,' she said. 'I'd be dead tomorrow if it weren't for you.'

'That's a bit dramatic, but it's okay. I'm not going anywhere.'

'Why, what did your brother say?'

'He told me to find out who I was up against.'

Daisy stared at him. 'And?'

'Now I know.'

Her staring continued. 'Know what?'

'We're going to work out. I'd even go so far as to say if we'd met at a different time, you'd have left him for me.'

Daisy laughed. 'You think I'd have left my husband for your pretty face? Like that's the kind of person I am?'

'That's exactly the kind of person you are. Your flaws are what make you so fucking fascinating.'

'I have no idea how to respond to that.'

Xander just grinned. 'So are you going to get drunk again tonight?'

'No.' She gave a little shake of her head. 'I have to move on, don't I? He has. I love him but... as you say, I'll get over it.'

'Does this mean we can go out on a proper date, not one where we're pretending to be just friends?'

'We are just friends, despite any deluded ideas you might have.'

'I'll wait.'

'You'll wait?' she asked, stopping outside Clara's cottage.

'Yes. But I'm not just going to wait. I've got a plan.'

'A plan?'

'Yes, Fitzgerald. A *plan*.'

Chapter Six

A rhythmic thudding woke Daisy. Without opening her eyes, she knew Birkin, the downright cutest alarm clock, would be sat beside her bed, his head to one side and his brown ears cocked as his tail flapped against the carpet. Every night, she'd leave him curled up on his cushion in front of the fire, but every morning, he'd sneak upstairs and wake her – like she minded.

Birkin provided a reason to get out of bed every morning and his visible improvement gave her hope. As his leg scars healed, her skin took on a healthy glow; as his weight crept up to somewhere near normal so did hers. Okay, Birkin still quaked at the sight of burly men, and Daisy might still cry for an hour if Finn popped up on TV, but together, they slowly recovered. And they did it under the watchful eye of Xander.

But he baffled her.

He point blank refused to elaborate on his *plan*, though it appeared to involve an army-worthy regime of walks with Birkin, followed by wholesome, homemade nutrition: grilled mackerel and Mediterranean salsa at Xander's, fresh pea and wild mint soup at hers or an impromptu picnic at Black Fell Tarn.

Often, he'd introduce her to alternative suicide methods: abseiling down cliffs, or kayaking down rivers, and for him she'd give anything a go, anything so long as it didn't make them seem like a couple. No meals in dimly lit pubs in case they erred toward romantic, no trips to the cinema, and no meeting his family. She never stated the rules out loud, but if Xander ever suggested popping to his brother's house, or dinner at the Miller's Arms, Daisy always found an excuse to go home.

But oddly, aside from the odd cheeky comment, Xander made no effort to sweep her off her hiking boots. Instead, he merely cemented his place as her Knight-in-Shining-Cricket-Pads. She began to think that's all he wanted to be.

Regardless of his motives, he achieved one goal – she hadn't touched a drop of booze since Finn's birthday.

'I ought to get up,' she said, rubbing Birkin's head, 'but what the hell does one wear when one doesn't know where one is going for the bloody day?'

All Xander would tell her was that she shouldn't make plans. On cue, her phone buzzed into life.

'Morning, Fitzgerald.'

'Morning.' She snuggled under the duvet, trying not to yawn down the phone.

'Are you still in bed?'

'Yes, it's only eight.'

'What are you wearing? Shall I come round?'

'Very funny. Are you ever going to tell me what we're doing today?'

'Meet me on the green at twelve. We're going house-hunting.'

'What houses, where?' She sat up.

He hung up.

Whatever his plan was, Daisy liked it. She liked it a lot.

After a foot-jiggling breakfast and a perfectly-timed walk over the common with Birkin, Daisy swapped her hiking boots for flip flops and headed out to meet Xander. The sky was cloudless, temperatures already hitting seventeen degrees and Daisy knew it'd be a perfect day. How could it not be when she was hanging out with her KSCP?

The church bells rang out and Daisy smiled hello to Lynda. Who wanted to be a nameless someone on the tube when you could walk across the village saying hello to your neighbours? Daisy's smile grew when Birkin's tail wagged ferociously – he'd spotted Xander on the opposite side of the green, sitting on a wrought iron bench.

'House hunting here?' she asked, glancing around the green dubiously. 'We have discussed my bank balance, right?'

'Have a little faith, because that...' Xander pointed to a huge double-fronted Georgian property. 'Is option one. Probably the most sensible option.'

A woman named Lorna ran a bed and breakfast but rented out rooms too. Not that Daisy had a burning desire to share a house with a daily influx of strangers, but the rent was incredibly reasonable and she welcomed dogs.

'What a lovely room,' Daisy said, brushing her hand over the chunky oak bed frame. The whole house was lovely. Lorna was lovely. She had no reason to say no, except... it just didn't feel *right*. But how could she turn down such a perfect place?

'Why don't you pop round tonight?' Lorna suggested to Daisy. 'It's wine o'clock at six in my house–'

Xander dragged Daisy out of there before she had chance to answer, leaving a slightly bemused Lorna yelling offers of lager in their wake.

'I would've said no,' Daisy said, a little too sulkily. Okay, her sobriety was helped by Xander staying with her until she went to bed most nights, but she could easily say no to booze. Easily.

'I wasn't taking the risk.'

'Where next?'

'We're here.' Xander leant against his car.

'Here?' She glanced to his cottage. 'You aren't serious.'

He pulled a key from his pocket and dangled it between them – no smile present, his gaze fixed on her.

'You know the deal. I have three bedrooms – one for me, one for you, one for handbag making. You pay half the bills. No rent. The obvious choice.'

'I'm not even dignifying the suggestion with the *whatever* it deserves.'

He laughed, hooking his arm around her neck and kissing her head. 'Can't blame me for trying. Time to see the unsensible option, Fitzgerald.'

'Moving in with you *wasn't* the unsensible option?'

'Not even close.'

And he wasn't wrong. Property Three sat in Gosthwaite Mills, midway up the Lum Valley – further out in the sticks than she'd ever planned, but God's best bit of the Lakes in her humble opinion.

'Oh... my... good God.'

The Old Forge originally housed the village blacksmith back in the Seventeenth century, and if Daisy squinted, a lot, it was the idyllic country home. Sadly, with her eyes open she could see damp walls, a rotting front door and foxgloves growing through the broken windows. Birkin jumped out of Xander's car, eagerly sniffing around the garden.

'Daze?' Xander dragged her attention to the grey-haired man hovering by the front door. 'This is Martin. He's from the ANA

Housing Association.'

Bemused, Daisy shook Martin's hand. 'But I don't qualify for housing association help.'

'We offer quid pro quo housing to the right people,' Martin replied. 'You get to live here, rent free, so long as you work on the place. Clean it up.'

'It needs more than cleaning,' she said, jabbing her toe into the dashing that sagged away from the walls.

Inside, Martin pushed open the living room door to reveal a multitude of pizza boxes, porn mags and enough beer cans to make her own recycling box seem reasonable.

'It does,' he replied, 'but it's a start. Local kids were using it as a den, and before that, the last owner went a little...'

'Insane?' Daisy said, reading the paranoid ramblings daubed over the walls in what she prayed was red paint and not blood.

'Why don't you take a look around? We can discuss terms when you're ready.'

Daisy wandered upstairs and down, staring open-mouthed at the Seventies, white veneered kitchen units, frowning with trepidation at the green, monolithic Aga, giggling at the aubergine bathroom suites. Finally, she crouched down, hugging Birkin and sighing with happiness at the view: the Miller's Arms was a two hundred metre, drunken stagger away. Now this was what living in the country was all about.

'I love it,' she said, grinning up to Xander.

'I had a feeling you would.' He glanced at the house, shaking his head. 'I can't believe you're choosing Skank Manor over me.'

'Sorry, but it has *two* bathrooms to tile.'

'At least it'll keep you out of trouble.'

Was that his plan? Unbelievably grateful, she stood up and threw her arms around his neck. 'Thank you.'

'You're welcome,' he replied, hugging her back.

Somehow, his fingers were in her hair, their lips a quarter head-turn from a kiss. Oh God, she shouldn't have hugged him, not like this – not for this long. It would be a mistake, ruin everything... but it was Xander who kissed her head and let her go.

Clearly, he really did just want to be friends.

'Scott and Clara are going to the barbeque tonight, at your brother's.' The words tumbled out of her mouth. Oh God, was she really going to say this. 'I was invited, but I'd said, no.'

Xander nodded before throwing a stick for Birkin. 'Like always.'
So he'd noticed her unspoken rules. 'I... was thinking I might change my mind.'

'You should. You'll enjoy it.' He turned away, ready for Birkin's excited return. 'We can go together.'

Her mouth opened, ready to say no, to say she'd meet him there, but he looked back at her, shaking his head, fighting a smile.

'I promise not to hold your hand, or do anything that might suggest we're anything more than just friends, Fitzgerald.'

She closed her eyes for a second, her cheeks burning. 'Sorry.'

'I'll pick you up at seven.'

But of course she was late – a wardrobe crisis. Jeans and ballet flats would be great to make the point of looking utterly *just friend*-like, but to meet Xander's brother, the *Sexiest Man in Town*? No. A simple white shift dress would be suitably demure and classy, but it would be tempting way too much fate not to spill red wine down the front.

'Seriously bored...' Xander called up the stairs. 'It's nearly half-past.'

Buggeration. Impetuously, she pulled on a slinky, red, backless top and slightly tatty, but skin-tight cropped jeans. Top half dressy, bottom half scruffy – surely the perfect balance?

'Two minutes then I'm dragging you out of here in whatever you've got on.'

With huge hoop earrings and the enormous wedge heels, she finished off her *just friends go to a barbeque* ensemble with aplomb, but worryingly earned a blatant once over from Xander.

'You'll do,' he said, shrugging.

Okay maybe the backless top, which prevented her from wearing a bra, might be a teeny bit outside the *just friends* remit, but it was worth it for the compliment: *you'll do*.

Still riding high, Daisy wandered into a quintessential country garden with her mouth gaping. Poppies, cornflowers and delphiniums filled the borders and a storybook scarecrow stood guard over the tidy vegetable patch. The traditional slate farmhouse might need twenty grand throwing at it to stop the roof from collapsing, but with horses and Herdwick sheep grazing in the fields, Low Wood Farm was Daisy's idea of heaven.

'Your brother lives here, really?' she asked Xander. 'It's like something out of a Beatrix Potter book.'

Xander looked around, affection filling his face. 'Grandpa and Grandma lived here. When she died, Grandpa rented it out. He said he couldn't live in the house, too many memories, but he didn't sell it because it meant so much to Rob and me. We pretty much grew up here. I'd rather hang out in the kitchen with Grandpa, but Rob preferred the horses. He took over Grandma's stock, mostly to annoy Dad, and Grandpa gave Rob and Van the farm as a wedding present.'

'It must've been lovely growing up here.'

'It was a lot more fun than home.' Xander flashed her the Colgate smile. 'Ready to meet my family, Fitzgerald?'

Before she had chance to answer, Xander took her hand and led her into the farmhouse kitchen where a tall woman with a perfect black bob chopped tomatoes and swayed away to an opera blaring out of a little CD player. Noticing them, she staggered a little, before turning the music down.

'Are you pissed?' Xander asked, laughing incredulously.

'Shush, don't take the mickey.' She had the loveliest Welsh accent. 'Since it's my birthday, I thought I'd treat myself to a glass of Buck's Fizz, only I think I've had half a bottle of Moet now.'

'Van, this is Daisy. Daisy, this is my beautiful sister-in-law, Vanessa.'

Crikey, was he right. Vanessa was all luminous skin, huge green eyes and bee-stung lips, her body encased in the simplest of black shift dresses. Though more oddly, despite her blatant supermodel qualities, Vanessa hadn't stopped blushing. Was she shy?

'Happy Birthday,' Daisy said, smiling politely as Xander sat her at the table.

'Thank you.' Turning redder still, Vanessa went back to her chopping. 'Sorry the place is such a pigsty. There never seems any end to the tidying these days.'

Stirrups, books, baby toys, CDs, rosettes and junk mail littered every surface, while the woodchip wallpaper could barely be seen for photos of children, horses and dogs. With the obligatory cat and fat Labrador lying in front of the Aga, it looked like a family kitchen should – chaotic and welcoming.

'Where's Rob?' Xander asked, pouring Daisy a mug of tea from the pot warming on the Aga.

Tea? Wasn't it a bloody party? Or was she still not allowed to drink?

'Where d'you think? In the yard. Bloody horses.' Vanessa threw the tomatoes in a bowl but only half of them made it; the rest landed on the floor. She scooped them up and her hands hovered over the bowl, but then she decided they ought to go in the bin.

'Let me,' Xander said, taking the knife.

'Oh, you are an angel. You'll do a much better job anyway.' She leant against the Aga, and again blushing, turned to Daisy. 'I can't believe you were married to Finn Rousseau.'

'I still am.' Though for how much longer?

'I used to have his poster on my wall, you know, when I was in the Sixth Form. He was in Hollyoaks then.'

'Van?' Xander didn't look around but shook his head. 'Remember that's the one subject we don't talk about?'

Mercifully, an uncomfortable pause was avoided when a little girl toddled into the kitchen, brandishing a bunch of daisies and buttercups.

'Xandy! Xandy!' she called, running towards him.

His smile grew as he crouched down and hugged his niece, the smile turning to laughter as he tickled her and she erupted into chuckles. How cute? He whispered something to the little girl, who nodded before tentatively walking towards Daisy. She held out the flowers, offering a shy smile.

'Thank you.' Daisy smiled.

'This is Matilda,' Xander explained. 'Tilly, this is my friend, Daisy.'

Blushing, Matilda gave a little wave then scampered off to hide behind her mum, but Daisy's attention was already switching to the slightly older, dark-haired version of Xander who'd walked in with a tiny baby asleep on one shoulder and a vast bouquet of wild flowers in his other hand.

Without acknowledging Daisy or Xander's presence he handed Vanessa the bouquet saying, 'Sorry I've been busy, angel,' before kissing her with complete disregard for anyone watching. When Robbie finally let her go, Vanessa stood blushing down at her flowers and he turned to Daisy.

'Hello,' he said, his eyes twinkling. 'It's *very* nice to meet you, finally.'

The guy was all faded t-shirt, ripped at the knee jeans and utter nonchalant confidence. Oh dear God, why did she feel fourteen, like the school heart throb had asked to her to help him with his science homework? Gingerly, Daisy shook his proffered hand, aware her face had to be the colour of the dropped tomatoes, but to her horror, he leaned closer, kissing her cheek. Clara was right; Robbie Golding absolutely was the sexiest man in town.

'Don't get any ideas,' Xander whispered to her as he unnecessarily topped up her untouched tea. 'He's married with three kids, Fitzgerald.'

Trying not to giggle, Daisy turned to Vanessa. 'How on earth do you have three kids and still look like Britain's next top model?'

Vanessa's mini-dress only left skin-colour to the imagination. She had no flabby stomach, no thickening waist, no droopy boobs – hell, she didn't even have grey shadows under her eyes.

'Amazing, isn't she?' Robbie smiled at his wife before pointing to a photo of a dark-haired girl flying over a jump on a bright bay pony. 'Tallulah's nine, going on fifteen. Matilda's nearly two and Pandora here–' On cue, white gloop erupted from the baby's mouth, trickling onto his shoulder. 'Is very nearly one month old. But thanks for that, Dora.'

'Honestly,' Daisy said to Vanessa, 'if I looked as good as you after three kids, I'd be wearing a sign saying, *check me out, child number three born only thirty days ago.*'

Robbie wiped his shoulder, grinning. 'I'm starting to see why my little brother's so keen for you to be his new... how does he put it, Van, *best friend?*'

'And I think my family have embarrassed me enough.' Xander wiped his hands, shaking his head.

Embarrassed him? Shown him in a whole new light more like. Where was the player who was suspiciously adept at unzipping a girl's pants, and who was this adorable *Uncle Xandy?* Or was this all part of the plan, to show her he wasn't a playboy?

Back in the garden, half the village milled around with glasses of Pimm's or bottles of lager, while Vanessa's salads sat on a table surrounded by mountains of bread rolls, coleslaw, sauces and foil-wrapped corn. On the far side of the neat lawn, a gazebo sheltered another table, one visibly sagging under the weight of more booze than even Daisy could drink in a year.

A drink. Finally, she could have a drink. Low Wood Farm really was her idea of heaven.

'So, OMG, the Old Forge,' Clara said, raising her eyebrows. 'Are you mental?'

Daisy joined her and Scott at a vast wooden picnic table, eagerly eyeing up the glasses Xander filled with champagne – well, half-filled.

'It's rent free and if I project manage the renovation, I get ten percent of the budget as payment.' Daisy sipped her drink, trying not to show how blissful she found the familiar tang of alcohol. 'I could make fifteen grand on it in nine months. That'd give me the deposit to buy somewhere.'

'Looking at the state of the place,' Clara said, wrinkling her nose, 'I'd want fifteen grand for living there. You should move in with your new BFF.'

'I agree.' Xander chinked his glass against Clara's. 'What's a BFF?'

'Best Friend Forever,' Daisy explained to Xander, making him smile.

'What are your acronyms for each other?'

Scott groaned. 'Has she told you yours?'

Xander nodded. 'KSCP.'

'Sorry, but it's better than RASCL.'

'Rich and Sexy Corporate Lawyer. I made up that one.' Daisy laughed. 'Clara is the BFG. It stands for Boyfriend Grabber because she's enticed more men away from their girlfriends than I've had bottles of wine.'

'And yours?' Xander asked.

'DAF, my initials.'

'It's to remind her of her awful middle name,' Clara said a little over casually. 'Angelique.'

Xander laughed. 'Daisy Angelique Fitzgerald? Were your parents drunk?'

'And...' Clara flashed a sickly sweet smile. 'It also stands for how Daisy spent Fresher's Week.' Daisy's best bitch glare had no effect on her. 'Drunk And Fucked.'

Xander almost choked on his drink but when he realised Daisy was laughing, he joined in.

'Did she really tile your bathroom?' Xander asked Clara, frowning when she nodded. 'Can't see it.'

'The day I met Daisy,' Scott said, 'she was wearing denim shorts and knocking down the wall between Clara's kitchen and living room with a sledgehammer.'

Daisy high-fived him, but Clara glared with fake anger at Scott.

'I'm amazed you remember the sledgehammer,' she said. 'You were so busy staring at her arse.'

Scott dismissed the claim by grabbing Clara and kissing her — he'd never been remotely interested in Daisy, or her him.

The evening melted into a blur of champagne, ludicrous cocktails and one too many chicken sheesh kebabs. Daisy had the loveliest time, helped by Xander being the most attentive of non-date dates. Constantly topping up her glass, he sometimes sat next to her, sometimes opposite, but was never far away. Unlike a date, however, he never flirted.

Clara, on the other hand, took to openly flirting with him. To begin with, it scared the life out of Xander, but after Scott explained that's just what she did, and Daisy explained they weren't a group of swingers, he relaxed.

'Bugger, I'm drunk.' Clara flopped onto the chair swing beside Daisy, taking the space Xander had vacated after he'd been summoned to say goodnight to his nieces. 'So, first he drags your skinny arse out of a vodka bottle and then he plays Kirstie and Phil. What aren't you telling me? Are you shagging him?'

'No.' Daisy leant forwards, grinning. 'But he said he thinks he loves me.'

'No freaking way,' Clara said. 'When did he say that?'

'Finn's birthday.'

'Why didn't you tell me, cowbag?'

'Because you'd make a big deal of it.'

'Do you think he meant it, or was he just trying to get into your pants again?'

'What do you reckon?'

'Pants, but are you really not ready to go out with him?'

'I know I shouldn't, but I still love Finn. Besides, Xander's too young and too good-looking. Everyone knows boys don't settle down until they're nearer thirty.'

'You're an idiot.'

'He'll move on to some leggy brunette.' Daisy sipped her caipirinha. 'I'm not falling for him. It's too risky.'

'An utter deluded idiot. He's a gorgeous piece of ass who says he loves you—'

'Said he loves me. Past tense and just the once. He doesn't even flirt with me.'

'Do you want him to?'

'No.'

'I can't believe you're not shagging him. You spend every day together.' Clara's eyes widened. 'If he does love you, do you think he's abstaining too? He can't be. He must be shagging someone. Is he?'

Daisy stubbed out her cigarette, scowling at the idea. 'How should I know?'

'Cake and eat it.' Clara turned to peer at Xander as he emerged from the house. 'But I don't know how you're not eating that particular piece of cake.'

'Well, a, he's not offering and b, you're not helping, Clara.'

'But it was good, wasn't it?'

Daisy frowned at her KSCP as she nodded. 'Thanks for reminding me.'

Grinning, Clara dragged Xander to the makeshift cocktail bar – undoubtedly to find out if he was shagging anyone, but mercifully giving Daisy the much-needed opportunity to banish the memories of him peeling off her top, his fingers running up the side of her body. She crossed her legs, unable to resist picturing his perfect torso and the happy trail that disappeared into his jeans.

Scott soon took Clara's place. 'He's okay, Daze. Not bad for you.'

'What do you mean, *not bad for me*?'

'Christ, well let's recap. Aside from the HMS, since I've known you, you've been out with some complete idiots. The three bad boys before the HMS were the most unsuitable blokes I've ever met. The heroin dealer?'

'He was not. Well only allegedly, and not when I was going out with him.' Daisy elbowed Scott in retaliation. 'Besides, I'm not going out with Xander. We're just friends.'

'Bullshit. Single, hot women and single, good-looking guys will never be *just* friends.'

'You're calling me *hot*?'

Scott pulled a face. 'No. It's just what he thinks.'

'How do you know what he thinks?' Daisy sat a little straighter. 'Please tell me you haven't had a *quiet word*?'

The day she'd met Scott, he'd assumed a big brother role after he used his six foot three bulk to fend off an over-zealous moron hitting on Daisy. After that, he'd had a *quiet word* with just about every bloke who'd shown the slightest interest in her. Finn included.

Scott shifted guilty in his seat. 'Look, rumour has it he's a total player, so I might've... had a chat before you went to his mate's party.'

Daisy sighed. 'So why do you think a *total player* isn't bad for me?'

'Well...' Scott frowned. 'He's a good bloke and... I think he's serious about you.'

'Why?'

'He's wagging you. You don't do that unless you're serious.'

'*Wagging me?* What the hell does that mean?'

Scott glanced to Xander, before swearing and leaning closer to her. 'Rob developed it from something he read years ago when he was a pick-up artist. It gave tips for pulling reluctant girls and guidelines for what a guy should do when he finds the girl he wants to marry. To make sure they say yes, when he asks. Rob took it a step further and had a full scale plan when he decided Vanessa was the one for him.'

'Xander said he had a plan.' Was this it? 'I thought only women were that conniving.'

'How the hell do you think I got Clara to settle down? Stage one, research and development. Talk to her. Listen to everything she has to say. Find out what she likes, doesn't like. If she's seeing someone, find out about him. Stage two, show and tell. Show her what a great guy you are, do nice things for her but never try it on. Treat her like a princess but never try it on. Tell her how amazing she is but never try it on. Remember when I took Clara to Edinburgh?'

Daisy nodded, laughing. Clara been utterly thrown by the time she'd come home – Scott had shown her a fabulous time, but they stayed in separate rooms. It drove Clara insane.

'Stage three?'

'Only for troublesome cases like Clara. Rob's tried and tested, last resort tip is to walk away.'

'Oh my God, that's why you stopped speaking to her for two months?'

'Well, it went on for longer than planned because she shagged Patrick, but towards the end, she was texting every day.' Scott kissed Daisy's cheek. 'Don't let it get to stage three, princess.'

After a long, slow stumble home along the bridleway from Low Wood Farm to the village, Daisy tottered up the garden path, clinging to Xander's hand for balance.

'Coffee?' she asked, full of faith in their platonic relationship.

She had every faith until she put her key in the door and Xander placed a finger at the base of her neck. Daisy froze. Slowly, he trailed his finger down the bumps of her naked spine. Oh dear God. She suppressed a shiver, hating that it only took a few drinks before her resistance fell apart. Why did she fancy him so much?

'Sorry, but I've been dying to do that all night,' he said quietly, his breath tickling her ear.

'Just friends, remember?' She turned to face him, appalled at her pathetic attempt to brush him off.

'You really don't make it easy to be *just friends*.' He tipped his head to one side and gave her a good coat of looking at. 'With your backless top and those ridiculous heels. Why do you wear shoes you can barely walk in?'

'You keep calling me a shortarse.' She tried to sound nonchalant, but when his hand made contact with her back once again, she ceased breathing.

'It's a term of endearment.' His fingers began drawing circles on her bare skin. 'Did you seriously think *just friends* when you got dressed tonight?'

'Yes.' Her back arched as she leaned into him, contradicting her earlier plans. Should she kiss him now, or drag him inside first? 'But that was about ten drinks ago.'

Xander's eyes looked heavenwards. 'You're hopeless, Fitzgerald.'

'It's better to regret something you've done, than something you haven't.'

'In your current state of mind, no, it's not.' He gently pushed her away and backed off, smiling amiably, but Daisy suspected he was a bit cross and probably hugely frustrated – she certainly was.

'What?' She folded her arms. 'I don't even get a kiss on the cheek?'

He laughed and planted a very slow, very deliberate kiss on her cheek. 'Good night.' He walked away.

In desperation, she called after him. 'Scott said you were wagging me. Is this stage two, all part of your *plan?*'

But Xander didn't stop walking. 'Fitzgerald, we've had to come up with a whole new plan for you. Night.'

She would've run after him, but what a stupid, stupid cow for wearing such ridiculous shoes. Ten minutes later, when she still wasn't on speaking terms with her Prada wedges, her phone buzzed – a message from Xander.

2 weeks ago I picked you out of the gutter. When you're sober maybe. x

He was twenty-two. Why didn't he ever just want a shag?

Chapter Seven

Parked outside the Old Forge, Daisy turned off the engine and the familiar desire to get wasted, to blot out her reality, surged over her. The lease was signed, the keys in her hand, but instead of the potential, the enormity of the project swamped her. The windows, the rendering, the floors, the walls, the kitchens the bathrooms... A cloud passed over the sun and she shivered.

Twelve months. She had twelve months to turn this hellhole around. Any later and she wouldn't earn the full project management fee. On paper, she could do it in nine months. In reality, she had to do it in less. She needed the bloody money.

In the hallway, Daisy kicked aside the charity mailings, most begging for just two pounds a month. As worthy as they may be, they'd have to get in line for her money. She hesitated at the starving little face pleading with her. Two pounds wasn't a lot for a destitute child. Surely, she could manage that.

With the flyer in her hand, she pushed open the first door, determined to see the positives. The pizza boxes and porn hadn't miraculously disappeared, but on the upside, the foxgloves growing through the broken window actually offered a cheery splash of pink now they were in flower.

'Well, this is it, Birkin. Home, sweet bloody home.'

The little dog sat beside her feet; even he appeared reluctant to explore such a hellhole.

Daisy leaned against the door frame, staring at Xander's number on her phone. If only he were here for this milestone occasion – they could have a cup of tea and giggle over the crusty porn mags.

Sadly, since his text on the Saturday night, she'd heard nothing from him. She'd called him but only managed to speak to his voicemail. She'd sent *are you mad at me* texts but her phone never buzzed in response. Twice, she bravely knocked on his door, but the lights were off, the cottage deserted. He was avoiding her. And Clara didn't offer much in the way of moral support.

'Cake and eat it,' she'd said. 'If you don't want to go out with him, stop messing him around.'

Daisy pressed dial.

'*I'm sorry. The person...*'

Ramming the phone into her back pocket, Daisy raised her chin. Well, if she couldn't hang out with her KSCP, she may as well get to sodding work.

By the end of day one, she'd emptied the easiest of the debris downstairs, but quickly realised trash bags weren't the answer; she'd need a bloody skip. On day two, with the skip half-filled she donned a facemask, ready to tackle the downstairs toilet. Twice, she had to evacuate the building, desperate for air. God, boys could be revolting creatures – how they peed in the tiny space, let alone spent *quality* time in there was a mystery. She carried a rigid magazine to the skip, trying not to appreciate *Kayleigh from Loughborough's* assets.

By day seven, the downstairs rooms were empty bar anything nailed down. She'd cut back the foxgloves, boarded up the broken windows and ripped up the disintegrating carpets – only the mental guy's paranoid slogans remained.

But Daisy still hadn't heard from Xander. Bugger it. She threw down her sweeping brush down and called him, her answer phone apology mentally drafted.

He answered.

'Fitzgerald, how the hell are you?' He had to shout over the music in the background.

'Bored.'

'Booty call?'

'No.' Thank God he couldn't see her ludicrous grin. 'Where are you?'

'Out.'

'On the pull?' It was meant as a joke, but it came out more bitter than she'd intended.

'With James. Jealous?'

'Bugger off. Where have you been?'

'Avoiding you.'

'At least you're honest.' Oh for a bottle of wine. 'Have a nice night.'

'When are you moving in to Skank Manor?'

'Friday.'

'I'll see you then.' He hung up.

Oh God, no. Her mum and dad would be there.

One hour. She'd left her mum and dad wrapping Clara's unwanted crockery and cutlery in old Hello pages, while she dashed to Tesco's for some vital groceries. One hour. Was it too much to ask that they'd still be there, still packing? But Clara's house was empty and Daisy's parents nowhere to be seen. Daisy peered through the window, her hand shielding out the light. Bloody hell, it *was* empty. Even the battered old sofas had gone, but Scott wasn't supposed to be shifting them until the following morning.

Thoroughly confused and unable to reach her mum or dad, Daisy climbed back into the MX5 and navigated her way down the now familiar winding lanes to Gosthwaite Mills. An odd sense of unease crept in and had her driving faster than she should, desperate to get to the Old Forge.

What if Xander had arrived already? Unease turned to downright horror as she pulled into the now ragwort-free parking area. Next to her parents' Prius was a Dowson-Jones furniture van.

Bugger, bugger, bugger.

Hastily, she fluffed her hair and checked for smudged mascara before taking a very deep breath and following the sound of happy voices. Despite her urgent prayers to God, the mini-housewarming party she found in the garden made her glad to be hiding behind enormous sunglasses. Her mum and dad were sitting cross-legged on the overgrown lawn, chatting to Xander, Marcus and James. The fact they all had glasses of wine didn't bother Daisy, but her dad lighting a joint while her mum giggled with Marcus certainly did.

Birkin was the first to spot her arrival, scurrying over, his tail a blur.

'Poppet, welcome home!' Her mum leapt up with a clatter of wooden bangles, her organic cotton summer dress wafting around her as she enveloped Daisy in an unnecessary hug – she'd only seen her seventy minutes ago, for God's sake. Why couldn't she wear jeans when she met Xander? Daisy inhaled her familiar lavender fragrance and sighed. And why couldn't she smell of Chanel No.5 when she met Marcus and James? At least her dad looked vaguely respectable in walking shorts and t-shirt. Why did her mother have to be so utterly mortifying?

Released from her arms, Daisy turned to Xander, desperate to be rescued, but after studying him and his friends, she gave up hope. Marcus peered at the wine bottle label, James sniffed like he'd done a couple of fat rails for breakfast and Xander took a long drag on the joint her dad passed him. The Playboy Removals team looked dreadful – all tired, pale and in desperate need of a shave. Daisy raised her eyebrows at Xander.

'I didn't think the MX5 would hold your shoe collection,' he said, looking her over without any hint of a smile. Was he *still* pissed off with her?

'Have you been on a five day bender?' she asked.

Xander dragged hard on the joint. 'It's actually a week now. Miss me?'

She ignored his question, saying hello to the others instead. James just about raised an eyebrow, acknowledging her existence, but at least Marcus managed a smile.

'Daisy, looking fabulous,' he said. 'Do you always move house in designer jeans and heels or just when Xander's coming to…' He tipped his head to the side, staring at her tits. '…help.'

Shut up, she mentally screamed. *You're sitting next to my dad.* Thankfully, her dad wasn't listening – he was too busy telling James about hiking in Nepal. Like James would give a hoot.

Daisy turned back to Xander. 'I don't think a van was entirely necessary. I only have a couple of suitcases and the odd box.'

'The odd box?' Xander laughed. 'The van's full.'

'Come on, poppet.' Her mum linked arms with her. 'Show me around.'

Resigned to a day of purgatory, Daisy unlocked the front door. Her mother loitered in the living room, quietly psychoanalysing the paranoid graffiti, while her dad wandered down to the kitchen. Daisy filled the new fridge she'd splashed out on with milk, Diet Coke and Hobnobs, then unlocked the kitchen door, watching Playboy Removals lounging in the sunshine.

'They're all so charming and good-looking,' her mum said, draping her an arm around her shoulders. 'But the last one I expected to be your Knight-in-Shining-Armour–'

'Cricket Pads.'

'None are wearing cricket pads. You really are a strange girl. Anyway, I said to your father, if I had to pick, it wouldn't be the grumpy one wearing the hat.'

Why was he wearing a hat? It was a warm September day and he was wearing an oversized beanie. He was always fabulously turned out, but this seemed a bit too fashion victim for him.

'He's barely managed a smile since they arrived,' her mum said, frowning. 'I thought Marcus would be more your cup of chai. He's a sweetheart.'

If only you knew, Mum.

Playboy Removals finally pottered into action, emptying the van as they emptied another wine bottle. With the last boxes dumped in the living room, the group gathered in the kitchen and Marcus handed Daisy a case of wine – albeit lacking two bottles. She thanked him with a dubious smile.

'Christ, are you actually going to live here?' James asked, sounding genuinely appalled as he looked at the kitchen. 'It's a dump, Daisy.'

She glared at him for dissing her dream. 'Well, lend me your butler for a week or three and I'll get the job done quicker.' One day, she'd show him.

Not bothering to respond, James shook her parents' hands and Marcus gave Daisy the most withering of looks as he leant in to kiss her cheek.

'It's customary to say thank you when people help you out,' he whispered.

Clearly, Marcus liked her even less than James, but did he really think she wasn't going to say thank you? What kind of person did he think she was? Despite now resenting the words, Daisy thanked James and Marcus, smiling as cheerily as Miss World runner-up.

Her mum went to the window overlooking the yard, watching Xander say goodbye to his friends. 'I met James' mother once. She was very beautiful. Such a tragic waste.'

'Tragic?' Daisy sipped her mum's wine. Oh, sweet nectar of the gods.

'Don't you know?' her mum asked. 'Ana, his mother, was a troubled soul. She took an overdose and died when James was still a baby.'

Daisy blinked. How did she not know this about India Dowson-Jones's mother?

'Petal,' her dad said, coming downstairs with his toolbox, 'I've put your bed together. You can do the rest. Your mother and I are going for a walk.'

'You're not staying?' *Wow, thanks.*

Her mum stroked Daisy's hair back. 'Poppet, we've helped you move seven times now. If I do any unpacking, you'll simply tell me off for putting things in the wrong place.'

Oh for God's sake, *that* old chestnut? Daisy folded her arms. The time she'd moved into the beach house with Finn, she'd snapped at her mum for putting the knives to the left of the forks in the cutlery drawer and she'd never heard the end of it.

'We'll be back to help you in the morning. Why don't you take Xander to the pub for lunch?' her mum suggested. 'Cheer him up.'

'Oh, he's fine. He's just sulking because I won't go out with him,' Daisy said.

'I think there's more to it than that,' her mum replied, glancing worried around at the decrepit kitchen. 'Are you sure you'll be okay staying here?'

'I'll be fine.'

'But–'

'I'm not twelve.'

Her mother shook her head and sighed. 'Clara told me Xander asked you to move in with him.'

'I'm moving in here.'

'I like him.' Her dad ruffled Daisy's hair. 'He's grounded. Just the kind of boyfriend you need. You should stay with him, at least until this place is habitable.'

'This is habitable.' More or less. 'And he's not my boyfriend.'

'But why not?' Mum asked. 'He likes you, you like him–'

'I do not.' She took a deep breath. 'I'm not even divorced yet. I don't need a boyfriend.'

'Poppy cock. If anything happened to your father, I'd be looking for a little company–'

'I'm still in the room, Laura,' her dad said, wagging a finger.

Her mum swatted his arm. 'Oh, Simon, you know no one would ever compare–'

'Please don't start talking about your sex life.' Daisy banged her head against the wall.

'Honestly, Daisy,' her mum said, 'I don't know where you get this appalling Catholic guilt. Just go out with him.'

'She'd get no argument from me,' Xander said, from his position in the doorway.

Oh God, how much of that had he heard?

When her Dad shook his hand, Xander finally smiled. Hell, he actually laughed as her mum hugged him and whispered something that sounded suspiciously like *good luck*.

'Always full of surprises, Fitzgerald,' Xander said when her parents finally left. 'From your materialistic values, I'd assumed you'd been dragged up by middle-class Tories.'

'No, a couple of new age hippies. Please don't take the piss.'

'I'm not. I like them. You look just like your mum.'

'I said don't take the piss. She might be fifty, but she's taller and prettier. I know.' Growing up with a model-like mother had never been easy.

'You really are very weird.' Xander shook his head.

Daisy nodded to the mattress resting against the wall. 'Help me with this? I'll buy you lunch.'

With downright profanities spilling from her mouth, they wrestled the new, dead-weight mattress up the stairs and into her bedroom, finally dropping it onto the reclaimed oak frame her dad had built. Breathless, Daisy collapsed onto the plastic wrapped bed and stared at the ancient beams, more than a little exhausted.

'I suppose I ought to get Marcus and James a little something to say thank you.'

Xander flopped next to her, laying on his front. 'It was my idea.'

'I'll get you a present too. What would you like?'

'You.'

'Stop it,' she said, horribly aware they were lying on her bed.

'Your eyes give too much away,' he said, his eyes narrowing as he studied her. 'Is that why you wear sunglasses so much?'

Daisy pouted, cross with him for being right. 'There's nothing to give away.'

'I've a question.' Xander rested his head on his folded arms. 'How come you're into sports cars and your parents are trying to save the world? Backlash to the yoga and organic vegetables?'

'Sort of,' she admitted, happy to change the conversation. 'They weren't always like this. Once upon a time, Dad was a shit-hot merchant banker and Mum worked for a PR company. He retired at thirty-five, burnt out, and they moved to Cheshire to live the Good Life. I was five. Over the years, they turned into Lib-Dem worthies, growing their own veggies and wasting time with painting classes and Pilates. They tried to get me into it all, but I was more interested in booze and boys.'

'Your parents seem spot on.'

'Don't get me wrong, I love them to bits, but we have nothing in common. They despair at my love of cars, and I despair when they tell me how bloody organic they are. My dad smokes weed, for God's sake.'

'He rolls a great joint.'

'I just want them to be normal. I bet yours are normal.'

'At least your dad likes you.'

'Why don't you get on with your dad?'

'It's like he has to disagree with *anything* I want do. It's always been the same. I was ten when I first ran away. When they sent me away to school, it got worse.' Xander pulled his hat a little lower, his eyebrows now hidden. 'I'd bugger off back to Grandpa's on a weekly basis.' He stayed quiet for a moment. 'Then, when I left school, Mum and Dad moved to the Yorkshire Dales, leaving me with Grandpa. It's bad enough wanting to leave home because your dad annoys you, but when he turns round and says actually we don't give a shit...'

What God-awful parents.

'So what was with the week-long bender?' she asked.

'I can't believe you're giving me a hard time for going out with my friends,' he said with a sulky tone. 'You're all the hassle of a girlfriend with none of the benefits, Fitzgerald.'

'Why've you been avoiding me?'

'Why do you think?'

'Are you still pissed off about the other Saturday?'

He tugged her hair. 'No. I needed to get away, but I wasn't pissed off with you.'

'Then why wouldn't you answer my calls?'

'I'm going away tomorrow.'

'Oh.'

'Work rang last week. We've got a booking to take the yacht around the Med.'

'How long for?'

'Fortnight, if I last that long. I might throw myself overboard.'

'Oh, it'll be fine. Think of the money.' Her words were flippant, but disappointment coursed through her. The past seven days had been rubbish. What the hell would she do without him for two weeks?

His face settled into a pleased smile. 'Are you going to miss me,

Fitzgerald?'

'Of course I'll miss you. Who's going to cook for me? I'll starve to death.'

Concern flashed across his face. 'You will be okay, won't you?'

'Brownie's honour.' She held up the three finger salute. 'Besides, I've got Birkin to keep me company. And Skank Manor to keep me out of trouble.'

'You're not going to miss me at all.'

'I promise I'll miss you every single day.'

'Will you answer when I call this time?'

Daisy nodded.

'Will you send me sexts?'

'Now you're pushing your luck.' But she couldn't prevent her relieved smile. She had her BFF back.

He glanced around the room. 'I can't believe how much you've done to the place, but do you really think this is a good idea? You have no carpets, no curtains. There are rats in the cellar, bats in the attic.'

'It's fine, an adventure.'

'Mental. What are you going to do first?'

'Joiner's coming in a couple of days to measure up for windows and the plumber–'

'Which joiner?'

'A local guy. Jack somebody.'

Xander groaned.

'What's wrong with him?' She'd only spoken to Jack on the phone. 'Is he a cowboy?'

'No. A part-time fireman.' Xander couldn't have sounded grumpier if he'd tried. 'And you'll like him. Van always turns into a giggling mess when he's around.'

'A fireman?' Daisy struggled to hide her grin. 'Wow.'

Xander tugged her hair, but finally the corners of his mouth twitched. 'Promise not to cop off with him while I'm away?'

'You're worried I'll pull if you're not here to chaperone me?'

He shrugged. 'It's a concern.'

Daisy laughed. 'Just because I'm not jumping into bed with you–'

'Do you have to remind me?'

'Doesn't mean I'm looking for someone else. I like being single. Fancy my new local for lunch?'

'You haven't got any other options,' he said, standing up. 'Are you aware you have almost no food in your new house? You don't even have crisps, which is very unlike you. All you have are ten bottles of very high-end wine, a box of Diet Coke and some biscuits.'

'Clara and Scott are coming round later. Fancy a party?'

'With you? Always.' He flashed the expected smile, but when it was gone, his forehead crumpled into a frown and from his pocket, he produced the key he'd offered her a fortnight earlier. 'If you get sick of the bats and rats, go to mine.'

'I'll be—'

'Just take the key, Daisy. Please.'

Wordlessly, she put the key in her back pocket, but her eyes never left his. Was Scott right? Was Xander serious about her? He genuinely seemed to give a fuck about her.

'Xand, I'd... well, I just want to say thank you. I mean whenever I've needed something you've been there... Birkin, Skank Manor, a shoulder to cry on...'

He didn't react. He didn't even blink. He simply stood there.

Impulsively, she stood on her tip toes and kissed his cheek. 'Thank you so much for everything.'

'I've got to go,' he said, backing off.

'What?'

He flashed a smile, but it never reached his eyes. 'Look, we'll have to forget lunch. Sorry, but I have an early flight. Got to pack. I'll call you later.'

She grabbed his t-shirt, refusing to let him leave. 'You can't just go. It won't be the same without you. High-end wine? Diet Coke? Please stay.'

'I can't,' he said, dropping a final kiss on the top of her head. 'Welcome home, Fitzgerald.'

And without another word, he disappeared downstairs, leaving Daisy standing in her new bedroom, somewhat stunned. How the hell had she pissed him off by saying thank you?

Chapter Eight

'Disaster has officially struck.' Daisy curled up with a mug of camomile tea, her phone tucked between her ear and shoulder. But despite her words and her body aching in places she hadn't previously known existed, a contented smile refused to leave her face.

'Did the rats stage a coup and evict you?' Xander asked.

From a super yacht cruising around the Med, came the now familiar sound of him flopping onto his bed and Daisy's smile grew. Even the occasional bout of dodgy reception didn't prevent his calls and if she had made him cross with her thank you, she never got a hint of it again. As he'd promised, he called her the evening before he left and every night since.

'It's way worse than *rats*.' Daisy smiled down at Birkin as his tail wagged at the word. He spent most days sniffing out the freaky-tailed creatures, but even if she spotted one, Daisy wasn't convinced she could call in an exterminator. 'I've got a full-time bloody job.'

Xander laughed. 'St Nick's?'

'Yes. Remember Ms St. Clement, the art teacher? She's knocked up.'

'Christ, I always thought she was batting for the other side. Isn't she about fifty?'

'No. Thirty-eight. Anyway, she's having twins and has to rest, so in desperation, they've asked me to do her maternity cover. I start the week after next.'

'Welcome, to the world of work, Fitzgerald. It sucks.'

She wouldn't argue with that. Okay, the money would mean she could afford rugs for the cold wooden floors, but working full-time would severely reduce her renovation time.

'What's *more* depressing,' she said, 'is Freya Dowson-bloody-Jones will be in my GCSE class. How the hell am I going to face her after James' party? It's utterly disastrous.'

Xander laughed quietly, clearly not buying into her distress.

'She's seen her mother do much worse, I'm sure. Anyway, how's life at Skank Manor?'

'It's good.'

In fact, life at Skank Manor couldn't be better. Instead of yearning for Finn, the Old Forge devoured her time. Daisy's days disappeared in a whirl of manual labour – be it knocking off crumbling plasterwork or doggedly stripping a century of paint from the skirting boards. She had way too much to do and couldn't afford to sit around obsessing over her soon-to-be *ex* husband's photo in *Heat*.

Though oddly, she'd always somehow kept half an eye on the clock, managing to tidy up before Xander rang.

'Did Jack turn up?' Xander asked, through a yawn.

'Yes,' she replied. 'We spent the afternoon shagging on the kitchen worktop.'

'You're not funny, Fitzgerald.'

Not that she'd admit it to Xander, but he was right. She did adore Jack. Twenty-seven, cute as a button and a fireman; what was there to hate?

'Actually,' she said, 'he drank more tea than he measured windows, helped himself to my cigarettes and didn't stop twittering about his girlfriend, Grace. But the little superstar has totally fixed my project plan.'

Based on her experience of renovating Clara's cottage and the Brighton beach house, Daisy had made a neat schedule and proudly put it on the kitchen worktop to show Jack. To his credit, he didn't actually laugh, but within minutes, he'd turned her A3 sheet into a spider diagram as he gave jobs realistic timescales, overlapped various tasks and knocked two months off the calendar time.

'I totally owe him a drink.' Daisy scooted under her duvet, her contented smile back in place.

'Are you in bed?'

'Yes, but if you ask what I'm wearing, I'll hang up.'

'What are you wearing?'

She laughed, but settled down, happily chatting to her KSCP until they were both too tired to stay awake.

On day seven, he didn't call.

Daisy stood in front of the cellar door, tapping her phone

against her leg. The plumber would be round on Monday and needed access to pipes throughout the house, so Daisy had to face up to the only room she'd actively avoided. Bats in the attic she could cope with, but rats in the cellar... even Birkin lay by the front door offering no moral support.

Why hadn't Xander called? It was almost eleven. She stared at her phone. Was it broken?

After filling a skip with junk, but thankfully finding no evidence of any rats, Daisy finally staggered to bed at two, accepting he wasn't calling.

He didn't call the next night, but buried behind a dubiously stained mattress, Daisy discovered a trunk of art supplies and a stack of vast, unused canvases. Surely, they'd be worth something to someone on eBay? And the ancient wardrobe and tallboy might need scrubbing with bleach to banish the mould, but finally, she'd have somewhere to put her clothes.

On day four of Xander's communications blackout, fed-up after a day of continual rain and discovering the roof leaked, Daisy window-shopped for fabulous things to decorate the house. She wish-listed large watercolours of lakes and mountains for the living room, random sketches of horses and dogs for the kitchen and some slightly sexy but very vague pastels for her bedroom. Sadly, she couldn't afford even a poster until payday.

Why would Xander stop ringing? Why wouldn't he reply to her messages?

Clearly he was avoiding her again and, utterly depressed, she cracked open one of Marcus' high-end bottles of wine, a crisp Chablis. On the upside, her drunken stab at art left her with rather successful reproductions of the sexy pastels she'd seen online, but for the first time since the barbeque, she woke with a hangover.

The following three mornings were no better.

The second hand on the clock hadn't moved, had it? Was the clock broken? How was it only twenty-five past – hadn't it been twenty-past last time she looked... about ten minutes ago?

'Okay, time to tidy up,' she said, perching on her desk. 'And Travis, a word?'

As the others conscientiously tidied their charcoals away, the school heartthrob, natural artist and resident bad boy, merely threw his into a box and sauntered over to her. Seventeen years-old... if she were eight years younger, she so would.

'Yes, miss?'

'I've just finished marking the class essays on Dali. Didn't see yours.'

He tipped his head, smiling slightly. 'Have you lost weight, miss? I mean, not that you needed to.'

'Well, actually...' Oh wait, was he hitting on her? And worse, was she actually blushing? Vaguely aware of the rest of the class filing out, Daisy attempted to deliver Travis a stern school-teacher scowl, the one Clara used with devastating effect. 'Travis, where's your essay?'

'The thing is, miss...' He tipped his head, frowning slightly. 'Maybe it's the light, but your bone structure, it's somehow more pronounced... I'd love to sketch you one day.'

Daisy folded her arms, trying not to grin. The guy was seventeen and he was making her feel about fourteen. Her amusement faded when Travis glanced down and a smile twitched at the corners of his mouth. Oh God, her tatty painting shirt, an old one she'd pinched from Xander, gaped open, flashing way too much cleavage, and way, way too much lace bra.

'Travis?' Freya stood in the doorway, her arms folded and her eyes blazing. 'What are you doing?'

Mercifully, Daisy's mobile lit up, buzzing on the table and bringing her back to reality. Xander? No. Robbie. Shaking back her hair, she raised her chin and jabbed a finger into Travis' chest.

'Your essay better be on my desk by nine o'clock on Monday, Mr McKillican, or you'll have a detention.'

His face broke into a scowl, but Daisy grabbed her phone and dashed into the supply room at the back of the class. Jesus, she'd nearly let a seventeen year-old boy sweet-talk her. What the hell had she been thinking?

'Robbie, how are you?' Daisy said.

'Have you heard from Xander?'

'No, have you?'

He swore and left the longest pause. 'The clients... had a fight and ended the cruise early. He's been home for two days. I'm in Scotland, but Van's... Will you go and see him?'

'In a heartbeat, but he doesn't seem to be speaking to me.'

'He doesn't seem to be speaking to anyone.'

'Why, what's going on?'

'I honestly don't know.' Robbie sighed. 'He does this from time to time. It started after the mess with Lucy Errington and to be honest, we thought he just needed to find someone new, but well, clearly... I could see it building. You must've seen the signs.'

What signs?

'The comfort blanket hats, getting wasted with James, generally looking suicidal... it's always the same.'

Xander looked suicidal? Whatever. He was just sulking because she wouldn't go out with him.

'You're friends... I thought he might talk to you,' Robbie said. 'Will you go and see him?'

'God, it's the least I can do.'

'Thank you,' he said, laughing a little. 'You really are a welcome change.'

'From what?' Even as the words came out, she knew she shouldn't have asked.

'From the unsuitable married women. Or worse still, girls who bear an uncanny resemblance to my wife.'

'Oh.' Daisy nibbled a thumbnail, her hands shaking. Vanessa – the epitome of a tall, utterly beautiful brunette. *And I'm another unsuitable married woman.*

'It's not a big deal. He's been in love with the idea of her since he was ten, not that he'd admit it of course. Don't tell him I told you that.'

'I won't.' But by God, it explained a few things. 'I'll go see him now.'

'Thanks, Daisy. Really, it means a lot.'

At Xander's cottage, lights were flashing from the TV, but when she knocked, there was no response. Reluctantly, she took out the key he'd given her and prayed he wouldn't hate her for interfering. As she turned the brass handle and the door relented, memories from June flooded back – that first kiss, those taut abs... Oh God, what if there were someone with him?

'Xand?' *Please, don't be with someone.* 'It's Daisy. Can I come in?'

'No. Piss off.'

Nice. 'Well, you gave me a key, so you're right out of luck, sunshine.'

Thick smoke filled the darkened living room and it wasn't from cigarettes. Stifled, Daisy opened the curtains a crack and the window a lot, but Xander, lying on the sofa, simply stared at the TV, not bothering to acknowledge she'd come in.

'You're smoking weed?' she asked, perching on the windowsill.

No answer, but looking at the ashtray, she'd say he had been since he got back. At least his clean clothes suggested he wasn't in quite the black gloom she'd been in on Finn's birthday. The empty bottle of whisky didn't bode well though. She held it up.

'Breakfast?'

He finally glanced at her. 'Pots and kettles? But no, ran out of booze two days ago. You drank it all, remember?'

All too well. The empty tequila bottle still stood in the fire place where she'd left it.

'I got you a present.' He tossed her a small box, which she managed to catch before her heart stopped. It was a ring-sized box. 'Don't get excited. I'm not proposing.'

There was a mean look in his eye, but reassured at the *not proposing* line, Daisy peeked inside the little box to find a beautiful moonstone and crystal daisy dangling from a silver belly bar. For a minute, she held her hand against her mouth. It had to be one of the all-time loveliest gifts she'd ever received – utterly beautiful and perfectly her.

Giving into a wholly uncool grin, she faced Xander. 'Thank you. It's amazing, really...'

He didn't smile back.

Far from it. Just peeking from under his over-sized beanie, his brow was furrowed in a deep frown and his eyes, those beautiful deep brown eyes were filled with... Oh dear God, she'd seen that look before – at the cricket, the day they met. He'd taken off that cricket helmet, tossed it aside and let out a huge sigh. She'd assumed he was bored, as if village cricket wasn't this thing. But look at his family, the fact he lived in Gosthwaite – village cricket was exactly his thing. It wasn't boredom; it was... palpable despair.

And that day, he'd suggested the vodka – he was as desperate as her to blot out reality. How had she never questioned why? Misery did love company after all.

But Xander wasn't in the black gloom she was in on Finn's birthday. No, this was worse. This was long-term gloom. But what the hell could be so wrong with his perfect life?

She moved to sit on the edge of the sofa, but as her hand touched his leg, he flinched. 'Xand, what's wrong? Can I help?'

Rather than ignore her again, he sat up and slowly looked her over. The complete lack of emotion on his face unnerved her, but as Daisy tried to back away, he reached up and gently pushed her stupid curls off her face. Shivers surged down her body and Daisy struggled to breathe.

'You can let me take your sexy arse to bed. Again.'

He kissed her.

With his hand behind her neck, she couldn't escape or stop herself kissing him back. Stop herself? She wanted to drag her fingers through his hair, to feel his hands under her top, drawing those circles on her spine. Instead, with extreme reluctance, she dug her nails into her palms and pulled away, her lips tingling, her cheeks flushed.

'Would that really help?' she asked, gazing into those deep brown eyes. She'd have to go through with it if he said yes. *Have to go through with it?* Jesus, ninety-eight percent of her body prayed he'd say yes.

'No.' He lay down and relit his joint as he turned back to the TV.

'Are you going to stay stoned all day?' Her heart pounded in her chest, still recovering from the kiss and the overwhelming disappointment that he'd said no. 'Xander, what's going on?'

Nothing.

'Robbie rang me. He's worried.'

Xander didn't even blink.

'Should I throw you in the shower and turn the cold water on?'

A reaction of sorts, he almost laughed and Daisy knelt down, reaching out to stroke his hair. The sadness in his eyes almost broke her heart.

'Can I look after you now?'

There was an almost non-existent nod but, all the same, it was a nod.

'Can I stay at Skank Manor?' he asked. 'I'm so fucking bored of these walls.'

Daisy nodded. Even a Knight-in-Shining-Cricket-Pads needed a Damsel-in-Distressed-Jeans at times.

Xander was stoned, really stoned, so she let him chill and eventually he fell asleep on the sofa. Thank God, she could finally turn off bloke TV. She'd had re-runs of *Deadliest Catch* and *Top Gear* all bloody day. He'd been asleep for an hour or so when Vanessa turned up.

'Is he here?' she whispered, peeking nervously into the house. Daisy nodded. 'I can't stay. New groom's keeping an eye on things.' She handed over a casserole. 'He said you weren't much of a cook so I thought you could use this. How is he?'

'Asleep, stoned, hasn't said a word.'

'Par for the course, I'm afraid. Tell him I forgive him. Thanks, Daisy.' She smiled her good bye.

The casserole smelled divine.

'Has she gone?' Xander yawned as he wandered into the kitchen.

'You could've said hello. She said she forgives you. What for?'

He glanced at the floor. 'I told her to piss off and leave me alone.'

'You'll have to apologise to her tomorrow.' *And me.* 'Thankfully, she brought food. I wasn't planning on rustling anything up and you don't seem too enthused either.'

Xander took the dish and peered inside. 'You don't seriously think I'd eat anything you cooked, do you? Clara told me you nearly killed Finn.'

'There are more important things in life than being tied to a cooker. Food is fuel.'

'Daisy, you think the lemon in your vodka is fuel.'

'And?'

'You're a borderline anorexic.'

She should send him home. He could deal with his own bloody problems.

'Do you have anything that doesn't have microwave instructions on the side?' he asked, rummaging through the cupboards.

Guilty as charged. 'Taking the piss, feeling better?'

'Actually, no.' He rested his head against the cupboard door. 'I don't know what's worse, being on that fucking yacht or being here.'

He was the one who asked to stay with her. She bit down onto her bottom lip until she'd calmed down. 'And what's so bad about being here?'

'Everything in the fucking world.'

How could she answer that? She stropped off, leaving him to

finish pimping dinner while she took Birkin for his evening walk.

They ate dinner at the kitchen table in deathly, uncomfortable, silence. Daisy tried to be calm, patient and super-bloody-understanding, but when Xander swore at Birkin and her little dog scuttled away, hurt and confused, she gave up.

'Okay, how long are you going to mope for?' she asked, trying not to raise her voice as she cleared the table. 'I want to help you, like you did for me, but I can't if I don't know what's wrong.' His jaw twitched, but he didn't look up. 'Do you think an ounce of skunk will make you happy?' He toyed with his glass. 'Do you think it's about time to sort out your own problems instead of mine?' Still no response. 'Oh for God's sake.'

She dropped the dishes in the sink, but before she could say something she'd regret, she scuttled off to hide in the living room with the rest of the wine.

Well, that could have gone better. Cursing herself for losing her patience, she drained her glass and lit a cigarette.

'I'll go.' Xander slouched against the wall, focusing on the logs burning in the fire. 'You don't need this. You have enough of your own problems.'

'No, I don't, thanks to you and you're not going anywhere.' She patted the sofa. 'What's going on?'

'I...' He sank onto the sofa, taking his time to refill her glass before letting out an enormous sigh. 'I hate my entire fucking life, Daze.'

Oh. 'Work?'

Slowly, he nodded.

'So get a new job.'

'It's not just that. I want...' He downed half her wine.

'And get your own glass.' She elbowed him. 'What do you want?'

'It doesn't matter.'

'For God's sake, you're twenty-two. The world's your oyster. What do you want to do?'

'I want to be a chef again.'

'So be a chef again.'

'You know I can't, not after Lucy.' He took a long drag on the cigarette and let out the smoke with another lengthy sigh. 'Besides it's not that simple. I want more.'

'Everything's that simple. How much more?'

'I want my own restaurant and I want... you.' He glanced back at her, shaking his head. 'Seriously, I don't know what you've done, but it's killing me. The other week I actually stood in Boots smelling shampoos, trying to find the one you use. It's coconut and lime, right?'

'Coconut, lime and macadamia oil. My mum makes it.'

He closed his eyes and laughed. 'I can't believe I've just told you that.'

She struggled not to grin, though there was nothing she could do about her burning cheeks. He was obsessing over how her hair smelled? 'But what's so difficult? Aside from the last one, they're all totally achievable. Your family has a chain of restaurants and you *are* a chef. Why don't you just do it?'

He swore and ran his fingers through his hair, staring at the ceiling. 'I'm too young. I need more experience. I can't do it.'

'Can't or scared to?'

'I've been sous chef for a genius head chef on that stupid yacht for two years. I can turn out top end food, fine dining. I trained with some amazing people. Anthony's got two stars now and Grandpa Oliver... have I ever told you Oliver's my middle name?'

'Alexander Oliver Golding.' The only way to say it was with a plum in ones mouth. She giggled. 'You're so public school.'

He smiled for a second. 'I don't want, well I'm not aiming for a Michelin-starred place, but I can't...'

'You can do whatever you want to do.'

He sighed. 'Back in the day, Rob and I used to talk about opening a restaurant.'

'Robbie, really?'

'He hates his job too. Can you imagine how much of the girls' lives he misses out on? He managed the bistros until he fell out with Dad.'

She nudged him. 'I dare you to tell Robbie.'

'Dares?' The frown still lurked, but at least he was smiling. 'I haven't recovered from your last one. Are you sure you're not achievable?'

'Oh, stop it.' She swatted his leg but laughed as he gently tugged her hair. 'I don't have my beer goggles on now, sunshine.'

God, she'd missed him. And two weeks in the Med hadn't done him any physical harm. His skin was chestnut brown and by the look of his t-shirt, the boy was buffer than ever. She'd forgotten how perfect he was, too blinded by her KSCP, the nice guy who'd saved her life. But sat beside her, his thumb running along the edge of the wine glass, was the Xander who'd kissed her for hours when they were coked up but didn't take advantage because he'd made a promise; the Xander who'd licked salt off her stomach before he'd knocked back a shot of tequila and gently taken the lemon from her mouth.

It was madness, but her heart thumped against her chest and she stared into his deep, brown eyes, desperate to do it all again. For months, she'd pretended she didn't fancy Xander, but who was she kidding? She fancied the pants off him. Literally. Oh God. By Xander's rules, she had to be sober. She was sober. Well, almost. Two tiny glasses of wine surely didn't count.

'What?' he asked, frowning in confusion.

And she watched it happen, the moment of realisation. Hope sparked in his eyes.

'Daze, what would've happened if I'd said yes this afternoon?'

She lifted her chin, refusing to blush. 'You would've taken my sexy arse to bed. *Again.*'

Still frowning, he sat up and spent a minute gazing into her eyes before slowly leaning forwards – so slowly she wondered if he might be taking the piss, that he'd laugh and say *whatever.* He didn't. He kissed her. Not counting the sofa kiss that afternoon, it had been two months since they last kissed. God, she'd missed it.

'Daisy...' Xander repeatedly pulled away to talk but his lips kept coming back for more. '...this... what about tomorrow?'

His hands were already under her t-shirt. Who the hell cared about tomorrow?

'Daze?' He dropped tiny kisses down her neck, clearly expecting an answer.

'What?'

She really couldn't concentrate or care less as shivers flew down her body, but Xander stopped, taking hold of her face in both hands.

'How will you feel about this tomorrow?'

'I don't know. I don't care.'

They were kissing again and this was the fast-track to shagging kind of kissing. Daisy's fingers skimmed down his t-shirt, desperate to take it off, to feel his skin against hers.

Xander grabbed her hand, stopping her. 'You don't care?'

'So?' *You're twenty-two, why don't you ever just want a shag?*

'So, I care. I don't want...' Xander leaned away and linked his fingers behind his head, a determined effort not to touch her. 'Do you remember after Finn turned up, when you told me I wasn't him and I never could be? You meant it, didn't you?'

Guilt swamped her as she nodded.

'I never, ever want to feel like that again, like I'm second best.'

'But you're... It's not like that.'

'Daisy, it's exactly like that.' Xander stood up and took a photo off the wall, one of her and Finn on their wedding day. 'Who do you really want, Daisy?'

He dropped the picture in her hands then strode out of the room, mumbling expletives.

How could he leave? The fire was lit and the wine poured; she had on good underwear and her legs were freshly shaved. For God's sake, they'd been a t-shirt away from shagging. *Again.*

Ignoring the urge to wail into a scatter cushion, Daisy stared at the photo. Okay, no excuses, no booze, no drugs, no dares – just yes or no... Did she want Xander, not Finn? Finn smiled back with an arrogance she'd not noticed before. *Why do I love you?* Oh God, she really did still love him; she couldn't help it. But loving Finn wasn't the only problem; what about the Has-beens, the devastated girls Xander left in his wake? Was she prepared to risk utter heartbreak for one night of sex – albeit, spine-meltingly fabulous sex if the last time was anything to go by?

'Well?' Xander was back, leaning against the wall.

'I don't know.'

'At least there's hope for the future.'

'What about now?'

He gave her a slow smile and the naughtiest glint appeared in those fabulous eyes as he gave her a blatant once over. Being second best was the last thing on his mind.

Barely dropping eye contact with him, she stood up and peeled off her t-shirt. He muttered something in response but didn't make a move, so she shot him the cheekiest of winks and popped open the button on her jeans as she left the room. Upstairs, she lay on her bed, wearing nothing but black lace underwear and the biggest smile. Xander wasn't far behind.

He leant against the doorframe, tilting his head to one side as he studied the paintings propped against the bare plaster walls. 'Soft porn art?'

Though her cheeks were on fire, she rolled onto her back, trying to look as seductive as she knew how. 'I made them.'

'Always full of surprises, Fitzgerald.'

Crossing her legs was her only response.

'I think almost three months of waiting is pretty good going,' he said, perching on the bed next to her. 'Pretty heroic actually.'

'You've always been my hero.' She abandoned seductive and gave in to the biggest grin as he trailed a finger gently down her arm.

'And we'll deal with tomorrow... tomorrow?'

She nodded, and although his eyes repeatedly glanced over her body, he was never going to start this. Instead, she pushed him back and knelt astride him, adoring how he closed his eyes and took a deep breath.

'But don't forget, it's always better to regret something you've done,' she whispered, her lips millimetres from his, 'than something you haven't.'

Chapter Nine

Xander rolled over, raising an arm to cover his eyes and the duvet slipped, revealing his perfectly toned torso. Praying he'd wake up before she gave in to temptation and perved at the rest, Daisy kept busy playing with his hair. Bugger it. She kissed the sleeping beauty. The second her lips touched his, he responded, kissing her back.

'Morning,' she said, resting her chin on his chest.

As he opened his eyes, a lovely, lazy smile took over his perfect face. 'I've imagined waking up with you like this for ages.'

'The bird's nest hair, morning breath and smudged mascara?'

'All perfectly sexy.' His hands disappeared under the duvet. 'How do you feel today? Regrets? Catholic guilt?'

'If I had any regrets, do you think I'd let you do that?' For the first time in seven months, when she woke, Daisy hadn't looked for Finn. Instead, she'd smiled because Alexander Golding was asleep next to her. 'I don't regret anything and it turns out I might not be Catholic after all.'

To prove her point, she kissed him and in seconds things turned as hot as they had been the night before. Xander flipped her onto her back, pushing the duvet back as he scattered tiny kisses over her midriff, one hand sneaking up her thigh. Oh dear God. His tongue flicked at her navel, making the moonstone daisy jingle. At around midnight, he'd carefully unscrewed the Pacha cherries and replaced them with the daisy he'd given her. It wasn't a proposal, she'd told herself. Just a piece of jewellery.

'So,' he said, kissing his way back up her body as she fumbled in her bedside drawer for a condom. 'Do we have to keep this secret until you're actually divorced, or can the world know about us?'

Us? Daisy froze, staring at him. Us? They were friends who'd had sex, nothing more. She didn't say it aloud, but clearly, from his frown, she didn't need to.

'Okay, what?' he asked, sitting up. 'No regrets but…'

But, I can't go out with you.

Oh, God. She really didn't want to go out with Xander – the

idea filled her with horror. He was twenty-two, stupidly good-looking and definitely not a long-term investment. Maybe they'd last a few months, being wildly optimistic, maybe even a year but eventually, he'd bugger off with a leggy brunette and she'd be left alone, heartbroken again. No way would she end up a Has-been like all those girls at James' party.

'Xand... I'm not ready for a new relationship. I want to be single.'

He leant forwards, his elbows resting on his bent knees. 'But bar the obvious, we're practically going out already.'

'No, we're not.'

He looked away, but she didn't miss his scowl. This wasn't going well.

'Please, don't be cross. It's not all bad.'

He laughed without humour. 'How the hell do you work that out? You've just said no.'

'Well, I'm kind of saying no.'

If he hadn't said anything, they'd be shagging by now. Oh God, how selfish could she be? She wanted her new best friend and she wanted the fabulous sex – she wanted both but without the break-up. Was it possible to shag Xander but keep him at arm's length? Was it possible to have and eat that particular piece of cake? She almost smiled until he turned to her, frowning as if she'd shot his puppy.

She took his hand, linking her fingers with his. 'Xand, I like what we have. Can't we stick to just friends but maybe with the odd night like last night? FWB?'

'FWB?'

'You know, Friends With Benefits?'

'I know what it means,' he snapped. 'But for Christ's sake, Daisy, I'm not looking for the occasional shag when there's nothing better on offer. I want *you* to be my girlfriend.'

There was a long, difficult silence, which she hadn't the first idea how to end but, eventually his thumb brushed her hand.

'Seriously, FWB? That's what you want?'

At her nod, he swore, slumping back against the headboard. Clearly, they wouldn't be spending the rest of the morning in bed. She tossed the condom back in the drawer and scurried off for a shower feeling worse than she had on Finn's birthday.

The orange tiles needed knocking off the kitchen walls, but Daisy sat on the worktop, next to the Aga, and texted Clara.

Girl talk needed. Ring me at morning break?

The kettle clicked as Xander appeared looking like an athlete. How the hell did he make leggings and trainers look sexy? She tipped her head to the side, watching as he moved through a series of stretches. If only his depressed frown wasn't back.

'Are you going running?' It struck her as far too much like hard work. 'I wondered how you stayed so fit in between your extreme sport trips away.'

'The treadmill's the only thing that keeps me sane on that stupid yacht.'

'Is running a good sign? Better than getting stoned, at least.'

'You walk up a sodding big hill when you want to think. I run.'

'I'm sorry. Have I made things worse?'

'No, but you don't make things easy. FWB.' He kissed her then gently tugged her ponytail. 'I've borrowed your iPod.'

He left, running effortlessly down the bridleway with Birkin trotting alongside. Daisy filled her mug without shifting her bum. She really ought to do more exercise. Or she could just go back to bed. She was knackered.

Well over an hour later, Xander jogged back into the yard and her arse was, once again, firmly planted on the worktop by the Aga. Thankfully, his frown had gone and his eyes sparkled. Birkin, his tongue lolling, flopped into his basket – too exhausted to muster a hello.

'You have some of the worst music.' Xander dropped the iPod on the table and a kiss on her lips. 'The first Take That album? Dolly Parton and Nancy Sinatra? Have you even moved?'

'Not much.' She'd tried sleeping, but then Robbie had called and she'd twiddled her thumbs, waiting for Xander to come back. She enjoyed watching him stretch again. It was like having a young David Beckham in the house. 'How are you?'

'Resilient. I'll play by your rules. You can call it what you like but basically it's no different than before. At least now, I can drag you to bed while I wait for you to get over your soon-to-be-ex-husband. It's a massive improvement.'

'I've realised, that this year I've shagged you more than I have my husband.'

'It'd better stay that way too.'

'Let's go to bed. Stay there for two days.' She grabbed his t-shirt, pulling him closer.

'Later, I promise.' He took a deep breath. 'But after I've had a shower, I want to see Rob. Is that okay?'

'He's coming round in about thirty minutes.' Daisy's lips brushed up Xander's neck. God, even coming back from a run, he smelled perfectly edible. Maybe it was a pheromone thing. 'Plenty of time.'

'No... later.' But as the words came out, his gaze travelled down her body. 'Do you dress like this on purpose?'

She grinned down at her clothes – a t-shirt and tatty denim shorts. 'Like what?'

'You're not wearing a bra and that's my t-shirt.' His eyes darkened. 'Pants?'

She shook her head and in a heartbeat, Xander's mouth descended on hers. Clearly, he was as up for this as her. Daisy wrapped her legs around him, pulling him closer until they were pressed together. Dear God, she needed them to get very naked, very quickly.

Oh, sod it.

Crossing her arms, she grabbed the hem of her t-shirt and slowly lifted it. She'd barely got it over her shoulders before Xander's hands were on her, his thumbs stroking, his lips brushing. The teasing, the playful nibbles... they sent waves of pure pleasure surging through her.

Her t-shirt lay discarded in the sink, his on the floor, and she wrapped her arms around his neck, letting him carry her out of the kitchen.

'What happened to *later*?' she whispered as they reached the hallway.

'To hell with later. How about now?' Xander put her down, his knee pushing hers apart. Not that they needed much encouragement. 'Right now, Fitzgerald.'

His gravelly tone tripped her switches, sending her from playfully horny to desperate. She dragged her nails down his perfect abs, eager to get him naked, but he flinched.

'No tickling.' He laughed and grasped her hands, pinning them over her head.

Instinctively, Daisy tried to pull away, but Xander had her wrists clamped against the wall. She was trapped.

No.

The air in her lungs wouldn't go in or out.

She couldn't move her arms.

Please, no.

His mouth was moving in front of her, saying something, but she could only hear white noise, her own heart thumping in her head.

Can't breathe.

'Daze... Daisy?'

She was free, sitting on the stairs with Xander kneeling in front of her, saying sorry, sorry, sorry, over and over. Sweet air filled her lungs and his hands held her face, his beautiful, brown eyes wide with blatant concern.

'I didn't think,' he said. 'I'm sorry. I'm so sorry.'

Daisy blinked, sucking in oxygen. Jesus Christ, she'd totally panicked. She reached up a hand, raking her fingers through his hair. 'I didn't mean to tickle you. Sorry.'

'No, it's my—'

She shut him up with a kiss.

Her heart still thumped at a million beats a second but his slow, sweet kisses, his muttered apologies, calmed her soul. Soporific, she closed her eyes, laying back on the stairs, her fingers still in Xander's hair as he kissed his way down her neck, between her breasts, over the moonstone daisy. Breathless and buzzing, she lifted her ass, helping as he removed her shorts.

'Seriously, you dressed expecting this,' Xander mumbled, his fingers brushing over her.

'Oh God, Xander...'

His mouth joined his fingers, tasting her, teasing her. Had anything ever felt that good?

'FWB is going to be the best thing ever invented.' She had no idea if the words tumbled out of her mouth, or if she merely screamed them in her head as she came. How could he do that to her so easily? It had to be pheromones.

'FWB?' Xander said, his breathing unsteady as his cock replaced his fingers. 'I'll take anything I can get from you right now, but just so we're clear, I intend to spend the rest of my life buried in you.'

Buried in her?

'I'll be in here...' He stilled, closing his eyes as her muscles contracted around him.

She wanted to crack a joke, to make him laugh, but her body was still out of her control and it was all she could do to keep her eyes open.

'I'll be in here...' He kissed her forehead. 'I want to be the first thing you think about in the morning and the last thing at night.'

Like he wasn't already? Daisy wedged a foot against the banister, struggling to focus as they moved together. Oh dear God, she was building again.

'And most of all...' His rested a hand over her heart, his eyes burning into hers. 'I'll be buried deep in here.'

Crying out his name, Daisy came again, hard and fast, and seconds later, Xander joined her. They lay there, shattered and shaking, the wooden stairs digging into her back, but Daisy couldn't stop her grin.

Buried. Buried was good.

'You're a dreadful influence, Fitzgerald,' he muttered as she came back from her second shower.

'Get up. Robbie could come round any minute.'

'More than I could. You've destroyed me.'

'Come on, this looks awful.'

'He'd only be jealous.' Xander lay across the bed with his head hanging off the edge. 'Are you sure that painting is the right way up? It's totally perverse from this angle.'

The doorbell rang and Daisy abandoned her own assessment of what she'd assumed were woman's legs propped against a wall. Instead she hurriedly pulled on her jeans and planted a kiss on Xander's cheek. 'Just get up.'

Still trying to dismiss a ludicrous grin before she faced Robbie, Daisy pulled open the front door, but instead of Xander's fabulous brother, Clara's beautiful face beamed back.

'Thank God,' Daisy said. 'We need to talk.'

'We certainly bloody do.' Clara's grin was bigger than Daisy's.

'Tea? How come you're not at school?'

'I'm off sick.'

Off sick and happy? The last time Clara looked so stupidly happy was when Scott agreed to marry her. What else would make Clara smile like...

'Ohmigod, you're *pregnant?*'

'It's due in March,' Clara replied, inciting a bout of squealing, hugs and kisses. 'I'm nearly twelve weeks and we were going to tell everyone this weekend, but then you texted...'

'When did you find out?'

'Day before yesterday. I was totally clueless. Just thought the bigger boobs were because I was due on, but the other day, I nearly threw up just looking at Scott's mum's cauliflower cheese. She put me straight.'

Daisy put the kettle on then leant back against the Aga. Clara didn't look anymore pregnant than she had at Oscar's Bar and Bistro. 'OMG, were you knocked up when we went to the barbeque?'

Clara nodded. 'Not ideal, but apparently the baby hadn't implanted by then—'

'Did you note my blank expression?'

'It wasn't attached by the umbilical cord, so it got no booze.'

'Ah, okay.'

'And in other mind-blowing news, Scott wants to get married before junior arrives and after what I've put him through, I'm in no position to argue, so we're getting married next month, October the twenty-third, so we can honeymoon over half-term.'

Cue more squealing.

'A month to plan a wedding?' Daisy took out three mugs and splashed milk into the bottom of each. 'God, there's a lot to do.'

Clara sat down at the kitchen table. 'You're telling me. We managed to get a venue but I haven't even thought about a dress and Scott's mum's already banging on about the seating plan.'

The doorbell shrilled before Daisy could ask Clara if she'd prefer a modern or vintage style dress and apologising, she ran to answer it, again expecting Robbie. To her utter surprise, Tabitha bloody Doyle stood on the doorstep, wearing leather jeans and a shy smile.

'Hello, Daisy-chain.' She peered past Daisy, wrinkling her nose at the bare walls and floors. 'How on earth are you living like this? Though I must say, from what James said, I was expecting it to smell like some hobo's armpit. Am I allowed in?'

What the hell. 'Yes, of course. Come in. Today's a good day. My best friend is pregnant and getting married next month.'

Tabitha's smile returned. 'How fab. I'm insanely jealous of her already.'

Daisy doubted that. Tabitha didn't strike her as the most maternal of women and after her eighteen month marriage to a New York rapper ended with an acrimonious legal battle, she'd publically denounced marriage as a ridiculous, out-of-date institution.

'Tabitha Doyle... the actress? Wow.' Clara shook Tabitha's hand, pretending to be oblivious to the Finn connection. 'I'm a huge fan.'

Daisy pouted. Why was Clara being nice to the wannabe-husband stealer?

'Can't stay, sweetie,' Tabitha said, taking the mug of tea Daisy handed her. 'I'm meeting Marcus for drinks and I've a chinwag with the Corrie folk this evening. I'm thinking of becoming a soap-star.'

As what? Brought up by an Irish poet and an English heiress, Tabitha struggled to disguise her ridiculous upper-class accent with anything other than her father's native tongue. Could she pull off being a Mancunian barmaid? Unlikely.

Daisy's dubious frown grew as Tabitha handed her two envelopes.

'For you and Xander, sweetie. James said he was here. We're bored silly and thought it'd be a hoot to play stage two.'

'Stage two?' Daisy raised her eyebrows.

'Of Forfeit, sweetie. The first party is on the first, for my birthday – no gifts, please.' She visibly shuddered, as if horrified by the mere idea. 'The second shindig is on Halloween.'

'Do we have to play silly dares?' she asked.

Tabitha turned to Clara. 'Last time, Daisy had to kiss Xander for five minutes. Hardly a chore.' She sighed with all the drama of a fifties heroine. 'Daisy-chain, I had to drink ten shots of bloody whisky. I puked for hours while you and Xander were snogging. I've seen the photos, sweetie.' She gave a cheery wink. 'Oh, come on. Say yes.'

Daisy shook her head. 'It's five hundred pounds to play.' And she didn't have fifty – not that she'd admit that to Tabitha bloody Doyle.

'Don't tell me you can't afford it. That handbag's worth over a grand.' Tabitha nodded to the Chloé bag hanging over the back of a dining chair. 'Flog that. I mean, what is it, like five years old?'

'Two.' *And a present from my husband – the one you tried to shag.*

Tabitha put her tea down without taking a sip. To be fair, Daisy wouldn't have touched it either. She'd filled it with resentment and just a drop of milk.

'Just think, if you win, you could buy a shiny new one. Clara, talk her into it, *please*.'

'Firstly, you all must have more money than sense. Secondly,' Clara said, giving a wink Tabitha couldn't see, 'Daisy never does dares.'

Cowbag. Daisy scowled. 'I did the last one.'

'Kissing Xander... ooh, how tricky,' Clara said. 'Dare you to play?'

'I'll be there.' How had she been dared to do a dare by her best friend?

'Fabulous.' Tabitha air-kissed them on her way out. 'Have to dash or I'll be late meeting Marcus. He's holed up at a hotel in Grasmere with three women. No need to show me out.'

Daisy watched Tabitha's leather-clad, perfect arse disappear out of the kitchen, with a mixture of amusement and irritation – she really didn't know what to make of that girl.

Clara's face broke into an evil grin. 'Isn't that the ho-bag Finn turned down last year?'

I love you, Clara. Once they heard Tabitha's car drive away, they erupted into evil giggles.

'Please, promise you'll do your dare?' Clara said.

'I don't have five hundred quid.'

'I'll lend you it.'

'What if I don't win?'

'You'd better. You have to wipe the practised smile off that posh bitch's face. You should watch her...' Her words petered out as she peered out of the window, distracted by Robbie climbing out of his Discovery. 'God, he really is the SMT, the sexiest man in town.' She straightened her top and fluffed her hair, frowning at Daisy with suspicion. 'Did Tabitha say Xander was here?'

Daisy only had time to nod before Robbie knocked on the door. 'Come in. It's like Piccadilly Circus round here today.'

Robbie's face softened into a lovely smile when he saw Clara.

'Scott's already told you?' she asked.

'Rang an hour ago. He said he can't concentrate at work and walks around like a zombie mumbling, *I'm going to be a Dad.* Congratulations, angel.' In the customary Golding fashion, he wrapped her in a hug and kissed the top of her head.

Clara mouthed, *I love him* and Daisy struggled not to giggle.

'Congratulations?' Xander asked as he walked in. 'Knocked up, Clara?' She nodded and he dropped a kiss on her head.

Clara took a long look at Xander, then Daisy, no doubt taking in their wet hair.

'The Golding Brothers need to talk,' Daisy whispered, dragging Clara into the living room before she had chance to put two and two together in front of Robbie.

'So do we, don't we?' She curled up on the sofa, nursing her tea. 'Why the hell is Xander staying here? You did it again, didn't you?'

'Well, that's not why he's here but, yes.' They suppressed their squeals. 'He's fed up and I'm looking after him, returning the favour.' She explained about the restaurant, praying Robbie would be up for Xander's idea.

'And how are you?' Clara asked.

'Well, not ready for a relationship.' Not with him at least. Daisy took a deep breath. 'We're going to be Friends With Benefits.'

'And he agreed? Scott told me to piss off when I suggested it years ago. That is so perfect, but why don't you just go out with him?'

Daisy picked at her nail polish. He wanted to be buried in her heart. Shuddering in his arms, post-coital, it seemed a great idea… but in the cold light of sensible? 'He's too young and too good-looking.'

'He's less than three years younger than you. You're an idiot, but at least you're getting laid again. And how was last night?'

Despite her burning cheeks, Daisy couldn't stop a huge grin. 'Amazing. How the hell does someone get that good at twenty-two?'

Clara raised her eyebrows. 'A lot of practice? Though I'd put it down to the Michelin-starred cougar. But surely he's not better than the HMS?'

Finn had been something else – he'd taught Daisy a trick or two, but often he'd wanted to venture a little too leftfield. 'Actually, yes. Much more me.'

'If I wasn't so blissfully happy, I'd be eye-gougingly jealous.'

'But you're having a baby.' Daisy looked at Clara's belly. 'Can you feel anything?'

'Other than sick and stupidly tired? No, not yet. But since I found out I feel... special.' Clara stared at the wall with a serene smile and Daisy realised how amazing it might be to be pregnant. 'And sick.' Serenity over. 'I'm going to be nearly twenty weeks at the wedding. Wasn't quite my plan to look like a whale in the photos.'

'Oh, what about an empire-line dress, something to hide the bump?'

After twenty minutes scouring the internet, laughing at thousand pound satin reproductions of toilet roll dollies and sighing over sleek silk-chiffon numbers that had the ominous words *Price On Application* beside them, Clara announced she had to go.

'Scott's taking me to buy paint for the nursery.'

Daisy buried her smidgen of jealousy with another bout of hugging and squealing. Clara deserved this, to be happy.

'It is so wrong to still fancy Robbie Golding this bloody much.' Clara sighed as they watched the Golding brothers chatting in the yard. 'I've told Scott that, pregnant or not, I would run off and leave him if Robbie offered to take me away from all this. He said he'd wish him luck, that he'd need it.'

After two massive hugs, Clara left and Daisy tore open the envelopes from Tabitha. The first invite was for birthday drinks at Oscar's Bar and Bistro, Xander's dad's place. Wasn't that a little downmarket for Xander's crowd? The second invite was for a Halloween-themed night at Tabitha's apartment – why couldn't she have a flat like normal people? Silly cow. When Tabitha made that very public pass at Finn, it'd been hugely embarrassing and even sparked the odd rumour she was shagging him. It was all utter nonsense and Finn had been mortified, but did it make Tabitha a bad person? Maybe Daisy should give her a chance.

Xander and Robbie came in wearing huge smiles. Were they doing the restaurant? Before Daisy could ask, Xander's phone rang and he disappeared, leaving her with Robbie.

'What the hell did you do to him?' he asked, wearing a very amused expression, but Daisy busied herself opening the last bottle of Marcus' high-end wine. 'Four bloody years I've put up with the mood swings and never got a word out of him. How on earth did you do it?'

'We just talked.' Daisy pulled a face. 'But I did lose my temper.'

'Never worked for me, but well done.' He took a glass of wine and sat at the table. 'We're going to do it. We're going to open a restaurant.'

They chinked glasses as Xander came back.

'Mum said hello,' he said to Robbie.

'Did you tell her?' she asked, reclaiming her position next to the Aga.

'Christ, no. She'd tell Dad. Will you help me trawl the estate agents this afternoon? We're looking for a gastro pub or decent sized restaurant.'

'With outside space,' Robbie added.

'But not in a town.' Xander grinned at his brother. 'Somewhere in Gosthwaite would be perfect.'

'You two don't ask for much,' Daisy said. 'Where's the money coming from?'

Xander's grin faded and he rubbed a hand over his hair. 'I'm going to sell my cottage. Can I come and live here?'

'If you need to,' she said before she'd thought about it. 'No,' she added when she had.

'Van will beg to have you back at ours. I often think she only married me for my brother's cooking.' Robbie downed his wine. 'Or buy somewhere cheaper in Haver... ton.' His smile grew to a hugely amused grin. 'Lost your temper, did you, Daisy?'

Xander had stretched, scratching his neck and revealing a love bite previously hidden by his jumper. She hadn't meant to do it, well she had but as payback for the one he'd accidentally given her.

Daisy blew Robbie a kiss. 'You can bugger off. I've had quite enough of you for one day.'

'But not my little brother I bet.'

A mock brotherly fight ensued as Xander threw him out, but they had a final hug before Robbie left.

'You might've changed my life,' Xander said, sheepishly smiling at the ceiling as he leant against the kitchen door.

'Well, that makes us quits.' She held out her hand, beckoning him over. 'Happy?'

'Are you kidding? I've got you with *benefits* and I'm going to open a restaurant.' He sat next to her and kissed her cheek. 'Thank you, seriously. I know I still have to go to work, but it'll be bearable. Telling Rob has made it real.'

'Robbie said you get like this occasionally.' She held his hand as he tensed. 'If it happens again, please let me know.'

Silence.

'Xand?'

'It's hard.'

'Same old problem on the same old people? Why not text me something so I'll understand? Text me DAF and I'll come running.'

'DAF?' He laughed, putting his arm around her. 'Why?'

'Remember? They're my initials? Drunk and—'

'I know what it stands for. I mean, why will you come running?'

'Because you were there for me.'

He nodded. 'I suppose I ought to go home. Leave you in peace.'

'But you promised me two days in bed.'

'In that case, can we go on a proper date? One where we're not pretending to be just friends. Just for tonight?'

'A proper date works for me, sunshine.'

Chapter Ten

The proper date – the one where they weren't pretending to be *just friends* – rocked. Okay, Daisy might've preferred to have ducked off home and got naked a lot earlier than Xander wanted, but how could she complain when his primary mission was to hold her hand in public? A simple pleasure he'd been denied for a month, he'd said. They'd dined at a cosy bistro in Haverton and later sat on the terrace of the Weir Wine Bar, drinking, laughing and chatting until way after midnight. The perfect date.

Two weeks later and there she was, sitting in the same spot on the terrace. It was like the only things that had changed were the colour of the leaves and her marital status: divorced. Five days earlier, it became official.

Daisy shivered. Not her smartest choice opting for a leather jacket and token scarf rather than her wool coat and thermals. But the appearance of Xander warmed her insides. Cocooned in a down body-warmer and an oversized beanie, he looked better than ever, especially since his left hand clutched a vast bouquet. Daisy tried not to grin. Friends with benefits totally rocked.

He didn't bother saying hello, before he leant down and kissed her with no regard for the couple sitting at the next table. But she was used to his public displays of affection. And she loved them. Thank God she was sitting down though, because the boy could still turn her bones to spaghetti.

'Thank you,' she said, taking the bouquet. 'They're beautiful.'

He glanced down, his hand stopping hers. 'And they're for Tabitha. Sorry.'

'Oh.' Daisy lit a cigarette as Xander sank into a chair and deposited *Tabitha's* flowers on the table.

'How was your spa morning?'

'Fabulous.' And horrifically expensive but drinks with Xander's friends for Tabitha's birthday surely warranted a facial and manicure. The flowers were pink roses, beautiful pink roses. 'How's your new hair?'

He pulled his hat down lower. 'Cold.'

'You never buy *me* flowers.' She shouldn't have said that.

Xander stared at her. 'What?'

'Well, you don't.' And that hideously sulky tone wasn't cool.

'You want the flowers?' Beneath the hat, his frown deepened.

Was it a trick question? 'Yes.'

Xander handed her the flowers. 'Enjoy.'

Well, now she couldn't, could she? She'd practically forced him to give them to her. Okay, she shouldn't have done that, but then again she shouldn't have to. She took a long drag on her cigarette, pointedly staring down at the river.

'What?' Xander asked. 'You wanted the flowers; you've got the flowers.'

'But I shouldn't have had to ask.'

He snatched the flowers back. 'Fine. Tabitha can have them. At least she'll say, thank you.'

'But I wanted them.' Now she actually sounded like a five year-old.

'Keep this up,' he snapped, 'and you really will be single.'

Still sulking, Daisy didn't recognise this wasn't the time to be pedantic and point out that she was officially single.

'You're what? You're not single.' He glanced across at the nearby couple and lowered his voice. 'For Christ's sake, Daisy, FWB isn't even real. When I agreed to it, I thought it'd be just like before. We'd spend a lot of time together and maybe when you'd get drunk, we'd end up shagging. But what's happened? We spend *every* day together. There've only been four nights in three weeks we haven't slept in the same bed and that's because I was away with work. To everyone except you, we're *going out.*' He stood up, his hands behind his head. 'Face it, we're not *just friends* and we haven't been since the day we met.'

'No, we're Friends With Benefits.'

He threw the flowers at her feet. 'You can make your own fucking way to Oscar's.'

She was still staring at the roses when he strode away.

The bang-on-trend wine bar set in the old Magistrate's court, buzzed with smiling groups and cosy couples, but despite already being twenty minutes late, Daisy lit a cigarette, summoning the courage to walk into the OBB.

Okay, maybe she'd acted like an overly pampered princess that afternoon, but it didn't excuse Xander forcing her to go a party with his friends on her own, especially since James and Marcus clearly didn't like her – they probably thought she wasn't pretty or posh enough to go out with Xander. God, she'd even said it herself. *Go out with Xander.* Was he right? Was FWB all nonsense? To the outside world, they probably did look like a couple.

Still, she didn't want to go to bed alone, so she'd dressed with Xander in mind, positive her mint green, shimmery boob-tube, second-skin jeans and the Louboutin heels would do a better job of creating peace than Kofi Anan.

Tabitha met her at the door of the OBB and Daisy smiled as apologetically as she could muster, handing over her gift. A fabulous present would've felt two-faced when she didn't really want to speak to Tabitha, so she gave the girl what she'd asked for – a chance. She'd made an Monopoly style card and written on the back:

It's your birthday!
Daisy will take you to lunch so you can prove you're not an utter cow.

Expecting Tabitha to laugh and take it as it was meant, as an olive branch, Daisy paled when the girl's eyes brimmed with tears. Oh dear God. Why couldn't she be dismissive, amused or even downright ungrateful? Now, Daisy felt awful for being late, awful for falling out with Xander and awful for misjudging Tabitha's apology at the party. Realising it put her in an even fouler mood.

'Is everyone here?' Daisy peeked around the corner, spotting James at the bar chatting with some redhead. Where was Xander? Chatting to India. Oh hurrah. India was there. Maybe this wasn't going to be such a crappy night after all.

'Yes, but listen. I need to–'

'Can it wait 'til I've got a drink? I'm absolutely–'

Finn.

Finn was there. And not just in the same bar, but sitting at their table, between India and Marcus. Daisy stopped, simply staring at him. Finn glanced up, toying with his wine glass, his mouth set in a grim line. Clearly, he was as uncomfortable with her appearance as she was with his.

'That's what I needed to tell you,' Tabitha hissed in her ear.

At least she'd tried to warn Daisy. Why hadn't Xander? Daisy willed her legs to move, terrified she'd slip or turn a heel on the wooden floor. She had to handle this with dignity and grace.

At the table, she took the chair next to Xander, and emptied the nearest bottle of red into a vast glass, determined to ignore Finn. Conversation around them dried up. Marcus swirled the wine in his glass, Tabitha checked her phone, but notably, Xander kept up his cosy tête-à-tête with India. He hadn't acknowledged Daisy's arrival in the room, much less said hello. She sat back, picking at a beer mat and spiralling into an ever blacker gloom. She knew she should say something, apologise, but how could she under Finn's insolent scrutiny?

Why was he even in Haverton, for God's sake? He'd signed the papers. Wasn't he supposed to be kiss-camming Brittney Carle in New York? Or was he finally getting the wedding anniversary present Tabitha had promised? Was that why the cow almost cried, out of guilt? Daisy glanced up at Xander. *Please talk to me.* India flashed an apologetic smile. God, she was so... tall, dark and incredibly beautiful. Daisy's stomach churned. Was India why Xander left Daisy in the car park?

No.

She would not dissolve into jealousy-fuelled paranoia. Finn could shag who he liked and Xander... well, this was precisely why Daisy refused to go out with him. Screw both of them. She'd come out for Tabitha's birthday. She'd drink the drinks, play the party game, sing happy-bloody-birthday and leave.

'I'm going for a fag,' she said to no one in particular.

'I'll join you,' Finn said, scraping his chair back on the wooden floor.

Oh marvellous. A public slanging match with her ex was just what she needed. Daisy knocked back her wine and followed his perfect arse out to the beer garden. Why was he the only bloke she'd ever met who could totally pull off skinny jeans?

Outside, his new Romeo-long hair flopped onto his face as he lit a cigarette but not once did he drop eye-contact with her. The whole, fell-out-the-Ramones look suited him. A lot.

'Why are you smoking?' she demanded. 'You gave up. You made *me* give up.'

'Yes, but I only gave up so you'd give up. You were on forty a fucking day. Sorry for not wanting you to die.'

Why did he always have to play Mr Righteous? 'And why are you here? Brittany's mummy and daddy not let her out this late at night? What is she, nineteen?'

Finn shook his head. 'Twenty-four, older than your toy boy.'

'He's not *my* toy boy.' *He hates me.*

Dignity and grace skipped merrily out of the window. She turned away, refusing to let Finn see her bottom lip wobble. If she nipped out the side garden gate, she could leave without any of the others seeing her smudged mascara.

'Hey... come here,' Finn said quietly, pulling her to him.

'No!' She slapped his hand away. The last thing she wanted was to be trapped in his arms again. 'Get off me, Finn.'

But he held onto her. 'I'm sorry, Dee.'

Sorry?

'About... Claridge's, everything. I'm sorry.'

And there it was. It had taken ten months and a divorce, but she finally had her bloody apology.

'Why did you do it, Finn?'

His arms tightened. 'It was your idea.'

'I suggested blindfolds and being teased with silk scarves and feathers, not two days of... humiliation.'

'I know, I know.'

'Then why? Why did you put me through that crap?' Tears loomed. She ought to hit him, yell at him, but instead she wrapped her arms around him, clutching at his t-shirt.

'I know things got out of hand, but... it wasn't all bad, was it?'

Her cheeks heated up, as did her traitorous body. 'No, it wasn't *all* bad.'

'But I'm sorry for the bits that were. We were wasted.'

Too much booze, drugs and lack of good sense – the story of her life. 'And... why did you throw me out?'

His arms tightened again. 'A pre-emptive strike? After Claridge's, I knew... we were over.'

Daisy nodded and for a minute, they simply held each other. Through the window, she could see Xander, still merrily chatting to India. If only he were the one hugging her, not Finn, but he hadn't looked her way once. What would he think if he saw her in her ex-husband's arms? Would he even care?

'This is hard, I know,' said Finn. 'But one day... I'd really like us to be friends again.'

'Is... is that why you're here?'

'Should I pretend it is?' He laughed but without any humour.

'We've been divorced for less than a week. Do you think I'd intentionally go somewhere you'd be with *him*?'

'So why are you here?' Daisy detangled herself, stepping away. 'Tabitha?'

'I knew that's what you'd think, but no.' He took a deep breath. 'India.'

'India?'

'But it's not like that.' He smiled a little sheepishly. 'Much. We're old friends. We were at school together.'

'Why didn't you tell me you knew her?' *You know she's my idol.*

'Well, I haven't seen her for years. It wasn't relevant.'

Relevant? Daisy pulled away from his arms. 'Whatever. I should go home. Tonight's been a disaster since this afternoon.'

'I take it your pretty boy's mad at you about something.'

'What on earth makes you think that?'

He smiled, glancing inside. 'He's done nothing but sulk and knock back whisky since I got here. It's only when we saw your taxi pull up that he started talking to India. She's tripping.'

'Why?'

'It's the first time he's spoken to her in almost ten years. Apparently, he really doesn't like her. Think he's doing it to wind you up?'

Daisy stared at Xander, willing him to come outside and talk to her.

'What did you fight about?' Finn asked quietly.

'I was a bit of a cow over a bunch of flowers.'

'Then you need to break the habit of a lifetime and say sorry.'

'Excuse me?'

'Well, you never said sorry to me. Ever.'

'That's just because—'

'You were never wrong?' Finn laughed. 'Dee, do me favour and just think about this: was anything ever your fault, really, and did you ever say sorry?'

'What difference will it make?' *We're divorced.*

'It might give you and him a fighting chance.' Finn pushed her towards the door. 'Now, go and say sorry, but no making up in front of me. There's only so much I can take.'

Daisy gazed up at him as he held open the door for her. Was this gent the same guy who threw her out on the street? Confidently, she strode back to the table, no longer fretting over her heels on the wooden tiles. Had she really never said sorry, ever? Why had Finn never mentioned he went to school with India? Surely Daisy must've mentioned her idolatry once or twice.

At the table, Tabitha and India visibly relaxed when Daisy smiled. Even Marcus managed to raise the corners of his mouth. This would be okay. Finn took his seat beside India and refilled her and Daisy's glasses. A little weird, but okay.

After taking a confidence boosting deep breath, Daisy placed her hand on Xander's thigh.

'Xand, I'm... sorry about this afternoon,' she whispered, 'I was a cow.'

Finally, Xander turned, looking her in the eye. 'Did you know he'd be here?'

'No.'

Slowly, he leaned closer, letting his lips brush her ear. 'Then you're forgiven.'

Delighted, Daisy relaxed. 'I acted like an absolute child. No idea why.'

'Rob reckons you were doing what most two year-olds do, pushing your boundaries.'

'Do you discuss everything with him?'

He laughed, his breath making her shiver. 'Yes. You're far too tricky to deal with on my own. But remember, you overstepped the boundary today. Please, don't do it again.'

'I promise.'

'What did you and Finn talk about?'

'Me. You. Saying sorry.' She glanced over at Finn, but he was engrossed in some enthusiastic, arm-waving conversation with Tabitha. 'Why didn't you warn me he was here?'

'When I saw him, I thought he was why you acted out today... I thought we were done.' Xander swirled his whisky around in its glass. 'Not the best day I've ever had.'

Disregarding Finn's request, she dropped a quick but emotion packed kiss on Xander's lips. 'I'm so not done with you. This afternoon was... it was just me being a pain in the arse. I'm really sorry.'

He grinned, his glazed eyes telling her just how many whiskies he'd had. 'I love you.'

And finally, she could relax. Well, she could for ten seconds, until Tabitha plonked the ominous wooden *Forfeit* box on the table.

Seriously, were they going to do this in public, in front of India? How mortifying.

'Oh, come on,' Tabitha pleaded with a yawning James. She snatched Marcus' phone, mid-text. 'It's fun.'

'Ohmigod,' India said, leaning over the table. 'Is that *Forfeit*?'

James leaned forward. 'How do you know?'

'What's *Forfeit*?' Finn asked, half laughing.

Daisy daren't look up. He'd think her a childish brat for handing over five hundred pounds to do a stupid dare.

'It's the ultimate game of dares,' India explained, her gentle, husky voice, sounding like a purr. 'My parents' used to play it when I was a kid. They'd have these totes cool parties—'

'Mum and Dad used to play?' James asked, his head already shaking, disbelieving her, but India nodded, her glossy curls bouncing.

'And Bella.' India sat back, grinning.

'*My* mum played?' Marcus leaned on the table, frowning.

'When I was about five,' India said, 'she rode a motorbike around the house. I watched through the banister at the top of the stairs. I thought mum would go insane, but she just shrieked with laughter.' Fleeting sadness washed over her face, but she soon replaced it with a fabulous smile.

'Bella rode a motorbike, in the house?' James shook his head. 'As if.'

'So can Finn and I play too?' India asked.

James glanced to Xander who gave an almost imperceptible shake of his head. 'No. Original players only. If you start it, you have to finish it. It's in the small print.'

India sulked. 'You're such a pedant.'

'Money, table,' James said to the others, his interest infinitely more piqued than earlier.

Under India's envious pout, Daisy merrily tossed five hundred pounds of Clara's money into the metaphorical pot. Five hundred pounds. One third of what her car was worth. Okay, Clara said she didn't want it back again if Daisy lost, but no way could Daisy live with herself if she didn't pay her back. And no way could she afford to pay her back. The only option was to win.

Daisy threw the Teetotum ball. It landed on nineteen, not a number she loved.

'Shit.' James said, scowling at his card. 'Well, that's hardly fun.

Or difficult.'

'What?' Xander asked, throwing the ball.

James screwed up his face. 'It says I can't let anyone know what I'm doing, or why.'

Oh, like the Kiss Dare had to be done in secret. Tentatively, Daisy opened her card.

Temperance.

No drink or drugs for 30 days.

'Oh, bollocks.' Despairing, she showed Xander the card.

'It'll do you good.'

'What is it?' Finn's eyes glinted as he sipped his wine.

Marcus whipped the card out of Daisy's hands. 'No drinking? Good luck with that.'

'She can do it,' Xander said, flipping a beer mat at his friend.

'I'd bet five hundred quid she can't,' James said, his lip curling in a mean smile.

'Bugger you,' Daisy snapped. 'Five hundred quid says I can.'

'You're on.' James leant across the table and held out his hand.

Oh, now this was fortuitous. If she did the dare, she was guaranteed to get Clara's five hundred pounds back and if she won the whole thing... well, hello, two and a half grand.

'Cigarette?' India asked, flashing a smile at Daisy.

Xander frowned and Finn fought a knowing grin, but like she'd turn down the offer. Finally, she'd get to hang out with India Dowson-Jones.

'This might sound a bit fangirl,' India said, linking arms with Daisy as they headed outside. 'But I've been *dying* to meet you properly.'

'Me?'

'I just adored reading about you and Finn,' India explained. 'Falling head over heels on a mountain top. Too romantic. And you always look so cool in magazines.'

'Too fat, too thin and too undeserving to be with Finn, more like.'

'You're only remembering the horror stories. You always seemed so unaffected by the bullshit that surrounds Finn.'

'You shouldn't believe everything you see in the papers.' Daisy laughed. 'But, actually, back at you. I wanted to *be* you when I was a teenager.'

India paused, cigarette in one hand, lighter in the other. '*Me?*'

Daisy nodded.

'I wouldn't wish that on anyone in the world.' India glanced down at her Miu Miu knee boots. 'Sorry for bringing Finn tonight.'

'That's okay. What's going on with you and him?'

'Oh, he's just killing time until he's back in New York. I'm devastated.' India lifted a hand to her forehead, feigning despair and making Daisy laugh. 'I've always had such a crush on him.'

'Really?'

India nodded. 'He was the school bad boy.'

'Yeah, it works.'

'Totes thought Tabby or James might've told me you'd be here.'

'James isn't my biggest fan and well, I'm not Tabitha's.'

'Welcome to my world.' India flashed a grin. 'He's a sulky pain in the arse and she's... well, Tabitha bloody Doyle.'

'OMG, that's exactly what I call her.' Daisy laughed, utterly determined to become India's new best friend.

For twenty minutes, they chain-smoked and knocked back cosmopolitans, giggling over Tabitha's overuse of the word *sweetie* and merrily debating the merits of vodka versus wine.

'So are you and Xander going out now? Marcus said you were just friends.'

After Daisy explained the events since James' party, India's black eyes narrowed and she glanced inside, all humour disappearing.

'Please, be careful who you trust.'

'Are you telling me I shouldn't trust Xander?'

She nodded to the bar. 'If I were you, I wouldn't trust anyone until you've known them for a lot longer.'

India opened her mouth to say more, but Marcus came out and glared at her. What was going on?

'Coming back in?' India flashed Daisy the most innocent of smiles.

Daisy shook her head, studying Marcus. The time had come to have words with Mr Dowson-Jones; she was sick of his withering looks. The second the door closed behind India, Daisy turned to him. His face held a mixture of intrigue and disdain.

'You don't like me, do you?' she asked before knocking back her drink.

'Not much.'

'Why?'

Marcus lit his cigarette, pausing for a moment, clearly deciding if he wanted to tell her. When he made up his mind, he didn't hold back.

'Maybe because you're a judgemental bitch who thinks she's better than everyone else. Or maybe because you're so self-absorbed you have no idea how your behaviour impacts those around you. You think you're this salt of the earth girl, but really, you're vain, spoiled and someone I'd rather my best friend stayed away from.'

Daisy took a long drag on her cigarette. How else could she respond?

'You think, James and I are bored, fickle players with less depth than one of your Louboutin fucking heels, but how do you know that? Have you ever tried to get to know us? Do you know what we do for a living? We do have jobs, you know. Do you think James just sits in his ivory tower all day, being rich?'

Daisy's only answer was to blink guiltily.

Marcus shook his head. 'He works for the furniture business and not as some chinless wonder. He's doing a design apprenticeship to learn the ropes. He'll take over the business one day. You made judgements about who we were at the party and you decided we're pointless rich kids. Well, I'll return the favour and judge you on that night. That leaves one of my best friends going out with a party-girl, a party-girl whose husband threw her out on the street because she didn't know when to put the shot glass down.'

What the hell? Was that what people thought?

'However, since I know Xander *is* a salt of the earth kind of guy, I have to assume you have some hidden depths and you're not just a good shag with a sexy, designer jean-clad arse. I've given you the benefit of the doubt, but it's a luxury you're not willing to waste on me. Has it crossed your self-absorbed mind that if someone as genuine as Xander can be friends with James and me then perhaps we have hidden depths too?'

He took a quick drag on his cigarette and Daisy stared, dumbfounded.

'And this leads me to my biggest concern. If you think Xander would be friends with shallow, pointless rich kids, then you have no idea who Xander really is. Deep down, you probably think Xander's shallow and pointless too. To sum up, I bet you a bottle of *1990 Chateau Latour Pauillac* that you're going to break his heart because you're too bloody stupid to see anything beyond your initial misconceptions.' A big smile flashed across his face as Xander stepped onto the terrace. 'Fag, Xand?' Marcus flicked his cigarette away and, swearing under his breath, buggered off inside.

OMG. Daisy stared at Marcus' departing back. Judgemental? She wasn't judgemental or vain, or self-absorbed. Okay, maybe a little vain, but that was a side-effect of being surrounded by beautiful people like Clara, Xander and her own bloody mother. It wasn't her fault.

Was anything ever your fault, really?

Oh God, was Finn right? And if he was right, what about Marcus? She had assumed he and James sat around being rich, but of course she didn't think Xander was shallow and pointless. He was... fun, easy-going. He was... what if she didn't understand Xander? For months, she'd never seen his growing misery over his job. What if she were missing something else?

She turned to where he sat on a table, his hands in his pockets.

'From the look on your face,' he said. 'I'm guessing Marcus told you how much he loves you.'

'You're my KSCP. Go and hit him, defend my honour.'

'No.' Xander laughed. 'It's his opinion and he's quite entitled to it.'

'He called me a vain, spoiled and judgemental party girl.'

Xander winced. 'Vain and spoiled are uncalled for, but you are judgemental and let's face it, if you had your way, you'd live in a Bacardi advert.'

'What?' More stunned. 'That's not... I'm not judgemental.'

'Yes, you are. Look at when we met, you called me a playboy. Based on what?'

Based on your ability to get into a girl's pants. Daisy sat on the table opposite him. But if Xander wasn't a playboy, what was he? The love of her stupid bloody life?

He wants to be buried in my heart forever.

Why would he want that? She was a shortarse, frizzy haired party girl who didn't know when to put the shot glass down. Sighing, she hung her head, shame filling her soul.

'Hey...' Xander stood in front of her, lifting her chin, making her face him.

'I'm sorry.'

'For what?'

'Being a horrible, judgemental pain in the arse.'

Xander laughed and kissed her briefly. 'Remember, it's your flaws that make you so fucking fascinating.'

'Your friend doesn't think so.'

'Marcus just hasn't seen your good qualities yet.'

'What? Like me being a good shag?' Clearly, they'd discussed her and Xander's sheepish grin confirmed it. 'What happened to no kiss and tell?'

'Sorry.'

'I want to go home.'

'No, you're going to go in there and talk to Marcus. You have to prove him wrong. If you win him over, he'll do most of the work winning James over for you.'

Whatever. 'I can't go back in there.'

'Yes, you can. Morning after the cricket match, I gave you the perfect opportunity to leave. You didn't take it. Why?'

'Lynda was outside... and I didn't want you to be cross if I bumped into you at the post office.'

'Exactly. Being brave is one of your good qualities. You face up to shit most people would run from. In fact, you're one of the bravest people I've met.'

'Really?' She relaxed against him as she ran her fingers through his hair. 'What other good qualities do I have?'

'You have the sexiest arse in the world.' He shot her a cheeky grin and slapped her backside. 'But will you *please* stop idolising India?'

'I'm not. We're just talking. She's nice.'

'Why don't you make this the start of your non-judgemental life? Don't assume she's nice because she's a minor celebrity and has the same handbag as you. Why don't you take some time to see what she's really like? Then decide if she's nice or... otherwise.'

With his mini-lecture, Xander made her feel about six but Daisy didn't care – at least he was speaking to her again. Gently, he brushed her curls off her face.

'I'm sorry about today, Daze.'

'It was all my fault,' she whispered. Why had she acted like such a sulky brat?

'Your head's messed up, but I've always known that. I shouldn't have walked away.'

As Xander kissed his apology, the flare of a lighter caught Daisy's eye. In the darkness, the flame illuminated Finn's face. She dragged her lips from Xander's, mortified Finn was watching.

'We should go in,' she whispered.

She had too much love and respect for Finn to make this any worse for him.

Back inside, Daisy took a big breath and sat beside Marcus.

'Xander tells me you like wine,' she said, praying she sounded honest and well-meaning.

Marcus tipped his head, studying her through narrowed eyes. 'And what do you know about wine?'

'Screw tops are a lot easier to open than corks.' She laughed at his disapproving frown.

'I'm a sommelier. Do you know what that is?'

Oh, so now he was speaking to her as she were six, but Daisy merely smiled and nodded. This was for Xander. She listened attentively and with increasing interest as Marcus explained how his mum owned a vineyard in Italy and had passed on her passion for wine to him. Now, he worked as a sommelier for a hotel near Grasmere.

'Tell you what. I'll send you a case,' he said. 'Free of charge, no screw tops, but you have to taste each wine properly, and make notes, as I'll be asking questions.'

Daisy sat back, her arms folded. 'Sounds divine, but I can't drink for a month.'

Marcus sat back, mirroring her pose, but with a grin not a scowl. 'But with wine-tasting, you get to spit, not swallow.'

How cruel could the bloody game be?

Chapter Eleven

'It's like God's being deliberately mean,' Daisy said, adoring Xander's unexpected call.

She tucked her phone under her chin and swept up debris from her Textiles class' dubiously successful autumn-themed embellishment project. She'd challenged the buggers to use the colourful season as inspiration, for beading or appliqué work, to personalise the basic skirts and waistcoats they'd made the previous week. But once Magda opted to entwine ivy into her micro-mini's hem, the others followed suit and before Daisy knew it, acorns had become buttons and beech leaves were glued on patch pockets.

'You don't even go to church,' Xander said. 'You can't blame God.'

'If it's not God's fault, then Marcus has to be to blame.'

At eight o'clock, she'd arrived at school ready to educate the twatty posh kids, when Glenys the Head's PA reminded her of the Parents' and Alumni Fundraiser that evening. As if working full-time and non-drinking weren't ruining her life enough, now she had to give up a Friday evening too. To make matters worse, the fundraising event was a wine-tasting organised by Marcus.

'It's the start of the worst month of my life. Ever. I should take it as a sign and wave the white flag now.'

'It's day six, Fitzgerald. You lasted longer than this in August. It's only thirty days.'

'Yes, but those thirty days include a wine-tasting event and my best-friend's wedding. I'll be the world's first *sober* bridesmaid.'

'You'll cope. You just need something to take your mind off wine.'

'Working full-time and renovating a hellhole of a house aren't enough?' she sat on her desk, a smile finally fighting through.

'For you, no. You don't know how to relax if it doesn't involve something with a percentage written on the bottle.'

'God, I could do with something to get me through tonight.'

'Need your Knight-in-Shining-Cricket-Pads to come to your

rescue?'

She laughed. 'I wish.'

There was a knock at her door. Surely not? But the door opened to reveal Xander, holding a shiny red apple for teacher, his grin matching her own.

'You're like every schoolboy's fantasy come true,' he said, slowly walking over. 'Shall we christen your desk, *miss*?'

So wrong, but seeing Xander in a crisply ironed shirt and smart trousers... Daisy crossed her legs, half-tempted to say yes. 'What are you doing here?'

'Hey, I'm an ex-pupil. I get invited to these events, you know.' He perched on the desk beside her, briefly kissing her hello. 'Is that what you're wearing tonight?'

Daisy glanced at her paint-splattered jeans and his old shirt. 'Kinda hot, hey?'

'On you? Yes.' He glanced behind them. 'Seriously, desk?'

'Seriously? No.' She elbowed him, but to her surprise instead of seeing a cheeky twinkle in his eyes, that God-awful frown had returned. 'I know the idea of wine-tasting with your teetotal not-girlfriend might not be quite the Friday night you had planned, but bearing in mind you can drink tonight...' She ran her thumb gently over the furrows in his brow. 'You look miserable as hell. What's up?'

'The estate agent rang this afternoon. I've got three offers on the cottage.'

'Wow, that's quick. How much?'

'Asking price.' He picked up a paintbrush, flicking the bristles against his thumb.

'So... are you wishing you'd asked for more?'

'No. It's just... a bit sudden.'

'Are you regretting selling it? There's still time to change your mind.'

'It's what I want and Grandpa would've approved, but it's... my home.' He let out a long sigh. 'And facing life baby-sitting at Rob's isn't exactly rocking my world.'

'So move into Skank Manor.' The words were out of her mouth before she'd thought about them.

'What?'

'Well, you offered me a roof over my head when I needed one. It's only fair I return the favour. I have three bedrooms. One for me, one for you, one for not-handbag making.'

'You said no when I offered. You wouldn't even dignify the suggestion with the *whatever* it deserved.'

'Things are different now.' *I know you won't fall into the house with some girl.*

'They are, but... I'm not sure it's a good idea.'

What? Daisy's stood up, turning away to hide the mortification filling her face. Oh good God. Why had she said that? 'I need to get changed.'

'Not so fast,' he said, pulling her back to him, his hand holding her face, coaxing her to look up at him. 'You know there's nothing I want more, but I don't want a bedroom for me and a bedroom for you, and if we lived together, it wouldn't be FWB. Are you ready for that?'

Yes, because who was she kidding, whatever they were, they weren't friends with benefits. But was she ready to admit it? Was she ready to let him bury himself in her heart?

'I don't know, but I don't want you to be unhappy.'

'And you've no idea how much that means to me, but... look, I've got what, six or eight weeks. Let's just see what happens.' His lips rested on hers, leading her into a slow, deep kiss. 'Now, seriously-seriously, what about the desk?'

Laughing and shaking her head, she headed into Ms St. Clements' little office where Daisy's parent-friendly clothes hung. Ms St. Clement's little office... Daisy only had permission to use it for filing the students' work, not as some kind of recreation room, but didn't that make things even more fun?

'Of course,' she said, already unbuttoning her shirt, 'you could serve your detention in here...'

The hallway echoed with the sound of Daisy's heels on the parquet floor. Shagging in the school – beyond wrong. She'd had to sneak off to the gym for a shower like some naughty sixth former. Xander waited for her, leaning against the wall, his satiated smile making her own grow.

'High heels and hair up...' He gave her a long, slow coat of looking at. 'Hold ups hiding under that tight pencil skirt... Do you do the whole Miss Moneypenny thing for the boys' benefit or is there some hot teacher you've got your eye on?'

'There's not a single shaggable bloke in the whole faculty.' Daisy stifled a giggle. 'And I hardly think teenage boys would be into me.'

'How many of them sit at their desks after the class has finished?'

They all legged it the second... Oh, Travis hung around the other day. And Logan. 'Maybe one or two, but–'

'Turned on by the teacher.' Xander took her hand, his fingers linking with hers, but Daisy shook him off, horrified.

'Not here.'

'I thought we'd moved on from no hand-holding in public.'

Daisy cringed. 'Well, it's hardly professional in front of the pupils.'

'There are none around.'

Bugger. 'And I haven't exactly... told anybody about you.'

'Why?' Xander frowned down at her.

'You're an ex-pupil. It's inappropriate.'

'I left six and a half years ago. And you weren't working here.'

'It's still weird.'

'Christ, you know how to trash my ego.'

'Oh, for God's sake.' She took hold of his hand and reached up to kiss his cheek. 'Happy?'

'Hello, miss.' Freya Dowson-Jones stood in the doorway to the Old Library rooms where the wine tasting would take place. She handed them leaflets about the outdoor stage they were fundraising for. 'I don't know why they're bothering with this. Mum told me she'd pay for it, but she wasn't being arsed sitting with a horse-faced bunch of old fogies. Nice to see you have your own boyfriend these days. Might keep you away from mine.'

The cheeky little... Daisy's cheeks burned and Xander trying not to laugh beside her wasn't helping. Daisy itched to take Freya down a peg, but the Bursar acting as Master of Ceremonies, hit the school dinner gong, reducing the majority of old boys and girls to fits of nostalgic, honking laughter.

Overconfident, twatty posh kids – thank God, she'd gone to a state run school.

The most divine Pinot Noir sat in her mouth, begging to be swallowed. Why had she made the stupid bet with James? The five hundred quid stake she might've been able to pay back to Clara in instalments, but the five hundred quid she'd owe James if she failed? He'd want it on October 31st or he'd undoubtedly take his pound of flesh.

Of course, who'd know if she swallowed the odd mouthful? No one except her.

No.

Daisy spat the wine into the spittoon.

Not a drop could fall down her throat because when she took James' five hundred pounds, she had to do it with a clear conscience. Stupid bloody game.

'... blackberry and mint undertones. Remember, Mrs Lovelace,' Marcus joked, 'swish and spit. We've still got seven wines to go...'

Seven? They'd already tried five. Daisy sipped her water. Wine, wine everywhere and not a drop for her to drink.

The one good thing about being the only sober person in the room was that Daisy heard everything. Pissed people wittered in so many circles, she could pay attention to Marcus' tasting notes, take in Olympic village tales from the ruddy-faced woman opposite her and keep an eye on the elderly gay chap hitting on the sixth former pouring their wine.

'They charged the poor rowing fellow she'd been seeing,' said the ex-Team GB women's hockey player, 'but we all knew, it was the gymnast. Roofied the poor mite but fell off the rings in the end. Rumour has it the rope was cut. Tragic loss to sport.'

OMG, was she on about the cycling girl who was raped? Who cut the rope, the rower? Daisy yearned to pry.

'But you must play rugby?' said the ancient man in a pink cravat. 'With thighs like those...'

'Sam?' Daisy beckoned the wide-eyed sixth former over. 'Could we get some fresh water, please?'

'Yes, miss.' He sagged with relief. 'Thanks, miss.'

Peach, pears a hint of citrus... though it pained her to do so, Daisy spat out the most divine white she'd ever tasted. God, this was simply cruel. Daisy scowled at Xander as he drained his wine in one gulp. He hadn't attempted to savour those flavours.

'What are you doing?' she asked.

His eyes glinted, glazed with alcohol. 'I'm going away next week.'

Daisy's heart plummeted, as much worrying for his mental well-being as for her own happiness. 'Why didn't you tell me?'

'I just did.' He sank the rest of her wine. 'I wasn't sure I was going to go, but it's money, right?'

'Every penny for your restaurant, baby,' she leant up to kiss him. The rest of the room would be too pissed to notice. 'A cruise?'

'Mountain biking in Portugal.' His arm draped around her, his finger twirling a curl. 'I'm looking forward to it. Rob's going too.'

'But who's going to keep me sober?'

'I'll ring you every night.'

'Will you send me sexts?' she joked.

'Now you're getting the hang of it.' He dropped a kiss on her neck.

'But you'll be back in time for Clara's wedding?'

'I'll be back on the Friday, I promise.'

'You'd better. Clara said the best man's second in line to Robbie for the Sexiest Man In Town title.'

Finally, bottle twelve sat upturned in the bucket, and Daisy donned her coat ready to leave, but Jennifer Lovelace, the head teacher beckoned her over.

'Do we have to?' Xander whispered. 'She still terrifies me.'

'She's my boss. Yes.' Daisy tried not to grin. 'She's actually very cool.'

'Great news,' Jennifer said. 'We've got the money for the outdoor auditorium. Now, do you think Finn might come and open it if we asked?'

Daisy forced a smile. 'Maybe.'

Xander clutched her hand, but Daisy had played on Finn's name to get the interview; it was only fair the school got Finn in return.

'And how are you, Alexander?' Jennifer asked, maintaining her duties as head, despite the purple tinge to her teeth.

'Good, miss—' He stopped himself, laughing before letting the confident, Colgate smile work its magic. '*Jennifer*, lovely to see you again. I swear you haven't aged a day in six years.'

The next time Jennifer gave her a dressing down for arriving a few minutes late to some stupid staff meeting, Daisy would remember this moment – how her boss, resplendent with a red wine moustache, flicked her hair back, fluttering her eye lashes at Xander. This woman could silence an assembly of chattering students with the slightest lift of an eyebrow, but now she simpered like a schoolgirl.

'I have to say goodbye to Marcus,' Xander explained. 'Please, excuse me.'

Jennifer shook her head, an affectionate smile reaching her eyes as Marcus and Xander shared a back-slapping boy-hug.

'Be thankful you don't have to teach boys like them.'

Daisy didn't respond. The trick to getting information out of pissed people was not to ask questions. You simply didn't need to. Give them silence and they couldn't help filling it.

'Heartbreakers, the pair of them.'

'What was Xander like at school? I gather he wasn't the most academic of students.'

'Bright as any, but couldn't care less about anything other than cooking.' Jennifer slugged her port and grabbed a stilton-topped cracker from a passing waiter. 'Idolised his grandfather, but his parents... a different kettle of fish. Never took to his mother. It's criminal that he left Anthony Errington. Genius chef.'

'Anthony?'

'Xander. His grandfather said the boy could become England's finest chef.'

'It's still his dream. He and his brother are going to open a restaurant. I seem to spend all my free time trying to find them a decent venue.'

'I take it you and he...'

'It's complicated.'

'You want to be careful,' Jennifer said, fixing a stern eye on her. 'Troubled thing he was, when he came here, and his year were an odd bunch. I blamed James Dowson-Jones at the time, but when Xander left at sixteen, James and Marcus settled down and behaved like any other sixth formers. It seems Xander was the bad egg. I'd never seen it, too swayed by his impeccable manners and – let's be honest – that boy can charm bees.'

Daisy bit back her questions, as a tall woman approached them. From her professionally coiffed, if unnaturally dark locks, to her LK Bennett pumps, she was a perfect Duchess of Cambridge wannabe.

'Ah... Cressida Marshall, Pippa's mother,' Jennifer whispered. 'Desperate for a chat with you.'

After a quick introduction, Jennifer darted off, muttering she must talk to Henry Dowson-Gunn to see if India really would foot the entire bill for the outdoor stage.

'Darling to meet you at last,' Cressida cooed, kissing Daisy's cheeks.

Daisy smiled, anticipating some serious parent-teacher gushing. 'Pippa's such a good student, a real asset to the school.'

The previous week, twelve year-old Pippa had produced a beautiful silk painting in art. A gift for her mum's birthday, she'd said, glowing with pride. But if Mrs Marshall had received it, she never mentioned it.

'Actually, I was hoping for a teeny favour. Are you still in touch with Finn?' She held a hand against her reddening neck. 'Only when he was at school with my eldest daughter, we were so very *close.*'

Did she mean close-close? Cressida had to be mid-forties. What was it with married cougars and teenage boys in the Lakes?

'And I wondered... do you have his number?' Cressida went on. 'I'm in New York next month and I'd *love* to meet up with him.'

No, no, no. 'I... um... don't think...'

Cressida grasped Daisy's arm, leaning forward to whisper conspiratorially. 'Quite frankly, he was the most fantastic fuck. You must be insane to let that man go.'

The old hag was completely and utterly clueless. Daisy glanced across to where Xander stood watching her with a concerned frown.

'Sorry, Cressida,' Daisy said, giving her most insincere smile, 'but part of my divorce settlement was that I'd promise not to give his number to desperate hags like you.'

As Cressida gave a marvellous impression of a goldfish, Xander joined them.

'Ready to go?' he asked.

'And actually, I'm not insane,' Daisy said, leaning in to whisper to Cressida, 'because *this* is the most fantastic fuck I've ever had.'

Being sober rocked.

Chapter Twelve

In a five-star, country house hotel overlooking Thirlmere, Clara and Scott's five years of on-off shagging was about to end. The guests took their seats with Cafe del Mar chill-out tunes just audible over their gently excited chatter. Sadly, the music didn't appear to chill out the groom. Scott stood up and sat down with reliable regularity while he fiddled with his cufflinks, straightened his cravat and ran his hands through his hair.

'Scott looks gorgeous. Terrified but gorgeous. Think he's having second thoughts?' Daisy asked, trying to peek through a door gap.

'No, he thinks I'm going to do another *volte face*.' For someone about to get married, Clara shrugged with disturbing nonchalance. 'But he'll have to suffer for another few minutes. The registrar said it's a tradition.'

It was a tradition for the bridesmaids to get hammered too. Daisy eyed the champagne an ill-informed waitress had delivered to the pregnant bride. It wasn't even eleven o'clock but weddings, like airports, were exempt from time-zones and in a parallel universe, parallel Daisy would be knocking back the champagne.

Okay, so her skin glowed with a previously unseen radiance, and maybe she'd lost a little flab from her hips whilst gaining awesome arm tone – the latter being more to do with sanding skirting boards. She looked great, she felt great, but as the minutes ticked by, her resolve dwindled.

Xander hadn't turned up.

The previous night, he'd rang around eight to say his flight was cancelled. Oh he might've promised to be back in time for the wedding, but it was pure luck that Clara happened to drop by as Daisy was examining the contents of the mini-bar. A swift reminder of whose five hundred pounds was at stake and Daisy curled up in bed with a stubby tube of Pringles.

Booze in T minus thirteen days.

'Stop fretting,' Clara said, standing up. 'He'll be here. He promised.'

Daisy peered through the door gap, but couldn't spy the KSCP or his bloody brother anywhere. Bugger it. 'Ready to get hitched, Miss Knight?'

Clara nodded and stood up. In a four thousand pound, dazzling white dress, with her blonde hair falling in tousled-waves half-way down her back, she looked utterly beautiful but not remotely pregnant. And all credit to her, she'd picked kick-ass outfits for her bridesmaids too – simple black strapless column-dresses and faux-mink shrugs. Jimmy Choo shoe-boots, gifts from the vastly overpaid and about-to-be-married corporate lawyer, provided the sublime finishing touch.

If only Xander were there to appreciate it.

Sadly, he wasn't and as Cafe del Mar gave way to Bach, Daisy slowly strode down the aisle, clutching her posy of blood red roses, determinedly smiling. The most important bloody day in her year and he wasn't there. She wouldn't mind, but he'd promised. This would be his first fail.

She stopped beside the registrar, smiling sweetly to Clara's sister, Juliet. Well, bugger Xander. This was her best friend's big day, her true BFF's big day. Daisy turned, smiling as Clara all but floated down the aisle. God, she looked happy – her grin as big as Scott's.

Yes. Bugger Xander. He let her down – just like Finn had.

Scott gazed at Clara, as if he'd never seen anything so beautiful, so precious and Daisy stared down at her posy. Three years ago, Finn had looked at Daisy like that, promising to love, honour and respect her. She knew he loved her, truly loved her. She believed he still did.

Yet I'm stood here. Divorced. Single.

How the hell had she buggered up her marriage so badly?

Tears pricked her eyes, but her smile remained pasted in place as Clara signed the register. Sadly, there was no fooling her best friend.

'Why are you crying?' Clara asked, smiling for the posed signing photos.

'It's a wedding.'

'I'm ready to cry,' Scott said through a gritted smile. 'How long do we have to do this shit for?'

'Swearing in front of the Registrar invalidates your vows,'

Patrick, the best man replied, equally gritted.

'You never cry at weddings,' Clara whispered.

The only option was to make a joke of it. 'Because my life's utterly tragic? I'm divorced and my date's stood me up. Utterly tragic.'

Patrick gave Daisy a long slow, looking over. 'Or un-fucking-believably fortuitous?'

'Leave her alone, Patrick,' Clara snapped, before smiling for the cameras again.

With her vanity soothed, Daisy's gloom faded. Patrick, the local vet, had the tall, dark and ridiculously hot boxes firmly ticked plus, from the glazed look in his eye, she reckoned he was coked up too. Every cloud...

'But Xander hasn't stood you up.' Scott turned to her. 'He and Rob got here an hour ago. He tried ringing you—'

'What?' Daisy scanned the congregation and then there he was, sneaking back into the room carrying his niece, Matilda.

'Why aren't you in love with that?' Clara sighed. 'He looks fabulous, even for him.'

'We're signing the wedding register,' Scott hissed, 'and you're eyeing up some other bloke. Nice.'

To the wedding party's delight, Clara kissed her new husband.

Daisy would've giggled along, but she was too busy ogling Xander. His dark grey suit showed off his tall, rangy frame while the ice-blue shirt and matching tie contrasted perfectly with his Algarve tan. And he'd had his hair cut short – US marine short. He really did look fabulous, even for him.

After the ceremony, with her grin firmly in place, Daisy patiently endured the ritualistic torture of wedding photos, and Xander, standing under an ancient oak tree chatting to his brother, never took his eyes off her. The boy hadn't let her down.

When photographic purgatory finally ended, instead of running like a maniac, Daisy strolled over to him with utter sangfroid.

'You were late,' she said, giving him a good coat of looking at.

'Flights were a nightmare.' He smiled apologetically as she ran her fingers through his crew cut short hair.

'It was worth the wait. You'll do.'

He laughed and with no consideration for the wedding party watching, he kissed her under that oak tree for far too long.

'Do you get any time off for bad behaviour?' he whispered, his breath brushing her neck.

The wedding breakfast wasn't for another hour. Who'd even notice they were gone?

Daisy kicked off her shoes and they ran away like teenagers.

'Do you think our wet hair gives the game away?' Daisy giggled.

'You look stupidly beautiful,' he whispered before showering her neck with tiny kisses. 'I missed you.'

'Really? I barely noticed you'd been gone,' she lied. It was better than heavenly to have him back.

They sauntered into the conservatory, and Daisy smiled hello to Robbie's family. Tallulah waved a nonchalant hand as she briefly looked up from her iPod and Matilda squealed, attaching herself to Xander's leg.

'Better now?' Robbie gave Daisy a cheeky wink then pulled an apologetic face at Xander. 'Bad news. Ex-hell.'

Xander frowned. 'Exhale? What?'

'No, Ex. Hell. You've just walked into it.'

Xander looked around the room in horror. 'You've got to be joking? Two of them?'

Horrified and intrigued in equal measures, Daisy looked around. 'Who?'

'On the sofa in the corner, Holly's the blonde in the pink, and at the table next us, the girl in the flowery dress? Sophie...'

'Sadie. She's Clara's cousin.' Daisy laughed. 'Utter tramp. She won't have a clue what your name is either.'

'It gets worse.' Robbie nodded to a girl in a fabulous red dress, weaving her way to Holly. 'Bethany Marshall's here.'

Xander swore. 'Three of them?' His eyes darted around. 'Can we leave?'

'No, it's Clara's wedding.'

Probability hadn't been her strength doing GCSE Maths, but she knew enough to know you had to have a stupid amount of exes to have three at one wedding.

'Why are they both here?' He nervously glanced towards Bethany and Holly, who had their heads together, talking but looking his way. 'I'm really sorry, Daisy, but this could get very messy.'

With a dismissive shrug, she smiled. 'Oh, don't be so dramatic. So there are a few exes here. Are they very recent?' He shook his head. 'Then stop worrying. Who's Bethany?'

He led Daisy to a quiet window seat and after staring at the immaculate gardens for a minute, he took a deep breath.

'When I was seventeen, training with Anthony. I'd just been dumped by Bethany and...' He blushed. Xander actually blushed. 'Bethany made some very... let's call it constructive criticism.' He laughed at her gaping mouth. 'Your face is a picture. I was seventeen.'

'But...' *You get an A these days, sunshine.*

'I made it my mission to get better. I studied hard.'

'Tutored by the Michelin-starred Cougar?'

He tipped his head, nodding.

'And Bethany?'

'When I was twenty, I met up with her again. It was mean because I walked away without so much as a goodbye, but she didn't have much else to complain about.'

'Enough. I get you.' Daisy couldn't help giggling. 'So what did she dump you for? Aside from being crap in bed.'

'Isn't that enough?'

'No man in the world has ever been dumped for that. There's always a real reason.'

He stared out at the gardens again. 'I messed around with her best friend, Holly. That's why this could get very messy.'

'You bastard,' Daisy said, but kissed his cheek to reassure him. 'Constructive criticism? Remind me to thank Bethany later.'

Xander's frown deepened.

Around eleven o'clock, high on her eighth cup of coffee, Daisy perched precariously on her Jimmy Choos. While the DJ played some romantic twaddle, Xander wrapped one arm around her, the other hand twirling a curl as they swayed to the music. It could hardly be called dancing, but at least no one could accuse them of another PDA.

'Do you always cry at weddings?'

Bugger, he'd seen the tears during the ceremony.

'When I was fifteen, a French exchange student called Thierry broke my heart. I cried over him for three days. Idiot. After that, I vowed never again and taught myself a mind trick.' She showed him how she jammed her fingernails into her palms. 'It stops me crying. After Thierry, I didn't cry over anything until I left the

HMS. Even then, it took four days and two bottles of chardonnay before I finally cried and nine years of repressed leakage finally came out. But, honestly, I'm fine. It's just a blip.'

'Thierry? You let an exchange student called *Thierry* break your heart?' He shook his head, smiling. 'Only you, Fitzgerald.'

'Do you love her?' A girl's voice asked above the music.

Daisy turned and Xander's arms tightened around her.

Holly's black feather fascinator bobbed as her eyes flicked wildly between Xander and Daisy. 'Does he love you?' she asked. 'I didn't think he was capable of it.'

Xander's arms loosened. 'Holly…'

She sniffed. 'I can see she's fabulous but I'm prettier.'

It was true, taller too and, by the looks of things, rocking much better tits.

Holly looked up at Xander. 'At first, when she was staring at you, we thought she was just obsessed. We've all been there. But, God, when you kissed her under the tree?' She looked at Daisy. 'He never kissed me like that.' A tear rolled down her cheek as she focused her drunken gaze back on Xander. 'You only wanted a shag. I thought you loved me. You told me you loved me. Why didn't you love me?'

The girl was a psycho. Daisy could see it – most of the wedding party could see it. Scott, Robbie and Clara, pissing themselves at the bar, could certainly see it. It was just a shame Xander couldn't.

'Holly, it was five years ago.'

The last syllable hadn't even left his mouth when Holly went from vulnerably teary to full scale Alex Forrest. Pointing a French-manicured finger, she yelled he was a complete bastard and ought to be locked up to keep him away from unsuspecting women. Xander sheltered behind Daisy as if she might protect him. Not a chance, Holly looked ready to claw her eyes out once she'd ripped out his *cold, dead heart.*

Someone had to stop her. Daisy looked around, but Clara and Robbie were still in hysterics. Fortunately, Scott took charge and, with Bethany, dragged Holly away as she wailed, 'Why do I still want him? Why? Why? Why?'

Xander walked straight to the bar, ordered a large whisky and held his head in his hands. 'If Bethany went off on one like that I could understand, but Holly? I never even went out with her and it was five years ago. Jesus, are all women mental really?'

Daisy nodded, trying not to smile. 'On the plus side, you must've been a better shag at seventeen than Bethany gave you credit for.'

'What on earth did you do to that crazy mentalist?' Clara asked.

'Nothing that deserved that, I swear.'

Daisy pulled a face. 'He shagged her when he was going out with her best-friend.'

Xander turned to Clara. 'I'm so sorry. I hope it hasn't spoiled your evening.'

'Spoiled my evening?' She kissed his cheek. 'That was the funniest thing I've seen in ages. Besides, you have nothing to apologise for. It's not your fault she's a mental case. I'm just glad it wasn't one of my exes.' She grinned. 'Absolutely priceless, every wedding should have one.'

They were all smiling, but twenty minutes later, Daisy found out just what he'd done to that mental case.

Bethany Marshall had her cornered. Daisy came out of a cubicle in the ladies bathroom and there she was, waiting. With her false nails and hair-extensions, she hadn't seemed Xander's cup of tea, but actually, Daisy had the same shoes and she'd coveted the red dress the minute she saw it. Maybe she was his type. Now for the million dollar question. Why was one of Xander's more significant exes standing in the ladies loo looking like she wanted a bloody good chat?

'What?' Daisy tried not to sound defensive. She failed.

'Sorry about Holly. It's not your fault.' Bethany studied her Rouge Noir. 'Scott said you're okay, so I wanted to warn you... about Xander.'

'I think I can make up my own mind.' Daisy washed her hands, watching Bethany through the mirror.

Please, God, don't let her be a bunny boiler like Holly.

'He started shagging his way around St Nick's the minute he arrived in Year Nine. It wasn't my turn until the Christmas party in Year Eleven. I was going out with James at the time.'

'I'd started to think he was gay.'

'No. He's a Machiavellian bastard. He'll screw whatever best suits his needs. We'd had a massive argument the morning of the party but looking back, I think he manufactured it so I'd shag Xander. I suspect James watched.' She knocked back half her wine.

'That about sums up the kind of guys they are.'

'But that's not when you went out with Xander?' Daisy should've walked out.

Bethany shook her head. 'I was in the sixth form then and he was training to be a celebrity chef. We were at one of James' parties. He stalked me the entire night, on a mission because I was playing hard to get. It's all about the conquest for Xander. He's quite the player.' She narrowed her eyes. 'Think I'm a stalker yet? A nut job?' Daisy nodded. 'We went out for six months and he was a fabulous boyfriend. Sweet, thoughtful, funny, but you know all about that, don't you?'

'So?'

'It's an act.' She raised her eyebrows, challenging Daisy to say otherwise. 'I thought I'd tamed the guy no one else could but it turned out he'd shagged a different girl every week, which explained the gifts he'd given me. Flowers, CDs, books... they were all guilt presents. He must've shagged over twenty girls while we were going out. Holly was the last. She came to see me, crying her eyes out and I finally knew why he'd gone out with me.'

Would it be rude to help herself to Bethany's wine?

'All along, he'd been using me to get to Holly. She didn't come to St Nick's until the sixth form and he couldn't resist a new girl. At James' party, when he first met her, she ran a mile because she'd heard all about him. So he used me to show her what a great guy he was.

'It took six months, but she ended up so hopelessly in love with him, she shagged him even though he was her best-friend's boyfriend. But that's all he wanted. He shagged her twice that week, to prove he could, then she never heard from him again.' She sucked in a shaky breath, clearly still close to crying about it. 'When I broke up with him, I really laid into him.'

'You told him he was crap in bed so he went away and studied. He told me.' Daisy started to feel sorry for the poor girl.

'I created a monster. He wasn't that bad to begin with. We were seventeen, for Gods' sake. What did either of us know? When I was twenty, I was home for Christmas and he swept me off my feet, pursuing me like he had at James' party. Once he'd taken me to bed and shown me his new skills, he threw me out. It still rates as the best sex I've ever had.' She stared at the wall for a second. 'Daisy, he made me beg for more then he slammed a door in my face, and I do mean that literally.'

'But he's different now.'

'No. It was only three years ago. He's the same person, still hanging around with Marcus and James. He's a total player and you need to be careful. You're Finn Rousseau's ex-wife. You're a score and Xander will be playing you, like he played me. Don't think I'm jealous, I'm not. I'm over him. You're a friend of a friend and I'd hate for you to go through what I did.' Draining her glass, Bethany held out her left wrist, looking Daisy in the eye. 'You deserve better. We all did.'

Daisy stared at Bethany's arm. *I need a drink, way more than I ever need five hundred pounds.*

She'd expected to see a scar so the tattooed black X came as a surprise but appalled her more. Okay, it was small and quite twirly, but it was still a black bloody X on her wrist. She was as mental as Holly.

'It's to remind me not to be so fucking stupid in the future.' Bethany flicked her hair back and forced a pleasant smile. 'He might look like an angel, but it doesn't mean he is one. See if you can find out what was going on in Year Eleven. He wouldn't tell me.'

She left.

Daisy walked out of the bathroom on wobbly legs to find Xander leaning against the wall waiting for her. With his face expressionless, he gave a sideways nod of his head and Daisy followed him to the dance floor where they inappropriately slow-danced to an upbeat R&B tune.

'What did she tell you?'

'Her version of events.' Daisy kept her face against his shoulder so she wouldn't have to look at him. 'Did you shag around the whole time you went out with her?'

'Yes.'

'Are you still?'

'No.'

'Am I a conquest?'

'The greatest.' He lifted up her chin. 'This is different.'

'You were an utter bastard.'

'I know, but I'm not now.' He never dropped his gaze from hers. 'Daze, I'll admit that I've done some appalling things, but I'm not that person anymore.'

'What happened in Year Eleven?'

'That was seven years ago.'

'It's all in the past, right?'

'You know I'd marry you tomorrow.' His solemn face told her he was deadly serious.

'The ink's barely dry on my last divorce. Not a chance, sweetheart.' He wasn't turning her into a nutcase like Holly.

'I've accepted an offer on the house.'

She stopped, frowning up at him. 'And?'

'Twenty grand above asking, no chain and a quick sale. I have to be out by mid-December.'

'What are you going to do?' she asked, her voice shaking.

'It depends. Does your offer still stand?'

Daisy glanced across the room where Bethany sat, glaring at them with undisguised loathing. 'Honestly? I don't know.'

His arms tightened around her, his lips kissing her head. 'You have to trust me, Daze.'

'I know.'

But could she?

Chapter Thirteen

'It's six o'clock...' Xander said, taking away her untouched cup of tea.

'I know, I know,' Daisy mumbled, her mouth full of dressmaking pins. She was on the last hem and she wasn't going to rush now. Xander still loitered in the doorway. 'What?'

'Nothing. It's fascinating watching you make a dress.'

'You need to get out more,' she said, trying not to swallow a pin.

To be fair, they both needed to get out more. Since the wedding, Xander had pretty much moved in and they barely saw another person for a whole divine week, banishing any thoughts of bunny boiler exes or what might've happened in Year Eleven.

Finished. She snipped the last threads from the hem, before stripping off her t-shirt and slipping on her latest creation. The dress code for the *Forfeit* Halloween dinner was *black* and Daisy hadn't a thing to wear – certainly nothing that stood up to dinner at some fancy-schmancy restaurant with Xander's condescending friends. But in her sewing arsenal was the most fabulous nineteen-eighties pattern, and three hours later, she'd created little black dress nirvana – minus the shoulder pads.

'Covers up way too much,' he said, scowling at the mid-thigh jersey frock with its high neck and long sleeves.

And importantly, it also covered up her navel. That morning, she'd taken out the daisy belly button bar while she had a shower, but despite repeated searches of her bedroom, she couldn't find it anywhere. What if it had fallen between the floor boards? What the hell would she tell Xander? 'It'll look awesome with my black python Gucci knee boots.'

'Out of interest, how much do black python Gucci knee boots cost?'

'A fiver shy of fifteen hundred quid. Guilt-ridden Christmas present off the HMS.'

Xander's smile grew as she turned, showing off how the dress draped open at the back, leaving the top of her neck to the very base of her spine entirely naked. 'You'll do.'

Clearly, he'd remembered the backless red top she'd worn to the Low Wood Farm barbeque, which had been her cunning plan.

Hair done, make-up immaculate, dress waiting to be slipped on at the last minute – this would be a good night. How could it not? After they'd finished the game, she'd have her first alcoholic drink in thirty days and she couldn't bloody wait.

Xander leant against the doorframe, holding a mug and fighting a smile, no doubt at her underwear and Ugg boot combination. 'Tea?'

Oh God, roll on dare o'clock. For the whole of November she'd only drink liquids with a percentage written on the side, but for the next few hours she'd keep up the brave face.

'You are the best boy...'

Xander raised his eyebrows expectantly. 'Say it.'

'You are the best *tea* boy a girl could have.'

He slapped her backside but still watched with utter amusement as she hunted for her boots. Three boxes sat in a tower at the bottom of her wardrobe. The Louboutin pumps at the bottom, the Prada wedges in the middle and the Jimmy Choos from Clara's wedding on top. But where was the fourth box?

'Xand, where are my Gucci boots?'

'Why the hell would I know?' He sat on the bed, checking his phone. 'Under the bed?'

They should be in the wardrobe in a huge bloody box. How could they not be there? Was she going mental, was this what sobriety did to her? In frustration, she dropped to her knees, peering under the bed. A jumper of Xander's, her Converse trainers and a ball of Birkin's. No Gucci boots. But a twinkle caught her eye. Just visible under her bedside table was the daisy belly bar. Oh, thank God. Surreptitiously, while she still lay half under the bed, she fastened it back in, relief flooding over her.

'Xand, help?'

He sighed and tossed his phone on the bed. 'When did you wear them last?'

'My birthday?'

'Not since you moved here?'

She shook her head. Oh God, had she even seen them since she moved house? What if they'd been thrown out with some of the other boxes? With so many people helping, anything could've happened.

'I've lost my boots,' she wailed.

'Daze, they're just boots, bloody expensive boots but still.' He looked her over, with a growing smile. 'Want me to take your mind off them?'

'No,' she lied. 'We'll be late.'

He shrugged and threw her onto the bed.

What boots?

Oak Bank, Xander had already warned her, was probably the swankiest, most discreet boutique hotel in the country with one of the best menus. Daisy wasn't convinced any of that were entirely true, but she couldn't fault its über-cool charms.

The recently renovated seventeenth century country house was kitted out with innovative, local artisan furniture – rustic oak tables were adorned with roofing slate plates and simple crystal glasses. Even the pumpkin lanterns littered around the place looked hand-carved by a master craftsman. The hotel oozed class but with a soupcon of frivolity. Framed mirrors, each no bigger than a postcard, covered the corridor leading to the restaurant – you could check your individual body parts but not all of them at the same time. Daisy adored the place.

'Come on, we're already late,' she said, giggling as Xander studied his reflection, smoothing a barely noticeable kink in his centimetre-long hair. 'I can't believe you're wearing those scruffy jeans to this place.' His top half was smart in a crisp black shirt and black cashmere sweater, but the bottom half was mid-wash denim, very tatty mid-wash denim. He shot her a wink. The boy looked a billion dollars and he bloody knew it. 'OMG, you're as vain as me. I'd never twigged.'

He handed his jacket to the receptionist and took one last look in a mirror. 'I have to stand next to you, Fitzgerald. I'd hate to let the side down.'

The maître d' led them to a quiet alcove where the others were already seated in high-backed oak chairs, knocking back aperitifs and looking at them with despairing eyes. Oh, so they were a bit late. Who cared? But Daisy's nonchalant smile faltered when Xander trailed a finger all the way down her spine, just like he'd done the night she wore the red backless top. She employed every milligram of self-control to keep smiling and not melt on the spot.

Tabitha gave her a warm embrace, kissing both cheeks. 'Fabulous dress and I love the boots, sweetie.'

The four inch Jimmy Choo shoe boots were awesome, but they weren't the black python Gucci knee boots, Daisy explained, fighting any obvious pouting. No way would she prove Marcus right about her.

There were ten for dinner. James had brought Lidia, a Polish model and BFF of Tabitha's – maybe he wasn't quite as gay as Daisy had assumed. Lidia seemed pleasant enough but with limited appetite and intellect, she made Daisy look like a greedy genius and feel wildly superior.

Tabitha's date was Bruno, a piece of Italian eye-candy who barely spoke a word of English. He and Tabitha, who surprisingly spoke Italian, spent most of the night flirting quietly with one another. Occasionally, Xander and Marcus' shoulders would shake with repressed laughter and Daisy realised they could both understand Italian, another surprise.

Marcus's date was Ella Andrews, a food columnist, and since she was sitting next to Xander the Chef, much of the talk revolved around food. While it couldn't be lovelier to hear Xander so enthused, all the discussion of local produce and seasonality bored the pants off Daisy. And she didn't like the uncomfortable way Xander kissed Ella hello. Clearly, they had history.

In response, Daisy ducked out for as many cigarettes as she dared – Tabitha joining her for as many as she couldn't avoid.

'You and Xander seem happier,' she said, lighting a cigarette. 'Wasn't it a nightmare Finn turning up like that? I could've throttled India. I mean, surely it should've crossed her mind that you'd be there. James never goes anywhere without Xander and these days Xander doesn't go anywhere without you, sweetie. It makes me wonder if she didn't have an ulterior motive. Shall we do lunch next week?'

'So long as it's mostly liquid, yes.'

'How's sobriety been? A nightmare, I should think, but you look horrifically healthy.'

'Worst thing is, I feel it too.' Daisy glanced inside. 'I don't think I could've done it without Xander. He went away for a week, but rang me three times a day and for most of each evening to keep me entertained.'

'I've never seen him like this before.' Tabitha took a long drag on her cigarette. 'Well, Aunt Lucy maybe.'

'Lucy Errington's your aunt?'

'Friend of my mother's. No idea what he was thinking back then.'

'We should go in,' Daisy said, stubbing out her cigarette and putting on a brave smile. 'He's going to kill me for sneaking all these fags, but if I have to listen to Marcus' bloody date twitter lyrical about the sublime seasoning for much longer, I will kill someone with my soup spoon. You won't tell them I said that, will you?'

Tabitha shrieked with laughter. 'No, I'm half tempted to tell her I said it. The food is fabulous, but they've been talking about the perfect balance of flavours for an hour.'

Giggling like naughty children, they headed inside to find waiters ready to pounce with the next course. Oysters.

Daisy pushed her plate away. 'I've tried and I don't like.'

Lidia nodded. 'Me too. I'd rather blow a dog.'

There were several choking noises and everyone howled with laughter – everyone except Ella. Either she didn't approve of the comment or she was busy thinking if she could get *blow a dog* in her next column. While the others marvelled at the delicate flavour balance of the mignonette, Daisy fished a notepad from her bag and turned to Marcus who was sitting to her right. Time to show Mr Dowson-Jones she'd done her homework.

'It was the all-time hardest thing I've ever done,' she said, 'swishing a mouthful of wine around and not letting a drop go down my throat, *but* I made notes, as promised.'

Marcus sat back, his eyes narrowing. 'Go on.'

Okay, she was no Olly Smith, but Marcus ate his seafood snot, listening intently, occasionally nodding or frowning at her comments. Finally, he leant back in his chair, the corners of his mouth twitching with a smile.

'You sound like a ten year-old describing jelly and ice-cream, but okay. The Shiraz is a tad spicy, I agree.' He poured her a splash of the Pinot Gris they were drinking. 'What fruits are in here?'

Obediently, Daisy smelled and tasted, just as he'd taught her. 'Grapefruit...'

'And?'

She had no idea. Gutted wasn't the word.

'Tropical fruits. You smoke too much. You're killing your taste buds, *tesoro.*'

Tesoro? Really? It meant treasure in Italian. Daisy tried not to grin. 'My ex-husband's mum used call him *tesoro*. Are you actually Italian?'

He scowled, undoubtedly because she'd understood his term of endearment. 'Yes. Well, my mum is. Now, in the case I sent, there's a rather nice 2008 Riesling. Appreciate it, please.' He turned back to Ella – the wine chat over.

Xander lowered his head to Daisy's. 'Do you know Marcus is the only male you don't flirt with? You never have.'

Why not? With his model-worthy looks, Marcus ought to be right up her street.

'Are we going to do these bloody dares so I can have a drink?' Daisy asked, poised for her last spoonful of dessert – a meadowsweet mousse with blackcurrant granite. The dessert was so impossibly light, she'd devoured hers and happily let Xander feed her his.

'Let's do it.' James dropped the money on the table.

'As you know, I had to stay sober for thirty days.' She threw her dare card down. 'Job done. Someone get me a glass of God-damned wine.'

'Oh, I don't think so,' James said, taking her glass away. 'The card says, thirty days. This is day thirty. If you want to be in with a chance of winning the pot and our bet, you have to stay sober until midnight.'

You utter, fucking twat.

Why did he have to be such a sadistic wanker? What exactly had she done to make him dislike her so bloody much? Daisy sat back, rapping her nails on the table, but never dropped eye contact with James. Whatever it was she had done, when she found out, she'd do it over and over again, just to wipe that smug, God-damned sneer of his face.

But for now, she'd smile. 'Fine.'

At least it earned her another kiss from Xander. 'I'm proud of you.'

This wasn't about Xander's pride; it was about taking five hundred pounds from his bastard best-friend.

'And what did you do, James?' she asked sweetly. 'Drown a bag of kittens?'

He tossed his dare card on the table. 'I had to fuck three people in twenty-four hours, one of them being a current partner.'

Ella leant forward, resting her chin on her hand. Daisy followed suit, eyes-wide as she reassessed Lidia. She'd assumed the leggy model was just some date to make up the numbers, but James regarded her as a *partner*?

'Darling, we've been together for over a year,' Lidia said, flashing a catwalk-confident smile. 'Let's face it, it wouldn't be the first time. When was it?'

They'd been going out for a year? So James really wasn't as gay as Daisy had assumed.

'Two nights ago,' James said, looking Lidia in the eye. 'Aren't you going to ask who?'

Another smile from Lidia said she'd play along, but as she sipped her wine, her hand shook. 'Okay, who were they?'

'Tabitha,' James said.

OMG, weren't they related?

'You bitch,' Lidia hissed to her newest *ex*-BFF.

Tabitha shrugged, but Bruno, despite his lack of English, seemed to grasp the gist of the conversation and threw his fork across the table, glaring at Tabitha.

'And the other?' Lidia asked, her unchecked fury now bubbling to the surface.

'Dominik.'

'My brother?'

Whoa, so maybe he was quite as gay as Daisy had thought. But any amusement at James' revelation was obliterated as Lidia visibly crumpled. She'd been humiliated, publically dumped by her boyfriend of one year. How could James be so bloody callous?

Xander sat back in his chair, staring at his wine as he swirled it in his glass. That was his only reaction to his best-friend treating some poor girl like crap? Of course it would be. Not too long ago, this was just the kind of stunt Xander would pull.

'You're a piece of shit,' Lidia hissed.

James merely smiled, lifting his glass to his lips.

Lidia was too quick. She grabbed the glass and threw the remainder of the wine into his face, shrieking in Polish. After a vitriolic outburst, she grabbed her handbag and fled.

'You *ees* all fucked up childs,' Bruno growled before following her.

He was very possibly right.

'Does anyone have the first idea what the Pole said?' James smiled without the slightest trace of remorse as he dabbed his face with his napkin.

'Here's hoping it was a Romany curse,' Daisy replied sweetly. 'Do you actually hate women?'

'Fuck you.'

Xander finally looked up. 'Pack it in, both of you.'

Tabitha gently chinked a knife against her glass to gain everyone's attention. 'Are we all finished worrying about emaciated Eastern-bloc models?'

She placed a box on the table, then lifted out a glass vase – the glass vase Daisy had unwrapped on James' not-birthday, one of his birthday gifts.

James scowled. 'That's my Lalique vase.'

'Value?' Tabitha the game show assistant displayed the vase for all to see.

'Fifteen hundred, maybe two grand.'

Tabitha popped it back in the box then produced a small hammer out of her handbag. 'Count of three? One...'

James eyes widened. 'Don't you dare. It's a Lalique, for Christ's sake. And it's mine.'

'Two...' Tabitha winked at him. 'Three.' She squealed with laughter as she hit the vase.

James winced and stared in horror at the broken glass. Break a girl's heart and he couldn't care less, but break a vase and he's appalled? Gay and definitely hates women.

'Marcus? What did you do?' Tabitha asked, still giggling.

Marcus waved a dismissive hand. 'I didn't do mine.'

Shock and disbelief passed around the table like a Mexican wave.

He shrugged, clearly unrepentant. 'The dare was to take an illegal narcotic I haven't done before.' Xander smiled knowingly, and Marcus turned to Daisy, grinning. 'Unlike you idiots, I don't do drugs.'

She saluted him. There was a lot more to Marcus Dowson-Jones than she'd ever given credit.

'Loser,' Tabitha said, giving her most saccharine smile.

'Xander?'

He left the room but returned seconds later carrying a large cardboard box he must've stashed in the car while Daisy had dressed. Notably, he didn't come back to his seat but hovered at the opposite side of the table.

'I had to steal something worth more than a grand.' He opened the box.

'My black python Gucci knee-boots!' Daisy squealed. 'You bastard. You stole my boots. Bring them here.'

'Promise you won't hit me?'

'No.' She laughed, kicking off the Jimmy Choos before opening the Gucci box as a new mother would unwrap their newborn.

'Boots? Over a grand?' James shook his head.

'Fifteen hundred, actually,' Xander explained.

'Some people have too much bloody money,' James said, 'and that is rich coming from me.'

Daisy zipped up the boots and lifted a leg in the air to show them off. 'Sublime, perfectly balanced boots.' She sent Tabitha a cheeky wink. 'And worth every single penny.'

Xander kissed her leg before leaning back in his chair, lazily grinning. And then it all made sense. She touched the daisy belly bar through her dress.

'Did you steal the daisy too?' she asked, thoroughly suspicious.

He nodded. 'But stealing your boots was more fun so I left the daisy for you to find.'

But, that meant the moonstone daisy was worth over a *grand*? And if it were worth over a grand, then that wasn't a crystal in the middle – it had to be a diamond.

'Is it *real*?' she asked Xander incredulously, because that was a bloody big diamond.

He dropped a kiss on her lips. 'As if I'd give you anything that wasn't.'

'So who wins round two?' Tabitha asked, her eyes glinting with hope.

'Not you.' James threw a sugar lump at her.

'Surely, Daisy should for her restraint,' Xander said valiantly.

'Nope,' James said, shaking his head. 'She's not finished the job yet.'

One hour to go. 'But I will.'

'Undoubtedly,' James said, 'But Xander completed the best

dare.'

The others murmured their agreement and refusing to come across as a bad loser in front of James, Daisy nodded. 'I agree.'

'I shall fritter it wisely.' Xander took the money from James.

'Arse, this means I've thrown away five hundred pounds,' Tabitha said.

James sent her a foul look. 'Well, I'm down a grand and a vase.'

'Game over?' Xander asked as he flicked through the pile of notes. 'No round three, agreed?'

'Yes,' Tabitha purred. 'I mean, five grand stakes, sweetie? It's over.'

James and Marcus nodded.

'Game over,' Daisy agreed.

This had gone far enough. The last month had been hell – no way would she put herself through something like that again. Or worse, treat someone the way James had treated poor Lidia.

Besides, Daisy would never have the five grand stake to play round three.

As coffee was served, the head chef and friend of Xander's came to say hello. Xander stood up to boy-hug his old work colleague, before introducing Daisy. Unlike the rest of Xander's friends, all public school rich kids, Jonty was a salt-of-the-earth Geordie and Daisy warmed to him instantly. There was much adoration for the food, service and wine before Jonty offered Xander a job, which he rejected with a polite laugh. Why would he do that? The second Jonty moved on say hello to Tabitha, Daisy asked.

'Why didn't you say, yes?' she whispered.

Xander blinked, as if the idea had never entered his head. 'It's not what I want.'

'It's a job as a chef at a top restaurant. It's not working a job you hate.'

'And it'd be for a fraction of the money I earn working the job I hate.'

'It's still a job.'

'Not a very well paid one.'

Giving up, Daisy dropped her dubious looking *Passion Fruit Cloud Lollipop* into her coffee and went out for a cigarette. Through the window, she watched as Jonty went around the table. He chatted amiably with each guest, but his eyes never left the second person he'd said hello to – Tabitha bloody Doyle. He gazed at her while he shook James' hand and she smiled her Elmlea smile. Poor Jonty didn't look star struck; he looked in love.

'Amusing, isn't it?' Marcus said as he joined Daisy outside. 'It's not a new thing. Jonty's fancied her for years. Of course, last time he met her, he was a lowly sous chef. Now, he's rumoured to be getting a TV show.'

'Does it matter that much to her?'

'We all have our motivational prompts. Tab's is her career.'

'Is Xander's money?'

Marcus narrowed his eyes. 'And yours?'

Daisy shrugged. 'I guess I like beauty.'

'Is that an indirect way of admitting you're vain and superficial?' He elbowed her, grinning. 'Taste is what matters to me.'

'Is that a polite way of saying you're greedy?' She elbowed him back.

He held out the large glass of white he'd brought out with him. 'It's five past.'

Was it? Where had the last hour gone? Daisy checked her watch and apprehensively took the glass. Was this some trick? Why was Marcus being so nice to her? Slowly, she inhaled the bouquet, savouring the peach and violet notes.

'Is this the viognier from the wine tasting?' she said.

Marcus' answering grin meant the world. 'You were paying attention.'

'It was the one I totally nearly caved over,' she admitted.

'Xander said.' Marcus lit a cigarette and handed her a fat envelope. 'You won.'

'Would it pain James too much to give it to me himself?'

'Afraid so.' Marcus tipped his head. 'You know Xander likes you, really likes you? He thinks you still don't believe him.'

'I met Bethany Marshall recently.' She took several gulps of the divine wine. 'It's hard.'

'No, you just need to trust him.' Marcus folded his arms, his face screwed up in concentration for a moment. 'Look, he might've shagged around in the past, but he's not who you think he is.'

'I thought you didn't like me.'

He shrugged, glancing away and trying not to smile.

'Ohmigod, you don't really hate me, do you?'

'Don't push your luck. I meant every word I said, but...' He glanced over at Xander. 'He's been looking for someone like you for a long time. When you admit you love him, *tesoro*, ask me again.'

Chapter Fourteen

The next morning, Xander was called into work so Daisy, dealing with her first hangover in a month, laced up her hiking boots, heading up Lum Crag for a serious cobweb-blowing power-walk and a bloody good think. Marcus' words played over and over in her head. *He's been looking for someone like you for a long time.* FWB really was nonsense, but could Xander really be more than a fling?

The next step would be moving in together, and not as some deluded-notion of flatmates, but the idea still terrified her. One day, she'd be a Has-been. One day, she'd be Bethany. The thought churned her stomach more than her hangover and she stood on the edge of Lum Crag, the wind whipping her hair around her face. She teetered on the edge and, for a few glorious minutes, she forgot everything, revelling in the adrenaline rush.

The rush. Wasn't that the point? Okay, one day her and Xander would be over, but going out with him was the most fabulous rush. Couldn't she enjoy it? It wasn't like they'd get married and have kids.

Hangover banished, she ambled home with Birkin trotting by her side and to both their delight, Xander's car was already parked up. Daisy hurried inside, but Xander was nowhere to be found. Maybe he'd gone to the pub? Her hope faltered when she spotted assembly instructions for a Solid Oak Chair-swing. She didn't have a chair-swing, solid oak or otherwise.

Out in the garden she found him buried in his coat, an over-sized beanie and a grim expression, rocking away and smoking a joint. She expected him to be down again but as she walked over, a lazy smile took over his face.

'Hello, beautiful,' he said.

Beautiful? Hiking boots and rats nest hair thanks to the wind, that was his idea of beautiful?

'Hello, yourself.' Daisy nodded to the chair-swing. 'As presents go, this is definitely the most unique.'

'I like chair-swings.' He put his arm around her as she cuddled up next to him.

'It's freezing out here. Why aren't you inside?'

'I like chair-swings.'

Okay, he wasn't in a good mood but at least he wasn't petulant. She took the offered joint and as small a drag as she could get away with. 'What's up?'

'Four weeks on the yacht sailing around the Caribbean.'

'Can I come too?' she asked, half-serious.

'I wish.' His arms tightened around her as he kissed her head. One day, there'd be a bald patch where he'd worn her hair away from kissing her head so much.

'It sounds heavenly if you ask me.'

'It's supposed to be.'

He picked up the latest *Diamond Adventures A/W* brochure, turning to a page featuring a zillion dollar yacht. How could he hate this? Talk about unreserved luxury. The spacious, opulent bedrooms, the classy deck, the hot tubs, the food, the gym…

'Why is living in such stupid luxury for four weeks, in heavenly sunshine so awful?'

'Because I'm trapped on board with the idiots who charter it.'

'When are you going?'

'Friday.'

'*This* Friday? Why do you never get a bit of notice?'

'Rich people get to go when they want to go.' He tilted his head to look at her. 'But knowing you'll miss me has cheered me up, Fitzgerald.'

'It'll be hell without you, but it's only four weeks. I'll cope.'

Absentmindedly, Daisy flicked back through the brochure. It certainly wasn't your standard holiday company. The website described hundreds of potential activities and locations, but there were no prices. Customers could choose from the yacht in the Med with stop offs for the Grand Prix, or a castle in Scotland for the Open. Manor houses in the Lakes, Chalets in the Swiss Alps, Diamond offered it all. Their slogan on one page was *ask and we will deliver*. Reaching the inside cover, Daisy laughed as Xander smiled up at her, looking every bit the hottest holiday rep in the world.

'OMG, you poster boy,' she said, smiling as he cringed. 'You look fabulous. You really could be a model.'

'Tried it but it bored the pants off me. Had a great week in Rome though.' He kissed her neck. 'And it's very depressing only being appreciated for your looks. Although being with you, I'm getting used to it.'

In retaliation, Daisy gave a playful kick to his shins. 'That reminds me. You and Marcus understood what Bruno and Tabitha were saying last night? Marcus told me he was half-Italian.'

'He's pretty fluent but doesn't let on. I only understood the good bits.'

'Sofia?'

'No, she's from Essex. I spent six months working in Portofino at a restaurant where no one spoke English. *Cara mia, tu sei il mio amore.*'

He flashed his super-model smile and Daisy had to focus on the brochure, pretending she wasn't wildly impressed. Laughing, Xander flicked through to the Austrian pages and pointed to someone on the top of a mountain.

Daisy squinted at the tiny figure. 'That's you? It could be anyone.'

'It could, but it's me.' With his finger, he drew an off-piste and fairly vertical path down the mountain. 'Two minutes after the photo was taken, I skied down there. Scariest thing I've ever done in my life.'

'I'd forgotten you like skiing. I haven't been for years, but I used to love it.'

'Austria's my job of choice, skiing every day, but Richard doesn't trust me not to bugger things up and a slightly better class of client book the chalets. We should go skiing. India has a place we could go to. We'd have to put up with her, though.'

'Why don't you like her?'

He scowled. 'She's trouble.'

'But why?' Daisy's stomach bottomed out. 'OMG, you and her...'

'Christ, no. She's ancient.'

Ancient? India was only four years older than her and hellishly younger than the Michelin-Starred Cougar. Daisy wanted to... well, argue India's corner, but Xander had already moved on, pointing to photos of Robbie. Mountain biking in one, a smiley rep in another, he looked every bit as model-like as Xander. In fact, every single face in the brochure was stupidly beautiful.

Daisy glared at a dark-haired Glamazon on the yacht. 'Are there any mingers working for this bloody company?'

Xander shook his head. 'Recruitment policy. As much as I like you being jealous, you've no need to be.' He buried his face in her hair. 'I don't want to go.'

'Oh, I don't want you to go either but you need the money for the restaurant.' Daisy sighed. 'Four weeks. Bugger, that really will be being single.'

He lit another joint. 'You'd better not act like it.'

'I promise.' She kissed him.

'At least I'll be back for my birthday.'

Birthday? She'd never thought to ask.

'You are awful, Fitzgerald. It's the tenth of December, thanks for not knowing. Yours is the fourteenth of March. You're a Pisces. I'm a Sagittarius by the way. According to one website, you're indecisive and and I'm selfish, but we have an intuitive and mystical connection.' He started giggling, which set Daisy off and they didn't stop for five minutes.

'Wow, you look amazing.' Daisy held Clara at arm's length to look at her again. In a clingy red tunic with skinny jeans and low heels, she'd gained no visible podge – she just appeared to have stuck half a football under her top.

'It might be *Next* not *Net-a-Porter*, but coming to lunch with you requires a new outfit these days in case I get my pretty face in *Heat* too.' She winked and twirled. 'Not bad for twenty weeks, don't you think?'

'What did you mean about *Heat*?' Daisy asked as they sat outside on the Weir's riverside terrace.

'You haven't seen this?' Clara pulled a magazine out of her bag. 'You're in the *Going Up* section this week. *Doing lunch with a BFF*.'

Appalled and excited, Daisy barely dared to look. OMG, she was in a magazine and it had nothing to do with the HMS. The photo was of Tabitha and her walking along the main street in Haverton and another of them laughing over cocktails.

'God, you can't tell but we were hammered.'

'Why on earth did you go for lunch with that posh cow?' Clara asked, frowning.

'She wanted to apologise. But calling it lunch is pushing the term a tad. We went to the OBB for BOGOF cocktails. I'm not convinced we ate anything.' They'd drunkenly chatted about Coronation Street, shagging and how Finn seemed to be getting on famously in New York. 'But actually, we got on like a house on fire. She apologised four times for trying it on with Finn. The first would've done because she was sober and I think she meant it. The other three were because we were so bloody drunk.'

'You're also in *Grazia*.' Clara handed her another magazine. 'This time it's the best dressed section so congratulations, all that *Net-a-Porter* plagiarism has paid off.'

Grazia said she looked cool? Daisy peered at the photo. Wow, her and Tabitha did look cool – skin-tight jeans, skyscraper heels, bang-on-trend scarves, enormous sunglasses and in Tab's case a lovely woollen hat. Magazines used to only feature Daisy to point out how thoroughly undeserving she was to be the HMS's wife – this was altogether a very pleasant change. She couldn't stop her inane grin and barely heard Clara twittering about spicy food meaning she was having a boy, or a girl – depending on which website you looked at.

Clara snatched the magazine's back. 'I knew shouldn't have let you look at those until after you'd ordered.'

Realising the waiter hovered, waiting for her, Daisy quickly ordered the same as Clara, but with a glass of Chablis on the side, not orange juice.

As the waiter disappeared, Clara leant forward, resting her elbows on the table. 'So what happened when he left? Did you faux-cry at the airport?'

'I didn't take him to the airport.'

'You really are a heartless cow.'

'His idea, actually. We'd planned to have a lazy morning in bed, brunch with Rob and Van, then I'd take him to Manchester. Only he'd totally lied to me about what time his flight was. He woke me at six and said Robbie was taking him because he couldn't say goodbye to me at the airport.' Daisy lit a cigarette and stared at the river. 'He told me he'd filled the freezer so I had no excuse not to eat properly and then he buggered off. Well, he told me he loved me and then he buggered off.' She stared at the river, remembering that morning, but Clara, the cow-bag, had her lips clamped together, trying not to laugh. 'There was no way I was letting him leave like that so I legged it downstairs just as he was about to get in the car.' Daisy's cheeks heated up. 'Not my finest moment. I only had on one of his jumpers with no shoes or anything. God, I hope Robbie didn't see my arse.'

'So, much snogging later, you cried and told him you loved him too?' Clara asked, still fighting laughter.

'Much snogging later, I didn't cry or tell him I loved him, but I did say I'd miss him like mad.'

Clara's eyes widened. 'Oh my God, you're lying. What really happened?'

Why was she so appalling at lying? 'Honestly, that's true. I didn't *actually* cry, but I nearly did and I *nearly* told him I loved him.' The grin on Clara's face was nauseating. 'Oh, stop it. He seemed really upset so it felt like the thing to do.'

'You love him.'

Daisy shook my head. 'It's different.'

'But you almost cried. You never cry.'

'I've spent ten months crying. Just because I miss him, doesn't mean I love him.'

'You're such an idiot.' She shook her head. 'But you do miss him?'

He'd only been gone eight days but, God, yes. She'd tried to keep busy with the renovations, but she lived for her evening phone calls.

'It's not too bad,' Daisy lied. 'He rings between nine and ten every night, late afternoon for him. Sometimes we talk for ten minutes, sometimes an hour. It depends how busy he is. The other night he could only talk for a couple of minutes so he rang back at three in the morning. I was in bed, he was in bed and it got *very* out of hand.'

'What is it with you and phone sex? You won't kiss and tell to me but you'll talk *ho* dirty if there's a boy on the other end of a phone.' Clara grinned for a moment, before settling into a more sympathetic mode. 'Why are you wearing the *death of my marriage* dress?'

Daisy looked down at the black cashmere mini-dress she'd lived in after Finn kicked her out. It'd been a gift from him, one of the first he ever bought her.

'Is this because of yesterday? Sorry I couldn't be there.'

'Honestly, it was fine. I had a kitchen designer come round and take my mind off it.'

Clara's eyes narrowed. 'You didn't get drunk?'

'Maybe a tad.' Daisy lit a cigarette, hiding her guilt.

'Because it was your wedding anniversary?'

Daisy groaned. 'No. Well, a bit. It was three o'clock before I remembered what the date was. So I put on the death of my marriage dress to get all Cathy-esque and yearn for my lost love.'

'But Heathcliff's got brown eyes these days, hasn't he?'

Daisy nodded. 'I love Finn, but right now... I want Xander back. I've even taken down the pictures I have of Finn. It's like I'm trying to bury a chunk of my life, but I feel...'

'Excited?' Clara asked.

Daisy took a deep breath for the next bit. 'Once I realised I'd moved on from Finn, I thought what the hell and... I'm going to ask Xander to move in. Properly.'

After she'd finished squealing, Clara hugged her. 'That's the best news.'

'Being realistic, he pretty much lives with me already. He's got a toothbrush and half of Clinique men's department in my bathroom.'

And she couldn't cross the bedroom without tripping over his discarded jeans and t-shirts. The boy was ridiculously untidy, but it was his mess and Daisy couldn't bring herself to tidy it away. She'd even taken to sleeping with a jumper of his. Incredibly tragic, but it smelled like him.

'Don't get me wrong, there're things about Xander that make me very wary. He's too young and he's too good-looking for a long-term thing.' Daisy drained her wine, wishing she weren't driving. 'Eventually, he'll get bored and push off with some incredibly beautiful supermodel, but I may as well enjoy him while I have him.'

'Oh, for crying out loud. He loves you. You love him. He'll make you happy. Why can't you see it?' Clara gave a despairing sigh. 'When are you going to tell him?'

'I didn't think it was something you do over the phone after necking a few vodkas trying to yearn for your ex-husband. I'm going to wait until he comes home. Besides, when he rang he was beyond excited. He'd been scuba-diving with manta rays off the Turks and Caicos Islands yesterday. Why that boy hates his job is beyond me.'

'Did that phone call descend into soft-porn too?'

Daisy merely grinned.

'So, if you're over Finn, ready to live with Xander, why are you wearing the death of my marriage frock today?'

Still smiling, Daisy held out a foot. 'Because it looks fabulous with a denim jacket and the black python Gucci knee boots.'

Finn really was in the past.

That evening, Daisy didn't drink in case she blurted out that she wanted Xander to move in, but at midnight she poured a hefty glass of chardonnay and stared at the phone. He hadn't called. He didn't call the next night either. To begin with, she sent texts. Then she rang, sometimes several times a day, but each time it went straight to voicemail.

Despite telling herself there'd be dead zones in the Caribbean where reception must be non-existent, she knew something was wrong. This was exactly what happened in September when he went to the Med. But he knew he could talk to her about being miserable, so why wasn't he? What if she'd done something to annoy him? What if he thought her a whore after the phone sex? What if he didn't even want to go out with her anymore, let alone move in? What if he'd met someone else?

It took the whole bottle of white to banish thoughts of the Glamazons in the Diamond brochure.

A welcome distraction arrived in the shape of Jack the Joiner. He turned up to fit the new hardwood windows, when Xander had been gone for two and a half weeks but got bugger all done the first day because he arrived to find Daisy almost in tears. Cue lots of tea and sympathy, her life story and a potted history of her relationship with Xander.

Three days later, the windows were installed and a new oak door adorned the front of the house. There was also a gaping hole in the kitchen where the cooker once lived. Jack knew someone who knew someone and as two dodgy looking men loaded the unfathomable Aga into a lorry, Daisy pocketed several thousand pounds. She was mulling over blowing the lot on a new handbag not a hardwood kitchen, when she finally received a text:

DAF BA1396.

Chapter Fifteen

Oh God, the DAF code word. Xander must need her. But why? Daisy stared at the text as if the nine characters held some clue. What was so wrong with his life? She just didn't get it, though on the upside, he was coming home early and she couldn't help a little happy dance. She could totally picture his delighted face when she asked him to move in properly.

The British Airways flight wasn't due into Manchester for a couple of hours, so she played dress up until she stood in a red cashmere sweater, skin-tight jeans and Gucci knee boots. As she wrapped an enormous scarf around her neck, she frowned at the Aga-less kitchen. What if Xander didn't want to live in a house with no cooking facilities? She'd simply have to keep him in bed for two days so he wouldn't notice.

The drive to the airport was interminably slow due to torrential rain but she'd left in plenty of time. She wanted to be the one waiting, so he'd know she was there for him. A few French manicured nails were distressed while she stood in arrivals but, finally, there he was – stupidly tanned, sexily dishevelled and looking absolutely miserable under his over-sized beanie.

'Christ, I'd like to cheer that up,' muttered a girl behind her.

You won't get to, sweetheart. But I will.

His eyes focused on Daisy's as weaved his way through the taxi drivers holding up signs and her heart lurched. Like she had before he left, she wanted to cry. She hadn't realised just how much she'd missed him until her was back in her arms. They kissed without any care for who the hell watched and afterwards she simply gazed into his puppy dog eyes. Was Clara right, was Daisy in love with him already?

'I'm so glad you're back,' she whispered. 'I... I've missed you.'

He rested his forehead against hers. 'Can we go home?'

Xander didn't say another word as they walked to the car and the second he closed the passenger door, he started rolling a joint.

'Where the hell did you get that from?'

'I've just flown in from Jamaica, where do you think?'

'You brought a bag of weed through customs? You could've been arrested.' Daisy stared at him, appalled, but he glared back. 'You can't smoke that in here. I'll get stoned driving.'

'Are you going to bitch all the way home?' He dropped the bag with a petulant sigh before closing his eyes and ignoring her for the rest of the journey.

This wasn't going quite as she'd planned.

'Fridge full of food as usual.' He opened a can of coke and lit his joint.

'You can't cook anyway.' She pointed to the gaping hole where the Aga once lived. 'Hated it.'

'New windows?'

She nodded. 'So what—'

'Can I go to bed? I'm knackered.' Without waiting for a reply, he disappeared upstairs.

This wasn't going at all as she'd planned.

He came down after a couple of hours, showered, shaved and looking thoroughly bad tempered. Daisy wasn't sure if he were cross with her or cross with the world, but whatever it was, she wasn't bloody asking.

'Pub,' he said – a statement, not a question.

She nodded.

In the Miller's Arms, they sat at their favourite table and she remembered the night before he went away. They'd sat in the same seats and gazed into each other's eyes, talking nonsense in front of the toasty fire. Now, she wondered if she could sit through the horrific silence. Turns out, she couldn't.

'Xander?' she raised her eyebrows, but he didn't react. 'What's wrong? You know you can talk to me.'

But he didn't answer. He yawned, white wires briefly visibly between his scarf and oversized bloody beanie. He was listening to an iPod? Leaning over, Daisy yanked the wires.

'Don't you bloody dare,' she hissed. 'You don't get me to pick you up from the bloody airport, sleep in my bloody bed, then sit here listening to bloody music when you're supposed to be having dinner with me.'

What the hell was going on?

'It's fucking freezing in here.' He shivered, scowling like it was her fault, but after a minute of staring at the fire, he sighed and leant forwards. Gently, he pushed her hair back, stroking her cheek with his thumb. 'I'm sorry, Daze.'

Grateful he wasn't angry with her, she wanted to talk but he turned back to the fire. Another couple sat opposite, their happy chatter a hideous contrast to her and Xander's uncomfortable silence. She picked at her wild mushroom risotto, willing him to talk and twice Xander opened his mouth to say something, but he went back to his guinea fowl and confit potatoes, not saying a word. Where was her Xander, the one she'd kissed goodbye at six in the morning just over three weeks ago?

Instead of wishing for what she clearly couldn't have, Daisy concentrated on what she could do to help. He'd said sorry so this couldn't be about her – it had to be one of his hideous mood swings, no doubt connected to his job. The waitress cleared their plates and the happy, chatty couple went into the bar so Daisy emptied the wine bottle into her glass, praying Xander would finally talk to her, or do something.

Sadly, he did. He reached into his pocket and tossed her a small box.

'Gift,' he said, leaning back in his chair.

Was this how it worked? He'd go away and come back miserable with a gift for her. She sighed before opening the Tiffany box. Inside were beautiful drop-earrings – simple inch long platinum stems with three diamonds captured in a circle.

'Xand, they're perfect, but you should be saving your money for the restaurant, not spending it on expensive presents for me. What were these? A couple of grand?'

'Four. It was tip money I didn't want.'

'Tip money? Christ, you are good at your job. What the hell do you have to do to get tips like that? Shag the…'

It'd been a joke but he didn't smile. Bethany's words bounced around Daisy's head. *He'd shagged a different girl every week, which explained the gifts he gave me.* Had he shagged someone else, had they *tipped* him? He looked her in the eye and she knew it was true.

'No,' she whispered.

'Yes.' He downed the rest of his drink.

'But that makes you…' She couldn't say it.

'I'm quite aware of what that makes me.'

She stared at him, waiting, but he didn't explain and he didn't apologise. He simply stared back, daring her to say something, ready for the fight. Daisy walked out.

The rain was heavier than ever, rivalling her power shower, and since she'd left her coat in the pub, it drenched her in seconds. She'd probably get pneumonia, but who cared? She shouldn't have worn heels. The walk took too long and she wanted to run home and get the vodka out. Did she have any? No. Wine would do. Which one? A red? It didn't matter so long as it had a percentage over thirteen. She'd reached the yard before Xander caught up with her.

'Daisy?'

She threw the Tiffany box, hoping it would hurt when it hit him. It didn't. To her intense irritation, he caught it one-handed like he had that bloody cricket ball back in June.

'Was this *tip* money too?' Her hand shook as she took out the belly button daisy, dropping it on the cobbles as if it burned her fingers. 'And you think that's okay? You go fucking other women then buy me presents with the proceeds? Guilt presents like you bought Bethany?'

She threw open the kitchen door and hunted in the larder for a suitable wine. Fourteen percent, bingo. All the time she opened the bottle, she kept eye contact with Xander, mentally begging him to tell her it wasn't true, that it was a joke. He didn't. He sat on the kitchen table, fiddling with the belly bar daisy and glaring at her with an arrogance she'd never seen before.

This man was a stranger.

'What bothers you most, Daisy? That it was for money or that I've shagged someone else? You're not my girlfriend. We're *Friends With Benefits*, remember?'

She kept her words emotionless, refusing to cry in front of him. 'The bed in the spare room is made up. You can piss off in the morning, preferably before I get up.'

Why were there no doors to slam downstairs? Why hadn't Jack fitted them already? With her bottle of wine and cigarettes, she ran upstairs to her bedroom giving that door, at least, a satisfying slam. Then, for the second time in a year, Daisy cried her eyes out over a boy who'd broken her heart.

She clutched her phone, needing Clara, but she wouldn't ring her. How could she admit what he'd done? She couldn't even say it in her head. To block mental images of him shagging beautiful women on that bloody yacht, Daisy sank the wine as if it were orange juice and swallowed one of the sleeping pills a concerned doctor had given her months ago. She hadn't needed them when her husband threw her out, but God, she did now.

With some nonsense film in the background, Daisy stared at the empty wine bottle, considering getting another, but she couldn't keep her eyes open.

Something was wrong. A gentle thud came from downstairs and the lack of ambient light meant yet another power cut. Marvellous. Just another thing to add to her pathetic excuse for a life. Burying under the duvet, she tried to hide from the world. Wait, had she covered herself with it before her coma? Or had Xander come in? The wine bottle and sleeping pills were on her bedside table. He'd been in.

Another thud. What was that?

With a very fuzzy head, she pulled on her jeans and crept downstairs. It could've been a burglar or axe murderer and sensibly, she should've sent Xander in first, but she was too angry to let him play the hero. At the bottom of the stairs, her bare foot hit water. What the hell?

'Xander, get up!'

She rolled up her jeans and stepped into the hallway. An inch of water covered the floor but in the kitchen, where the floor dropped down two steps, a foot of water sloshed around. Birkin sat looking thoroughly confused on a kitchen chair and the thudding noise she'd heard came from small waves bashing the little plastic compost bin against the fridge.

Waves. She had waves in the kitchen.

'Oh God, please let this all be a Valium-induced dream.'

'Jesus.' Xander hid from Daisy's glare as he pulled on a jumper.

It would transpire that after two days of rain, rivers everywhere had burst their banks and half of Cumbria was under water. But Daisy didn't care about the rest of the county, just the little bit she'd worked so hard to make home.

Her buckets, her ladders, her paint brushes... She'd left them in the porch, but now they floated around the yard, in danger of being swept away.

Swearing, she dragged on her coat and Hunters before

venturing into the flood water. It whirled around her feet, about four inches from the top of her boots, making it almost impossible to walk – carrying a ladder and three buckets didn't make the job any easier.

'Let me,' Xander said, taking the ladder.

By the time he'd secured the ladder and Daisy had rescued all the paintbrushes she could find, the water had risen another three inches. The rugs she'd blown half her wages on would be submerged, the ancient sofas she'd bought from a junk shop and lovingly reupholstered would be ruined. Beaten, Daisy stared down at her Hunters, now with barely an inch left visible above the over the water, and burst into tears.

Why was this happening to her? Was this some kind of karmic payback for her previous sins? Did she deserve this? All she'd wanted was for Xander to move in, but he was a fucking man-whore and all her hard work in the house was ruined. She stood sobbing until he scooped her up and, while she wished it wasn't bliss to be in his arms again, she clung to him, breathing in the remnants of his aftershave. She wanted to hate him, but she couldn't and she really didn't want him to leave.

Inside, they sat on the kitchen worktop, leaning against the wall in silence. With no cooker or electricity, they couldn't even make a cup of tea but then she'd already considered hitting the wine again. It was only eight o'clock.

Xander tentatively twirled a curl around his finger but, resisting the urge to be comforted, Daisy watched the rain pouring down and hugged her knees. It was time to deal with him.

'It has to stop,' she said, lighting a cigarette with shaking hands.

'It will. I've never seen this bit of the valley flood before.'

'I mean you. It. It has to stop.'

He stopped the twirling. 'Yes, I know. It has. I'd say I've lost my job anyway. I buggered off the yacht without telling anyone.'

'Stopped because you've stopped, or stopped because you've lost your job?'

'Stopped because of you.'

'Do they know? Work?'

'Do we have to do this now?'

'If you ever want me to forgive you, then yes, we have to do this now.' She wanted to see repentance in his eyes, but she could only see the top of the woolly hat. He wouldn't look at her. She couldn't blame him.

Finally, he swore into the collar of his jacket. 'Yes, work knows. The company provides *anything* the client wants so when you get on that fucking yacht you leave your morals on shore. Nights out, parties in, booze, drugs, the entertainment... it's our job to sort it out, wherever in the world we are. It's not just me, which is why there are only pretty faces in the brochure. Some of the girls make a fortune.'

'Robbie?'

'Don't be ridiculous.'

'Does he know?'

'About me? I hope not. About the others? Of course.' Xander glanced up. 'You might think he's a saint but I know my brother. He's worked for Diamond for ten years. I bet it was his idea in the first place.'

Oh dear God. 'Why didn't you tell me?'

'It's hardly the news I've been dying to tell the love of my life.'

'Why did you tell me? You've lost your job, I'd never have known.'

He finally looked her in the eye and she knew he was sorry.

'Daze, I'm not proud of what I've done, but you know what, it's who I was and since I met you, I honestly can't do it anymore. I'm not saying it never bothered me before but now I feel so dreadful, so guilty, I had to tell you.'

Oddly, his frown had finally gone, as if the confession had eased his conscience. So, this is what had tormented him for the last three years. He pulled her into his arms and she let him.

'I'm so sorry,' he said, resting his head against hers, 'and not just about dropping this bombshell but about yesterday. I'm really sorry I treated you like that.'

His lips were against her cheek and she almost smiled. 'Was it one or lots?'

'Don't.'

'Old? Young?'

'Seriously, don't.'

'Did you fancy them?'

'Don't do this. You don't really want to know anything.'

'How much money?'

'Stop it.'

'But this is why you turned Jonty down, isn't it? For this

money.'

'Two grand.'

'Two grand?' She turned to him. 'Two grand for what? A night? OMG, I must've run up one hell of a tab.' From nowhere, she laughed and then couldn't stop. Hysteria. It took her a couple of minutes to calm down. 'Honestly, I don't know where this leaves us but promise me, never again?'

'Never ever, I promise.' His body relaxed, the tension gone. 'You've no idea how much I've missed you.'

'I've missed you too.' Daisy curled against him, enjoying the bliss of having him back.

'Do you want to see what happens when I drink far too much rum in Barbados?'

The happy switch had been thrown and her Xander was back, but after the first bombshell she was more than a tad hesitant to say yes. He unzipped his jacket and lifted his jumper to reveal a long, thin tattoo running down his left side. The lettering and twirly design made it almost impossible to read the writing.

'Does that say... DAF?' Daisy clamped her hand over her mouth to stifle her giggles. 'OMG. How glad are you that I haven't thrown your sorry arse out?' It really was very sexy but a tattoo of her initials?

Xander grinned. 'There was some sentimental twaddle being said at the time about how you'll *always be by my side*, but in the squiggles it says *Drunk And Fucked* too. Which, incidentally, is what I'd be if you do throw my sorry arse out, so it works both ways.'

'I hope you don't think I'm going to return the sentiment and plaster your initials all over my body...' Like Bethany. 'Did you know Ms Marshall has a black X tattooed on her left wrist? It's to remind her not to be so fucking stupid in the future.'

He dropped his head back, closing his eyes.

'Xand, what happened in Year Eleven?'

'Not today.'

'But—'

'No, Daisy. Please?'

What, so he could finally admit to charging women two grand a night for sex but he wouldn't tell her what happened seven years ago at school? An uncomfortable silence followed until he kissed her head and apologised again.

'Well,' she said with a positivity she didn't feel, 'trying to count my blessings, it's stopped raining and the water's stopped rising. The kitchen is the worst hit, but that was a disaster area anyway. Thank God this happened before the new one went in.'

'You're getting a new one? When?'

Daisy hopped down from the worktop with an oddly satisfying splash and dug the CAD designs out of a drawer. 'The week after next.'

Xander frowned again when he saw the plans. 'But this is…'

'Exactly what you said I should get?' She fished a can of Diet Coke from the debris bobbing around under the sink. 'Have you any idea how often you doodle the kitchen layout while you're on the phone? You're obviously going to design a much better kitchen than me so I just asked for everything you did.'

His eyes devoured the plans as a genuine smile took over his face – the smile she'd expected to see when she asked him to move in.

'What are you going to do about work?'

He shrugged. 'But half a million will land in my bank account in a few weeks.'

'Xand, that's for the restaurant. You can't live on it. You need a job. Why don't you talk to Jonty? It might not be two grand a night, but it'll pay the bills.'

He frowned, pushing his hat lower. 'But what if I fuck it up again?'

'You won't.'

'I don't want to let you down, Daze.'

'Don't do it for me. Do it for you. Do it so you can go to work with a genuine smile on your face and earn money you want to keep.'

Doubt filled his face. 'But you want all *this*.' He gestured around the kitchen. 'You want to live in a cottage with stables in a sought-after village. You want to party with India Dowson-Jones. We can't afford that.'

No, they couldn't. When the job was finished, she'd be out on her ear, able to use her commission as a deposit on a house, but it'd be for some flat in Haverton, not a detached period property with three acres.

'This really hasn't turned out how I planned.'

She paddled through to the living room and, standing in four inches of muddy floodwater, she stared at the photo of them she'd put up, replacing the one of her and Finn. Finn had thrown her out and Xander had been shagging women for money.

'Two days in bed, Fitzgerald?' Xander leant against the wall, but followed her gaze until he smiled at the photo too. The smile turned to confusion and he frowned at her. 'Fitzgerald?'

Oh, she already knew she'd forgive him but did she really want him to move in? 'I was going to ask you to move in. Properly. No spare rooms.'

He sank onto the sofa with his hands behind his head. 'Oh Christ, please tell me that I haven't completely fucked everything up.'

She'd known him for just over five months and she'd swear he'd aged at least two years in that time. It was the frown. She hated seeing him so sad. All she wanted was for him to be happy, for them both to be happy.

Slowly, she shook her head and smiled, loving his relieved laugh.

'Move in?' she asked, sitting astride his knee.

His smile was bigger than the one he'd had for the kitchen plans. 'No more FWB?'

'No more FWB.' She laughed as his hands got the next two days in bed under way. 'Are you ever going to take that bloody hat off?'

He cringed, smiling. 'Want to see what happens when I get really stoned in Jamaica?'

Chapter Sixteen

Daisy ran her fingers through Xander's amusing, mini-Mohawk, loving the contrast between its velvet-soft sides and gel-roughened centre stripe. 'Miss me?'

'Not even slightly,' he replied, still trying to kiss her hello as he shut the front door. 'How's my kitchen?'

'*Our* kitchen,' she corrected, poking him in his rock hard abs. 'You'll love it. Have you finished packing?'

'Just about.'

Seeing the hallway, stripped of Xander's family photos, sent an unexpected wave of nostalgia flooding over Daisy. The little house was crammed with memories for her – from the x-rated one night stand to the thoroughly domesticated, yet stupidly romantic past two weeks.

Poor old Skank Manor needed to dry out if Jack were still to fit the kitchen as planned, so Daisy twisted arms and fluttered her eyelashes, and finally persuaded Stan, her superhero of a plumber, to fit the new boiler and central heating the minute the water subsided. It would mean a week with no heating or hot water, so Daisy and Xander decamped to his cottage.

The move had cemented her decision to ask him to live with her and finally, the bittersweet, final night at his cottage had arrived. On the upside, the next day they'd be able to cook in their new kitchen and fall asleep together in their bed, but on the downside, Xander would hand over the keys to his Grandfather's cottage to a couple retiring to Gosthwaite. And if Daisy would miss the place, she could only imagine how Xander must be feeling.

'You okay?'

He nodded. 'Come on, time to make dinner.'

Daisy groaned dramatically to hide her smile. For some reason known only to him, Xander had undertaken the herculean task of teaching her to cook.

On day one, he announced she was his *sous chef* and taught her how to chop an onion. He said it was like teaching a three year-old

– if she did it wrong, she certainly behaved like one.

On day two as his *sous bitch*, as Daisy called herself, they moved on to julienne vegetables. She sulked for thirty minutes after he rated hers as kindling, not matchsticks.

On day three, she *prepped* leeks and nearly severed a finger. Only a nail tip was harmed in the making of the stew, but they both saw what might have happened and he gave her the night off.

On day four, he gave Daisy her own *special needs* knife. She asked if he'd got her some round-ended scissors too, but he said she wasn't fit to use them and should still ask an adult for help. After she pointedly ignored him until he apologised, he finally realised the enormity of the task he'd taken on.

'What's for dinner, chef?' She rolled up her sleeves, secretly loving the challenge.

'Pasta arrabiata, but you're making it this time.'

Ah, the same pasta dish he'd cooked on the one night stand in June, making it the perfect meal to have on their last night in his house. He smiled at the floor, clearly embarrassed by his romantic gesture, but Daisy held up the prosecco she'd brought – the same prosecco they'd drank at the OBB marquee. Sympathetically loved-up, they indulged in a very long kiss before he handed her a garlic clove and her knife.

'Do your thing, *commis*.'

Ah, she'd been vastly demoted from *sous chef*, but just as he'd taught her, Daisy sprinkled salt on the chopping board and squashed the cloves with the back of the knife. The garlic turned to mush and she couldn't resist marvelling at her own brilliance.

'Well done, Fitzgerald. You can crush garlic. You're a real chef.' He kissed her neck, making up for the sarcasm. 'What're you getting me for my birthday?'

'What do you want?'

'You.'

'You can take that as a given these days. What else?'

'You wrapped in a big, red bow. Have you found me a restaurant yet?'

From his cheeky grin, she knew he was joking, but he didn't know the hours she'd devoted to the search. While he rustled together marinated olives and figs wrapped in Parma ham, she filled him in on her estate agent obsession while he'd been away.

'Thank you.'

She turned back to the tomatoes on her chopping board, her cheeks flushed. 'I haven't found anything yet.'

'No, but you looked. It's... well, it's very nice of you.' He popped an olive into her mouth.

'You do know I'm already getting fat living with you?'

'No, you're starting to look healthy.'

Fat. At least arrabiata sauce didn't require cheese.

'Daze, why don't you eat?' He tried for nonchalant but his tone couldn't have sounded more strained.

'Do we have to talk about this?'

'Yes.'

'Well, if you think I'm doing it sober, forget it.' She pointed to the empty glasses on the worktop. 'I do eat.'

'Not properly.' He obediently poured the wine. 'If you had your way, you'd live on Hobnobs and crisps, topped up with Marmite on toast and a vineyard of white wine.'

'I'm not an anorexic. I know you think I am, but I'm not.' The chilli succumbed to her knife – hardly perfect squares, but at least the pieces were tiny. 'Look, I know I don't eat five a day or have a balanced diet, but I'm so much better now you're feeding me.'

'But you do realise you're very skinny? I've seen photos from when you lived with Clara before you got married. You weren't this skinny then.'

'Try living in the shadow of an actor in the limelight.'

She gulped the wine, wishing she could smoke, but Xander had pleaded with her not to smoke in the kitchen when they were cooking. *Pleaded*, for God's sake.

'And you've seen my mum,' she went on. 'She makes me look podgy, but I'll admit things got worse when I married Finn. The magazines loved to report how *refreshingly curvy* I was. I was a size eight for God's sake. I've never been curvy in my life. Apparently, I have okay tits and a good waist to arse ratio, which stops me looking like a boy, but I'm hardly Playboy material. Then I became a size four, which in US sizing is the hideous size zero, but that was too skinny. The magazines had a field day, saying I was anorexic. Eventually, I settled at a six. This year has been a bit... up and down though.'

Xander shook his head, tipping a handful of bronze spaghetti from its pack. 'Just to be clear, you have perfect tits and an excellent waist to arse ratio. And believe me, you look nothing like a boy. Christ, you'd be the hottest Playboy Bunny ever, but... I think you probably looked better before.'

Oh, so what, she was hideous now? Daisy's cheeks flamed and her defences kicked in. 'This is bullshit. Like you'd have plied me with prosecco if I had a size fourteen arse.'

He wagged the spaghetti at her. 'Don't judge me by your standards, Fitzgerald. You might be more interested in what someone looks like than who they are, but I'm not. I bet you'd still be wishing you hadn't filed for divorce if I wasn't this *pretty*, which I really don't like being called by the way. Actually, I fucking hate it. I care more about *you* than the size of your arse. Sexy as it is now, I bet it looks better as a size ten or twelve.'

Daisy snatched up her cigarettes, but his face was the picture of parental disappointment. Bugger. Letting out a huge sigh, she dropped the pack into her handbag – her restraint earning a hug and another long, indulgent kiss.

'Ready to cook?' he asked, handing her the spaghetti.

He issued directions and Daisy focused on softening the garlic, trying not to worry about how skinny and hideously superficial she'd become.

With dinner over, she sat cross-legged in front of the fire still basking in the glory of her surprisingly good, *seasoned to perfection*, pasta arrabiata. They were on the second bottle of prosecco and Xander lay on the rug, smiling up at her.

'What?' she asked, self-consciously dragging her hair back.

'You're the most casual I've seen you in months.'

'I think you've seen me in tatty jeans a few times.' She sipped her wine. 'It's funny though. Until this year, I used to live in battered jeans and Converse trainers, or shorts and flip-flops. Surfer chick Daisy. The HMS was a bit more that style, I suppose.'

'What am I? Skin-tight jeans and high heels?'

'No, but *I* am these days. I adore the sexy jeans and silly heels. Which do you prefer?'

He shrugged. 'But I meant *you*, not your clothes. Your hair's longer, a bit less curly, but you look... relaxed, like you did in June.' He raised his eyebrows suggestively. 'And with more clothes on.'

She'd sat just the same, but wearing his t-shirt, and he'd lay there looking fabulous in his jeans, prompting her to start the tequila body shots. The empty bottle still stood in the fireplace.

She'd tried to throw it away but Xander, without saying a word, had taken it off her and put it back.

'Who'd have thought a rather random one night stand would have ended up here?' she said quietly. Back then, she'd wanted Finn back so badly, it hurt. Maybe what she'd really needed was affection. Maybe she'd *needed* Xander.

'That was not a one night stand.' He played with her fingers.

'Well, no because we're here, but at the time it was.'

'Even at the time, it wasn't a one night stand. We clicked and you know it.' He tugged a curl. 'Still, I'd liked to have met you later, when you'd got over the HMS already. It would've made my life a lot easier. Or better still, before things went tits up with you two.' He had the cheekiest grin. 'Then you'd really know the truth.'

'The truth?'

'That you're in love with me.'

'I'm so not in love with you.'

'So are.' His grin grew. 'And one day, you're going to realise you love me more than you ever loved him.'

Daisy glanced away, trying desperately not to grin. She didn't love him. She really didn't, but every day she spent with him made it that little bit harder to believe she wouldn't.

'God, this house holds such a lot of memories,' she said. 'Must be ten times worse for you.'

He nodded.

'I'm sorry you had to sell it.'

Again, he merely nodded.

'But I'm glad you're getting to make your dreams come true.' She stared down at her glass. 'Must be nice.'

'What's your dream?'

'I don't have one.'

'You must've at some point.' Xander topped up their glasses. 'What about when you were with the HMS?'

'Well, I did up the beach house, but he was on tour a lot, so I went with him.' She frowned up at the ceiling. 'I loved the travelling, but every time he'd get excited about a new character, or a script, I'd... God, I'd get so jealous. I wanted something to get excited about.'

'Okay, before him. What did you want to be?'

'I know you joked about me making my own handbags, but at uni that was my business plan, to make high-end handbags out of recycled leather. Hard to believe I got a First. God knows what I'll do when I grow up.'

'What if you're doing it?'

She stared at him, horrified. 'I'm not going to be a teacher forever.'

'You're quite a good one, apparently.'

'Look, it's... it's not as bad as I make out, most of the kids aren't overconfident, twatty or posh, but it just... well, it doesn't set my world on fire.'

'I meant the house. You've already done an incredible job on it. What if that's your calling?'

'The next Sarah Beeney?'

'Why not?'

'Because I'd need capital to buy, renovate and sell. Plus, the market's just not viable at the moment.'

'Listen to you. You know this shit. You could take the commission from Skank Manor and do it again.'

Daisy gave him an inquisitive frown. 'I take it from your blasé attitude to losing your job you weren't exactly reliant on it. How minted are you, Golding?'

'Today? Pauper. Ask me tomorrow when over half a million lands in my bank account.'

'Do you *need* to work?'

'Of course I do. I have to hang out with the Dowson-Jones'. But okay, I have a private income.'

'Poor little rich boy. Pocket money off Mummy and Daddy?'

'Even if it were offered, I wouldn't take it. It'd give them too much control. I have a trust fund from Grandpa Oliver. It's not much, but it pays the bills.'

'When did he die?'

'When I was nineteen, bang in the middle of the Lucy Errington mess. If there'd been a cliff handy, I'd have happily jumped off it.' He paused before smiling up at her. 'I could've done with you then.'

God, she'd loved to have spent that summer making him feel better. They could've messed around, enjoying the Indian summer until she met Finn in the September.

'Xand, this is a question you might want to say is none of my business but, if you have a private income and don't *need* to work, why did you keep working for the immoral company when you hated it?'

He stared at the fire. 'Seriously, I hated seventy-five percent of my time with Diamond, but I've been to places and done things most people only dream about. Blast around the track at the Monaco Grand Prix, Champs Elysees on the last day of the Tour de France, VIP at Glastonbury.'

'Doesn't matter who you are, there'll always be mud at Glastonbury.'

'Not your thing, festivals? Heels get stuck?'

She laughed for a moment then asked what she'd been dying to ask for two weeks. 'How did it start?'

'What?'

'Your *tip money* career, how did it start?'

'Don't.' He drained his Prosecco, scowling at her. 'What, are we going to start discussing exes next? Are you going to ask how many girlfriends I've had? Then I'll ask how many guys you shagged at university? Don't do this, Daisy.'

'I can guess yours. Actual girlfriends you've had? Not many. Girls you've shagged? Probably hundreds. The answer to mine is a lot more than I should have but a lot less than I could have.' She narrowed her eyes, refusing to back down. 'I don't want the gory details, just how it started. Surely, you don't wake up one day and think, how I can make a few quid... ooh I know. Or do you?'

'Daze, I don't want to talk about it.' He swore as he lit a cigarette. 'Christ, this is like the Year Eleven thing. You won't let it rest, will you?'

'No. It bugs me.'

Sighing, Xander lay down, drawing heavily on his cigarette as he stared at the ceiling. 'One day, this woman... her husband was shagging the model their son had been seeing. It was a very messy cruise. The wife asked how much I'd be to tempt the mistress away. Then jokingly, asked how much I'd be to take her mind off the mistress. I asked what she was offering and she told me. I thought, fuck it.'

'Literally,' Daisy said, her tone unsurprisingly bitter.

'You asked. The next morning I felt...'

'Like a whore?' Daisy suggested, trying not to smile.

'I will hit you. I felt dreadful so the next time someone asked, I doubled the price. And the next time, I doubled it again. I have wondered how much someone would pay.' He looked up at her, smiling. 'What are *you* offering?'

'Think I've got about six pounds fifty in my purse.' She leaned down, dropping a quick kiss on his perfect lips. 'And you'd be worth every penny.'

'Thank you.'

'Why did you keep doing it? Clearly it made you miserable.'

He took a deep breath. 'I... the money's addictive. For the last three years, I've earned a minimum of fifty grand a year, at least half of it tax free, cash in hand. What was that? Two, maybe three times what you can earn? Last year, I stopped counting.'

OMG. 'I can't believe I'm going to ask this, but what's the most you earned on a trip?'

He looked at the fire. 'Don't.'

'It's fine, tell me?'

Despite his reservations, he smiled. 'My car.'

'In a week?'

'In a weekend.'

'Maybe I should start pimping you out. I miss my TT–'

In retaliation, Xander pulled her to the floor, tickling her. 'I'll pimp you out.'

Grinning, she relaxed against him, breathless and flirty, knowing exactly where things were heading. 'Xand... what did happen in Year Eleven?'

He gave her a look she hadn't seen since she was fifteen when the Head caught her behind the customary bike sheds with a prefect. 'I swear I really will hit you.'

'Oh, come on.'

'Don't, Daisy.'

'For God's sake,' she snapped. 'Just tell me.'

Xander swore under his breath as he detangled himself from her, topping up their glasses once again. 'Did Bethany tell you anything?'

Daisy shook her head. A gulf of silence filled the room before he looked her in the eye and told her what he'd refused to for over a month.

'I shagged all the girls in Year Eleven for a bet.'

He did *what?*

'It started as a joke at the end of Year Ten when Marcus realised how many of the girls I'd already... copped off with. He wondered if it was possible to shag all the girls in our year. Russ

Bracknell said it wasn't.' Xander's gaze had shied from hers. 'Russ bet me I couldn't. I bet I could. I could and I did.'

'You shagged every girl in your year for a *bet*?' OMG. 'Was it for a lot of money?'

'That wasn't really the point.' Xander scowled. 'But Marcus did run a book.'

'Every girl?'

'Come on, it's not a big school. There were less than fifty girls in my year.'

'Mingers?'

Xander nodded, his frown growing.

'Weren't some gay?'

Xander flashed an arrogant smile. 'Not in my year, Fitzgerald.'

She threw her lighter at him, missing by a foot, making him laugh. Unable to resist, she joined in, but dear God, was there anything that boy wouldn't do for money? And, if he'd shagged sixtyish girls by the time he'd left school at sixteen, just how many girls had he shagged by the ripe old age of twenty-three?

'What?' he asked, his smile dropping.

'How many girls have you shagged?'

'I knew this is where your head would go next.' He sank down to the floor again, rubbing his brow. 'You still don't trust me, do you?'

'Sorry, but you're too young, too good-looking, too perfect, too... everything.'

'And too in love with you. You should trust me.'

'Look, I'll get over it. It's not like we're going to get married and have kids, is it?' She almost laughed at the mere idea, but Xander's devastated face had her stifle her amusement.

'For fuck's sake, Daisy. When are you going to realise that...' He put his hands behind his head, staring up at the ceiling. 'Christ, at this rate, you never will.'

Clearly, she'd just ruined the last night at his Grandpa's cottage.

'Clara's lost count,' she said, trying to rescue the situation. 'She stopped pretending to keep track years ago. And she has another three years of bad behaviour on you.'

Xander turned to her, his frown in place. 'But hasn't she been with Scott for years?'

'They've been on and off since she was twenty. Her dad smacked her mum around, so Clara refused to let another man control her life and she shagged around to prove it. Scott's put up with her getting up to all sorts of mischief, sometimes right in front of him, but he loves her.'

'I'm starting to feel slighted I was left out.'

'You're too *pretty*, I'm afraid.'

Finally, a smile tugged at his mouth. 'You're so going to pay for that later.'

Daisy grinned. Friends again. 'When I left the HMS, Clara realised just what a good thing she had. She told Scott she loved him, she was sorry and she wanted to get married.'

'And?'

'I'm not saying I'm happy about it, but no matter how dubious your past is, my best friend is probably on a par and I've *never* judged her.' Daisy ran her fingers through his hair. 'I'm sorry for asking about Year Eleven and how many girls, but I just don't want any more bombshells.'

Xander propped himself on one elbow, studying her. 'Okay, let's do it your way. Tomorrow night, I'll tell you anything you want to know.'

'Are you sure? It's your birthday.'

'It's kind of apt.' He nodded as if he'd made the right decision. 'But after that, you have to start trusting me.'

'Deal.' To make up for almost spoiling their lovely night, Daisy knelt astride him. 'Xand, why are you keeping that empty tequila bottle?'

'Isn't it obvious?' he said, relieving her of her t-shirt. 'It's a reminder of when everything changed. You'd buggered off to the bathroom and I thought you'd come to your senses, that you'd go running home, full of regret for drunken shagging. I really didn't want you to go. Instead, you waltzed back in wearing my t-shirt and bugger all else, waving that bottle. For about the tenth time that day, I thought you are full of surprises. You'd rocked my world, Fitzgerald.'

The next morning, after the removal men drove away, Daisy held Xander's hand as he locked the door to Grandpa Oliver's cottage for the last time. He wouldn't look at her, but the return of the frown gave him away. Xander was a lot more upset at selling his Grandpa's house than he'd admitted, maybe even to himself.

He kissed her briefly then walked to his car without saying

goodbye. If he wanted to deal with this on his own, she'd let him, but back at Skank Manor, she lit a fire and waited for her boyfriend to come home, praying that telling her anything would finally allow her to trust him. But did she really want to?

Chapter Seventeen

For Xander's twenty-third birthday, Daisy suggested they sneak off for a dirty weekend in Paris, but he'd shaken his head. What he really wanted to do, more than anything in the world, was to cook in the new kitchen. Utterly mental, but from the smile on his face, as he effortlessly produced a romantic dinner for two, Daisy knew it was the perfect way for him to spend his birthday. Nutter.

Besides, it wouldn't all be slaving away over a hot stove. Underneath her innocent-looking grey jersey dress, Daisy hid ludicrously seductive scarlet underwear, all part of his birthday treat. That boy was so getting her wrapped in a big red bow after dinner.

'Have I told you how much I love this kitchen?' he said as he grabbed a rolling pin out of the drawer next to him. 'Everything is *exactly* where it should be.'

Daisy sipped her wine, trying not to giggle. He'd only told her about a hundred times. But any amusement was wiped away when he put the first plate in front of her. It bore no resemblance to the relaxed, bistro-style dishes he knocked up on a nightly basis, and Daisy just stared, first at the food and then at him.

The mini red onion and goats' cheese tarte tatin sat amongst a dainty scattering of baby salad leaves she didn't recognise, and he'd splattered the pear jus in a Pollock-esque manner across the plate.

'Xander, it's...' She paused, still blinking in surprise. 'Well for a plate of sustenance it's beyond beautiful and as a work of art... it's perfectly edible.'

He smiled as if she'd told him she loved him. This food thing really did mean the world to him; she had to find him a restaurant, and soon.

'You should so be a celebrity chef,' she said as she gazed in tummy-grumbling delight at the main course he laid before her. 'The TV people would die for you.'

Xander blushed, running a hand through his hair.

'What?' she asked. 'You've got the pretty... you look the part and this...' She waved a hand over the ballotine of chicken with pomme puree, chanterelle mushrooms and Madeira sauce. 'Even I know this is stupidly fantastic.'

'Look, I've been there, done that and it didn't go well.' Xander sat back in his chair, nursing his wine. 'Cooking under the scrutiny of very scary chefs and several cameras did not bring out the best in me. The only good thing about the entire experience was that I was so bad, none of it appeared on TV. Professional Masterchef, I was nineteen.'

Oh she'd pay to see that.

'Do you remember what you first cooked?' she asked, hopping up to sit on the worktop as he compiled dessert.

'Off.' He backed up the order with a sideways nod of his head.

Since he'd moved in, they'd agreed to a few rules. She wasn't allowed to smoke in the kitchen while he was cooking or in the house while anyone was eating, but he always had to put the toilet seat down. He was solely responsible for buying food, but even if they both cooked, she had to tidy the kitchen. If he ever expected her to do his laundry, he had to put dirty clothes in the washing basket rather than leave them on the floor. Oh, and kitchen worktops were for food, not her arse. The last rule was the only one still under debate – she'd formed quite a habit of sitting near the cooker since the Aga days. Still it was his birthday, so she hopped down.

'Thank you.' He kissed her. 'Macaroni cheese.'

'That's what you first cooked, really?'

Lately, Xander had become the most appalling food snob. He mocked her on a daily basis for eating salt and vinegar crisps, but she'd discovered he had three guilty pleasures: lager, mint Aeros and macaroni cheese.

'Hey, I was five. I wanted tinned Heinz stuff, but Grandpa said I should learn to make it myself, from scratch. I never touched the Heinz stuff after that.'

Daisy watched in awe as Xander trailed lines of chocolate sauce across the plates.

'Listen, I've been thinking about asking Jonty if that job offer's still good.'

'Even though it's not two grand a night?' she teased.

Trying to look cross, Xander dotted her nose with a blob of

chocolate, but then kissed it away. 'To be honest, it wasn't really the money. I wasn't sure if I wanted to work for someone else in a professional kitchen again.'

'Scared?'

He nodded. 'But after tonight, I definitely want to. I want to show I can do it and that... I'm not who I was when I was nineteen.'

'Oh, just think, in four days' time, St. Nick's will break up for Christmas and you can go to work while I laze around in bed.'

'I think you'll find, I've been walking your dog and packing.' He carefully placed the poached pears alongside the chocolate stripes, swearing as a microdot of the poaching jus marred a plate. 'I've probably had two glasses of wine more than I should have to do this.'

'It's okay. There's only me to appreciate it and I'm an utter philistine.' Daisy marvelled at the speed with which he used two spoons to mould ice cream, homemade of course, into little rugby balls. 'Cute.'

'Not cute, *quenelle*. It amazes me how clueless you are. You must have gone to some good restaurants with the HMS.'

'Occasionally, but he's more of a burger and chips kinda guy.' Which suited her down to the ground. 'Want me to carry one?'

'No, you'll drop it.'

'Your faith in me is touching.'

'As is your trust in me.'

Ouch. Point taken.

With the table finally cleared and the kitchen immaculate, Daisy wandered into the living room with a mixture of trepidation and sheer bloody nosiness coursing through her veins. *I'll tell you anything you want to know.* She smiled as Xander swore at his shiny, new iPhone, his birthday present from James.

'What are you doing?' she asked.

'I'm trying to get this thing to recognise your printer. I need to print an email.' He swore at the phone a few more times.

'Why not send it from your laptop?'

'Because this is my new toy and it should do as it's told.' He finally smiled as the printer lit up. 'Right, get your sexy ass into the kitchen. I'll have a beer, please. Hell, get me two. I'm going to need them.'

He didn't need to tell her twice to get more booze, and minutes later, she returned with a fresh bottle of Chablis and two bottles of Becks. Nervously tapping his foot, Xander almost downed a bottle in one as Daisy sipped her wine, drawn to the printed sheets of paper sat on the coffee table.

'What's the email about?' she asked.

'If you tell me a secret, a real secret, something you need to trust me to tell me, I'll show you the list.'

'What list?'

He looked at his beer, the muscle in his jaw twitching. 'To prove the Year Eleven bet, James kept a list. Who and when. This might seem a bit weird, but he's kept it up to date.'

'A *bit* weird? Oh my God, why are you friends with him?' Daisy sank her first glass without taking breath. 'What if I don't want to see it?'

'Then you don't want me to tell you everything.'

Confused, she lit a cigarette, watching as he finished his beer. If she said no, she'd always wonder, but if she said yes then she'd know, but she might not want to know, not really. The whole cigarette had gone before she made her decision – one she made for Xander as much as herself.

'Finn made me do a threesome once. I mean, he didn't hold a gun to my head but there was a lot of emotional blackmail.' With the coffee table between her and Xander, Daisy sat cross-legged on the floor, alone and exposed but the twinkle in Xander's eye almost made her smile. Boys were so predictable. 'You can wipe that look off your face, baby, it won't happen again. I hated it. I nearly left the next day. With hindsight, I should have.' The twinkle had gone, replaced by an angry scowl. 'Not even Clara knows about that.'

He opened his second bottle, cursing her ex-husband. 'What the hell else did he make you do?'

There was no point lying, Xander would see straight through it. 'You said one secret.'

He took a deep breath. 'Okay, but there are rules...'

The deal was she could ask anything she wanted and he'd tell her the truth, but she wasn't allowed to get angry, jealous, mean or ask about the names with stars next to them.

Each page of the list covered a year, with it all starting on his fourteenth birthday – *Imogen* had the dubious honour of being number one. A few months after her, several names filled each month. Each name was numbered. By the end of Year Nine, there were sixteen names. OMG.

Xander lit a cigarette. A sign. He was tense.

Daisy's eyes flicked over Year Eleven, trying not to look disapproving. Those girls were for a bet. Jesus. But Year Eleven had nothing on the post-school years when he worked for Anthony Errington. Did she really want to know this?

'Why keep the list? It's very weird.'

'James just kept adding to it.'

'Meaning you tell him about everyone?' She couldn't help her snappy tone.

'Remember the rules.' He gave Daisy a warning look. 'Not like that. I don't ring him up and give him a rundown on the previous night's events but, you know, we talk. Don't pretend you don't tell Clara everything. I didn't tell him about you.' He smiled at her raised eyebrows. 'Seriously. I promised I wouldn't kiss and tell so you weren't added to the list until October.'

The page ended with Lucy Errington, number two hundred and sixty-eight. Jesus Christ, that was five months after his nineteenth birthday. Daisy flicked over, expecting the endless stream of names to continue.

It didn't. The majority of the page was blank. It wasn't until December, his twentieth birthday that the names started again. The last she recognised – Sofia, the woman she'd hung up on in June.

The next two pages shocked her more. Aside from the starred names, which had to be tip money encounters and she didn't dare count, the pages were blank. They were blank until June, until her. Number three hundred and eleven.

'Is this true?' she whispered. 'Just Sofia, and me?'

He nodded.

'But...'

'Remember Marcus' little lecture? When he called you judgemental?'

As if she'd ever forget it.

'The day we met,' Xander said, leaning forwards, 'you assumed I was a playboy, right? That I went out every weekend knocking damsels in distress off their high heels?'

'In my defence,' she replied, holding up the list, 'you were.'

'No, I was a teenager who shagged around. There's a difference.'

Was there? Daisy flicked back through the pages. Okay, so he hadn't shagged around recently. 'What happened, the Michelin-starred Cougar?'

He nodded. 'After her, I wanted ... something else.'

'And you thought Sofia, another married cougar, was it?'

'No, but, for two years, she was the only one.'

'I can't believe I hung up on her. I'd say sorry, but of course I'm not.'

'Me neither.' Grinning, he put out his half-smoked cigarette. 'After you left that morning, I rang her and told her I'd met someone else.'

'Bit over-confident.'

'Until I got my heart trashed by you, I was.'

Daisy gave an overly dramatic sigh, but couldn't help her smile. 'And since June, there's just... me?'

And the stars. But she wouldn't say that out loud.

'You were the only person I wanted to drag to bed, but you wouldn't let me.'

'Unless I was drunk and then you'd come over all heroic.' Daisy stared at him. 'But that means...'

'Nearly three months of celibacy for you, Fitzgerald. You've no idea how many miles I had to run to keep that up. Remember the barbeque, with your backless top and high heels?' He'd relaxed, leaning forward with his chin resting on his hand.

The eight names after hers were all starred. Several in June, two in August, one in November, the Caribbean yacht trip, and two in September. *Two* on the Med yacht trip?

'Xander, how much did the daisy belly bar cost?'

He smiled, reluctantly, but he'd promised honesty. 'Eight grand.'

She passed out at that point. Well, not really, but nearly.

Bravely, she turned back to page two and looked for Bethany Marshall. She was number thirty-two when he shagged her as part of the Year Eleven bet but, by the time he went out with her a year and a half later, he'd notched up over a hundred girls. There seemed to be an endless stream of names for the next six months, a lot more than the twenty-odd Bethany had assumed.

Cressida Marshall.

'You've got to be kidding?' Daisy's shaking finger hovered over the name. 'Pippa's mum? Is she Bethany's mum too?'

Xander closed his eyes and nodded.

'You fucked your girlfriend's mother?'

Again he nodded.

Were there no depths he wouldn't sink to?

'What is it with that woman?'

'Mrs Marshall's...' Xander's cheeks reddened. 'An education.'

'Yeah, I gather Finn thought so too. Remind me to keep you away from my mother.'

'I was seventeen, Daze.'

She shook her head. 'But why did you do that to Bethany? Was it really just to get to Holly?'

The embarrassed exterior gave way to a twitching jaw as he nodded. 'I met Holly at James' party. I thought she'd do for the night, but she'd heard the rumours and wouldn't go near me. That was a red rag to a bull so I went out with Bethany to win Holly over. It took six months.'

'You're an absolute, utter bastard.'

'No, I'm not.'

'You played them both. God, if I'd heard those rumours, I'd never have gone near you either.'

He reached across the table, putting his hand behind her neck and gently pulling her towards him. 'Daisy, you couldn't stay away if you tried.' He kissed her, proving he was right. 'Look, I'll admit I wasn't very nice to Bethany, but I was seventeen. What were you doing at seventeen?'

Mostly Sam Underwood but the least said about that the better.

Xander laughed at her guilty cringe. 'What were you doing, Fitzgerald?'

'A not very close friend's boyfriend, on and off for about a year. He was a bad boy, the one who introduced me to class-A drugs and dance music. I found him impossible to say no to. Obviously the friend and I fell out eventually but it wasn't a huge loss.'

'Another bad boy?'

'The first of many.'

Xander raised his eyebrows with an expectant smile; clearly, he aimed to get as much information out of her as she would find out about him. 'What's the worst thing you've done?'

'Morally speaking? You.'

'You were already separated.' His eyes narrowed. 'You're lying. What did you do?'

'I kissed Scott.'

Xander's face said it all.

'It was a year or so ago. Clara had just shagged Patrick, you know, the best man at the wedding. Payback for Scott refusing to talk to her for two months, and Scott was devastated. Finn and I were on shaky ground and I thought... Scott is a total super-hero. And after the briefest of kisses, we both pissed ourselves laughing. We so don't fancy each other.'

'So why is it the worst thing you've ever done?'

'She's my best-friend. You don't kiss your best-friend's bloke, even if she is pretending she doesn't love him.'

'And you've never told her?'

Daisy's eyes widened in horror. 'No.'

'Don't. You'd only be easing your conscience, not making her life better.'

Daisy glanced back at the paper in her hands. 'Shall we get back to your appalling past?'

His post-school years were ludicrous. There must have been a hundred names in his eighteenth year alone.

'Age sixteen to nineteen, you must have been exhausted, sunshine.'

'I was a chef at a five-star hotel. There were a lot of guests, hotel staff, waitresses and weddings every Saturday. Have you any idea how up-for-it most girls are at weddings?' He grinned. 'Of course you do, you've been one of them.'

Daisy hit him with the list. 'So which are the girlfriends? Real girlfriends, not the married cougars?'

'Number one. Imogen's, the Headmaster's daughter.' He pointed to number four. 'Samantha North was my girlfriend at St. Nick's. It wasn't a serious thing, but she was certainly the best of a bad bunch. A good laugh and pretty much up for anything.'

'I don't want to know, thank you.'

'She knew about the bet.'

'And she didn't mind?' Nice girl. 'Who else?'

'Bethany.' He flicked through the list. 'Ciara, she was a rebound job after Lucy, and you.'

'That's it?'

He shrugged. 'Three hundred girls and I'd say the majority were self-absorbed, shallow princesses with massive confidence issues.'

Hadn't he just described her? 'Did you like anyone? I mean, did you not meet any girls that you thought, *wow*.'

'Three hundred and eleven certainly got a wow rating.' He grinned. 'There was a girl in Italy I really liked. Emanuella, but she's not on the list, too Catholic. And Imogen.' He sat back, smiling up at the ceiling. 'Headmaster's daughter at the school I went to before St Nick's. Christ, we were like Romeo and Juliet. Unfortunately, her Dad kicked me out after... well, there was a sexting incident that would put yours to shame. If he hadn't, I might never have shagged another girl. I have wondered what would've happened if I'd stayed at that school.'

Well, we wouldn't be sitting here. Daisy owed Imogen's dad a drink.

'So what changed? Why did you go from a nice, settled down, one girl guy to the school *ho*?'

He flashed Marcus' trademark withering look. 'I got to St Nick's, where I didn't know anyone and I missed Imogen like mad so I pulled anything I could to forget about her. It turned out I could pull anything I wanted to and messing around with girls was way more fun than watching football or smoking behind the bike sheds. I bet you spent a bit of time behind the bike sheds.'

Guilty as charged and not always smoking. 'Why were you so reluctant to tell me about the Year Eleven bet?'

'Because I regret it.' He sat back with his hands behind his head. 'Some of the girls, like Bethany, were utter bitches but some were... there were a few half-truths told and some downright lies. A few girls, nice girls, got hurt. Christ, I've never admitted this to anyone. Zara, number seventy-one, was a bit of a tortured soul but a family friend I'd known since I was a kid. After we'd—'

'I don't need the details.'

'Well, the next day, I'd already moved on to the next girl and Zara took an overdose. She survived, but over the years she cut her wrists, drank a lot and, when we were eighteen, she finally took enough prescription drugs to finish the job.'

'What, because you dumped her?'

'I'm not saying it was my fault, apparently she had issues, but if—'

'Is this why you can't resist a damsel in distress? If you rescue you me, you make up for Zara?'

'That might be reading a bit too much into things. I just wish...' He downed his drink. 'So, that's me being honest. You know everything. The truth and not just some picture you have in your head.'

'I did think you were a playboy, a total player. Sorry. I really am judgemental.'

'At least you're aware of it now.'

'Is that why you showed me the list, to show you don't shag around?'

'I showed you the list so you'd know I'm serious about you.'

'But you're too young to think about settling down.'

'My brother was twenty. I'm not too young. My problem is getting you to believe that.' Then he smiled, his eyes daring her. 'So, what number am I?'

Bugger, she hadn't prepared for that. 'I have no idea. My best friend isn't obsessed enough to keep a list.' She left a dramatic pause before doing what any sensible girl would do. She lied. 'Twenty-ish?'

'Even you don't believe that.'

'Okay, maybe nearer forty? Those summers clubbing were hedonistic to say the least.'

'Not exactly a virgin, are you?' He swatted her with the list, trying not to laugh. 'Tramp. So shall we burn it? Ceremoniously?'

'Bugger that, I want to keep it.' She snatched the list back.

'Not a chance in hell. I said you could look, not keep. I don't want this around forever. I want to put it behind me. Behind us.'

'A fresh start. I'll go for that.' She started looking over the names. 'Is there anyone on here I know? Is Tabitha on here?'

'She's practically a sister. No, she's not.'

'What happened with Imogen? Did you never see her again?'

Xander took a deep breath. 'Actually, I met up with her in July, after I met you.'

'And?' Daisy asked, not sure she wanted to know the answer.

'I hadn't seen her for nearly ten years, but I always thought that one day, I'd meet up with her and... that'd be it.' He stood up and pulled Daisy to her feet. As he gazed down at her, one hand stoked her hair back while the other snuck under her t-shirt. 'Look, Imogen's still beautiful, still the amazing girl I went out with, but I came back here determined to make you forget about your ex-husband. Imogen's why I rang Clara when you wouldn't answer my calls. Imogen's how I knew what I really wanted. Finally.'

Stunned, Daisy wrapped her arms around his neck, her fingers raking through his hair. She couldn't tell him she loved him; would he accept being worshipped?

'Get married and have kids?' Xander said, shrugging. 'But I don't see why not, because we are going to live happily ever after, Fitzgerald.'

Despite everything, she laughed. This was her boyfriend. The guy who expected her to trust him even though he'd shagged over three hundred girls, sixty of them for a bet. He'd charged rich women for sex, but said he loved her. That night, she kept him up very late to prove to him, and herself, that the past didn't matter. She could trust him.

Or at least she'd learn to.

Chapter Eighteen

Two o'clock. Eight and half hours until Xander would be home. Even school staff meetings had never dragged so interminably. Daisy had endured five days without her official boyfriend thanks to his new job and God, did she miss him.

The Tuesday after his birthday, he'd come home with a new haircut, announcing Jonty had all but begged him to take the job as *sous chef* at Oak Bank starting that night. Initially, Daisy had been delighted, but by the end of week one, she started to wish he still worked for the immoral holiday company.

In five days, she'd spent the grand total of fourteen and half hours with him, giving her the niggling worry she'd wind up spending much of the Christmas holidays alone. Each morning, she'd get up at eight to walk Birkin, but by the time Xander had dragged his ass out of bed, they would barely have chance for a coffee together.

All she could do was keep busy until he came home.

Trying to summon a little enthusiasm, Daisy stared at the paint charts she had scattered on the kitchen table. Maybe she should just paint the walls Brilliant White. It'd save her the equivalent of a new washing machine. But it'd ruin the aesthetics of a period home.

Wordsworth Yellow would be cheery in the kitchen.

But it didn't cheer Daisy.

Why? This should be the bit she loved; it was the bit she could do. Painting, tiling, finishing touches. *Finishing.* Was that why painting was so depressing, because it meant the end was nigh?

She grabbed her handbag. The end wasn't nigh. She had a lot of bloody work still to do; painting was only the start of it. Second fix joinery, floors, two new bathrooms, the garden. No maudlin. And *Mallard Egg Blue* would be perfect in the spare bedroom.

Singing along with Arcade Fire on the radio, Daisy whizzed her little car along the road out of Gosthwaite. Lilac for her bedroom or a deep sultry red? Definitely a soft green for the living room. But all thoughts of period paints fled from her mind as she spotted five firemen chatting at the side of the road. Three of them were in their forties, but Jack the joiner and another guy were keeping the demographic to somewhere near fit. Daisy pulled over, smiling at Jack. With his coat open and a sooty smudge on his cheek, he looked fabulous, and God, did he know it.

He shot her a wink as he leant against her car door. 'If you wanted to see me in the uniform, you could've just asked.'

She swatted his arm, trying not to giggle. 'What's going on?'

'Fire at the old slate workshop,' he replied, nodding behind him. 'Between you and me, we reckon it's an insurance job. This place has been closed for months.'

Intrigued, Daisy took a peek. The workshop was a detached slate building, a similar size to Skank Manor. Thanks to the fire, it lacked a roof, but Daisy picked her way over the soaking ground absolutely entranced.

Gosthwaite Slate, The Bobbin Mill, Gosthwaite.
Slate workshop, Retail Outlet and Café.

The faded water and fire-damaged sign sat propped against the front doors. Daisy peered through the windows, appalled at the devastation, but couldn't stop a smile spreading over her face, especially when she clocked the remnants of a stainless steel kitchen at the back of the building. Was this it?

The Bobbin Mill would be a great name for a Lake District restaurant. Her mind raced with ideas for windows, flooring, light fittings, door handles and a crazy idea struck her. What if Xander were right, what if property renovation was her dream job?

Maybe it was sheer luck, or maybe it was shit-hot planning (thank you, Jack), but Skank Manor was on schedule and on bloody budget. Even a major flood hadn't derailed her plans. Skank Manor would be completed in a few months, by which time the Bobbin Mill could fill her non-working time.

Already imaging opening night, she took several photos then rang her best legal genius.

'Scott, I know property isn't your thing, but do you know someone shit-hot who can help me with a top secret project? They may need to be brutally persuasive.'

'How brutal?'

'I need to make Xander's dreams come true.'

The lights from Xander's Golf briefly lit up the living room and Daisy dived on the sofa, trying to look terribly nonchalant. She expected Xander to be anything but, since she wore nothing but hot pink underwear. Clearly, she wasn't playing things even slightly cool, but they both had two days off, his last free weekend for the foreseeable future, and she planned to spend every minute of it with him – preferably in bed.

The second he clocked her, Xander stopped dead and the most amused smile took over his face.

'Hello, honey. I'm home.' He picked up the glass of wine she'd already poured him and sat on the opposite sofa, never taking his eyes off her. 'Had a good day?'

'Yes, thank you. Plus, you're home so right now, life's all good, baby.' She uncrossed her legs and he lasted another ten seconds on the other sofa.

God, she was good at being bad.

Afterwards, they lay on the sofa Xander lit a joint and it took all her restraint not to tut. He'd come home after his first shift at Oak Bank absolutely psyched – Tigger would be a fair comparison – and rolled a joint explaining if he didn't, he'd be awake until one. After shift two, a pattern emerged. He'd come home around half-ten and smoke a joint while she patiently listened as he recounted the last twelve hours at Oak Bank.

That evening, she'd hoped they might skip the smoking stage and move straight to the shagging your girlfriend stage then go to bed. Turned out, she was wrong.

It wasn't that Daisy was morally against weed, but it made Xander a little... dull. Or maybe that was just his adventures in a stifling kitchen that bored the pants off her. With a slightly forced smile, she listened attentively as Xander, full of pride, explained how he'd suggested serving the venison with wild mushroom ravioli and it'd sold out half-way through service. Kate said it was the best thing she'd ever eaten. Kate? One of the waitresses, he'd replied. He'd been very dismissive of Kate, but she got four mentions in that evening's tales of Oak Bank.

'And what have you been up to?' He glanced at the new white walls. 'Painting, obviously.'

'Coat one of three downstairs, done. It's going to be like

painting the Forth bridge though.' She daren't mention The Bobbin Mill to Xander. No way she could risk getting his hopes up when the place wasn't even for sale. 'So, after week one, how is it working for Jonty?'

'I prefer to think of it as work *with*. I'm better than him and he knows it. It's just like when we worked at Anthony's. Jonty and I started work the same day. He came after catering college but I started as soon as I left school, fast-tracked because I'd been trained by my Grandpa and I'd worked at Oscar's during the holidays. I was the golden boy, streets ahead of Jonty and most of the others who'd been there for a year. Anthony's favourite.'

'Until you shagged his wife?' Daisy tried not to giggle.

'Actually, I don't think he minded that nearly as much as when I went off the rails and quit. I'm not sure he likes her really.'

'What's she like?' Daisy asked, unsure if she wanted to know. 'Tall, dark and utterly beautiful?'

'What? You've never Googled her?'

'I meant to, just never did.' Daisy glanced at her phone.

'Go on. You'll be surprised but don't read too much into it.'

Daisy quickly typed *Lucy Errington* into Google and clicked on *Images*. Most of the photos were of Anthony, but on row three he stood smiling with his petite, blond wife.

'She looks like *me*?'

Back in June, she'd asked what Lucy was like and Xander had brushed her off. Now, she understood why. He hadn't wanted to tell her she looked like the love of his life. OMG. No one would mistake them for sisters, but the general concept was the same – short, skinny and very blond. Her wavy hair looked a lot neater than Daisy's wayward ringlets but neither woman could be described as model pretty. Lucy was *quirky* too. Daisy had always wondered what Xander saw in her. Now, she knew.

'I'm the poor man's Lucy Errington,' she whispered.

'I said not to read too much into it.' His arms tightened around her. 'But no, you're not. It certainly made me pay attention to begin with, but early on I realised you were nothing like her.'

'How early on?'

'The day we met? Maybe when you hung up on Sofia? Or when you agreed to get drunk with me in the first place?' He tickled her ribs, making her squirm. 'Or maybe when I mentioned kissing you and your face said, *don't let it stop there, baby.*'

Daisy elbowed him. 'You're flattering yourself. It said, *maybe* after another few beer goggle drinks. How are we different?'

Xander laughed. 'Are you fishing for me to tell you why you're amazing, or do you want to know how rubbish she is in comparison?'

'Both.'

'You, as you well know, are sexy, confident, very good fun and an utter tramp. But what most people don't see, is that you're also incredibly kind, generous and I still can't get over how supportive you are of me.' He brushed her hair back and kissed her nose. 'Lucy, on the other hand, likes to think she's a delicate artist, a creative soul, but she's actually cold, manipulative and selfish. Not that you'll admit this, but you'd have left the HMS for me because you love me. She liked to think that she loved me, but she wouldn't have dreamed of leaving her husband because she didn't want to give up the life and status of being a Michelin-starred wife. That do you?'

Daisy nodded, loving how he made her sound. To hide her smug grin, she peered at a photo of Lucy sat at an easel. 'God, does she actually sit around in drawing rooms, drinking herbal tea and painting ghastly watercolours?'

'Not far off.'

'What did you see in her?'

'Damsel in distress?'

'Did you love her?'

'I thought I did at the time, but now, I know I didn't. I love you.'

Satisfied, Daisy tossed her phone back onto the table. 'What are the girls like at Oak Bank? Any hot waitresses you've got your eye on?'

'If you think I'm even entering that minefield, you're mental. Whatever I say will be wrong.' He toyed with a curl again. 'What've you got planned for tomorrow afternoon?'

'Don't care so long as it's with you.'

'Then can we get a Christmas tree tomorrow?'

Daisy laughed. 'Ohmigod, you total child.'

'Don't care. I fucking love Christmas. What are you getting me?'

'What do you want?'

'You.'

'Wrapped in a big red bow?' Laughing, she dragged him to bed.

By two pm the next day, as they finished lunch at the River Cafe in the village, Daisy gazed at Xander, happier than she could remember. Ever. Her life was great, beyond great. And as Xander gazed back, she knew he was thinking exactly the same thing. They must have looked like a pair of dopey teenagers to the diners around them.

Earlier, under grey skies, with their breath forming clouds in the frosty air, they'd held hands on a long, slow walk through the woods before buying a lovely, slightly wonky Christmas tree. Daisy, full of empathy for such a quirky little tree that surely no one in their right mind would want, pleaded with Xander. He'd wanted a glossy, seven foot Nordman, but when Daisy fluttered her eyelashes, he dropped the utterly beautiful tree and picked up the little Norway that was filled to bursting with character. It even started snowing as they popped into town to buy fairy lights.

In Haverton Garden Centre, Xander had over-casually dropped a single bauble in the basket, causing Daisy to chastise him.

'I'm making popcorn garlands. I want natural, not trashy gold, daubed with glitter. What does it say, anyway?' She picked up the bauble and giggled. *Our 1st Christmas.* 'OMG, you are such a hopeless romantic.'

'And you're an unfeeling cow.' Totally unashamed, he'd slapped her arse, earning himself a quick, checkout queue kiss.

Was it their first Christmas, or their only? Bethany and the bombshell had convinced her Xander was a temporary thing, a stepping stone, but maybe it would be okay. Maybe this would be the first of many. Oh, God, this was how she'd felt the morning he left for the Caribbean – a step away from telling him what he desperately wanted to hear, that she loved him.

'What?' He leaned forwards, taking hold of her scarf. 'You look–'

'I was thinking we should make mulled wine this afternoon. It's the *best* thing to have while you're putting up Christmas decorations.'

He pulled her closer, his eyes sparkling. 'Liar. That's not what you were thinking at all.'

The kiss, slow and lingering, promised the world: it told her he'd be buried in her forever.

Then his phone rang.

'It's Jonty,' Xander said, smiling apologetically as he answered it. 'Your timing's awful... No, carry on... Is he okay? Of course. I'll see you later.' He hung up and pulled a face. 'Marco's burned his arm on the steam oven. Jonty asked me to go in.'

Thankfully, they'd chosen an outside table which meant she could light a cigarette and God, did she need one. Taking a long, deep drag, she glared at Xander.

'Poor Marco,' she said. 'I do hope he gets better really bloody soon because strangely, I didn't hear you tell Jonty to piss off. You're supposed to be spending a much needed day with me.'

It had stopped snowing.

Chapter Nineteen

Play coy with skinny jeans and a cute top? All out sexy, wrapped in a big red bow? She grinned. No. Something more conniving. He loved conniving, he always saw through it and he always appreciated her efforts. That night... how about accidentally sexy? Ripped at the knee work jeans, a slash-necked t-shirt that slipped off her shoulder, showing a red bra strap... oh, and a smudge of dirt on her cheek.

At twenty-past ten, with her hair in a loose plait, a few strands escaping, she took her position on the stairs and got to work, sanding the banister spindles. *Oh is it that time already*, she'd say. *I'll just finish this spindle.* So of course, he'd sit on the bottom step, chatting to her as he smoked his stupid joint, then they'd get naked and relive that time on the stairs. She had it planned to the last detail.

Except for one – timing.

By quarter to eleven, she'd fine-sanded three spindles and refilled her glass twice. Where the hell was he? He was usually home for half-ten. Maybe he had to stay late, crisis in the kitchen, a staff meeting... a drink with *Kate*. Bloody Kate.

Daisy lit a cigarette and abandoned her sandpaper.

Every night, she'd smile and nod at the right times as he bored her to death with his tales from the Oak Bank kitchen, but no matter how hard she tried, every time he mentioned Kate the waitress or the latest addition to the narrative, Nadia the receptionist, Daisy couldn't fight the urge to sink another massive gulp of wine.

Okay, she'd gleaned that Kate was a redhead, not an utterly beautiful brunette like his sister-in-law, but what if he were looking around? What if now he *had* Daisy, he didn't want her? What if she were just a challenge, like Holly?

No. She couldn't think like that. He'd shown her the list to show her he was serious about her; he'd told her the truth so she'd understand him, so she'd believe him. Being jealous was nothing but destructive. She mustn't sink to that level. Mustn't.

Lights flashed outside the house. Finally.

She moved up a step, and busily rubbed the fourth spindle, smiling when he joined her in the hallway. As expected, after a kiss where he looked her over with an amused look in his eye, he sat on the bottom step and skinned up.

'You're late,' she said.

'Discussing the staff party. We're having it in the New Year.'

'What do staff at a fancy boutique hotel do? Feast upon high-end food and vintage wines or devour fish and chips and get hammered on Stella?'

'Night out in Newcastle.'

Didn't see that coming. 'Clubbing?'

He nodded. 'Nadia's organising it.'

'Is she?' Daisy couldn't help her bitchy tone.

Xander paused, his half-rolled joint in one hand. 'What does that mean?'

'Nothing.'

'Daisy, what?'

'You spend more time with that Polish bloody receptionist than you do with me. I never see you anymore.'

'I'm working.' He stared at her, wide-eyed.

'Well, I assume you're working. And how's *Kate* today?'

Xander's brow creased into a deep frown. 'What's going on?'

Don't do this. 'You're never here.'

'This is the restaurant business. I know the hours aren't exactly social, but that's just the way it is.' There was no apology, no repentance. 'This is what I do.'

'I miss you. We've just got together, but I may as well be single.' She threw her sandpaper down, feeling worse than ever. She should've kept her stupid mouth shut.

'I'm sorry,' he said quietly. 'It's the job.'

She took a deep, if shaky breath. 'Have you decided what you want to do on Christmas Eve? Clara's for dinner, or the pub?'

He glanced at his feet. 'I... Marco's still—'

'You're *working* Christmas Eve?' That he'd agreed to work until three on Christmas Day was bad enough, but Christmas Eve was his day off. He hadn't had one since Jonty's bloody phone call. 'I should've gone to my brother's with my parents. At least I wouldn't be on my own.'

Xander moved up, sitting on the same step as her. 'It won't be so bad. Come on, it's just Christmas Eve.'

'It's not *just* Christmas Eve. Everyone else will be out having fun. What am I supposed to do, go to midnight bloody mass? Maybe I should. It'd be better than sitting here waiting for you to come home to tell me how bloody marvellous Kate and Nadia are.'

'What the—'

But Daisy stormed off, striding into the kitchen. Why was she letting this bother her so much? Finn had girls throwing themselves at him on a daily basis, but she'd never doubted him. Trying to stay calm, she sat on the table, impaling her palms with her fingernails. It didn't work. The tears tumbled out.

Oh God, she didn't want to be jealous. But she was jealous — utterly, tragically jealous. Xander worked at a five-star hotel, a five-star hotel full of pretty waitresses, customers and hotel staff. Last time he did that, he also did a couple of hundred girls in three years.

'Daze?' He stood in front of her, wiping away her tears.

'I'm sorry.' She tried to look up, to offer a reassuring smile, but she couldn't look him in the eye.

'Kate and Nadia are just people I work with.' He kissed the top of her head. 'You should see how bored they look when I've been banging on about how bloody marvellous you are for the thousandth time of the day.'

'I'm sorry,' she whispered, wrapping her arms around him. 'I'm being an idiot.'

'You are. You know how I feel about you.' He held her tight, his thumb brushing her bare shoulder. 'Were you really sanding the stairs?'

'Yes and no.' Thank God he couldn't see her blushes. 'Do you remember that day?'

'Like I'd ever forget it.' He leaned away, lifting her chin so she had to face him and he placed a finger over her heart. 'And I still mean it. Buried here forever.'

She wanted to believe him, she really did, but the sad reality was Daisy just didn't trust him. The list hadn't helped. It had made things worse.

Gosthwaite Hall had been transformed into a Dickensian postcard. The enormous Christmas tree sagged under the weight of little wooden toys, handmade paper chains and ginger biscuit stars. They'd even gilded the holly with a dusting of faux-snow.

Why the hell had she come to a Christmas bloody fayre? To buy a bag of chestnuts or a side of wild boar for Boxing Day? Would Vanessa really thank her when she unwrapped organic felt-boots for Dora's Christmas present?

Someone shoot me now.

At the least nauseating Swiss chalet-style stall, she bought a *glühwein* from *Frau* Butterworth. It was a little naughty since Daisy had driven to the village, but it was the only way to cope with the saccharine sweetness of the stall-holders in traditional Victorian garb. Near the festive tree, she sat on a bench and lit a cigarette, ignoring the appalled looks from the middle-aged woman sat ten feet away.

Oh, bite me. We're outside.

At a stall selling hand-painted decorations, a couple giggled over a bauble – a sickening reminder of how Daisy had teenager-gazed at Xander, looking forward to his two days off. Days off? She slugged the surprisingly good *glühwein*. Boxing Day was his only day off until New Year's Eve.

And after her outburst the previous night, why would he even want to spend time with a whining cow? For God's sake, like the other Has-beens, she'd become a mental idiot. Where had her self-respect gone? She had to stop being so jealous – it really didn't suit her. She downed the rest of the *glühwein*.

'You look bored.'

The hat and unshaven face might've hidden him to the rest of the crowd, but Daisy could name that man from the first syllable he uttered. Finn. He stood a few feet away with his hands in his pockets, looking sexier than ever. And despite the unreasonable behaviour, despite Xander and his work colleagues, Daisy found she was smiling genuinely.

'What on earth are you doing here?'

'Bit on the twee side, isn't it?' Finn raised his eyes to the heavens, shaking his head. 'The olds are staying at the cottage. They fancied a *real* Christmas. Are you bored?'

She nodded.

'Lunch?'

'Thanks, but I shouldn't.' Xander wouldn't like it.

'It's only lunch. Of course you should.' He held out a hand, his smile making his eyes twinkle. 'Mum and dad are dying to see you.'

That was a look she hadn't seen in a long time, but it was a look he used to have all the time. For a while, she'd made him happy, ridiculously happy. How the hell had they lost it so easily? Was it because she never said sorry?

'Daisy,' Fabien Rousseau strode over, his arms wide. 'Mon petit chou!'

Vicky St. Michael, Finn's mother wasn't far behind, peeking from under a fur hat. 'How darling to see you. Join us for lunch? We're walking to the village. Fabien simply adores the homemade steak pie at the Alfred.'

Unable to resist their company, anyone's company, Daisy relented. 'But I have to drive home later so don't let me drink. Much.'

Finn laughed and placed a hand on her back to guide her around the stalls. He really was an absolute gent. Leisurely, the four of them walked through the woods, heading along the bridleway.

'Where's the youngster today?' Finn asked, stripping the twigs off a stick he'd picked up.

'Work.'

'Xander works? Really? I assumed he sat around looking good.'

'Be nice.' Daisy tried to frown but ended up giggling. 'How's Brittany?'

'Touché.' He flashed a rueful grin. 'You'd like her, a lot.'

'Ohmigod, we should so double date.' Daisy laughed, but when Finn tapped her arse with the stick, she pouted in mock-outrage. She really shouldn't be going for lunch with him, but God it was good to see him again. 'Did I really never say sorry? Ever?'

'Not even that time you didn't defrost the chicken and nearly killed me.'

'But that wasn't my fault–'

'Which is kind of my point. It never was.' Finn glanced back at his parents, but they'd stopped, cooing over the view up to Lum Crag. 'None of it was ever your fault, was it?'

'But...'

'I know you think...' Finn went back to stripping twigs and bark from his stick. 'I pushed you too far, but Dee, you said you were totally up for the three–'

'I did not.' With her cheeks burning, Daisy turned to check Fabien and Vicky couldn't hear. 'I never said anything–'

'Yes, you did.' Finn's brow creased. 'Remember, that night we went to Boujis?'

Quite frankly, no. A few weeks after their doomed anniversary night out that Tabitha ruined, Finn suggested they give it another go, this time in a swanky London club. Surrounded by minor British royalty, and more A-List celebs than Daisy could read about in *Heat*, they'd knocked back pills she never bothered to ask the name of with bottles of Krug.

'We were trashed. I could've said anything.'

Clearly, uncomfortable, Finn nodded. 'Looking back, that's when I should've... done something.'

'Done what?'

'Stopped you drinking.'

'Oh for God's sake. I wasn't that bad.' Daisy scowled. '*You* overreacted. We were both partying hard, that's all.'

'But I didn't want to party...' Sighing, Finn draped his arm around her shoulders, pulling her closer. 'I just wanted... us.'

Was it all her fault? Certainly she'd be the one who'd suggest they go out, the one who'd order the tequila, the one who'd never say no to pills or powders.

If you had your way, you'd live in a Bacardi advert.

She looked up at him, his eyes so serious, so filled with sadness. All he'd wanted was to settle down, to have a family and be with her.

'Finn–'

Suddenly smiling, he pressed a finger against her lips and kissed her nose. 'Let's not do this today. It's so good to see you again, and I... let's enjoy lunch.'

Daisy relaxed. 'Okay.'

Lunch was a blast, not least because Finn and Fabien seemed to have a tag-team routine for topping up glasses. She'd be walking home.

'How's the play going?' she asked Finn.

'Reviews are wonderful,' Vicky gushed. 'You should come out in the New Year, darling... stay with us.'

Before Daisy could respond, her phone rang. Oh, Jesus, it was Tabitha, exactly the last person to mention in front of Finn. Daisy smiled apologetically to his adorable parents.

'Tabitha, how are you?'

Doyle? Finn mouthed, his brow contracting. Daisy nodded, moving to sit three tables away.

'Oh, just wanted to say hello, sweetie.'

Actually, it turned out what Tabitha wanted to do was give her the latest on the Coronation Street part she was after. Daisy listened dutifully to her ego-trip, grateful to Finn for topping up her glass.

'And how are *you*, sweetie?' Tabitha asked. 'James said you're not exactly loving Xander's career move.'

'Well, yes and no. He's busy, that's all. Honestly, it's fine.'

'Really?'

She glanced back at Finn, but he was laughing with his mum, not paying Daisy any attention. 'But can you believe he's working Christmas Eve? We had a fight about it last night.'

'But, sweetie,' she said, through a tinkly laugh, 'please play out with me. I have something lined up which will suit you down to the ground.'

She wouldn't say what, but with no other invites on the table, Daisy reluctantly agreed. After, Tabitha mwah-mwah'ed her, Daisy hung up, already anticipating Finn's questions.

'You're *friends* with Tabitha?' he joined her, perching on the table.

'Well, she's friends with Xander's friends and she's... okay.'

'After everything you've said—'

'But I was right. She totally admitted to trying to get in your pants.' Daisy drained her glass. 'She also apologised for it. Several times.'

'Fair enough.' Finn nodded. 'Now, what's up with you? And don't brush me off. I know you too well. You're not happy.'

'I'm fine.' She flashed a smile. 'But I should go. I need to take my dog for a walk, but thanks for dragging me to lunch.'

'Really, you have to go?'

She nodded.

'Let me drive you home, at least.'

She shook her head. 'The walk will sober me up. When are you going back to New York?'

'Couple of days.' He stood up, pulling her with him. 'It's been great to see you, Dee.'

Impetuously, she threw her arms around his neck, hugging him. 'You too.'

'Ah, Vicky,' Fabien said, 'Maybe they are like us… married, divorced, married…'

Trying not to giggle, Daisy detangled herself and said goodbye to her ex-parents-in-law. God, it was good to see them again. With a final hug for Finn, she kissed his cheek and walked away, only turning back when she reached the door.

'Hey, Finn?'

He looked up.

'I'm sorry.'

The smile he answered with prompted her to blow him a kiss, and spend the afternoon pondering *what ifs*. What if Tabitha hadn't ruined that anniversary? What if Daisy had gotten pregnant? What if she'd not given up so easily on that whole *for better or for worse* vow? Because simply having lunch with Finn had been the highlight of her week.

'What if,' she muttered, gazing at the photo of her and Xander stood under that oak tree at Clara's wedding. 'What bloody if?'

At ten-fifteen, Xander's car pulled up and Daisy leapt out of the bath. He was early. Bugger. She'd totally planned on an innocently sweet knitted dress and leggings combo, hoping to talk like a rational adult. Hell, she'd even avoided wine for the whole night so she didn't succumb to alcohol-induced jealousy. But her smile couldn't be more genuine as she wrapped herself in a towel. Accidentally half-naked could never be a bad thing.

'You're early,' she called as she dashed downstairs. 'Sorry, I was in the bath.'

He didn't answer, so she headed into the living room, only to be faced with the most enormous bunch of flowers.

'OMG, you got me roses?'

And not just any roses, shocking pink ones – her absolute favourites. Were they to apologise for him working Christmas Eve? Absolutely thrilled, she breathed in their fabulous, sweet bouquet. He might not be around much at the moment, but at least he thought about her. Daisy turned to him but dropped her smile. He wasn't smiling. Far from it, he was drumming his fingers on his leg, smoking a joint and staring at her.

The flowers weren't from him.

'They were left by the front porch. There's a card.'

Goosebumps covered her skin. They must've been delivered

while she was out with Birkin and she'd used the back door when she came home. Her hands shook as she opened the card.

Enjoyed today. Happy Christmas. Finn x

Fuck.

'Where have you been today, Daisy?' His voice was low, quivering with anger.

She touched the beautiful roses. Oh, why couldn't they have been from Xander? Why? Simple answer really. He'd stopped buying her presents ages ago. The last gift she'd received was a pair of diamond-encrusted guilt earrings.

'Could you at least try not looking delighted with his fucking flowers?'

Slowly, Daisy turned around. 'The roses are lovely, but I wish they were from you.'

His fingers stopped drumming.

'Today, I went to a stupid Christmas Fayre. I got you the most God-awful Christmas jumper, which I expect you to wear.'

A smile twitched at the corners of his mouth.

'And I had lunch with Finn.'

'And you forgot to mention any of these plans this morning, when I asked what you were doing today?' He set about shredding a Rizla paper into tiny strips. 'Painting the bathroom is what you said.'

'I changed my mind. I'm sick of sitting here, waiting for you to come home. I saw an advert in the local paper and just went. It wasn't planned or anything. I bumped into him and he insisted on taking me to lunch.'

'Insisted?'

'I knew you wouldn't like it, but it was just lunch.'

'Of course I wouldn't like it,' he snapped. 'That's why you shouldn't have fucking gone. Or is this some kind of payback because you don't like me working?'

'No.'

'Then why did you have fucking lunch with him?'

'I was bored,' she said angrily.

'Bored?' He shook his head. 'So this is about me working.'

'No. I went...' *Because I miss you.* 'I went because I was bored and he had his parents with him. They're good people. I miss them.'

Xander drained his bottle of Stella. 'If it was just lunch, why's he sent you flowers? To wind me up?'

Daisy scowled. 'Well, it's working.'

Shaking his head, Xander strode out of the room, pushing past her. What was the big deal with her having lunch with Finn anyway? It wasn't like she was shagging him.

After a minute, Daisy braved hunting Xander out. She found him in the kitchen, pouring a hefty measure of Glenfiddich. He knocked back half of it, his eyes glaring, filled with hurt and anger.

'Xand, you're always asking me to trust you. You've given me plenty of reasons not to, but I try really hard. This is the only time you've ever had to trust me. Could you try, please?'

'Seriously?' He laughed without the slightest trace of humour and sank the rest of the whisky. 'Daisy, you flirt with every bloke you meet. I have to trust you every single day, but you know what? I'd trust you to have lunch, dinner and breakfast the next day with pretty much any bloke in the world. But not him.'

'Oh my God, Xand. I divorced him. Why would I shag him?'

'Because you still think you're in love with him.'

Xander leant on the breakfast bar, his head in his hands and guilt swamped her. The last thing in the world she wanted was to make Xander miserable. The guy had all but saved her life, surely he deserved better from her?

Quietly, she went over to him, taking a moment to run her fingers through his hair, kissing his head. 'Baby, I'm sorry. I swear it was just lunch, totally harmless. Finn and I are friends, that's all, but if this… I won't see him again.'

When Xander turned, his frown was worse than ever. 'Do you mean it?'

She nodded. Of course she meant it. Besides, how could she see Finn when he was in New York shagging Brittany Carle?

In a second, Xander's lips were on hers and Daisy tugged the edge of her towel, letting it drop to the floor. She knew Xander needed reassuring and dear God, she was happy to give him what he needed. More than happy. Her fingers deftly unhooked his belt and he lifted her onto the breakfast bar. More than, more than happy.

'I'll have nothing to do with Finn ever again,' she said, dropping her head back as Xander's lips and teeth assaulted her neck, his stubble grazing her sensitive skin. 'I promise.'

Chapter Twenty

At ten to seven on Christmas Eve as the taxi took a left, Daisy stopped rapping her nails against her handbag.

'We're going to Oak Bank?' she asked Tabitha.

'Bingo, sweetie,' she replied, applauding. 'Jonty invited me and said I could bring a friend. We get a night out, he's paying and *you* get to see Xander. What could be more perfect?'

Nothing could be more perfect. God bless Tabitha.

Stupidly excited at surprising Xander, Daisy even managed to smile über-politely to Nadia the Receptionist. Nadia recognised Tabitha, but if she knew who Daisy was, she did a bloody good impression of hiding it. Glad to escape her immaculate, Slavic-cheek-boned, glossy dark-haired presence, Daisy let Tabitha drag her to the bathroom while Nadia buzzed through for Jonty.

'I know it's Michelin-fabulous here,' Tabitha said, producing a pretty glass vial from her Prada clutch, 'but for God's sake, it's Christmas Eve, sweetie. Want to party?'

Daisy shook her head. 'I have to deal with three small children tomorrow, but don't mind me.'

At least her hair still sat perfectly corkscrewed and, actually, the frothy layers on her turquoise chiffon mini-dress were sexy *and* cute. Okay, Tabitha probably persuaded her to wear the little Oasis number because it was high street and she was in a sequin Hervé Léger dress, but Daisy didn't care – she rocked. God, it was amazing what half a bottle of pink champagne could do for a girl's self-esteem.

'Jonty's out front,' Nadia said, poking her head around the door. To her credit, her immaculately plucked brows never even raised at the sight of Tabitha cutting lines, though perhaps that was down to Botox, rather than an unshockable demeanour.

Daisy hovered beside the reception desk, as Jonty gave Tabitha a long, flirty hello. God, that boy adored her. It was really rather sweet, if slightly get-a-room worthy. Annoyingly, Daisy had to wait twenty minutes for her hello with Xander, and when it came there was nothing sweet about it.

As a waiter placed a second round of champagne cocktails on the table, Xander crossed the room, all pleasant smiles for the other diners, but his eyes never left Daisy. And if she wasn't very much mistaken, he was furious.

God, she hated those bloody checked trousers and stupid white jacket. The whole ensemble didn't suit him, far too uncool. Or was it merely uncool because he seemed to love wearing it more than he loved her these days?

'What the hell are you doing here?' he hissed, crouching beside Daisy's chair.

'Aren't you even going to say hello?'

'Seriously, why are you here? Not for the food obviously.'

He hadn't kissed her. He always kissed her hello.

'You don't seem very pleased to see me.' Why hadn't he kissed her hello? Was he afraid someone might see, like Kate or bloody Nadia?

'I'd be more pleased if you hadn't been caught doing coke in the toilets the second you got here.'

Nadia was a grassing cow, but he was just assuming she'd taken some too? She hated Xander being cross with her but equally, she hated that he'd simply accepted she'd done coke, without checking the facts.

He went to stand up, but Daisy grabbed his hand.

'What do you think we're going to do,' she said, 'dance on the bloody tables?'

He stared at the floor, the muscle in his jaw twitching like mad, but at least his fingers had curled around hers.

'Come on, Xand.' She tugged his hand. 'We're honestly here for the food. *Your* food. I'm not here to make your life hell.'

He relaxed slightly, managing a small smile before he mouthed, *behave* and headed back to the kitchen. She relaxed, thank god he'd calmed down, but seriously, where the hell was her kiss?

'Bugger, I shouldn't have come.' She drained her cocktail and smiled at the drinks waiter. *More booze, mister.*

'What on earth is going on?' Tabitha asked.

As a waiter delivered the first course from the Twelve Days of Christmas themed taster menu, Daisy explained how Nadia and Kate were all Xander talked about. Sympathetically nodding, Tabitha picked at the six tiny quenelles of Goose-liver pate – but

Daisy barely nibbled a bread roll, miserably sending the dish back untouched.

'Sorry, Tab. Hardly the best fun, am I?'

'No, but then that's why we have friends, to get us through the bad bits.' She squeezed Daisy's hand and grateful, Daisy returned the gesture. She'd become such a good friend.

'My real problem is that I've been spoiled,' she said. 'I've basically had Xander to myself since August. Okay, he's had a few trips away and random days at work, but mostly he's been there when I get home from work. I miss him. He loves working here, but it's hard pretending I'm happy for him. The reality is I want to tell him to quit so we can hibernate until spring.'

And she could keep him away from bloody good-looking Polish girls. Nadia, with her perfect skin and enormous green eyes, looked far too beautiful to be a receptionist, Poland's Next Top Model maybe.

'Grin and bear it, sweetie,' Tab said. 'Don't be a bitch, don't be jealous and don't moan or you'll drive him into the arms of that sassy redheaded waitress who clearly fancies him.' She studied Kate the waitress for a moment. 'She looks like I did at twenty. Cheap and unbelievably bloody trashy.'

Daisy's smile returned and grateful, she chinked her glass against Tabitha's.

'Of course, I was rebelling against my parents' wealth and lifestyle. What's her excuse do you think?'

Daisy could've kissed Tabitha for keeping her spirits up. And the waiter for keeping the spirits flowing.

Feeling positive, and hoping to prove she was there for the food, his food, Daisy sipped her way through all eight *Dancing Ladles of Soup* and studiously ate at least half of each of the other courses. But by the time the waiter served coffee and *petit four calling birds* she'd most definitely consumed more mouthfuls of champagne than she had solid food.

Sadly, with the coffee gone, Tabitha also disappeared, whispering she wanted to say goodbye to Jonty. Glancing around the room, Daisy caught Nadia smiling piteously from her maître d' table. Cowbag. With equally appalling timing, Kate came out of the kitchen, carrying desserts and sending a flirty wink back through the closing door.

Oh God, what if that was to Xander?

Grabbing her bag, and the half-empty bottle of Krug, Daisy ducked outside to hide. She should've stayed at home; she should've gone to midnight mass. The night had been a disaster, another #*fail* to add to her car crash of a life. It was all she could do not to cry.

'Xander will be out in five minutes,' Nadia informed her with a very sulky tone.

Grassing cow. Hang on, it was half-nine; he didn't normally finish work until ten. What did he usually do for that extra half an hour? Oh God, what if really was shagging Nadia or Kate, or both?

Mercifully, before Daisy actually succumbed to tears, Tabitha appeared, sans any lipstick.

'OMG, what have you two been up to?' Despite her own appalling evening, Daisy couldn't help but be pleased for Tabitha. Jonty seemed a poppet – a salt of the earth treasure. 'You like him then?'

'It's tricky,' Tabitha said, running a hand through her bedhead locks. 'I've been told he's shagging the supermodel receptionist *and* the redhead waitress.'

Jonty was shagging Nadia? 'So why the hell are you snogging him?'

'Because he's going to be a massively successful chef, rumour has it, with his own TV show.' Tabitha peered into a compact, reapplying her lipstick. 'It's just a shame that I couldn't trust him to keep it in his pants.'

'I know that feeling.'

'Daisy, Xander isn't like that.'

'He was.' Daisy sighed. 'Oh, I do trust him, but it's a bit bloody harder with twenty year-old redheads batting their eye-lash extensions at him.'

'Sweetie, when you get home, hop on his knee. In that dress, he'll be putty in your hands.' She eyed up Daisy's chiffon layers. 'I might have to borrow it so I can get some High Street Fashion *Grazia* inches.'

'Or you could buy your own. It was only fifty quid.' She didn't have the heart to tell Tabitha it was a size six and she'd never get her fake tits into it.

Together, they walked out, arm in arm, and when Nadia wished them good night, Daisy sent her a death glare. 'Bloody tell-tale.

That's her acronym, NTT. Nadia the Tittle-Tattle.'

'Or she could be a Naudi TT,' Tabitha giggled.

It was an awful joke but had them in stitches. Thank God for friends like Tabitha.

'Happy bloody Christmas, Tabby-cat,' Daisy said, bear hugging her.

'Happy bloody Christmas, Daisy-chain.'

'Where are you off to anyway?'

'Club in Manchester,' she said, climbing elegantly into her taxi. 'Want to come?'

Beyond jealous, Daisy shook her head. 'I can't moan about never seeing him then bugger off on Christmas Eve. Tempting as it is.'

Shooting a wink, Tabitha snuck her coke stash into Daisy's hand. 'To cheer him up,' she whispered, glancing behind Daisy. 'Happy Christmas, Xander.'

He forced a polite smile then jerked his head at Daisy. 'Let's go.'

'Why don't you normally come home this early?' She asked as she climbed in the car.

'Don't.'

The rest of the twenty-minute journey home was in silence.

The second they got in the house, Xander sat on the sofa and lit his stupid joint while Daisy stood in front of the fire staring at him. He stared back, the muscle in his jaw working overtime.

'I really didn't need you rocking up tonight and doing lines,' he said. 'Thank fuck it was Nadia who saw you and not a customer. You two could've ruined the restaurant's reputation. And mine. Fortunately, Jonty's so desperate to get in Tabitha's pants, he couldn't give a fuck.'

'Whatever.' She didn't deserve this. 'So what if a famous actress and her friend get a bit wasted at a five-star über-chic hotel? It'd hardly trash its reputation, more likely enhance it. But you know what, I didn't do anything to ruin anyone's reputation and Jonty couldn't really complain since he invited Tabitha.'

Xander's angry glare turned to a doubting frown as he took a long drag. 'Why didn't you tell me you were coming?'

'Because I didn't know. Tab wanted to surprise me. Did you think I was checking up on you?'

He stared at his fingers as he picked the label off his lager bottle. 'What's going on, Daze? With us.'

'I have no idea, but it's Christmas Eve and you're home. We should make the most of it.'

He looked her over but gave a little shake of his head. 'You're high.'

'Like that would stop you. What exactly did that Polish cow tell you? Because here's the thing, sunshine, I didn't do any coke tonight. Tab was doing a couple of lines when Nadia walked in, not me.'

He swore and rubbed his forehead. 'She said you were in the ladies, powdering your nose.'

'But you didn't ask *me*, Xand. Tonight, I drank a bit too much and didn't eat a lot. That's nothing new. There was no need for you to be so angry with me.'

It was Christmas Eve, for God's sake. They should be shagging under the mistletoe, not arguing to the Vegas-style blinking of the stupid fairy lights that didn't seem to have a static setting. Taking a slow breath, she walked over to him and followed Tabitha's advice. Her skirt rode up to indecency as she sat astride his legs, but his instant reaction suggested indecent was just what the doctor ordered.

'I'm sorry,' she whispered, shivering as his hands ran up her thighs, pressing her closer to him.

'No. This was my fault. I'm sorry.'

As her fingers made light work of the buttons on his jeans, he rested his forehead against hers, his breath coming in unsteady waves.

'Since it's practically Christmas,' she whispered between teasing kisses. 'Shall we call a truce?'

'Having fun?' Xander stood in the doorway, smiling down at Daisy and Matilda as they watched the Peppa Pig Christmas special.

'Xandy, Xandy!' Matilda beamed, clearly as delighted to see him as Daisy.

'Actually,' Daisy said, as he joined them on the sofa, 'I've had a great day.'

'Really?'

She nodded. 'I went for a long walk, had a bath, then your brother came to pick me up and kept forcing bucks fizz down my neck. It's been horrific. But I missed you.'

'I missed you too.' He rubbed his nose against hers, both grinning at the overly sweet gesture.

The night before, they'd gone to sleep happily wrapped around each other after a lengthy making up session. They were okay again. He'd woken her at eight, enticing her downstairs with the promise of coffee, a fire and sparkly gifts. The loved up feeling was back.

They'd raced down to the tree and ripped open their gifts as if they were five. He was forever asking her the time, terrified he'd be late for work and let the team down, so she'd blown a considerable chunk of her wages on a fabulous Tissot watch. He'd put it on instantly, grinning at its titanium awesomeness. She only hoped he didn't Google it to see how much it cost or he might insist she return it. Who needed a cam belt for her car anyway?

Her smile had faltered when he handed her a turquoise blue box tied with white ribbon. It was another Tiffany box – the same size and shape as the last. Inside were earrings very similar to the tip money earrings from November. Little drop earrings with a few diamonds in each. The tip money earrings had circles at the bottom; these had hearts.

'I know you really liked the other pair, but you'll never wear them,' he'd said. 'They're upstairs if you ever wanted to, but I thought you'd like some that were... more honestly earned.'

She'd thrown herself at him, showering him with a million thank you kisses, and when he'd left at ten-thirty, she'd waved goodbye, honestly not minding that he'd be spending the next few hours with Nadia and Kate.

The second Peppa Pig ended, Matilda scampered off, leaving Daisy alone with Xander. Sadly, their lips had barely met when a screaming match between Tallulah and Robbie ruined any romantic or lust-filled ideas, and they wandered through to see what was going on.

Tallulah stamped her feet, claiming her stupid iPod was rubbish in comparison to Matilda's pony. Robbie yelled at her, calling her a spoiled brat. Dora, startled by Daddy's shouting, cried, prompting Vanessa to comfort her six-month-old. Matilda, jealous of the attention her little sister received from their mother, then hit Dora. Vanessa tried to scold Matilda but could barely be heard over

Tallulah's shrieks and Robbie's bellows.

Xander quietly took over the cooking and Daisy hovered nearby, sipping her wine and watching the Golding's do their thing.

'It's a hell of a birth control method, seeing them in action,' she said, her legs firmly crossed at the ankle. 'You still think married with kids is a good idea?'

Xander laughed. 'Don't panic. I think we're a few years off that yet.'

Thank God.

'But it has its upsides too.'

Robbie and Vanessa changed tactics and swapped kids. He told Matilda she wasn't to hit Dora then whispered she was his favourite anyway. Vanessa glared at Tallulah, explaining the iPod cost twenty pounds more than Matilda's little Shetland and peace reigned.

With a twinge of guilt, Daisy thanked her lucky stars she hadn't got pregnant with Finn – that could be her battling with a two year-old. But just as she let out a sigh of relief, Matilda wrapped her arms around Robbie's neck and he closed his eyes, smiling the sweetest smile as he hugged her back. Xander was right; married with kids did have its upsides.

One day.

By the time Vanessa brought out the flaming Christmas pudding, Daisy had taken to gazing at Xander with teenage adoration and Robbie had a permanent, *you're so in love with him* smile. But who cared? It was Christmas Day. Peace on earth and goodwill to all men.

Mr and Mrs Golding senior rang when Robbie and Vanessa were putting the two youngest kids to bed, so Xander reluctantly answered the phone. Daisy, though engrossed in the final of a best of three KerPlunk battle with Tallulah, gave him a supportive smile at every opportunity. She couldn't hear much, but Xander appeared to say *no* an awful lot. Five minutes and the conversation was up. Xander handed the phone to Tallulah, grabbed his jacket and walked out. Bugger this. Daisy pulled out a stick and followed him, the clatter of marbles drowning out Tallulah's hellos to her grandparents.

Outside, Daisy found Xander rocking gently on a chair-swing and smoking a joint.

'So this is why you like chair-swings,' she said. 'Habit?'

'Not allowed to smoke near the house or kids.'

She wrapped her scarf a little tighter and snuggled next to him. 'How are your parents?'

'Same old.'

'Do they know about me?' she asked carefully.

Her mother had taken to chatting to Xander for a good ten minutes every time she called, flirting for at least eight of them, but Daisy had never even said hello to Xander's mum or dad.

'Not really. Do you mind?' He took a long drag on his joint. 'They know my girlfriend is here, so Rob must've said something, but they don't seem to know anything about you. That's a good thing. My foul father has a brilliant knack of buggering things up for me, and we have enough going on without him helping.' He offered her the joint, but she shook her head. 'Plus, you have a tendency to want to fix things and I'd rather you didn't get involved.'

'Excuse me? I do what?' Daisy took the joint.

'Well, usually it's one of your good qualities. You like to make people happy, to push things like you did with me and the restaurant. I don't want to make mine a happy family.' He frowned down at her. 'Sorry, but do you understand?'

Actually, she did. Ever since he'd explained about Mr and Mrs Golding moving to Yorkshire, she'd wanted to tear a strip off them for being God-awful parents.

'I understand.'

He sat twirling a curl for a few minutes. 'I'm so glad you're here.'

'Me too.'

'Happy Christmas, Fitzgerald.'

'Happy Christmas, baby.'

'Despite everything that's gone on, since the minute I met you, I've been the happiest I've ever been.'

The sincerity in his eyes... He meant it, but it wasn't a sentiment she could return. She'd gone through some of her worst days since she'd met him, days he'd picked her up from. She should say something, tell him how grateful she was, what he meant to her.

He put a finger over her lips. 'I know.'

He knew? Oh God, did he think she was about to tell him she loved him? His eyes twinkled, his smile growing, but she couldn't ruin this moment by correcting him. Instead, she smiled back, because no matter what she felt, making Xander smile really did mean the world to her.

What if?

The next day, they left Low Wood Farm laughing, kissing and armed with gifts. Daisy was happy, stupidly happy. The kind of happy she knew would never last.

Chapter Twenty-One

With Birkin taken out for a token walk and promised a longer one later, Daisy kicked off her Hunter's and happily picked up the waiting glass of Buck's Fizz off the kitchen table – at nine o'clock in the morning, anything else would be wholly inappropriate. Xander had come up with the rather fabulous idea of spending the day *DAF* style and, since he'd already poured the booze, clearly he was as keen as her to get the day of iniquity underway.

Her phone beeped.

Followed by Xander's.

He didn't take any notice. After a huge yawn, he stretched, treating her to a snippet of the happy trail. Oh dear God. She absolutely shouldn't get too wasted too quickly that she couldn't *fully* appreciate the kick-ass shagging that was no doubt coming her way.

As if he'd read her mind, Xander looked up as he licked the edges of the cigarette papers and Daisy saw all manner of promises in those fabulous brown eyes. Love, play, downright filth. She had no idea what he had in mind, but knowing he'd never push her where she didn't want to go, Daisy sat on the table and slowly peeled off her t-shirt.

'You are... without doubt...' Xander leant against breakfast bar and took a maddening amount of time to light his joint. 'The *un*sexiest thing I have *ever* seen.'

Playing to his teasing, Daisy crossed her legs, shaking her hair back. '*Un*sexiest... Ever?'

Xander wandered over, taking a long drag on his joint and checking his phone. 'Ever-ever.'

In an effort to maintain her air of *un*sexiness, Daisy slid her bra straps off her shoulders. They were so doing it on the kitchen table. Although, Xander was actually frowning at his phone, and possibly not in some faux way pretending to play hard to get.

'What the fuck?' He looked up, his frown in place. 'Daze, check your phone.'

Oh for God's sake. Doing as she was told, Daisy grabbed her phone. A Facebook notification sat on the screen.

Forfeit invited you to their event – The Ultimate Games of Dares: Round Three.

What the hell… They'd all said they didn't want to play again. They'd all agreed.

'And who do you think sent these?' she asked with bitter sarcasm. She'd bet five grand James was bored silly again.

'I'll ring the others.'

31st December. Oscar's Bar and Bistro. 20:00 until 21:00. Going (0) Maybe (0) Invited (5).

Join? Maybe? Daisy scanned the Facebook event page. Where was the *Not A Chance In Hell* option? James was such an arse.

'No one's answering,' Xander said, tossing his phone onto the worktop. 'Let's just ignore it. Now, get that fine ass back on the table.'

Daisy hopped back up, but she couldn't shake a niggle of unease. Even Xander taking off his t-shirt didn't help. Okay, it helped a little. As did him pushing her back onto the table, scattering a million kisses up her body.

Beep, Beep.

She groped for her phone.

'You're killing me, Fitzgerald.'

'It might be an explanation.'

'I've got my girlfriend half-naked on the kitchen table… it'd better be a fucking good explanation.'

Shaking her head at his schoolboy sulking, she sat up and checked her phone.

Forfeit has sent you a message.

Oh, here we go.

Daisy, you didn't click 'Join'. Mistake. You see, if you had, I wouldn't have needed to send this message.

You might've decided to end the game of Forfeit in October, but I'm afraid the game hasn't ended. You will attend on New Year's Eve. You will do your dare. You know why?

Yana.

The words blurred and Daisy blinked to refocus. Oh God no.

Yana hasn't kept her word. She's ready to tell all about the night she spent with you and Finn Rousseau. Right now, she's keeping her mouth shut thanks to a sizeable fee. The fee expires on January 1st unless you play the game.

Take care, poppet.

'Daze?'

Pushing Xander away, she thrust her phone at him and stalked around the room, trying hard not to throw up. Why was this happening to her?

'Who's Yana?' he asked, quietly. 'The threesome?'

Daisy topped up her glass with champagne, not bothering with the juice. Who cared what time it was? 'She's a *friend* of Finn's from before we were married, someone he trusted to keep her mouth shut. She's a Ukrainian model. Well, let's be honest, she's a Ukrainian high-class call girl.'

'I'm sorry.' Xander wrapped his arms around her, kissing her head. 'But don't let it get to you. It's a stupid sex story, that's all.'

Daisy sheltered in his arms. 'It's not just the threesome. If whoever's doing this has talked to Yana then they know what happened at Claridge's.'

'But—'

'Yana was there too.'

'What did happen at Claridge's?' he asked, holding her so tight, his words were muffled in her hair.

Beep, beep.

It was Xander's phone this time. For a second they clung to one another, but sighing, he let her go and picked up his phone. As he read the message, his frown deepened.

'Do I want to know?' she whispered. 'Another bombshell?'

'There are no more bombshells,' he said softly. 'It's just about the tip money. Names, dates... prices.'

So why was his voice so shaky? It was just a sex story, right?

'Who's doing this, Xand?'

He shrugged, relighting the joint.

'I don't get it,' she went on. 'Why someone would want us to play again? Surely none of the others are doing it for money, to win the pot?'

'You and I would be the most poverty stricken out of the five of us and it isn't me, Fitzgerald.'

'Then who would do it?'

'I don't know.'

'But they're your friends.'

'Yes they are, and that's why I know they'd never blackmail me.'

'But James hates—'

'Do you really think James could be arsed to set up a Facebook event, just to annoy you?' Xander handed her the joint. 'What about one of the others? Someone who knows about the game but wasn't playing? I can't see Ella being interested–'

'She is a journalist though. Anything for a story?'

'Lidia? Looking for payback?'

Daisy sighed. 'It could be Finn.'

'Why him?' Xander folded his arms. 'Why does your *ex*-husband have to be the first bloke who pops into your head?'

'He wasn't. James was. But it couldn't be James, because he doesn't know about Yana.'

'And Finn doesn't know about the tip money. Not unless you told him.'

Daisy's head snapped to attention. 'Of course I didn't tell him. What, do you think I like telling people my boyfriend, until very recently, charged two grand for sex?'

Xander hung his head for a moment, his hands shoved in his pockets. 'But who else knew about Yana? In my message there are names listed, names no one knows.'

'Me, Finn, her and you. But I never told you her name.'

'And I've only ever told James and you.' His frown was back. 'So who the hell could do this?'

'I don't know but if we can't find out, I have to turn up on New Year's Eve. After the text message fiasco, the last thing I want my dad to hear about is... and there's my job. How much would St Nick's put up with?'

Xander kissed her head. 'It's okay, I know. We'll work it out.'

'Then again, I can be blackmailed until the end of time, but I'll never have five thousand pounds to play Round Three.'

'Unfortunately, I don't have that excuse at the moment.'

Daisy sagged in his arms. Happy bloody Christmas.

The next morning, Daisy pottered around in her Ugg boots and Xander's jumper, shivering against the cold. For the first time she was grateful she'd hand Skank Manor back in August, because despite the new heating system and new windows, the house was bloody freezing in winter.

Beep, beep.

Daisy's heart stalled, but tentatively she glanced at her phone. Scott. Letting out the breath she held, Daisy had to stifle a squeal when she read the most magical words:

Have details of Mill. They'll sell.

Surely finding Xander his dream restaurant would utterly make up for the Forfeit nightmare? Stifling her smile as Xander came downstairs, she quickly texted Scott back, telling him she'd be pop around later. God, she so couldn't wait to see Xander's face when she showed him the photos.

'What are you smiling about?' Xander asked, his suspicious tone too amusing for words. He'd love the surprise later.

'Clara. I'm going to see her this afternoon.'

'I've lit the fire,' Xander said, slumping against the cooker. 'If it wasn't so fucking cold in this house, I'd consider phoning in sick. I feel awful.'

After the hideous *Forfeit* messages had arrived, they'd ended up spending Boxing Day as they'd planned – *Drunk and Fucked* – albeit not in the same spirit. Using booze, weed and the coke Tabitha had given Daisy on Christmas Eve, they blotted out reality.

'We could go back to bed,' Daisy suggested. 'It'll be warm there.'

Beep, Beep.

'I'm broken.' Xander laughed, rather over-casually as he picked up his phone. 'You've officially worn me out.'

'I'll take that as a compli–'

'Jesus Christ.'

Daisy peeked over his shoulder, but had to clamp her hand over her mouth to suppress a scream. His iPhone screen, with its retina display crispness, showed Daisy, her head thrown back, her skin glistening with sweat and her nipples like bloody football studs.

'Who the hell took this?' Xander asked, his voice ominously low.

Daisy backed away, worried by his tone, the muscle twitching in his jaw. He wasn't going to like her answer. 'Finn.'

'That fucking–' Xander walked away, his hands on his head. 'When? After the Christmas Fayre?'

If he'd been three feet nearer to her, she'd have slapped him. 'No. It was over a year ago.'

He still stared at the photo.

'Delete it, Xander.'

He glanced up for a second, before swearing and hitting delete.

'Now,' she said, her voice dripping with sarcasm, 'is it okay that my ex-husband is the first bloke I think of this time?'

Without waiting for Xander's answer, she grabbed her phone, her fingers shaking as she pressed call. It rang. And rang. And rang.

'Hello?' Finn said, his voice rough with sleep.

'It's me.'

'Dee? What's up? Are you okay?'

'Did you send the photo to anyone?'

'What photo?' There was some muffled rustling. 'Fuck, Dee. It's four in the morning.'

'The one you took of me... in Ibiza.'

More muffled rustling and him shushing someone. 'You're calling at four in the morning for this?'

'Someone has that photo, Finn.'

'I never sent it to anyone. Cross my heart.' He swore. 'But Dee, I lost the phone. The text messages...'

Oh God, no. She sat heavily on the table next to Xander. He lost the phone. Someone... out there had that photo. But was it just the one? He'd taken dozens, but promised to keep just one, one they'd both agreed on. 'Finn, how many of photos did you keep?'

'Just the one, like you said.'

She'd never believed he'd be so restrained. 'Finn... I need to know the truth. It's really fucking important right now.'

The silence stretched across the Atlantic Ocean.

'Four,' he finally admitted.

There weren't enough expletives in the world, but God, did she try to use them all.

'I'm so sorry, baby,' he whispered.

'Finn, who is that?' said the distinct husky drawl of Brittany Carle.

Daisy hung up.

Xander's brow was more furrowed than she'd ever known. 'The photo was on the phone he lost?'

'Four of them.' Tears welled up, as she wrapped her arms around herself. 'Xand... I daren't even guess which ones he kept and *someone* has his phone. They put the text messages I sent on Twitter. They'll do it again.'

'No, they won't.' Xander kicked the nearest chair, sending it across the flagstone floor. For a minute or maybe ten, he stood, his hands on his head, his eyes closed. Stunned, Daisy daren't move, waiting for him to come back from wherever he'd gone. Finally, he turned back to her, his eyes still blazing with fury. 'I'll tear down the world before I let anyone hurt you again.'

And then he did it; he opened the Facebook app on his phone and pressed *Join*.

Ten seconds couldn't have passed before Daisy's phone lit up.

Beep, beep.

Reluctantly, she typed in her passcode.

Forfeit *has sent you a message.*

But of course he had.

Xander's playing. Ready to see what'll make you join the party?

She refused to reply.

No, you don't need to see what I have, do you, Daisy? You know everything he's done, right? That is right, isn't it? Because I've got something... good.

She hit *Join*.

'But just so you know,' she hissed at the words on her screen. 'I don't have five thousand pounds so I won't be playing your fucking game.'

Xander's hand rested on her back. 'Leave it, Daze.'

She threw herself into his arms. 'Do you have to go to work?'

'You know I do. Do me a favour, stay here today, just so I know you're safe?'

'I have to see Clara.'

'Why?'

'It's Christmas,' she lied. *Please don't push this. Don't ruin the surprise.*

'Please, Daisy.' His frown worsened, his tone less pleading and she understood how serious he was.

'Okay. I'll stay at home.'

She even meant it for a while. But after standing in the shower, unable to stop imagining the photo going viral via Twitter, and painting her toes, picturing her dad reading about her sexploits in the Guardian, Daisy caved.

She needed to get out of the house, for some normality. She needed to see Clara and Scott. She needed to get the information on the Mill. But most of all, she needed to picture Xander's face when she showed him the Mill photos. She needed to, because she hated the image currently burned into her eyeballs, the one of Xander's face as he ogled the photo of her tits while her then-husband screwed her senseless.

Especially since a surreptitious check proved Xander hadn't deleted the photo.

'OMG, you're enormous,' she said, hugging Clara. 'Fabulous but enormous.'

The half-football had been replaced by half a beach ball but from the back, no one would guess she was pregnant.

'So does it kick?' Daisy asked.

'*He* does.'

'Definitely?'

They hugged again, this time with squealing.

'Daisy's here then,' Scott said as he wandered in. His grin was short-lived as he peered at her. 'Jesus. You look awful. Drugs at your age?'

'You're only jealous because you're nearly forty.' Daisy kissed his cheek and they hugged. Scott was only twenty-nine, but she did like to mock.

'Need some tea and Hobnobs?' he asked, already heading to the kitchen.

'Like you wouldn't believe.' She flopped onto the sofa, smiling at Clara's vast bump. 'Have you picked names, now you know it's a boy?'

Clara sat next to her, studying her, leaving Daisy nowhere to hide. 'You do look awful.'

As if Daisy didn't know. The indulgence of the previous day was etched across her face – too much sex, drugs and booze. Even Touche Éclat struggled with the suitcases under her eyes.

'I asked about names first.'

Clara smiled, gracious in defeat. 'We went through the top ten, then the top hundred, looking for something not too made up and chavvy but not stupidly popular either. Jack, Oliver, Charlie, Harry, Alfie. All out. I quite liked Dylan but Scott reckoned it was a dog's name. His mum liked Max but that was my old dog's name. Then Scott liked Edward, but do you remember the Edward guy at Uni?' Daisy recoiled in horror. 'Then he suggested Sam.'

Daisy laughed. 'The guy who turned gay after you ruined his life?'

'That's the one,' Scott said, leaning against the doorframe. 'We went through the top thousand boy's names and crossed off any dog names and anyone Clara had shagged. That left William.' He ducked back into the kitchen as his wife threw a scatter cushion.

William? Daisy raised her eyebrows and Clara smiled with utter innocence. Appropriately, she appeared to have forgotten all about the Will she'd shagged in Amnesia.

'William, Will... it's a great name.' She leant towards Clara's beach ball and said hello to William. Clara laughed. 'What?'

'He's converting a try.' She took Daisy's hand, holding it against one side of the beach ball. 'He's kicking. Talk to him again.'

'Hello, Will.'

Then Clara's stomach *moved*. Daisy shrank backwards, watching as something moved under Clara's skin. Okay, she knew it was Will, but it looked like something out of *Alien*. Daisy crossed her legs. No, thank you.

'What were you up to yesterday?' Clara asked. 'You haven't looked this bad since you left the HMS.'

'Xander and I had too much of everything bad yesterday. He's such a bad influence on me.' Like she could tell Clara the truth.

Clara opened her mouth but unusually for her, a lecture or wise advice didn't follow.

'What?' Daisy asked.

'It doesn't matter. So how are things with you two?'

'One minute we're gazing at each other like Romeo and Juliet, the next he's accusing me of shagging Finn, and I'm convinced he's copping off with the one of the girls at Oak Bank. How can I trust him now I know that the last time he worked at a five-star hotel, he shagged about two hundred girls? Aside from Tabitha, I never doubted Finn and zillions of girls threw themselves at him. The problem is Xander's—'

'Too young and too good-looking. I know, I know.' Clara exhaled a long, slow breath. 'You're an idiot, Daisy. Xander's the best thing that ever happened to you. Trust isn't usually an issue. I think you want an excuse not to admit you're in love with him.'

'Why on earth do you think he's too good-looking?' Scott asked, handing Daisy a mug of builder's strength tea. 'You're beautiful when you're not on a coke comedown. His idea or yours?'

It was a sly question, snuck in so she didn't get to compose a lie face. 'Mine, of course.'

'Then don't try making it Xander's fault,' Clara said.

'And he's no younger than you when you got married,' Scott

argued.

What chance did Daisy stand when they worked together like this? 'But Clara always said I was too young when I married Finn.'

'Yes, but really I didn't want you to run off with the HMS when you'd only known him for two months. I didn't trust him.'

'How is Xander any different?'

'Because he's Xander, not the HMS.' Clara held her hands up in defeat. 'But you know what? I give up. And I need a wee. Don't you two have secret legal matters to discuss?'

Outside, Daisy lit a cigarette and smiled as Scott opened the file on the Bobbin Mill. It couldn't be more perfect. Surely Xander and Robbie would think so too.

'It's a fantastic place,' Scott said. 'What's it for?'

'Xander's restaurant.'

He laughed. 'You're so in love with him.'

She so wasn't, but Daisy asked him something she never thought she would. 'How do you cope with Clara's past?'

'What's the real issue, Daze?' He took an illicit drag on her cigarette.

'He's shagged over three hundred girls. He's done some awful things.' *And most of it for money.* Daisy checked Clara wasn't about to walk out. 'Do you really trust her?'

'I wouldn't have married her if I didn't. Clara might've put me through hell at times, but at least she was honest. Do you think he's honest?'

Daisy nodded.

Scott wrapped an arm around her shoulders. 'Then you have to give him the benefit of the doubt. His brother used to be a total player, but look at him now.'

'Robbie?'

'He would have a girlfriend, another on the side and one lined up for later, but after he met Vanessa, he never looked at another girl.'

'Really?'

'Really.' Scott nodded. 'If I were you, I'd give it a serious go with Xander. He's a hell of a spin-bowler and makes fantastic ice cream. Jesus, I'd marry him.'

With the stereo blaring, Daisy drove home, planning how she should tackle Xander. Should she just delete the photo and never mention it again? Or should she raise holy hell because he'd effectively lied to her?

A car appeared behind her, and since everyone knew the road to Gosthwaite Mills better than her, she pulled over as soon as she could to let them pass. How odd? The Range Rover didn't overtake.

Tentatively, Daisy set off again, glancing in the rear view mirror. Who had a Range Rover and lived up the valley? Well, they were stupid not to have taken their chance to overtake her, because she refused to feel rushed. Actually, they weren't tailgating her. Maybe they were tourists who were happy to follow a local. But if that were true, how had they caught up to her to begin with? She shook her head, trying to banish her paranoia. Just because it was dark, she didn't need to freak out. Besides, crazy people couldn't afford Range Rovers.

Take care, poppet.

Oh God, what if this was about *Forfeit*? What if someone were following her? Okay, she had to stay sensible. It could be anybody. She simply had to drive another mile, turn left, and in a few hundred metres she'd be home. The Range Rover would most probably carry on to the Miller's Arms, not knowing it didn't open until six. Or they could be going to a house further up the valley. There were masses of reasons why they might be driving up this road.

Her heart raced as she turned off, praying she wouldn't be raped and/or murdered in her own home. She just had to get inside and lock the doors. Easy.

The Range Rover carried on.

What a stupid, stupid cow? Of course, they weren't following her. God, she could be melodramatic. Sighing to herself, she slowed, about to pull into Skank Manor when lights flashed in her rear view mirror.

The Range Rover had pulled up twenty metres behind her.

Chapter Twenty-Two

The Range Rover really was following her. Daisy's shaking fingers struggled to lock the car door as she looked at her completely unlit house. Should she go in? Run for cover? Or would that make her the B-movie heroine everyone could see was about to be murdered in the basement?

No phone reception. Bugger. She drove on a little, passing the gateway drive. Fabulous, three bars. Less fabulous, the Range Rover edged forwards too, still far enough for her not to see the number plates or who was inside, but near enough to know they were there. Daisy dialled Xander but, unsurprisingly, he didn't answer. He'd be busy in the kitchen at Oak Bank.

The little Mazda MX5 seemed tiny with the Range Rover's lights shining in her rear-view mirror. Bugger it. She'd embrace melodrama and laugh at herself later. Turning the Kings of Leon up, she set off, quicker than before. She'd go to the village. She'd be safe there.

The Range Rover stayed behind her, regardless of her speed. Oh fuck. She was driving too fast; no point getting away from a psycho only to plough into a dry stone wall.

'Siri?' she said to her iPhone. 'Dial Low Wood Farm.'

Thankfully, Robbie answered.

'It's Daisy. I know this sounds absolutely mental but someone's following me.' Her voice cracked and she struggled to breathe. Oh God, she was actually terrified. 'Really, they are. I've detoured past my house, but Xander's at work so I didn't stop.'

'Calm down. Where are you?'

'Heading to the village.'

'Come here. You'll be fine. Just concentrate on driving. Now, who would be following you?'

'No one. Why would anyone follow me?' Even *Mr Forfeit* had no reason to. She'd already said she'd rock up on New Year's Eve.

'Fuck, fuck, fuck,' she squealed as a corner loomed far too fast. Thank God for the MX5's awesome handling. 'I need to slow down.'

'You'll get to the crossroads soon. Go straight on, through the village. It's longer that way but more houses.'

'Okay.'

'What kind of car? Tell me about it.'

Robbie's voice was so confident, so soothing, she took a deep, slow breath. *Get a grip.*

'It's a Range Rover. Silver I think.'

'Reg number?'

'It's dark. I can't see. His lights are in my mirror and he's too far away.'

'There's a man driving?'

'What? I don't know.' She couldn't stop her right foot pressing down. The MX5 might be old and small, but in theory it could outrun the Range Rover. Sadly, she never seemed to gain any ground. 'I can't see but... and I know I shouldn't say this, but I've never seen a woman shift a car like that.'

The only lights she could see were behind her, so without slowing she ploughed straight over the crossroads. As did the Range Rover.

'He's still there, Robbie.'

'You'll be fine.' His voice oozed reassurance. 'Can you see anything else? Dealership stickers? Air-fresheners, like those Magic Trees?'

Despite her panic, Daisy laughed. 'No, clearly they have taste. Okay, I'm at the village.'

She slowed to a respectable speed and the Range Rover hung back, further than before. Daisy looked up at the faux-Victorian street lamps. He didn't want to be seen. The relative safety of the village gave her courage and she slammed her right foot down, braking hard. The Range Rover disappeared down a side road.

'They've gone.' She took a deep shuddering breath. Had she imagined it? Read too much into the situation?

'Daisy,' said Robbie, 'are you out of the village yet?'

'Nearly.' She took a left onto the road bypassing the village, but before she'd reached a decent speed, lights flashed into her mirror. She blinked. The vehicle was practically behind her.

Oh God, no.

'Daisy? What's up?'

Had she screamed out loud? With her foot pressed to the floor, the MX5 flew away, it's acceleration making a mockery of the Range Rover, but it would be short lived. On a decent road, the Range Rover could do eighty in first gear. She had to get to Low Wood Farm.

'Daisy?'

'The Range Rover just appeared, really fast.'

'You're okay. They probably went down the side street so you couldn't see them.'

'I can see your drive.' Thank God, Low Wood Farm didn't have a gate.

She hit the brakes, praising the MX5's cornering ability and, once she was cruising down the drive, she dared to look in the mirror. The Range Rover had stopped at the end of the lane with its lights off. Who was in there? She pulled up in the yard, the Range Rover drove away and she finally allowed herself to cry.

Vaguely aware of Robbie pulling her from the car, Daisy sobbed her thanks, tears pouring down her cheeks. He soon had her sitting on the sofa beside the fire, repeatedly doing his bit for the bald spot on the top of her head. Why wasn't he Xander?

'I thought I was being silly, but when I got home the house was dark and Xander's at work and the Range Rover just sat behind me.'

Vanessa bobbed down, pressing a vodka and tonic into Daisy's hands. 'I've phoned the police.'

The police? Oh God, what the hell could she tell them?

'Shall I phone Xander?' Vanessa asked.

'No,' Daisy replied, shaking her head. 'Marco's still off. They need him.'

'You need him,' Vanessa argued back.

'Honestly, I'm just being melodramatic.'

'For God's sake, Daisy,' Robbie snapped. 'We saw the car at the end of the drive. Whoever that was, they were following you.'

The debate whether to ring Xander or not was still raging twenty minutes later when the police arrived. Hardly *Inspector Morse*, PC Andy Chapman was a local boy who protected Gosthwaite from speeding cars and teens drinking in the playground. Oh, she might not be worthy of *CrimeWatch* airtime, but at least Andy patiently asked questions and she told him everything she could remember.

'One thing to consider is... a jealous or angry fan,' Andy said.

'A fan?'

'Of Finn Rousseau or Brittany Carle.'

She scowled at him. 'What are you talking about?'

PC Andy shifted uncomfortably. 'Well, it's just she's pretty upset.'

'Who is?'

'You haven't seen the papers, or seen *HeatWorld*?' Robbie asked.

Daisy shook her head, dreading what was coming next. Sure enough, Robbie handed her a copy of the Guardian and on page nine was a photo of a puffy eyed Brittany Carle in the back of a car, sitting next to a stony-faced Finn. Apparently, the day before, HeatWorld posted a piece about Finn's romantic reunion with his ex-wife. Romantic Reunion? It was nothing like, but the accompanying, slightly blurry photo showed Finn with his arms around Daisy while she laughed.

OMG.

'There are more photos on HeatWorld,' Robbie said quietly. 'I take it Xander's not seen any of this yet.'

Daisy slumped into the sofa, shaking her head. 'And I hope to God he doesn't. I can't believe what that looks like. I was saying goodbye, that's all. Bugger. So you think maybe some crazy fan might be pissed off with me, really?'

PC Andy stared at his notepad. 'Or you could have your own crazy fan. The beach photo's fairly... you know... revealing.'

The beach photo? 'Please don't tell me they're the bikini shots?'

PC Andy nodded. Oh God, she couldn't have a conversation with him now she knew he'd seen her sat astride Finn on a Cancun beach while she threatened to take off her skimpy and practically transparent bikini top.

'So Andy, now what?' *Please leave.*

'Well, we have the car description, but without a registration I can't promise–'

'That you'll find out anything. I wasn't much help, sorry.'

Andy left, saying something about getting in touch should she find herself murdered in her bed, but she stared at the fire, not really taking it in. The thought of some sex-starved perv drooling over her photo repulsed her. Thank God she hadn't stopped at home.

Out on Xander's chair-swing, Daisy tipped the last of the wine into her glass, just as his car pulled into the yard. Thank God, he was finally there. Despite his fabulous family's best efforts, it was Xander she desperately needed the hugs and reassurance from.

She didn't get it.

He stalked towards her, but the closer he got, the more he scowled. He was in a foul mood.

'I asked you to stay at home.' He ran a hand through his hair, swearing. This wasn't a foul mood, he was full on furious. 'Why the fuck haven't you answered your phone? Have you any idea how worried I've been since I missed your call?'

Her phone was on the kitchen table and reception in there was non-existent. She hated that she'd made Xander worry, but as her mum had said many times, Daisy never reacted well to being chastised. Obviously, he'd not yet spoken to Robbie. If he had, he wouldn't be cross. Or would he? Daisy stared at him, unable to answer back in case she lashed out.

'Have you seen this?' He tossed her his phone, *HeatWorld* already loaded. 'Doesn't look perfectly fucking harmless to me.'

'He was hugging me goodbye. That's all.'

'You were flirting.' Xander shook his head.

Daisy sipped her wine and glanced over the rest of the webpage, trying to ignore his frosty, arrogant attitude.

'Where the hell have you been?' Xander sat next to her and lit a cigarette.

'Clara's,' she whispered.

'Thing is,' he said, his tone deadly serious. 'You were being secretive this morning and I think you're lying now. You haven't just been to see Clara, have you? So where the hell have you been today?'

'Well, I haven't been shagging my ex-husband. He's in New York apologising to Brittany Carle.' Daisy slugged more wine. 'I'm not shagging anyone else and I've not been to lunch with anyone else. I went to see Clara. End of.'

'I don't believe you.'

She took a deep breath to stop herself from screaming at him. 'Do you want to hear what actually happened today?'

For a second, Xander's anger faltered.

'Well, go ask your brother.' She pushed him off the bench. 'Go on, piss off and ask him since you don't believe me.'

Minutes later, Xander came sprinting back across the lawn to hug the life out of her. He kissed her head, muttering the words of reassurance she desperately needed, but he didn't apologise. Neither did she.

'What did you tell the police?' he asked. 'Did you tell them about *Forfeit*?'

'Are you having a laugh? Like I'm going to tell your brother we've been playing a stupid game of dares. Besides, it's hardly like the Met rocked up. It was PC Andy.' She took a long drag on her cigarette. 'Look, I was thinking of telling them but then Andy told me about the photos on *HeatWorld* and suggested it was some weirdo. It made sense.'

Xander picked up his phone, smiling a little at the photos. 'Marco doesn't believe you're my girlfriend.'

'I thought Marco was off work, injured?'

'He came back yesterday.'

'So why were you in work today? This should've been your day off.'

'Mike needed to swap a shift.'

'Oh.' *Would you actually rather be at work than with me?*

Xander sighed, leaving the biggest pause before he crucified her with nine words. 'What's happened to us? Things aren't brilliant, are they?'

Oh God, no. The edges of her world were disintegrating. Or was she already a Has-been?

'I did go to Clara's this afternoon. I know you asked me not to, but this was too important. Come on.' She strode back to the car with Xander in tow, and took out the Bobbin Mill folder Scott had given her.

Things aren't brilliant, are they?

He'd leave her soon.

'I hate spending every night alone,' she said as they headed back to the house. 'I hate you working every day even when you don't have to. I hate the stupidly pretty girls you work with. And I hate that we fight all the time. I might really hate you being a chef because it's ruined my fucking Christmas, but I know it's important to you.'

She dropped the folder on the kitchen table and fanned out the contents, trying to steady her breathing. She mustn't cry.

'I wanted to surprise you tonight,' she said, 'but since you think I've been doing lunch and possibly my ex-husband, we'll do it now.

I think it'd make a fabulous restaurant.'

She called for Robbie to join them and he instantly began sifting through the floor plans and photos, a smile creeping onto his face.

'Is this for sale?' he asked.

'Well, it wasn't, but if you don't ask you don't get, and my lawyer was quite persuasive. Put in a sensible, realistic offer and it looks like you can have it.'

'It's a disaster zone.' Xander dismissively glanced over the photos.

'The Bobbin Mill,' she said, trying not to get annoyed at his lack of enthusiasm, 'was gutted in a fire a few weeks ago. It was a slate workshop and retail outlet, with a café. It even has the remains of a kitchen. The gardens have potential and it's next to the river. It's on the main road between Gosthwaite and Haverton with ample space for parking.

'The fire wasn't an insurance job as some suspected, but a genuine electrical fire. The owner's devastated but can't afford the rebuild because they let their insurance lapse after the place was flooded in November. Stupid him, lucky you. I've had a solicitor make some very discreet enquiries and this year was the only time it ever flooded.'

'Will they sell?' Robbie asked, smiling at her as if she were an angel.

Daisy nodded.

'But it's a hell hole,' Xander argued, staring at her as if she were mental.

'It needs renovating.' She focused on Robbie. He got it.

'What are they asking?' he asked.

'Offers around three hundred. Of course, it'll take six months and another two hundred grand to put it right.'

'It's like the OBB,' Robbie said, then laughed. 'Christ, you've got me talking like you now. Oscar's looked like this when Dad bought it.'

'Are you two crazy?' Xander didn't get it.

'Xander,' Robbie said, 'your fabulous girlfriend has found you a fucking restaurant. You ought to say thank you.'

'Look, forget the mess.' She picked up one of the photos. 'It has four solid slate walls. In a couple of months, a team of builders will have it cleaned up and reroofed. It has plumbing, electric and, because it had a café and a car park, planning permission isn't a problem. Xand, I've looked for months for potential restaurants and gastro pubs. This is the best thing I've seen by miles. It'll come in under your budget and it's on your bloody doorstep. Most of the properties I've seen are too far away and the skankiest things ever. You'd still have to do an enormous amount of work on them just to make them habitable, and you'd be confined to the layouts they already have. With this, you'll have an empty box. You can do whatever you want. Do you get it?'

A smile started at the corners of Xander's mouth as he spread the photos out. He nodded. Thank God. Xander pulled her to sit on his knee and Robbie promptly disappeared.

'Sorry.' Xander rested his forehead against hers. 'I am so sorry.'

'I'm sorry too. I hated being secretive, but I didn't want to get your hopes up. One of Scott's colleagues had the file, I had to collect it.' She wrapped her arms around Xander's neck. 'Look, I know things aren't brilliant, but I'm not shagging anyone else. I still believe in you and your restaurant.' *I still want you to be happy. Even it makes me miserable.*

'Thank you,' he said, peering at the photos. 'I can't believe you've done all this. Can we really have it? Seriously?'

She nodded. 'Can we go home now?'

'I just need to have a word with Rob.'

'I want to go home.'

'Just ten more minutes,' he promised.

She swore, and not under her breath, before taking a bottle of wine from the rack, her phone off the table and her miserable ass back out to the chair-swing. This would be the start of things to come. If he'd rather be at Oak Bank than with her, she didn't stand a chance against the bloody Bobbin Mill.

Itching with a masochistic desire to read the *HeatWorld* article, Daisy unlocked her phone, but the first notification waiting for her was **Forfeit** *invited you to like the page Forfeit – the Ultimate Game of Dares.* Her finger shook as she clicked the link. Eighty-one Likes. What the hell? Liked by who? Who knew about it?

On Saturday 24th June, five hedonistic twenty-somethings each tossed fifty pounds into a pot, gambling on their ability to do a dare. Follow their progress as they get ready to play the final round.

Who the hell would be interested? Eighty-two people, one of them a friend of hers. Clara had *liked* this nonsense?

In Round One, birthday boy James Dowson-Jones collected bras...

The names were hyperlinks. Daisy clicked hers. Daisy Fitzgerald – Forfeit Player. It wasn't her own Facebook page, but another set up by someone else. It had a shot from James' party as the profile picture. Vague details about her. And comments. People had posted comments on *her* wall.

Do the dare!

Hope you play!

Do the dare #forfeit

It had a hashtag? Oh God. It did. This wasn't real. It couldn't be real. But over on Twitter, *@ForfeitHost* had almost a hundred followers, the hashtag dozens of tweets.

@polilrichgal: Daisy's a Fugly Ho #forfeit

@1_D_fangirl_1990: hate her too, but so want to play #forfeit

@skizzerd_love: bet they don't turn up on NYE #forfeit

@wineinachippedmug: she's alright, I reckon. Daisy to win.

At least someone was on her side.

Daisy scoured the tweets, the comments, the messages. Ninety percent of it was people discussing dares they'd done or forfeits they paid, but the other ten percent? Bitchy comments, mostly decrying her as totally unfit to kiss the feet of Xander or Finn.

By the time she'd chain-smoked her way through half the bottle of wine, the Facebook page had almost three hundred Likes and *@ForfeitHost* over five hundred followers. This crap was going viral before her eyes, not hurt by the Daisy/Finn/Brittany story.

Pay the stake, Roll the dice, Do the dare.

The tweet had come from *@jellyfishmommie* at 10:45. By 11:30 that quickly became a mantra tweeted and retweeted with horrific regularity. Daisy hoped the jellyfish mommy had her jellyfish babies taken away from her. Pay the stake…

'I don't have five thousand pounds, you stupid cow.'

Pay the stake, Roll the dice, Do the dare.

At a little after three in the morning, Daisy clicked the Facebook app. Six hundred and twenty-nine Likes. That was six hundred and twenty-nine people who'd instantly get to see her tits unless she somehow found five grand by New Year's Eve.

Bethany Marshall? She'd commented on Xander's page, but mentioned Daisy. *I hope <u>Daisy's</u> dare is along the lines of James' in Round Two. She can give you a taste of your own medicine.*

The rest of his page seemed filled with girls cheering him on, listing their phone number and generally offering themselves up for his sexual pleasure. He had over a thousand *Likes*. Marcus three hundredish, James the same, Tabitha nine hundred, Daisy fifty and she assumed most of them were only because there wasn't a *Dislike* option. Why did everyone hate her?

Even Xander hated her. She glanced over at his sleeping body, his back turned to her. They'd barely spoken on the ride home.

Things aren't brilliant, are they?

How much longer would they last? How much longer would it be before he looked elsewhere, to one of those girls posting cleavage shots on his Facebook page?

Her head pounded and her mouth was so dry, even her perfume looked drinkable.

What's happened to us?

What had happened to them? On the tenth of December, his birthday, they were blissfully happy. Eighteen days later and they were a disaster. It was his job. It was killing them. Well, his job and knowing the number girls he'd shagged were killing them. And bloody Finn wasn't helping.

She needed a drink.

Quietly slipping out of bed, she pulled on Xander's jumper and padded downstairs for water and some headache pills, but sleep felt a million miles away.

She simply didn't trust Xander. Why the hell would she? Bugger, was it really bad to want wine at three am?

Twenty tweets in the time she'd been downstairs, each telling her to pay the stake, roll the dice and do the God-damned dare.

'Oh fuck off,' she growled at the phone. 'I'd like to see you lot put your money where your mouth is.'

A slow smile grew across her face. That was it. If they wanted her to do the dare, then they'd have to put their money where their bloody mouths were and pay her stake. Tying her hair back into a scruffy bun, she opened up her laptop and put the kettle on.

A bolt of agony made her cry out as Daisy tried to lift her head.

'What are you doing down here?' Xander said quietly, massaging her neck.

Daisy blinked, focussing on her surroundings. The kitchen. She'd fallen asleep at the kitchen table.

'Have you been reading those crappy messages all night?' he

asked.

'No. She's been a very clever girl.' James picked up the kettle. 'Tea?'

'Careful, James,' Daisy said. 'That sounded distinctly like a compliment.'

'Don't let it go to your head. Remember how the masses really don't like you. *Fugly ho.*'

'Will you two pack it in?' Xander snapped. 'And what the hell are you talking about?'

'Daisy has raised the five grand she needs to play the game. It's genius. Why waste our own money when it seems there are thousands of people willing to let us waste theirs.'

'Wait,' Daisy said, still rubbing her neck. 'I've raised it?'

James nodded.

'All of it?'

He smiled.

Daisy woke up her laptop and went straight to the crowdfunding site where she'd spent almost two hours setting up a *project.* She had set four days to raise the money, she'd hoped she could do it in time – she never dreamed she'd do it in five hours.

Her project had a green light. *Funded. Amount raised: Fifteen thousand three hundred and fifty pounds.*

'Oh my God,' she whispered. 'They paid up.'

'Who?' Xander asked, more than a little frustration in his voice.

'I set up a crowdfunding project then I told all those bitches badmouthing me on Twitter that if they wanted to see me do a dare, then they'd have to pay for it, because I didn't have five thousand pounds.' Daisy refreshed the page. Another fifty quid – that was for a Daisy-based slogan t-shirt of the bidder's choice, *Fugly Ho* was proving the runaway winner. 'There are different bid levels from a pound to five hundred and you get different treats in return. Well, you don't get anything for a pound, but for five hundred, I'll have dinner with the bidder.'

'Are you insane?' Xander asked, staring at her.

'No, it's genius.' James said. 'Marcus and I set up projects this morning. Of course, the bad news, Daisy is that you have fifteen thousand pounds of proof that no one likes you.'

Daisy refreshed again before flashing James a hearty smile she didn't feel. 'It's sixteen thousand now, and I'll take that hatred and turn it into a new car.'

'Why are you talking about getting the money?' Xander snapped. 'We're not going along with this. We're contacting Facebook and reporting it.'

Daisy's foot tapped on the floor. Okay, that had been the plan they'd discussed the night before, but it was the holidays. When would Facebook and Twitter respond by? And even if they took the pages down, that didn't stop that twisted @ForfeitHost from putting her photo on a bunch of Readers' Wives websites.

'We should phone the police.' Xander said.

'Be realistic,' Daisy said, 'the police were bugger all use when someone followed me home and they're going to be less fucking use when we tell them horrible people have given me fifteen thousand pounds.'

'You're really going to go out for dinner with any random stranger who's willing to pay five hundred pounds?'

Daisy raised her chin. 'Last time I checked, there was a Facebook bidding war going on for a night with your *pretty* face. Looks like your rate has gone up, sunshine.'

'Fuck you, Daisy,' he snapped, kicking a chair over on his way out.

'That was uncalled for,' James said, handing her a mug of tea.

Daisy frowned up at him. 'Maybe, but he let me down yesterday and I don't think he even realises.'

Things aren't brilliant, are they?

No, sunshine, they're bloody awful.

Chapter Twenty-Three

Even a second glass of pink champagne wasn't improving Daisy's mood. She lay on the bed in lovely red, silk underwear, trying to summon the enthusiasm to get dressed.

Things aren't brilliant, are they? Those five words played in her head on auto-repeat for the last three days. Her relationship with Xander was disintegrating. Since the car chase and *fuck you* moment, they'd tiptoe around each other until he went to work and invariably, by the time he'd get back, she'd be pissed, snippy, or quite often both.

Ten thousand pounds sat in a plain brown envelope on her dresser. What the hell was happening to her? In five days, she'd be *celebrating* the anniversary of the death of her marriage and in a few hours, she'd handover five grand so she could get a dare she was bloody certain she wouldn't want to do. If only she had some of Tabitha's coke left. How had this become her miserable existence? What happened to a quiet life in the Lakes, away from the drama of living with Finn?

'I thought you were getting dressed.' Xander leant against the bathroom door, fresh out of the shower, a towel wrapped around his waist.

They'd barely kissed each other in three days. These were definite eggshell times but dear God, he was sexy. She gave him a slow wink and arranged herself like an underwear model on the bed. 'Come and play?'

'We'll be late.' Still leaning in the doorway, his gaze swept over her, the red silk underwear clearly doing its job and Daisy rearranged her legs, aiming for more *Playboy* than *La Senza*.

'Xand, if there's ever a night to be late, it's tonight, baby.'

They were late and Daisy couldn't care less. The dalliance proved to be just what they needed to break the tension. For the first time in days, they were happy.

Just before they went into the OBB, Xander stopped, pulling

her to him for a kiss and she enjoyed a few minutes of inappropriate, very public snogging. The second he let her go, she gazed up at Xander, wanting more, but he had the most arrogant smile as he looked through the window into the OBB. The crowd at the table in the window were watching, two of them taking photos.

Daisy faux-swatted Xander with her handbag. 'You don't need to stake your claim for the world to see.'

'Fun though,' he said, struggling not to laugh as he draped a proprietary arm around her shoulders as they went into the bar.

On a merciful front, the bar wasn't crammed with Facebook and Twitter followers as Xander had feared. It seemed *@ForfeitHost* had kept the *invite* to the players. And what a miserable bunch they were.

Usually there'd be air-kisses galore, but tonight no one seemed willing to put in the effort. James, looking fabulous in a beautifully tailored tuxedo, the tie undone, ignored Daisy, his usual bored scowl never slipping as he drummed his fingers on Tabitha's bare leg. She gave a brief smile to say hello but went back to studying her nail polish and occasionally knocking back large mouthfuls of what Daisy suspected was neat vodka. By her rather glitzy black cocktail dress, Tabitha looked to be heading to the same party as James. They made a stunning, but terribly languid pair.

At least Marcus managed a cheery hello and massive hug. He glanced over at the window table, several of whom were still snapping them.

'Xander giving them some material so he gets the column inches, not the ex-husband?' Marcus whispered, trying not to laugh. 'Excellent moneymaking scam, by the way. Loved how they were paying for you to come here. You didn't even promise to do the dare.'

'I'm going to powder my nose.' Tabitha looked to Daisy. 'Coming?'

'Maybe later.' Daisy shot her a wink, before handing James a gift bag. 'Happy birthday for tomorrow.'

He took the bag, giving Xander a brief smile. 'Thank you.'

Xander laughed. 'Like I'd buy you a present. All Daisy's work.'

If James was shocked, surprised, or even mildly incredulous, he didn't show it on his face, but the bag sat on the table, untouched. That hurt. Knowing James was Xander's real BFF, Daisy had spent weeks looking for the perfect Lalique vase – to replace the one Tabitha smashed on Halloween. Daisy had planned to sell the tip money earrings to pay for it, but as it turned out, a hundred or so strangers who wanted her to do a dare paid for it instead.

'Marcus,' James demanded, 'go to the bar and order another bottle.'

Daisy, still smarting from the rejection, raised her eyebrows at Marcus and prayed he'd tell James to piss off. Disappointingly, he didn't. Marcus merely did as he was told.

As another camera flashed, maybe pointing at them, maybe at someone else, Xander perched on a tall stool, pulling Daisy to stand between his legs. She loved and resented the Neanderthal protectiveness in equal measure.

'I can't believe we're doing this crap,' he said.

'Why are you complaining?' James replied. 'You've got twenty grand in the bank and you only have to have dinner with three people.'

'Yeah, but what if one of them is a bitter Has-been?' Daisy said, kissing Xander's cheek. 'Have you seen the *He's No Angel* Facebook page Bethany Marshall started? She's using it as a therapy centre for all the girls whose hearts he's broken.'

'It crossed my mind,' Xander said, frowning around the room, 'so I ended the project.'

Daisy glanced at the envelope on the table, her eyes wide. 'So that's... *your* money?'

'I'm not promising anything to anyone for a few hundred...' He looked Daisy in the eye. 'Or even a few thousand pounds.'

'But why are you throwing away five grand of your restaurant's money?'

'Same reason we're all here,' James said. 'Because we can't say no.'

Daisy studied James. 'What do they have on you?'

'Haven't you got it?' He topped up her glass with champagne. 'The first message was a tease, to get us to pay attention. It's not about the things *we've* done. The second message was the real leverage. What were you threatened with, something about Xander?'

Daisy paused, her glass hovering before her lips. 'It was a photo of me.'

'No.' Xander shook his head. 'The photo was sent to *me* to

make *me* play. They know I won't let the photo get out there.'

Then why the hell haven't you deleted it?

James tipped his head. 'So your second message, Daisy... who does it hurt?'

'I joined before they sent it. I didn't want to know what...' *Xander had done.* 'I didn't want to know what it said. The photo was enough to make me play.'

James chinked his glass against Xander's. 'And that, says it all, my friend.'

Says what? Daisy stared, bewildered at the pair, but mercifully, Marcus returned with Tabitha in tow, her nose powdered.

'Any idea who's behind this?' Xander asked.

Heads shook.

'What bugs me,' Daisy said, 'is *why* someone would do this? Where's the benefit in getting us to do stupid dares? I could understand if it were one of us hoping to win the final pot, but none of you lot need the money.'

'So this is your way of getting another handbag?' James asked with absolute contempt.

'Bite me. Thanks to my *genius* crowdfunding idea, I can buy a handbag without fleecing you, sweetheart.'

'Play nicely, kids. It is New Year.' Xander tugged her hair, smiling.

'Anyone aiming for noble resolutions?' Marcus asked.

'I can't persuade him to ditch the weed,' Daisy replied, 'but Xander's going to give up cigarettes.'

'Again?' Marcus laughed. 'He says that every year.'

'Hey, I've done really well this year,' Xander said, faux-punching him on the arm. 'Meeting Daisy-chain-smoker hasn't helped, but by this time next year I'll have totally given up.'

'You say that every year too.' James finally cracked a smile.

'Good, I want him to fail.' Daisy laughed. 'Born again non-smokers are a pain in the arse.'

'Thanks for your support.' Xander kissed her neck. 'You could always give up too.'

Not dignifying his suggestion with a sarcastic retort, Daisy smiled at the remarkably silent Tabitha. The grubby, hair-needs-a-wash look was back and no amount of make-up could hide how tired she looked.

'You okay, Tab?'

She looked up from her beautifully manicured nails and for a moment, her eyes flashed with loathing. Shocked, Daisy blinked, but Tabitha gave a little shake of her head and the murderous look vanished. What daydream had she woken from?

'What are your resolutions, Daisy?' she asked.

'Oh, I don't do them. My October resolution was to be a better person.' Daisy winked at Marcus.

'You could give up wearing dresses that don't cover your arse,' Tabitha said, without any hint of mirth.

Xander patted Daisy's backside. 'I said no to that one.'

An hour ago, when she'd finally dressed, Xander's appreciative smile said the red-satin, Diane von Furstenberg copy met his approval. Not too big a surprise since it was the shortest dress she'd ever worn. But how dare Tabitha pull anyone up for showing a bit of leg? She'd flashed her tits for anyone who could afford a cinema ticket. Daisy opened her mouth to say just that, but Marcus mouthed, *fag* and all but dragged her outside.

'What's up with her?' Daisy asked, sulking. 'On Christmas Eve, she was my new best friend.'

He lit her cigarette. 'She and James had a tiff.'

'Aren't they related?'

'Not really. Distant cousins via marriage. They've been together since we went to Oak Bank and he ditched Lidia, but Tab went all weird at Christmas and he thinks she's shagging someone else.'

'Jonty,' Daisy said. 'I guess she doesn't mind him not keeping it in his pants.'

'Well, she's tried to back out of the party they're going to which isn't helping James' hideous mood.'

'Why do you put up with him being such a horror to you?'

'He's my brother.'

'Whatever. If my brother spoke to me like that, I'd kick the crap out him and he plays for the Harlequins.'

Marcus tipped his head. 'You don't know, do you?'

'What?'

'The sordid Dowson-Jones saga.'

'Apparently, not. Tell me?'

He sighed. 'James resents me because our father left his mum for mine.'

'OMG. I just assumed they'd hooked up after she topped herself.'

'I'm three months younger than James.'

'Oh.'

'Their mother, Ana, was a nutcase. Indy can tell a few stories. Dad met my Mum, she got pregnant and he left Ana just after James was born. Dad rarely talks about it, but he once told Indy that Ana's jealousy and histrionics drove him away. It's a rubbish reason to leave your wife and children but, whatever, here I am and he's devoted to my mum.'

She so shouldn't have pushed the conversation, but since she had, she may as well carry on. 'I heard James was a baby when she killed herself.'

'India was the one who found her. She was seven years-old. Still has nightmares, asking her mother why she didn't love her enough to want to live.'

'Oh my God.'

'Just for a little extra drama, Ana did it on James' first birthday. That's why he has the party in July. He always has.' Contempt dripped from Marcus' words. 'He and Indy will get wasted tomorrow and my mum will be there to pick up the pieces. I stay out of the way.'

Daisy peered back into the bar where James sat sulking with Tabitha. No wonder he was so messed up. The poor guy.

'Why doesn't Xander like India? I think she's amazing.'

Marcus laughed, shaking his head. 'It's New Year's Eve, let's get drunk.'

'Mission accepted, JC.' She saluted.

'JC?'

'When you admit you adore me, then I'll explain.'

'Never.'

'Why no date tonight?'

He shrugged. 'There'll be girls at Rob's party.'

Ah, that explained why he was kitted out in distressed-effect designer jeans and a cutting edge shirt, his and Xander's standard going out wardrobe, rather than black tie like the others. He was coming to the Low Wood Farm house party.

'Why don't you have a fabulous girlfriend?' she asked, truly intrigued. 'You're always with hot models but not, you know, real girls.'

'When too much is on offer you don't respect it. I'd rather wait until something kick ass came along. Like Xander did.'

It was a massive compliment and coming from Marcus, it meant the world. How much had she misunderstood this charming, intelligent, adorable guy? She hearted Marcus like a little brother. Maybe that was why she didn't flirt with him.

Back inside, the others had moved to a room off the main bar. Word had got out and a small crowd had gathered, peering through the steamed up window. Management threatened to bar anyone who even looked as if they were taking photos – a perk of Xander being the owner's son and ninety percent of the staff being in love with him.

For all the warnings, as Marcus and Daisy weaved their way through to the side bar, conversations stopped and phones were raised, lights flashed. She should've made the skirt six inches longer.

Daisy pushed past a gaggle of overly made up girls, all pretending to casually chat amongst themselves whilst never taking their eyes off Xander. Daisy gritted her teeth.

'Going to do your dare, bitch?'

Daisy's head shot around, desperate to see who said it, wanting to know why they said it, but Marcus' arm wrapped around her shoulders.

'Don't rise to it,' he whispered. 'This might be the hardest thing you ever do, but don't ever rise to any of this shit. If you don't, it'll be over in a week. We're nobodies. They'll forget us.'

In the side bar, Xander, James and Tabitha sat on leather sofas around a vast mahogany table. Oh God, the wooden *Forfeit* box sat open, ready for them to play. Daisy surreptitiously wiped her palms on her dress.

For the first time since she'd had the crowdfunding idea, she had doubts. For days, she focussed on what would happen if she couldn't play because she didn't have the money, but now she worried what would happen if she *did* play? What kind of dare would you have to do for a five grand stake?

'Right,' James said, dropping a fat envelope on the table, 'let's do this, then I can piss off somewhere fun.'

He rolled the Teetotum ball, took the dare card, read it and smiled. Okay, maybe the dares weren't so bad. Several flashes went off outside and in as Tabitha took her turn.

'Daze, it's New Year's Eve,' Xander whispered against her ear, 'let's not read the dares tonight.'

An excellent plan. She nodded and threw the gambling ball. Fourteen. Well, that couldn't be a more lovely number; her birthday was the fourteenth. She popped the card into her little clutch bag without dreaming of sneaking a peek and Xander pocketed his, swiftly followed by Marcus.

'If I ever find out any of you did this,' Xander said, his quiet voice deadly serious, 'I will kill you.'

James and Marcus tried to protest.

Xander held up an apologetic hand. 'I know, I know, but when that guy followed Daisy home, well that's a step too far.'

'Someone followed you?' Tabitha blinked and became animated for the first time that evening. 'When was this?'

With Xander's arms reassuringly snug around her, Daisy explained.

'Ohmigod, I didn't realise it was so serious.' Tabitha had decamped to her family's technology-free estate in the Highlands after Christmas Day, only discovering the *Forfeit* blackmail threats when she returned.

'Who's nursing the twenty-five grand?' Daisy asked.

'Who do you distrust the least?' James scowled.

She scowled back. 'Me.'

'I'll put it in the safe at work,' Marcus said. 'Look, this stage is supposed to have a year time limit but I can't see the point in dragging it out that long, or ruining another Christmas. What about six months? Meet up on July the first?'

They all agreed. Here's hoping @*ForfeitHost* didn't mind.

Facebook Likes: 2145. Twitter followers: 3762.
@*polilrichgal: Enjoy your dare, Fugly Ho* @*daisy_fitz* #*forfeit*

At Low Wood Farm, the hours passed in a blur of pink cava. The music rocked, the booze flowed, the people mingled. All the boxes were ticked for the perfect New Year's party, but as the big hand edged nearer to midnight, Daisy completed her third circuit of the house. Xander wasn't there.

Chair-swing, was all Robbie said when she asked if he'd seen his brother.

Armed with a freshly opened bottle, Daisy pulled on her jacket and headed outside. Sure enough, bundled up in his coat and an over-sized beanie, Xander sat on the chair-swing, rocking it gently with his long legs.

'It's nearly midnight,' she said, sitting beside him.

'I know.'

She didn't want to ask, but this was a *must do* situation. 'What's up?'

'You'll deny this,' he said, 'but you're drifting away. You don't think we're going anywhere and nothing I do is changing your mind.' He put a finger over her lips before she could respond. 'We live together, but you still put all your energy into your ex-husband.'

'I do—'

'Shush,' he said quietly. 'Just shush, Daisy. Please.'

How could she not? His eyes pleaded with her. 'Go on.'

'Finn. I've seen you looking at his photo, at the *HeatWorld* photos. You're thinking the grass is greener, that it'd be different with him now.' His finger prevented her from arguing. 'Please be careful because I don't think it will.'

She pushed his hand away. 'I'm not going to run off with my ex-husband, Xand.'

'Okay.' He smiled, humouring her. 'All I want is that... if that is what's going on, just be honest about it. You might need to be honest with yourself first though.'

He sat back, his bloody awful frown in place and relit the joint. Smoking weed, oversized beanie, chair-swing... Oh God, she was doing this to him. She was making him miserable. She was making him as miserable as being on the yacht and shagging rich women for money.

'The grass isn't greener, Daze.'

10... 9...

She opened her mouth to protest her little socks off, but he stopped her with a kiss. With a hand behind her neck, he kissed her the whole time the people in the house yelled the countdown. He let only let her go when they reached one.

'Happy New Year, Fitzgerald.'

'Happy New Year.' She stared at him. 'I'm sorry.'

Like he'd never said a word about grass being greener, he lifted her legs to drape them over his then examined her feet with a smile. 'More high-end shoes?'

Lanvin 1950s style skyscraper heels, tomato red with a pink

CAROLINE BATTEN

ankle strap, courtesy of a bunch of strangers. 'Like them?'

'I do actually. Pretty sexy.' He pushed her hair back and tipped his head to the side, studying her with curiosity. 'Have you read your dare?'

'No. We agreed not to. Why, have you?'

'Couldn't resist.'

'And, what is it?'

'Something that'll never happen.'

She'd seen him with a worse frown before, but she'd never seen him look quite so sad.

On New Year's Day, Daisy left Xander making bread while she headed up Lum Crag to walk off her hangover and process what he'd said the night before. He'd crucified her with *things aren't brilliant*, but now he'd thrown six new words at her: *you're thinking the grass is greener.* It wasn't true. *Be honest with yourself.* Okay, she'd seen a different side of Finn, and herself in recent months, but Finn was in New York with Brittany Carle, no matter what the media reported.

The northerly wind whipped her hair across her face and the dark clouds threatened rain, or maybe snow – it was bloody cold enough. The dull grey light sucked the vibrant orange from the old bracken. Winter was definitely the worst season.

Sitting on her favourite rock, Daisy took out her cigarettes and the little dare card stashed inside the packet. It took two cups of tea before she finally felt brave enough to read it. When she did, the black handwritten ink swam in front of her eyes. This had to be a joke. She blinked, several times, not believing what she saw.

'OMG.' She laughed, actually laughed.

Not a chance in hell. Not doing it. No way.

Daisy watched a vast charcoal cloud swirl over the valley before reading the card again.

Kindness: Prove your ability to love unselfishly. Create life. Get pregnant – or get someone pregnant.

Don't tell anyone what you're doing.

A kiss, Dry-Tober and get pregnant. Her three dares. The first was a doddle. The second she pulled off, quite proudly too. But the third? Well, she wasn't even going to attempt it. She lit another cigarette off her last and sipped her tea.

Get Pregnant.

Hell, she didn't fancy doing that when she was happily married. She certainly didn't want to do it when her boyfriend was about to bugger off because *things aren't brilliant.*

Could she just forget it? Forget about the blackmail? Forget about the hundreds of people who paid for her to pay the stake, roll the dice and do the dare? She flipped the card in her fingers. It was just a cream card. The handwriting on at least two of her dare cards was different. More than one person must've written the dares back in the day. Daisy could make up a new one. She could, but what? Did it matter? When it got to June, she could pick something monumental she'd done anyway.

Daisy headed down the sodding big hill with a smile on her face.

She'd fake her dare.

Too easy.

Just before she reached the edge of the village, she crossed paths with a family. Mum, dad and a little girl sat on his shoulders. The girl, who looked about the same age as Matilda, gave Daisy a cheery wave.

But doesn't that look nice?

Daisy leant against a dry stone wall, watching the backs of the departing family. The second she closed her eyes, she saw a little girl running around Skank Manor, her blonde curls bouncing, her high-pitched laughter filling Daisy's head. *Mummy, Mummy, help. Daddy's going to tickle me.* Daisy opened her eyes. What the hell was that? Was that what she wanted? A little girl, and a daddy to go with her? Should her little girl have big, brown eyes just like her father?

Daisy laughed at herself. Xander was twenty-three. He wasn't a potential father; he was potential heartbreak. Amused at her own stupidity, she wandered down the bridleway, imagining telling Xander he was going to be a dad. How quickly would he run? Maybe that's why he practised so much.

Still, Xander's entire family were bloody good-looking. As gene pools go, it wasn't a bad one to dip her toe into. Bloody hell, she wasn't intending to do the dare so why contemplate raiding Xander's gene pool? Besides, the rate things were becoming less and less brilliant, he wouldn't be around long enough for any gene pools to get raided. Daisy plodded the last hundred metres feeling more despondent than ever, and ended up sitting on the yard gate, reluctant to go into the house.

Through the kitchen window, she could see Xander cooking. Why had they become so utterly doomed? They were good friends and living together couldn't be easier – so why were they so appalling as a couple?

But what if... what if they had a reason to always be connected? Still friends, still having fun but not going out, like... *Parents With Benefits?* Had that actually crossed her mind? She'd be better off trying to make Xander see that things *were* brilliant.

He came to the sink and glanced out of the window, smiling when he spotted her. Oh God, she was a stupid cow. She couldn't lose him; she had to make this work. Finally smiling again, she jumped off the gate and jogged into the house.

'Have fun?'

She kissed him hello. 'Absolutely. All the fun a girl can have with an enormous hangover on top of a windy hill in January. What're you making?'

'Your favourite hangover cure.'

'Homemade pizza with... prosciutto, wild mushrooms... artichokes and olives?' Her absolute favourite things. She kissed him again when he nodded. 'God, sometimes I really love you.'

Xander grabbed her arm. 'Only sometimes?'

She didn't miss the hope sparkling in his eyes. 'I didn't... I just meant...'

He shook his head and let her go, swearing as he turned back to his chopping board. 'Don't want to hear it, Fitzgerald.'

Bugger. So making it work had lasted for how long? Two minutes? God, this was hopeless.

The next morning, Daisy stood in the bathroom staring at her pill packet and, after a quick peek at the sleeping gene pool, she popped the little blue pill out of the foil packet, letting it drop down the plug hole. Most likely, nothing would happen. Nothing had happened with Finn. She'd learned you didn't get pregnant at the first go.

But it did feel very underhand when she woke up the gene pool with a glint in her eye.

Chapter Twenty-Four

Forfeit Likes: 2451
@ForfeitHost followers: 6587
*@daisy_fitz followers: 2584 which was a massive hike from the 13 she
had before Christmas*
New hate tweets received: 25
Most reported Twitter handle: @polilrichgal

Up to her ears in off-white tedium, Daisy put down her paint roller
and picked up her phone. Her finger hovered over the Facebook
app, but she closed her eyes, picturing Xander's face.

With the gene pool *thoroughly* raided, he'd left for work wearing
a contented smile, but only after kissing her repeatedly and making
her promise not to obsess over Facebook likes or to check her
Twitter account.

'I promise,' she'd said.

'I love you,' he'd replied.

And then he'd kissed her with one of those face-holding kisses
which without fail turned her legs to spaghetti. She couldn't break
her promise.

Dear God she was bored.

Was it wine o'clock yet? Quarter to six. Surely that was near
enough. But as she pulled the cork on a bottle of peppery Grüner
Veltliner – an Austrian white Marcus was in love with – her phone
lit up.

'Want to come over?' Tabitha asked quietly. 'Please?'

Even if Daisy hadn't been bored beyond reason, she'd have
agreed. She'd never heard Tabitha do meek before and she was
dying to know what was going on. Hoping for some wine bar
action, Daisy changed into a pair of black wash jeans, off the
shoulder cashmere sweater and the black python Gucci knee boots
then she headed over to Windermere.

'Oh, I could so live here,' Daisy murmured, her heels sinking into the deep gravel driveway as she stared up at Tabitha's flat.

Once, Houghton Manor would have been a crumbling money pit that no one could afford, but a well-financed developer turned it into eight exorbitant apartments that a select few could afford. And hurrah, the beautiful Grade II listed building was saved.

Or maybe not she couldn't live there. Five minutes later, clutching the stitch in her side, Daisy banged on Tabitha's door. She daren't guess what Tabitha's top floor apartment cost, with its roof terrace and uninterrupted lake views, but for the money Daisy would've expected a bloody lift. Xander had persuaded her to go running with him a few times, but trying to jog upstairs in heels wasn't quite as easy. By the time she got to the third floor, she was a breathless, sweaty mess.

'Come in,' Tabitha yelled.

Still struggling to breathe, Daisy slumped onto the cream suede sofa and gazed in awe at her surroundings. The enormous ceiling rose and original cornices contrasted brilliantly with the contemporary furniture, although it lacked a few homely touches, like junk lying around. Fabulous living room, but it felt a little like a high-end hotel.

'Well then you'd better fuck off!' Tabitha shrieked from another room.

Daisy sat up. Was Tabitha telling her to get out? Daisy turned, just in time to see some trustafarian, complete with beard and dreadlocks, dash out, slamming the door behind him. He didn't look Daisy's way, but she did clock his very nice arse.

'Tab?' she called, stripping off her coat and scarf. 'Who was that?'

'No one that matters,' Tabitha purred as she leant against the doorframe.

'OMG.'

Tabitha's hair was nearly as famous as her – thick, luscious and auburn, she'd never needed extensions to bulk out her locks. Two days ago, they'd tumbled halfway down her back. Now she had one, maybe two, inches left.

'You look absolutely incredible,' Daisy said. Tabitha's cheekbones and huge emerald eyes took over her face. 'Did you have that done today?'

'At a party last night. Not sure what I'd taken and I'm not sure what I think. It seemed a good idea at the time, but it's taking a teensy bit of getting used to.'

She clutched at it with her fingers. On New Year's Eve she had perfectly French manicured nails, but now she'd bitten them all down and painted them the darkest purple. Not that Daisy was looking her best, but with pallid skin and enormous black shadows under her eyes, Tabitha looked as if she were being subjected to ritual abuse.

'What's going on and who the hell's Mr. Dreads?'

'He's just some guy.' Tabitha flopped down on the sofa.

'Marcus said James thought you were seeing someone else.' Daisy took a slug of Tabitha's wine. 'Are you?'

She shrugged. 'I'm not seeing anyone.'

'And how you can you be shagging James anyway?' Daisy asked, lighting a cigarette.

'We go back a long way.' She laughed at Daisy's raised eyebrows. 'I was twenty-two. He was sixteen. Perfectly legal and very fun. Do you want to go out for dinner or just get wasted?'

'Wasted.' How could she not love Tabitha? 'I'll ring Xand in a bit. He can pick me up on his way home from work. It's funny, I'd assumed James was secretly gay.'

'He'll do either.'

'So why don't you go out with him?'

'His heart belongs elsewhere.' Her face broke into an evil smile. 'That's why he hates you.'

'Xander? He loves Xander?' Daisy stared at her for a moment. 'Please tell me they never...'

'Fuck no. Xander's as hetero as they come.'

'So, what's up?'

'Ugh. Where's all the fun gone, Daisy-chain? Fuck the consequences kind of fun. Everything's so serious. Even the silly *Forfeit* game has had the fun sucked out of it. What happened when you got followed?'

As Daisy explained, Tabitha's frown worsened.

'What would have happened if you'd gone home? Would he have come into your house do you think?'

'I try not to think about it. Oh, thanks for this.' She took Tabitha's little silver coke tin out of her bag. 'Life saver over Christmas.'

'You're welcome, sweetie. Want to grab a bottle of fizz?'

'Don't need to ask me twice.'

Tabitha's fridge, a retro number, sat at odds to the rest of the kitchen. Like the living room, the white, high gloss units were pristine and clutter free but on the fridge, a billion mirrored star magnets held up photos, invites, notes and lists. Finally, proof Tabitha actually lived there.

The fridge contents were similar to Daisy's pre-Xander – two bottles of champagne, three white wine, a four pack of Red Bull, mineral water and a soothing eye gel-pack. Nostalgia for the lazy days, dossing at Clara's, washed over her. She mourned for her liquid fridge. These days it was full of rare breed pork, goats cheese and weird looking mushrooms.

'OMG,' she said, moving a photo of Tabitha and James to one side to peer more clearly at a pair of red tickets underneath. 'You have tickets to Chapter for *tonight*? The Swedish House Mafia versus Avicii, in *Manchester.* How is that even possible?'

'Gold dust tickets. Should've sold them on eBay, but couldn't be arsed.'

That was the hottest club in Manchester and Daisy had never been. If only. She pouted for a second, but the pop of the champagne cork did wonders to ease away her sulkiness. As did the sight of Tabitha doing a couple of lines. Two remained.

'So how's life with Romeo and Juliet?' Tabitha asked, handing Daisy a rolled up twenty.

Xander wouldn't be impressed if she went home coked up, but bugger it.

'It's okay,' Daisy lied, before hoovering up her lines. 'Living together works really well. He's dreadfully untidy so I wander around after him, checking out his arse and picking up his clothes. He spends his non-working hours trying to concoct the tastiest creations to tempt me to get fat.'

'Have you got over your jealousy?'

'Pretty much. It's his turn now. Apparently I flirt.'

'Like no one I've ever seen before,' Tabitha said, tinkling that laugh. 'It's so bloody effective, I've started taking notes.'

She rearranged herself to sit exactly as Daisy was and then pulled off a better than plausible impression of her: accent, voice, actions.

'But I thought you could only do posh or Irish harlot?'

She stuck out her tongue. 'I did a dodgy Welsh accent when I was twenty and no one lets me forget it. These days I do Irish or posh because it's so God-damned easy and I've become too God-damned lazy. But if the Corrie thing happens, that'll do for a few years. I'm keeping my actual acting skills under wraps until my looks start to fade. Then, when they think I'm over, I'll come back with a powerhouse, character performance and wow every single bastard who said I couldn't act. I'll reinvent myself and be the biggest success this country has ever seen.'

Was she wildly driven or utterly deluded?

'Can I try on your sequined Hervé Léger dress?' Daisy asked, adding her best pleading smile.

For the next two hours, they acted like teenagers at a sleepover, trying on clothes and giggling over how great they looked in *Grazia* and *Heat*. Like Daisy, Tabitha had kept the copies too.

Xander rang at nine.

'OMG, you must be psychic, I was about to ring you,' Daisy said, tottering around in a red leather mini skirt.

'Where are you?'

'Tabitha's. Can you pick me up on your way home?'

'I'm already home.' He sighed. 'I finished early. Marco owed me.'

Daisy frowned, as much at his news as at how pale her legs were. 'But I can't drive.' Tabitha mouthed, *Stay.* 'Tab said I could stay here.'

'Well, if that's okay?' He sounded... pleased.

'Oh, okay. I'll see you tomorrow then.'

'I'll miss you. Have a good night.'

I'll miss you? But he usually said, *love you* before he hung up. And why did he sound relieved?

'Night.' Daisy hung up, staring at her phone. 'Now we're back to me being jealous. He sounded positively chipper when I said I was staying here.' She frowned at Tabitha. 'He's shagging someone else, isn't he?'

She laughed her tinkly laugh. 'Of course he isn't and I'd know because he'd tell James, and James tells me everything. He's probably looking forward to watching a bit of porn and getting a decent night's sleep. I hear you keep him awake a lot.'

Or maybe he's shagging Nadia.

Daisy pottered to the fridge, needing more booze to block mental images of the Polish tittle-tattle undressing Xander. Her glossy black hair, her stupidly long legs... Oh, the shiny red tickets for Chapter. They couldn't. They shouldn't.

But she wandered back to Tabitha holding up the tickets.

'Really, sweetie?' Tabitha asked, her eyes glinting.

'Let's go party before we're thirty and time starts crawling over our faces.'

'Won't Xander mind?'

'Things are so bloody awful between us, probably yes.' Daisy took a deep breath. 'You know, it's almost a year since I left Finn.'

Tabitha stared at the rug. 'Daisy...'

'It's okay.' Daisy didn't mean to make her feel bad. 'But I could do with the escapism before I deal with it. I think Xander will understand.' Although it'd be a lot easier if she never told him. 'It's not like we have to go wild. We'll just go for a dance.'

Tabitha nodded. 'Let's find something to wear.'

Daisy was already heading to Tab's extensive, high-end wardrobe, because if the gene pool did get raided then this could be the very last time she'd get to go clubbing. And she fully intended to enjoy every bloody second of it.

In a micro-short white Balmain number of Tabitha's, opaque black tights and the Gucci boots, Daisy stood at a Chapter bar with an insouciant attitude only a couple of lines could give. She'd piled her hair in a scruffy up-do and hid behind seventeen layers of black eye-shadow. Tabitha looked unrecognisable in black velvet shorts, matching halter-neck and bright red killer heels. With lashings of green eye make-up, she looked ready for a photo shoot in Vogue. They were so going to be in *Grazia* the following week.

Why hadn't she been clubbing for over a year? The bass from the house tunes battled for control of her heartbeat and, God, being a VIP in this club rocked. Styled as an old-fashioned library with leather armchairs, huge oak tables and actual books on the wooden shelves, Daisy was in heaven.

'You've pulled,' Tabitha said, nodding discretely to the end of the bar.

Daisy glanced over, trying to hide her smile, but the cute guy smiled back. A seven? She turned to Tabitha. 'I came here to dance, not cop off with something half as good as what I've got at home.'

'What about something twice as good?' asked a guy behind her.

Finn? Daisy turned, absurdly pleased to see his gorgeous face.

To hell with nonchalant, she gave him a huge smile and a bigger hug.

'If what you have at home is so good,' Finn said, whispering in her ear, 'why's it at home and you're here?'

Self-consciously, she glanced around, detangling herself from his arms. 'You sure you want to be seen with me?'

His eyes creased as he smiled. 'Hell, yeah.'

'Why aren't you in New York?' Tabitha asked sweetly.

He nodded up to the DJ. 'Dee, it's Jesus. I wouldn't miss his first big gig for anything. Especially not when he's warm up for the Mafia.'

Daisy squinted against the lights, grinning when the DJ waved to her. He'd been Finn's BFF for years. 'Brittany forgiven you yet?'

'Xander forgiven you yet?'

'It was a hug goodbye. There's nothing to forgive.'

'Exactly.' He high-fived her. 'Sooner people realise that we're just friends, the better.'

'Then, can we dance?' Daisy asked, already bobbing to the beat.

Finn grinned.

Within thirty minutes, Tab had abandoned them, whisked away by Todd, a DJ friend of Finn's from New York, and Daisy spent a glorious hour dancing her socks off with her ex-husband. It was like old times, the good old times. Her best dancing buddy ever.

No. Xander was her best dancing buddy. *I promise.*

'I need a drink,' she said, glancing at her watch. Eleven o'clock. Okay, maybe this wasn't such a good idea.

Taking her hand, Finn weaved his way through to the bar. Oh, so Tab had pulled. Todd had his hand on her arse and Tabitha raked her hair back, laughing sexily as he spoke in her ear. That left Daisy with Finn.

Daisy's unease grew when Finn asked for a bottle of Evian and produced pills. Oh God.

'They're only Es,' Finn said, grinning at her wide eyes. With a small, speckled pill between his finger and thumb, his eyes never left hers as he dropped it into her mouth.

Only Es? What was she doing? Ugh, and why did they have to taste so vile? She knocked back several mouthfuls of water, still grimacing, then frowned at Tabitha as she wound her arms around Todd.

'Don't you dare leave me alone with Finn,' Daisy hissed.

'I'll be glued to your side,' she purred, never once taking her eyes off Todd.

Daisy looked to Finn for reassurance, but as he necked a pill, desire pulsed through her. When had they ever come up in a club and not ended up shagging in the toilets? The timing had to be spot on to appreciate the full rushes of coming up, yet not to be so trashed you couldn't come. The last time had been amazing.

Finn's eyes burned through her. He knew what she was thinking. And she knew he was thinking exactly the same.

'No,' she said, shaking her head. 'Not a chance.'

'You're no fun.'

Thankfully, rather than try anything on, Finn just proved why he'd be an eternal BFF, nearly as much fun to dance with as Xander. Why had Xander been so happy for her to stay at Tabitha's? She shook her head, simultaneously banishing the image of Nadia dropping to her knees in front of Xander and triggering a massive head rush. Delicious tingles surged over her scalp, down her neck and spine – these were bloody good pills. She smiled at Finn and lost herself in his eyes.

Drowning in blue...

Oh, the grass wasn't greener, but God it was fun. Fuzzy edge, forget the real world, dance 'til your toes bled kind of fun.

Out of control...

And fuck she'd missed him. It. She'd missed this, clubbing, getting high. Not him.

'Addicted you,' they sang together, his arm hooked around her neck, his forehead rested against hers.

I'm addicted to you.

They sang along to the Avicii track grinning like idiots. There'd be no flirting – just dancing, hardcore dancing. It was only midnight; they could do this for hours yet.

By two, the bass had taken control of her heartbeat, her face ached from smiling and she didn't care if she looked a sweating, bedraggled mess. She was a goddess and Finn her absolute best friend. Their fingers were firmly linked together as they returned from a cigarette break, dancing their way towards Tabitha who, for once, wasn't snogging Todd. He was cute, but Daisy itched to cut his chin length hair and pull up his jeans.

Why was Tabitha staring like that? She stood perfectly still while the crowd bobbed around her. Finn's hand held hers a little tighter and Daisy's heart fluttered out of sync to the bass. Even waving a hand in Tabitha's face didn't change her friend's wide-eyed stare.

'Tab?' Finn asked.

Her eyes rolled back and she collapsed. Finn caught her before she hit the ground, scooping her up in his arms. Terrified, Daisy followed as he ran behind the nearest bar, down a corridor and into the back rooms. Staff appeared, security type people, someone did first aid, someone said an ambulance was on the way, someone stressed this was Tabitha Doyle and someone asked what she'd taken.

Daisy admitted to the coke and an E. Finn said she'd taken two. Two? One of those little speckled buggers had Daisy trashed.

She sat on a table in the corner, praying her unconscious friend would wake up. What if she died? They laid her on a sofa, her pale skin blue under the LED lights – her red hair and the green eyeshadow luminous in comparison. Finn sat beside Daisy, motionless as he stared at Tabitha.

'You gave her *two*?'

'Get real. I didn't *give* her anything. Tabitha did what she does best. She demanded. Besides, she knows her limits.'

'Apparently not,' Daisy hissed.

Finn flinched as if she'd slapped him. Oh God, he already must feel guilty as hell; he didn't need her to make him feel worse.

'I'm sorry.' She took hold of his hand and his fingers closed around hers.

'Me too.' His eyes never left Tabitha.

Where the fuck was the ambulance?

Minutes passed, but they felt like hours. The staff were brilliant and by the time the ambulance arrived, Tabitha's eyes had begun to flutter. Daisy almost cried with relief.

'I'll be back in a sec,' Finn said, darting over to the paramedics.

She stared bewildered as Finn chatted with the paramedics and stroked Tabitha's brow. Alone, half-dressed in a Manchester club… what the hell should Daisy do now? Mercifully, Finn soon came back over, his relief palpable as he engulfed her in the longest hug.

'They think she overheated. She'll be kept in overnight, but she's okay.' He looked down at Daisy with nothing but concern in his eyes. 'Are *you* okay, Dee?'

Daisy nodded and they followed the stretcher. How the hell would she get home?

'Daisy?' Tabitha tugged the oxygen mask off. 'I had an awesome time. Shall we do it again next week?' She tried to give her silly, tinkly laugh but as it faded to a cough, she let the paramedic put the mask back over her face. Tabitha had never looked more fragile or bizarrely, more beautiful.

Relieved her friend would be okay, Daisy braved checking her phone. Six Facebook notifications waited. She'd been tagged in three photos. Bugger.

'Hey...' With a gentle hand, Finn lifted up her chin. 'Do you want to get a drink at the bar next door?'

'I have to go home.' Daisy showed him her phone. 'He's going to find out about this and he's going to kill me.'

Finn stepped closer and slipped a hand around her waist. 'Then don't ring him.'

Oh shit. 'I have to go home.'

'No, you don't.'

His hand drifted down, over the curve of her arse and Daisy fought not to drag her fingers through his hair, not to press her body against his. That familiar aftershave, those mesmerising eyes... What if?

'This is a very nice dress,' he whispered, 'but you'd look much better out of it.'

The hand slid up her back then moved forwards until his thumb skimmed over a rock hard nipple. Oh dear God. His eyes dared her to stop him.

She didn't.

'I have a suite at the Lowry,' he said, his breath brushing her cheek.

Oh Christ, he'd pulled her closer. Or had she moved? Only millimetres of hot, electric air stood between them.

No.

Now, why hadn't she said it aloud?

'Dee?'

She reached up, running a hand through his hair. He closed his eyes and she gave in, pressing herself closer. His heart thumped in his chest as her thumb traced over his lips, so familiar, so perfect, so fucking snoggable. He kissed her lingering thumb, just kissed it, but he may as well have stuck his hand in her pants. She wanted him. Badly. And the love of her stupid life wanted her just as much.

This was it, the answer to everything. Her and Finn. It wouldn't be like before. They'd be different. They'd have kids, she'd say sorry, they'd be happy. Why had she ever bloody left?

Because he kicked me out. The grass isn't greener.

'No.' She turned away and rang Xander.

'Daze? What's up?' he asked, his voice full of sleep and confusion. 'Time is it?'

'I... it's half-two but, Xand, I need you to pick me up.'

'Can't you get a taxi?'

'No.'

There's no way she'd trust her half-dressed body with a taxi driver for an hour long journey into the countryside. Suddenly, she burst into tears. It had to be the adrenalin.

'Thing is,' she sobbed. 'I'm in Manchester. I went clubbing with Tabitha, but she took too many pills and collapsed. She's gone to hospital. She's going to be fine, but I don't know what to do.'

To her surprise, he didn't yell. More worryingly, he remained ominously quiet. She daren't look at Finn.

'Please come and get me, Xand. I'm scared.' *I'm scared I'll shag my ex-husband.*

'I'll be there in an hour,' he said, softly. 'Be outside.'

Daisy was still thanking him when he hung up. What a disaster. Slumped against the wall, she took out her compact and set about wiping away the seventeen layers of eye-shadow which had formed black streaks down her cheeks.

'Perfect again,' Finn said, adding a smile before he nodded to a door marked Private. 'This goes to the bar next door. We can get a drink while we wait for your boyfriend. Fuck knows I need one.'

How was he taking her rejection so happily? 'Sorry.'

'Don't be.' He glanced down at his feet, but not before she'd seen his sheepish grin. 'I think you just stopped us from making a *very* stupid mistake.'

Oh.

'Come on, Dee. We need a very strong drink.'

Within ten minutes, they were sitting on a secluded terrace bar having a cigarette and a bloody good chat. She told him all about the house, the work she'd done, and he described life in New York – the traffic, the noise, the awesome delis. Daisy sat cross-legged, her head resting on the back of her chair.

'I wish we'd gone together.'

He glanced down at his Jack Daniels and nodded. 'Me too.'

'Did we give up too easily?' she asked. 'I think I did.'

'I think so too.' He kissed her cheek. 'But no sad talk. How's the old school?'

Daisy fought a naughty smile. 'I bumped into Cressida Marshall last term.'

'Oh.'

'OMG, you're actually blushing. You *never* blush.'

'Shit, what did she say?'

Daisy flashed her eyes at him. 'She asked for your number.'

'You didn't give it to her, did you?'

As they both fell apart laughing, Daisy looked up to see Xander stood on the edge of the terrace, with his hands in his pockets, his jaw twitching.

'I said, outside.' Xander gave Finn a murderous look. 'What the fuck is he doing here?'

Daisy jumped up to say hello and to put some distance between her and Finn. 'Hi.'

'Car,' Xander snapped.

'Thanks for everything.' She quickly hugged Finn. Xander swore, practically dragging her away. 'What? He's been looking after me.'

'Must've done a bloody good job. You don't look very fucking scared now.' He marched her towards the exit, handing her a pair of sunglasses. 'Photographers.'

Sure enough, as they walked out, the flashes were seizure inducing. What the hell? They weren't even famous. Xander handed the doorman a twenty and Daisy dived into Xander's car which was parked on double yellows outside the club.

'You're taking the points for any tickets I get tonight.' He frowned at her jiggling feet. 'What have you taken?'

'Coke, E.'

Wasn't she allowed to have fun? Was it her fault Tabitha took too much? This was all Tabitha's fault. If she hadn't been such a greedy cow, they'd have had a marvellous time dancing until dawn and Xander would've been none the wiser.

He turned up the radio so they couldn't talk and Daisy relaxed. They shouldn't talk. She wasn't sure what might come out of her mouth. It could be anything from *I love you* to *Fuck you*. Thankfully, the M6 whizzed by at a steady 110mph, sometimes more, rarely less. She'd so be copping for a driving ban.

At home, she expected him to dive off to bed, leaving her to watch MTV until the bloody drugs wore off. Instead, he sat on the sofa and skinned up. Daisy stood in front of the fire watching him, waiting for the lecture. Maybe she should leap in first with a sorry, or thank you?

'No,' he said, stopping her as she opened her mouth. 'Get me a beer, please. I'm going to smoke this, then you've got some making up to do.'

Making up to do? She tried not to look too pleased.

He laughed, without much humour. 'You'll be horny as hell, if I know you, and I'd prefer to get it out of your system than have you sit here thinking about that bastard all night.'

Well, she didn't see that coming, but she couldn't see any issue with obeying either instruction. Maybe this wasn't so bad after all. 'Aren't you going to yell at me?'

'What's the point? You're off your tits.' He looked her over. 'But so we're clear, I fully intend to take every advantage of the situation.'

Her body fizzed with excitement and she smiled her most dazzling smile. 'Bring it on, baby.'

Chapter Twenty-Five

She was awake, wide awake; from comatose to clarity in one vast leap. She ached all over. Who the hell had removed all her internal organs? She winced as her tongue brushed the bit of her cheek she'd accidentally bitten the night before. The night before? Oh fuck. She closed her eyes... Finn, Xander... *I promise.* She wanted to throw up and it had nothing to do with the E-comedown.

What a stupid, stupid cow. Why did she always think it was better to regret something she'd done than something she hadn't?

Poor Xander. She'd dragged him out of bed at half-two in the morning, getting him to drive for an hour to rescue her and how had she rewarded him? By practically sitting on her ex-husband's knee. But not once did Xander yell at her and although he'd threatened to take advantage of her loved up state, he hadn't. In fact, it rated as the most fabulous sofa shagging ever. Ever-ever.

Even that morning, when he told her he'd already walked Birkin, he didn't get cross. He just quietly told her to get some sleep. He looked so sad; sad like the day she admitted she'd been to lunch with Finn. Was this the final nail?

Tears loomed, but she forced them back and her arse out of bed. Xander would be home by half-ten – she had five hours to turn herself into a decent person.

After a long sin-absolving shower, she moisturised every inch of her skin before putting on a grey cashmere mini-dress and knitted leggings. Last time she'd worn the outfit, Xander said she looked adorable. She tied her hair in a loose plait, hoping he'd think the same again. To add an air of innocence, she limited her make-up to a layer of mascara, but couldn't resist a little Chanel No.5, Xander's favourite scent.

Tabitha still hadn't responded to her messages. Daisy should've gone with her to the hospital. What kind of friend was she? If she had, she wouldn't be in half this mess.

Oh, please be okay, Tabby-cat.

With the discarded clothes in the washer, ashtrays emptied and the bottles in the recycling bin, she removed any evidence of the previous night's debauchery. A quick vacuuming and a scrub of the kitchen left the place looking like a show home.

Daisy? Adorable. House? Immaculate. Soul? A little less black.

Finally, she headed down the bridleway for Birkin's evening walk. The frosty air and starlit sky lifted her mood and after a bowl of Xander's vegetable and lentil soup, her cheeks had a healthy glow once again. By ten-fifteen, when she curled up on the sofa with her first vodka and tonic, she finally felt vaguely human.

Only, Xander didn't come home at half-ten. Or half-eleven when she poured her third drink. He walked in at midnight.

'Hi.' She took a long, nervous drag on her cigarette as he sat on the opposite sofa. 'I'm sorry.'

He lit a joint but didn't speak.

'I'm sorry for going out and I'm sorry for dragging you out of bed. Thank you so much for coming to get me.'

'Are you sorry for... whatever the hell you were doing with your ex-husband?' He stretched his long legs out, a hand behind his head, trying to look relaxed and confident but that little muscle in his jaw twitched away. 'You promised.'

I know, I know. 'Xand, we were just talking. But, if you want, then I'm really sorry I was talking to him.'

'*Talking* to him?'

'Yes, *talking* to him.' She hadn't shagged him, for God's sake. She could've, but she hadn't. But she mustn't lash out. 'Where the hell have you been 'til now?'

'Don't start, Daisy. You're... I went to talk to Rob.' His shoulders sagged as he stared at his hands, the faux-confidence abandoned, replaced by the same sad look he'd had that morning.

Bugger this. She moved to perch on the sofa next to him.

'I'm sorry I went out. I had no idea Finn would be there. It's just Tabitha had the tickets and I haven't been clubbing for such a long time. I'm sorry for everything, but I just needed to go out, to let my hair down like when it was James' birthday, because... there's a bad day coming.'

Xander raised his head, his eyes filled with concern and she dug her nails in her palms. This was underhanded and a lie – the same lie she'd fed to Tabitha to justify going out. What had she turned into? When did she think it was okay to lie? No, it wasn't like that; this was self-preservation.

'The fifth is when *it* happened,' she said, staring at the ceiling. 'I just want to forget. Finn wasn't exactly the person I wanted to see, but he did look after Tabitha. And me.'

Xander held her hand. 'Okay.'

She'd been forgiven, but her soul had gone back to black. They headed up to bed, still holding hands, and she silently vowed that her life would revolve around making Xander happy and their relationship work. She needed to become girlfriend of the bloody year. She needed to do whatever it took to make him like her again. She needed to say *I love you.*

Yes, that was it. She'd lie and tell him she loved him.

The girlfriend of the bloody year mission didn't get off to a great start when she woke late. As she towel dried her hair, she watched Xander through the window, walking back down the bridleway with Birkin. She really wanted to get her good behaviour off to a good start – having him walk her dog, yet again, wasn't how she planned to do it.

Dressed and wandering downstairs, she wrapped a pashmina around her shoulders, protecting herself against the cold, austere house. Oh God, Xander had taken all the Christmas decorations down. What time did he get up? Muttering a hundred swearwords, she poured coffee and rang Tabitha.

'Finally, how are you?' Daisy asked, relieved she was alive. 'I must've sent you twenty messages yesterday.'

'I've never felt better, darling. I checked into a clinic and they gave me the most amazing vitamin drip. I look and feel really rather fabulous.' She sounded it.

'Xander's a tad annoyed with me.'

'Mmm, I can imagine.'

In the yard, Birkin jumped up as Xander threw a ball in the air. Xander laughed. Daisy smiled. 'I'm so glad you're okay. It was the scariest thing, watching you keel over.'

After Tabitha went over her ordeal – the trauma of seaweed body wraps and sedatives on demand – Daisy hung up, a little miffed as she seemed to have come off worse than Tabitha.

With her stomach grumbling, Daisy popped a slice of bread in the toaster and, sipping her coffee, picked up the copy of *Cumbria Life* lying on the table. Not something they usually had in the house, but the post-it note marking a page near the back piqued her nosey nature.

Under a sumptuous photo of Oak Bank, Ella Andrews had written a glowing review. Couldn't see her getting *blow a dog* in *Cumbria Life*.

God, she heaped praising simile after praising simile on Jonty's food but, more fabulously, she'd returned for a second visit after she heard *third generation chef, Alexander Golding, grandson of Michelin-starred Oliver Golding* was now working there. She proclaimed the quality, imagination and presentation had improved twenty percent and any of her tiny criticisms from the first visit were now obsolete. Oak Bank was *on the map and hotly rumoured to be listed as a Rising Star in the forthcoming Michelin Guide. With Alexander Golding on the team, surely a star has to be on the cards next year.*

OMG.

Xander came in, laughing with a thoroughly over-excited Birkin and Daisy smiled with pride. Sadly, the second Xander spotted her, his smile dissolved into the worst scowl.

The toaster popped.

Daisy jumped, bashing her hip against the cooker, but she gritted her teeth and held up the article. 'This is fantastic.'

'It is,' he said, nodding before picking up a tabloid newspaper, 'but this has taken the edge off it.'

He dropped the paper on the worktop next to her and stabbed a finger at the large photo on page five. She blinked but the photo didn't change. Oh, fuck. The photographer's focus might've been on Tabitha but Xander's finger pointed at Daisy. Despite the grainy image, no one could miss her cosy smile as she looked up at Finn. He had one arm around her, the other lifting up her face. She knew Finn was being sweet, asking if she wanted to dance or drink, but to the rest of the world it looked like he was about to kiss her, or he'd just finished the job.

'It wasn't like... I didn't...' Hemmed in by the kitchen units with tears looming, she turned from Xander's emotionless stare. Two holdalls and a large box sat by the door. She glanced around the kitchen and her stomach went into freefall. His knives had gone from the block. 'You're leaving?'

'Yes.' His expression didn't change. The muscle in his jaw didn't twitch.

Her heart hammered in her chest, but after Thierry when she was fifteen, Daisy didn't sit in toilets crying; she fought back. Joe, a boyfriend who dumped her just before their A-Levels, received a tirade not unlike the one Bethany Marshall gave Xander. But Xander hadn't left. She mustn't lash out.

'Why haven't you gone already?'

'I don't know.' He leant against the island. 'I keep hoping there'll be some… explanation, just something.'

'Nothing happened.'

'What are you doing tomorrow?'

She shrugged, last day of the holidays? 'Hairdressers.'

He closed his eyes for a second and folded his arms. She'd failed to answer the million dollar question correctly.

'That photo isn't the half of it,' he said. 'James came round this morning to fill me in. The photos online are something else. Do you want to see them?'

She shook her head. She'd done nothing more than dance with Finn, but no doubt the evidence would look much more incriminating, especially if someone had snapped them talking in the corridor. But she'd turned Finn down. The grass wasn't greener.

'Shock horror it was James. What, did he waltz in carrying the paper and a hip flask, saying I told you so? He never has liked me.'

'Fuck off. If Clara had seen a photo of me with my arms wrapped around another girl, wouldn't you expect her to tell you?'

'But nothing happened.' How many times did she have to say it?

'Because Tab collapsed? What if I hadn't come to pick you up?'

He stared into her eyes like he was looking for the answers of the universe, but she had none to give. Her eyes burned as she stared back.

Nothing would have happened because he's… not you. I would never, ever cheat on you. You are…

She blinked, trying to focus her thoughts.

Xander turned to look out of the window. 'You don't know. You have no idea what you'd have done, do you?'

Yes, I do. Nothing would have happened.

Why couldn't she just tell him? Why were the words in her head but not coming out of her mouth? And why wasn't her unable-to-lie face not telling him?

Her hands shook as she lit a cigarette. 'And what did you do that night? You were very keen for me to stay at Tabitha's. I'm not stupid.'

'What?'

'Nadia?'

He ran his fingers through his hair. 'I can't do this anymore. I love you, but I can't.'

She poured herself a large vodka, not bothering with tonic, just three ice cubes and a squeeze of lime. A big mouthful bolstered her courage and she turned to face him, taking a long drag on her cigarette.

'If you really did love me, you wouldn't be leaving because I got wasted and hung out with my ex-husband. That's not what love is.'

'Like you'd know. You still love the manipulative bastard who threw you out of the house.'

'He's not manipulative.'

'Really? You can't stand having your hands held above your head, so to prove who's in charge, he tied you to a bed for two days.'

She frowned.

'Daisy, I know you. There are several things you're really not into, but he did them all, didn't he?

She took another long drag on her cigarette.

'Fuck. I'm right, aren't I? That fucking...' Xander put his hands behind his head, taking a deep breath. 'He tied you to that bed and did whatever the fuck he liked.'

Slowly, she exhaled the smoke, not having a clue how to fight back.

'You do know what that's called, don't you? It's called rape, Daisy.'

'It wasn't like that,' she said, her words little more than a whisper.

'Wasn't it?' Xander shook his head, his frown worse than ever. 'Or is that just what you tell yourself?'

No, it wasn't like that. But she merely stared at him, unable to talk.

'Even the other night... I'd never push you where you don't want to go. Or is that the problem? You want another bad boy.'

Daisy still had no words as she watched him light a cigarette, swear and put it out. Even when he was about to leave her, he was sticking to his New Year's resolution.

'Stupid fucking me,' he said, moving to the other side of the island, getting away from her. 'I've spent hours on eating disorder websites trying to understand you. He treats you like crap and you love him. I treat you like a princess and you still think you fucking love him.'

No, not anymore. She stubbed out her cigarette and poured another vodka.

'Daisy, it's half-ten. Is that your answer, to get shitfaced again?'

She shrugged, staring at the glass. She was a Has-been. It was her turn. But she wouldn't lash out like Bethany or go crazy like Holly. She'd handle it with dignity and grace.

'You know you never loved him, not really.'

'What? Of course—'

'No. I don't think you even like him.'

'Don't be ridic—'

'What are you doing tomorrow, Daisy?'

'Going to the hairdressers, I've already...' Oh God, was tomorrow the fifth? She had no idea what the date was. Her eyes burned again.

'You don't give a fuck about it being a year since you left him. It was just an excuse you used so I'd forgive you. Seriously, do you give a fuck about anyone but yourself?'

She turned away from him before the tears started tumbling out. Dignity and grace. Xander came to stand behind her, resting his head against the back of hers. She dug her nails into her palms, swallowing hard and taking deep breaths. *Stop crying.*

'Daze,' he whispered, 'do you give a fuck?'

He turned her to face him and she looked up. Of course she gave a fuck, but he was too young and too good-looking. He was always going to leave her so it may as well be now.

'I went out clubbing. It wasn't planned and aside from taking a few illicit drugs, I didn't do anything wrong. I didn't lie to you, or shag anyone else. Yet, you're leaving.' She wasn't lashing out. This was very grown-up of her.

'I'm not leaving because you went out. I'm leaving because you don't give a fuck about me.'

'So why haven't you left already? Or were you hoping to make me beg, like you made Bethany?'

Anger flashed across his face. 'I haven't left already because I've been waiting for a fucking miracle. We could've been perfect, Daisy, but you've never given us a chance because you think I'm too young and too good-looking. You don't trust me, but I've done nothing to make you think that.'

'Are you taking the piss? There are three hundred and eighteen reasons and twelve grand of diamond encrusted tip money jewellery that tell me not to trust you. I've only flirted and you don't trust me. You fucked *every* girl in your year for a bet and you expect me to trust you.' His shoulders dropped. She shouldn't have mentioned the bet. 'But you're still here?'

'Still waiting for a miracle.' His eyes shone with tears as he turned away, leaning on the worktop.

That's when she understood why he looked so sad yesterday morning. He'd known he was leaving then.

'You'd decided this yesterday,' she said quietly. There'd be no more shouting, no more recriminations. There was no point. They were over.

'Not really. I'd hoped...' He turned, facing her again. 'But you're killing me, Daisy. You're literally ripping me apart. Bethany's going to be delighted.'

She'd contributed a hundred pounds to Daisy's crowdfunding project, *hoping you'll get to give that bastard a taste of his own medicine.*

Xander, as he'd done so many times before, stood in front of Daisy and pushed her hair back. And like all the other times, she stopped breathing for a minute and stared into his fabulous brown eyes.

If she told him she loved him, he'd stay. She had to tell him, now.

'Daisy, I love you, but I can't live with you anymore. I can't live with someone who won't love me back. It's too hard.'

Tell him.

He dropped a lingering kiss on the top of her head then walked away.

He'd left.

She wanted to run after him, to beg him to stay, but after lighting a cigarette with shaking hands, she clutched her glass and sank to the floor. Tears poured down her cheeks, but she behaved with dignity and grace.

Chapter Twenty-Six

A year ago, Daisy came home to find her husband had packed her bags. A day ago, she got up to find her boyfriend had packed his bags. Next year, she'd stay in bed for January.

The salon junior combed her hair and Daisy stared at the horror looking back from the mirror. Grey skin, a spot on her chin, black circles under her eyes. Okay the lighting in the hairdressers made everyone look dreadful, but Daisy was in worse shape than Tabitha after New Year's Eve.

Much of the previous day was a vodka-induced blur, but snippets like Robbie calling would pop into her head, making her feel sicker than her hangover. He'd begged her to go round, to apologise to Xander, but she'd told him to *fuck right off*.

No. She mustn't think about Robbie or Xander while she sat in front of the mirror.

The heat and chemical stench of the hairdresser's threatened to overwhelm her, but Daisy forced a pleasant smile for the teenaged assistant.

'What does your tattoo mean?' Daisy squinted, trying to make sense of the swirls on the girl's inside of teenaged assistant's forearm.

'It's roman numerals of my son's birthday. I got them off the internet.'

Roman numerals? She knew eleven would be XI, which seemed fortuitous, but she had to dig out her phone to Google the three hundred. For the first time that day, Daisy smiled and asked the salon junior where she had her tattoo done.

Haverton Ink, here I come.

Clara hugged her the minute she stepped into the house. 'How are you?'

'Being a divorcee, one year on? Fine. Boyfriend walking out? Fine.' She held Clara at arm's length. She looked so beautiful – vast but beautiful. 'Bump's looking good. How are you?'

'Concerned. He's walked out and you're *fine*?'

'Can I say I told you so?' Daisy wandered into the kitchen and put the kettle on. 'I told you he'd leave and I told you he'd try to break my heart like he did all the others. This is exactly why I refused to fall in love with him and his pretty face. He left yesterday.'

'I know.'

Daisy paused as she took the mugs out of the cupboard. 'You *know*?'

'He phoned to ask me to keep an eye on you,' she said. 'Hair looks good. How's the hangover?'

'Bloody awful,' Daisy admitted, hating Clara knew her so well. Still, her hair did look awesome. She'd had six inches chopped off her layers and the curls, no longer weighted down went wild – a white blond cloud of corkscrews and ringlets tumbled to her shoulders. 'Check this out.'

She lifted her hair and peeled back the plaster, showing Clara the tattoo running down the back of her neck. It looked ace but getting it done had hurt like hell.

'Jesus. Is that real?' Clara asked.

'Bethany Marshall has an X on her wrist but this is way cooler.' Gently she put the plaster back and shook out her enormous hair. 'It's a reminder not to be so fucking stupid in the future.'

'What, by being fucking stupid now? You've just branded yourself with a tattoo that says *CCCXI*.'

'I thought it would look better than 311. Five hundred and ten would've been perfectly apt, DX, our initials. If he'd have shagged around for the last few years like he did at eighteen, he could've hit over five hundred easily.' She poured the boiling water on the teabags. 'It's only one or two a week since he was fifteen.'

'Have you actually lost your mind? It's a tattoo, Daisy.'

'Did I tell you he has one? He had it done in Barbados. It says *Drunk And Fucked*. I bet he's regretting that now.' She couldn't look at Clara, but stared at the wedding photo of her and Scott on the wall. Xander had kissed Daisy under that same tree.

'What have you done, Daisy?'

'It's a tattoo, not the end of the world.'

Clara took the milk out of the fridge, sighing. 'No, I mean to Xander.'

'I didn't do anything. He left, not me.' The tears stung Daisy's eyes but she wouldn't cry. Instead, she poured the milk in the mugs, blinking furiously.

'Look at you. You're completely in love with him.'

'No, I'm not and I don't want to love him.'

'Why on earth don't you want to love him? He's fabulous and he's in love with you.'

'I don't want to be a crazy Has-been like Holly or Bethany.'

'Well, you're a tattoo in their direction.' With her eyes focused on the ceiling, Clara sighed, no doubt trying to form a diplomatic response. 'Daisy, you need to sort your head out before you lose him for good.'

Was she mental? 'But I don't want him back. He was always going to leave.'

'Oh for...' Clara banged her mug on the worktop. 'You're wearing a shitload of make-up to hide your puffy red eyes. You've been crying because it's killing you that he's left. And it's killing you, because you love him.'

Daisy turned the lighter over and over in her hand.

'When the HMS threw you out,' Clara went on, 'you barely shed a tear. Do you know why?'

As if Daisy could stop Clara when she was in rant mode.

'Because you don't love Finn. You never did.'

'Of course I loved him. I wouldn't have spent six months trying to kill myself with alcohol if I didn't.'

'Yes, you would,' Clara said with uncharacteristic bitterness. 'It's what one *fucking* does when one's husband throws you out on the street.' Ah, the very words Daisy had yelled last April when Clara told her she was drinking too much. 'Getting divorced was a really good excuse for you to get drunk and start smoking again, but we're not at university any more. This is real life.'

'You're supposed to be on my side.'

'I am. You know that. But Xander told me what he said yesterday and I think he's right. About everything.'

'No.' Why was she doing this? Daisy rubbed the heel of her hand against her temple. 'He said Finn was a manipulative bastard–'

'Yep.'

'That I never loved Finn.'

'Totally right.'

Daisy laughed without any humour. 'What about me having an eating disorder, is that right too?'

'D'you know what that tattoo should say?' Clara asked. 'I'm a freaking idiot.'

Daisy gave the door a satisfying slam as she left.

At home, after she finished the vodka, Daisy managed a bottle of wine before she was sick. The tears poured out again as she sat on the bathroom floor remembering the last time she threw up after drinking far too much. Xander had hugged her better. He'd hugged and hugged her, and a few hours later, he'd said, *I think I love you.*

Pay the stake, roll the dice, do the dare.

Daisy hovered in the doorway, staring at the words written on the blackboard. The Year Nine kids sat at their desks, heads down, a few shoulders shaking with suppressed laughter.

No, no, no.

The tweets, the Facebook comments, she could just about cope with them, but not to her face. They'd stuck the bikini shot underneath it.

Not here.

That morning, she'd woken with swollen eyes, horrendous breath and a hangover worse than the day before. The alarm had beeped away, but she'd barely registered it as she stared at the empty pillow beside. He'd left her. School, she'd hoped, would keep her brain busy, to stop her thinking about him.

With her head held high, she strode into the classroom. 'You do realise, I can use your last assignments to match the handwriting.'

The majority fidgeted, a few gave away telltale glances, but Daisy sat on her desk, determined to stare each twatty posh kid in the eye.

'Whoever wrote that has until the end of class to 'fess up. After that, I'll work out who wrote it and you'll be reported.'

She stood up and turned to pick up the board rubber.

'Nice tat, miss.' That was Rex Maguire.

'Finn like it, miss?' Jacinta Moore added.

Should she report the whole bloody class to the head? Slowly, she erased the Forfeit mantra. But what difference would it make? They no longer respected her and who could blame them? She was some failed fashion student who wasn't even qualified to teach in state schools. The only reason she'd got the job was because she was married to Finn. She was a fraud – a drug-taking, superclub-frequenting fraud.

Then again, she was a fraud with ten grand in the bank.

'You know what?' she said to the ceiling. 'I don't need this fucking shit.'

Students followed her into the corridor, some giggling, others taking photos on their phones. Utterly against the school rules, but not her problem anymore.

'Alright, miss?' Travis McKillican loitered in the doorway to the photography lab, blatantly giving her a coat of looking at, and spending far too much time over her tits. 'Have a good New Year?'

No respect and they'd all seen her in a nigh-on transparent bikini.

'Total TILF.' She suspected that was Joe Cohen, but no way was she looking around to check.

'TILF,' said another in agreement.

'Fugly ho,' chipped in a girl.

Daisy stopped, wheeling around. Freya Dowson-Gunn. How could she have been so stupid? 'The ultimate poor little rich girl... You started the Twitter campaign.'

'I didn't start anything.' She folded her arms, facing up to Daisy. 'You're a fugly ho cougar. Stay away from my boyfriend.'

As she walked away, Daisy's nails pressed harder and harder into her palms, but she would not cry.

Not here.

By the time Clara turned up at one, Daisy had retreated back to bed. The comforting arms of her best-friend induced a fresh flood of wailing, but Clara didn't say a word. How many times over the past year had she soaked Clara's shoulders? Too many to count. Eventually, Daisy calmed, taking shuddering gulps of air.

'I've lost my job,' she whispered.

'The overconfident, twatty posh kids have already splashed it all over Facebook and Twitter.' Clara broke out a smile. 'But you officially have TILF status now.'

Wiping her tears away, Daisy laughed. 'Every cloud and all that.'

'That painting's the wrong way up and it's obscene. I love it.' Clara shifted, making Daisy sit up. 'I wasn't very tactful yesterday, sorry. Are you ready to listen? Even if it's not what you want to hear? This might hurt.'

Daisy nodded and Clara handed her a photo. It showed the two of them on a Cornish beach the summer before she met Finn. Of course, Clara looked fabulous in a black strapless tankini, but she'd reluctantly lent Daisy her all-time favourite, stupidly flattering, white Dolce and Gabanna bikini. That day, Daisy looked sexy as hell – the first time and only she'd ever looked better than Clara. She'd pulled TJ, the cutest Aussie lifeguard, that afternoon, starting a rather lovely holiday fling.

'Yes, you looked amazing. Way better than me.' Clara laughed, nudging Daisy before taking the D&G bikini out of her bag. 'Now, put it on. You need to see the truth. I said this might hurt.'

With the photo in hand, Daisy stood before the mirror wearing the little white halter-neck bikini. In the photo, she was slim but sexy, and in her head that's how she still looked.

The reality was horrific.

She had to hold the pants up to stop them falling down. She could see ribs, hip bones, collar bone, chest bone... Name a bone and it was visible. What she couldn't see were any of the sexy curves she had in the photo. Turning sideways, tears trickled down her cheeks. Her hip bones stuck out nearly as much as her tits. How had Xander ever fancied her?

'Crying's a good sign, shows you're not too far gone.' Clara handed her a jumper of Xander's. 'You do look like you have an eating disorder. You look awful.'

Daisy pulled on the jumper, wincing as the intoxicating scent of Xander hit her, and she hugged her knees, wishing they were him.

'I don't think you are anorexic for the record,' Clara said, 'but you have gone too far. The last year has been hard, but you use drama as an excuse to drink too much and stop eating. Xander's worried about you and he's right to be. Are you below a six?'

Daisy rested her heavy head on her knees. 'Yes.'

'Can you understand why he thinks you have an eating disorder?'

Daisy nodded.

'Ready to discuss the rest?'

'Yes, but can I take this bloody bikini off first?'

'I'll make tea.'

After Clara buggered off downstairs, Daisy braved the mirror, this time safely hidden under Xander's jumper. How had she let herself get to a size zero again? The rest of the British population had put on half a stone over Christmas, but she'd managed to lose it, with a bloody chef in the house. It had to stop.

Dressed in her favourite feel-good jeans and Xander's jumper, she ran downstairs, handing Clara the bikini.

'Thank you,' Daisy said, gratefully taking a cup of tea and a milk-chocolate Hobnob.

'Don't thank me yet. You haven't heard what else I've got to say.' Clara smiled, no doubt trying to reassure her. 'Who do you want to start with, Xander or Finn?'

'Finn,' she said, but not without a good dose of trepidation.

'You don't love him. You never did.' Clara held up a hand as Daisy opened her mouth to argue. 'Just listen. Please.'

Too weary to fight, Daisy lit a cigarette and sat back, determined to hear out her very best-friend, because she had to do something other than cry.

'You were blown away by Finn, because he's the Hollyoaks eye-candy you used to wet your pants over when you were sixteen. Going out with him, getting married after two months... It was like you were on some gap year. He meant you didn't need a job, or to pay off your student loans, but do you actually like him?'

She did, didn't she? Daisy took a long drag on her cigarette. Of course she did.

'Think about it, Daisy. If he'd been just some bloke, would you have kissed him on top of that mountain?'

Probably not. More tears trickled down Daisy's face and she pulled her feet up to sit cross-legged. God, this wasn't pleasant but it felt more productive than hiding in bed. Had she really been such a deluded idiot for the last three years?

'Something happened, didn't it?' Clara asked, picking up a Hobnob. 'Before he tied you to a bed for two days.'

Daisy couldn't tell her about Yana. Clara had done the

occasional three-way, but she'd always be the most beautiful girl in the room. She'd never understand how horrendous it was to watch her husband kiss someone as stunning as Yana.

'What do I do about Xander?' Daisy whispered.

'Do you want him back?'

Daisy nodded, unable to stop the sobbing again. 'But it's never going to work. He's too young and too good-looking.'

Clara hit her with a scatter cushion. 'Do you actually believe that?' Daisy nodded and she sighed. 'Okay, one, he's perfectly grown-up. Didn't the list tell you anything? He played the field for years, but then he wanted to settle down. He knows who he is and what he wants, which is more than I can say about you. Two, he's not too good-looking.'

'But he's perfect and I'm not.' Worried about her protruding bones and lack of tits, Daisy picked up another Hobnob.

'No, you're not perfect but neither is Xander. He's very good looking but too... footballer.'

Daisy laughed. Clara preferred her men rugby-player big – she'd fancied the pants off Daisy's brother for years.

'Daisy-chain-smoker, you married an eye-candy actor. You're every bit as fabulous as Xander. You've got your big curly hair that doesn't need highlights and you've got that body. I work my arse off to stay fit but you? Jesus, even seriously under-weight, you still have an hour-glass figure.'

'I look hideous.'

'You just need to stop drinking and start eating. Look, I know you don't think you're conventionally pretty, but you're more than that. You're sexy pretty.' Clara paused, nibbling the corner of a Hobnob. 'Now, what's the real reason you're trying so hard not to love him?'

'I don't trust him.' Letting her head fall back against the sofa, Daisy sighed. 'How can I? The Year Eleven Bet? Three *hundred* and nineteen girls by the time he's twenty-three?'

'Scott told me you'd asked if he trusted me, cow-face.'

'Sorry.'

'Maybe it's because I've been where he is, but I think you can trust Xander. And I want you to make it work with him because he's made you happier than I've seen you since pre-HMS. He lets you be you. He puts up with the awful bits and brings out the good bits.'

Clara had just about finished her Hobnob. Daisy had eaten four. How was she the anorexic one?

'But things have been hideous,' Daisy said. 'He thinks I'm shagging Finn and I think he's shagging half the hotel. We just don't work.'

'What really happened in Manchester? Did you shag Finn?'

'He offered, but I said no. '

'So even though it looks like you copped off with Finn, you *know* you'd never shag around because you like Xander so much. You need to trust him. It doesn't matter what he's done in the past, he loves you and he'd never shag around either. You need to realise you love him too.' Clara poured more tea. 'Let's say you are in love with Xander, when did it start?'

'The morning after James' party,' Daisy said without hesitation. God, they'd spent hours on that floating deck, chatting, even sleeping in each other's arms.

'You've never trusted Xander because you've been scared he'd leave you, but you're the one who's made it happen.' Clara frowned as she peered out of the window. 'Bugger, it's snowing.'

The snowflakes drifted down, just like they had at the day Daisy and Xander had bought the Christmas tree. 'Last time it tried to snow, I almost told him I loved him.'

'Then it's time to decide how you really feel and tell him.' Clara pulled on her coat. 'Sorry, but I'd better get out of the valley before the roads get treacherous.'

Daisy hugged her, wishing she could stay. 'Thank you.'

'He'll come back, Daze. He loves you.'

After a lunch of reheated casserole from the freezer, Daisy sat on the worktop, watching the snow fall. There had to be three inches on the ground already. If Xander were there, they'd be getting excited, hoping they could build a snowman. If he were there.

Daisy turned her phone over in her hand. She could call him, just to talk. But, then again, he only wanted to hear three little words. Could she say them? When things were right, they were amazing. She felt connected to him. She always had. Why didn't she at least tell him that the day he left? Sighing, she lit a cigarette. She didn't tell him because she was imploding. He'd asked if she cared. Of course she cared. She cared so bloody much, she couldn't get the words out. Surely that meant she loved him.

Call him.

Her phone lit up, the ringtone startling her. It was the landline at Low Wood Farm. Oh dear God. Her heart stopped as she said hello but then plummeted to her stomach when the wrong Golding brother spoke.

'It's Rob. I just wanted to check—'

'I'm so sorry for telling you to fuck off the other day.' *Is Xander there? Is he okay?*

'I'm not forgiving you.' He sighed. 'You're going to be snowed in if it carries on like this. Are you okay? Do you need anything for Birkin? I'm assuming you're well stocked with wine and vodka?' He swore, but his words were muffled. 'Do you need anything?'

Just your brother. 'No,' she said quietly and he hung up.

Who was she kidding? She couldn't just ring Xander, have a quick chat and expect everything to be okay. Robbie could've been her ally, instead she'd alienated him. She stared at the bottle of Pinot Noir sitting beside the cooker. No.

For the rest of the day, she watched nonsense on TV and didn't dare ring Xander in case he told her to piss off. That's if he even bothered to answer the phone.

At nine o'clock, she received a text from Marcus, *1990 Chateau Latour Pauillac.* The wine he'd wagered that she'd break Xander's heart. She opened the Pinot Noir and shed a few more tears. She'd broken Xander's heart and she'd lost Robbie and Marcus's respect. That ripped her apart more than any tweet or Facebook comment.

She was a hideous person.

Day three in the big idiot house. Utterly determined to go and talk to Xander, Daisy opened the curtains wearing a short-lived smile. Aside from the cornflower blue sky, everything had been blanketed in white. She wasn't going anywhere.

To keep herself busy and to make up for drinking a bottle of wine the night before, she made a batch of vegetable and lentil soup, just like Xander had taught her. Using her special needs knife, which she adored, she chopped the vegetables – not into the perfect cubes he always asked for, but acceptably even in size. Obviously, the end result wasn't a patch on the soups he'd made, but it tasted pretty good and she'd been remarkably tidy making it.

Beep, beep.

She closed her eyes and prayed. *Please be from Xander.*

It wasn't, but Tallulah came in a close second. How would the grown-ups feel if they knew she was texting the enemy? The photo in the message showed Tallulah, Vanessa, Matilda, Dora and the enormous snowman they'd built in the descending darkness the day before. In the background, Xander sat on his chair-swing, arms folded, watching his beloved family having a whale of a time. Daisy zoomed in on his desolate face. His hat, pulled over his brow, hid his frown, but the dejection was clear to see. A tear splashed onto the phone. She needed to hug him, to make him happy again. Wasn't that all she'd ever wanted?

Oh dear God, it was true. She really did love him. Why was she such an idiot? If she loved Finn, really wanted him, she'd have gone back to the Lowry that night in Manchester. But she hadn't. She'd already known then – the grass wasn't bloody greener. Tears continued to roll down her cheeks, but the biggest smile took over her face.

I'm completely in love with Xander.

She had to tell him.

She glanced out of the window, swearing at the unploughed road. No way could she get the MX5 out.

But there were footprints on the bridleway. She could walk.

If she wrapped up warm, it'd be fine. It was what, three miles? Might take her an hour and a half, maybe two in the snow. What if she slipped and died? No one would discover her body until it was too late. Oh for God's sake, she needed to see Xander. Walk. Run. Just go.

She swapped her jeans for two pairs of leggings then layered on a fleece, down jacket, mittens and scarf. With her hair in pigtails to look girlish and endearing, she pulled on an over-sized beanie and rang Clara.

'Okay, I might die,' she said 'but I'm not letting the snow keep me from Xander. I love him and I'm going to tell him.' Daisy grinned as Clara squealed. 'I'm going to walk to Low Wood Farm. If I don't ring you in two hours, please can you ask the Mountain Rescue to come and find my cold, dead body?'

Chapter Twenty-Seven

Despite the blue sky and dazzling sunshine, the temperature hadn't risen much above zero, but after two days cooped up in the house, Daisy happily sucked the crisp, cold air into her lungs. It couldn't be a better day for getting Xander back.

Should she say *I love you* first, or *I'm sorry*? Would it matter? She'd walk up the Low Wood Farm drive and Xander would come out of the house, smiling as he waited for her. There'd be hugs and kisses – clearly he'd appreciate the risk she'd taken, trudging for miles in the snow just to say *I love you*.

'I love you.' She tried it out loud. Birkin raised his ears and wagged his tail. 'Yes, poppet. I love you too.'

In the midst of kissing, she'd say *sorry* and *I love you* about a million times. Then they'd get Robbie to bring them home in his Discovery. Robbie. Bugger. I'm not forgiving you, he'd said. Robbie hated her. What if Xander hated her? What if after three days he'd realised he was better off without her? Daisy upped her pace to a power-walk.

Okay, this would be fine. Oh please, God, let it be fine.

Her heart rate increased with every stride she took down the driveway of Low Wood Farm. Had she ever felt so nervous? Maybe when she ran off with Finn? No. Her dad had given her an emergency credit card and made a point of saying she could always come home. But there was no coming back from this. Xander had to love her.

She texted Clara to say she'd made it alive then smiled as the front door opened, just as she'd imagined. Only she hadn't imagined Robbie standing there looking ready to bludgeon her with a blunt instrument. About ten metres from him, she stopped.

'Hi,' she said.

Slowly, he shook his head, the murderous scowl never leaving his face, then turned back into the house. Fighting nature's instinct to flee, Daisy followed him. In the kitchen, Vanessa told Tallulah to take Matilda into the living room.

'It's not bloody fair,' Tallulah whined. 'I never get to hear what's going on, all I've done is take–'

'Now,' Robbie snapped.

She scarpered with Matilda who waved, giving Daisy a toothy grin. At least someone was happy to see her; Vanessa fussed about, making tea, clearly refusing to look at Daisy. With no one else to turn to, Daisy straightened her shoulders and faced Robbie.

'Can I talk to him?'

'No.' His jaw muscle twitched just like Xander's did when he was cross. 'He's not here. You're about seven hours too late.'

Daisy sank onto a dining chair. 'What?'

'When he realised you weren't going to turn up, he buggered off. He didn't even say goodbye. I could fucking kill you.' Thankfully, before he gave into temptation, Robbie stormed out, slamming the door behind him.

'But Xander can't just leave,' Daisy whispered. 'He can't. Where's he gone?'

'We don't know.' Vanessa finally turned, wiping her hands on a tea towel. 'We took the girls sledging this morning and when we came back, he'd gone. He'd left that on the table.' She pointed to a screwed up piece of paper resting against the teapot.

With shaky hands, Daisy flattened the crumpled note and his scruffy, boy scrawl gave her a rush of love stronger than any she'd had on that bloody E.

Sorry for not saying goodbye but I have to get out of here. If I stay, I'll go back. x

ps. Make sure she's okay.

Her tears fell onto the paper, smudging the ink. *Make sure she's okay.* He still cared about her, but he'd gone.

'Oh my God, what am I going to do?' Daisy stared at Vanessa. 'I need him back.'

'Daisy, you've really hurt him.' Vanessa sat down at the table, not bothering to hide the anger in her eyes. 'What did you do?'

'Don't you know? I thought Xander told you everything.'

'He used to 'til he met you.' She screwed up her face. 'To tell you the truth, I was a bit miffed to begin with, but I realised Xander needed advice on how to win you over and let's face it, pulling girls is Rob's area of expertise.' She tipped her head and narrowed her eyes, the look she gave Matilda to check if she'd really eaten her peas or stuffed them in her socks. 'Did you sleep with Finn?'

'No, of course I didn't. Xander left because I'm this hideous selfish person who didn't love him.'

'What? That's it? You didn't do anything dreadful?'

'Well, breaking his heart is pretty dreadful.' Daisy wiped her eyes and read the note again. *If I stay, I'll go back.*

'You need to talk to Rob,' Vanessa said.

'Not a chance. He'll kill me.'

'He's just upset.'

Haven't *just upset* people been known to murder the people they were *just upset* with? After a great deal of stalling, Daisy wandered into the yard looking for Robbie. He came out of a stable smiling but slammed the door when he saw her, kicking the bottom latch so hard it bounced back.

'Get out of my fucking sight,' he snarled. 'I might actually hit you.'

'That's not going to help Xander.' Amazingly, her voice held more confidence than she felt in her entire body. 'You really don't know where he's gone?'

'No. Which means I can't look out for him. You know what he gets like when he's down... and if he doesn't come back, if he gives up on his dream again—'

Enough. She fled. She stumbled through the snow, wanting to run home but getting only as far as Xander's chair-swing. The last time she'd sat there was on New Year's Eve – the night he said the grass isn't greener. God, was he right. How many times had he been right? How could he know her better than she knew herself?

Curling up on the swing, she hugged her knees as she sobbed.

'You do love him then?' Robbie sat down beside her.

Daisy nodded, wiping her eyes. 'Yes, of course I do. I've been such an idiot, but I honestly didn't realise until Tallulah sent a photo of him.'

'I sent the photo.'

Daisy laughed through her tears. She ought to have known. 'Christ, you're good.'

'Don't you ever forget it.' He put his arm around her and grateful, she huddled against him.

'What did he say?'

'Nothing really. He ran, watched TV or sat here smoking 'til all hours of the morning.' He took a deep breath. 'I'd told him to leave you.'

'You did what?'

Robbie's arm tightened around her shoulders. 'Xander's been miserable since that bloody awful mess with Lucy Errington, but you made him happy again. You just needed something to make you realise what everyone else in the world has known for months, that you're perfect for each other. I'd expected you to come running here the next day, that's if you'd let him leave in the first place.'

'Stage three in the Wagging plan?'

'Who the hell told you?'

'Not telling.'

'I bet it was Scott. Traitor.'

Daisy smiled for a moment, relishing Robbie's friendship. 'What am I going to do about Xander?'

'He'll come back. He hates being away from home.'

'When?'

'Week? Maybe two.' A slow smile spread over Robbie's face. 'Of course, when we find out where he is, you're going to show him you love him and drag him back.'

'What if he tells me to piss off?'

'If you're lucky enough to find true love, you have to be brave enough to fight for it.'

She really ought to have swooned, but instead, she giggled. 'OMG, you really are a dreadful romantic.'

'Nothing dreadful about it,' he said, totally unabashed. 'Have you tried ringing him?'

She shook her head.

'Well, get on with it.'

'I can't.'

'Just ring him.'

'I need to work out what the hell I'd say, first.' She braved looking him in the eye. 'I'm really sorry for swearing at you the other day.'

'You're forgiven.' He dropped a kiss on her head. 'Let's go inside. I'm freezing. Did you walk all the way here?'

'No other way. To be honest, I would've crawled here on my hands and knees if it were the only way.'

'Now who's the dreadful romantic?' He grinned, holding open the kitchen door for her.

With hope on her side once again, Daisy reread Xander's note. *p.s. Make sure she's okay.* Surely that meant he still loved her. Surely.

Just ring him. That night she should've called Xander but of course, she didn't. She called Clara, cried some more, drank a bottle of wine, watched nonsense on TV, smoked a lot but never came close to dialling his number. The next day, Robbie popped round and hid his disappointment admirably when she admitted she hadn't rung Xander.

'Please, Daisy. Just ring him.'

The idea almost made her physically sick.

It didn't take Clara long to join in with the *Just Ring Him* mantra.

'Just call him,' she almost yelled down the phone, her patience beyond tested by Daisy's incessant dithering.

'But what if he tells me to piss off?'

'Then you have to take it on the bloody chin, but just ring him.'

But still Daisy couldn't do it.

Three days later, six days after Xander walked out, Robbie gave up on mantras and hiding his disappointment. Instead, he came round with Tallulah. She handed Daisy a card, decorated with a big purple heart she'd painted and a lot of glitter.

'Matilda helped,' she admitted. 'But Dad said you needed a big dose of courage, like the cowardly lion.'

A ten-year-old had given her a bravery card. 'Did you set this up to make me feel obliged?'

Robbie raised his eyebrows to Lulu who stomped outside with Birkin, muttering how she never got to find out what was going on.

'What's up?'

Robbie leant on the worktop, rubbing his forehead. 'He still won't answer my calls and they've accepted the offer on the Mill. I have the contracts, but if he doesn't sign in the next two weeks, they'll put it on the market.' Robbie helped himself to a cigarette. 'I'm off to Italy on Saturday. Daisy, you *have* to ring him.'

There was no way she'd let Xander sacrifice the Bobbin Mill. 'Okay.'

Robbie hugged her, kissing her head and doing his bit for the bald spot. 'Thank you.'

As soon as he left, she picked up her phone. But put it down while she poured a glass of wine. And lit a cigarette. Bugger. She curled up on the sofa. What would she say? *I'm sorry* or *I love you?*

Okay, she'd dial, the solid beat from FUN's *Tonight* would sound, the ringtone he had for her, then he'd pick up the phone and she'd say... something. She pressed dial.

The person you have dialled...

Fuck.

She threw the phone to the other end of the sofa. Either he was somewhere with no reception, he'd turned his phone off or, more likely, he'd just blocked her call.

For the next four days, she called him at eight in the morning, three in the afternoon and at midnight on two wine-induced occasions. She sent *I need to talk to you* and *Robbie needs to talk to you* texts but the messages went unanswered and her calls only ever reached his answer machine.

Despairing, she rang Tabitha.

'Xander's left me. Totally buggered off.'

'Oh sweetie, that's awful. Where's he gone?'

'No one knows. Robbie said James is claiming ignorance. Do you know anything?'

'Haven't heard a dicky bird.'

'Tab... please can you work your magic on James, see if he knows? I'm going to see Marcus.'

'Leave it with me.' She gave her silly, tinkly laugh. 'Ooh, I feel like cupid.'

'Thank you so much, Tabby-cat.'

'You're most welcome, Daisy-chain. I really hope you get him back. You so deserve each other.'

God, to think she gave Tabitha a *Chance* card. Daisy blushed at her own egotistical bullshit. She was definitely buying Tabitha a massive present to say thank you for being such a good friend. The crowdfunding project could pay for a Chloé handbag, maybe.

Chapter Twenty-Eight

While she waited for news from Tabitha, Daisy registered with *ludicrouslyexpensivewines.com* and, six hundred pounds of crowdfunding cash later, she pulled up at Dowson-Jones Manor, otherwise known as Hawthwaite Hall. The previous July, the house had been stripped of its splendour but now, with a crystal chandelier the size of a small car hanging in the centre of the double height ceiling and a Jackson Pollock original on the wall, opulence wasn't the word. Marcus met her in the hallway where the Radio One DJ had held court and she'd danced for hours with Xander.

'Do you seriously think you can win me over with a bottle of wine?' Marcus asked, his withering glare turned up to nuclear winter.

Daisy almost balked, but Marcus repeatedly glanced to the *1990 Chateau Latour Pauillac* in her hand. 'I'm merely paying my debt. It seems you were right. I'm a vain, judgemental party girl who didn't understand what she had.'

Nodding, Marcus took the wine. 'But if you think I'm cracking this open for you to get drunk on, you're very, very wrong. This is going in my collection. Come in, *tesoro*.'

As the sun dropped behind the grey and orange mountains edging the lake, Daisy fought tears of relief. *Tesoro.* Marcus led her to a large sitting room where India, in a white woollen shift, reclined on a vast burgundy velvet sofa.

'Daisy!' She jumped up to bear hug her. 'The parents have flitted off to Prague so we're behaving badly, smoking in the house like naughty teenagers. Marcus, pour her a glass, darling.'

'I'm driving...' It was a feeble attempt.

'Stay the night,' India suggested and Marcus nodded. 'Tabitha's coming over too.'

'Maybe just the one.' No less feeble.

'It's been an age. We totes ought to have lunch next time I'm up.'

Daisy's ego soared. India Dowson-Jones wanted to hang out with her. '*Totes*? You talk like Freya.'

'Actually, the bloody little copycat talks like me. She's forever stealing my clothes *and* my best lines. I'm devastated about her malicious tweeting.'

Daisy glanced around. 'She's not here is she?'

'Lord, no. Until the little horror 'fesses up and apologises to you, she's not allowed weekend leave.'

Daisy frowned. 'But what if she's telling the truth?'

'She's fourteen. She doesn't know the meaning of the word.' India lit a cigarette. 'Have you heard Marcus is in love?'

'Hot model?' Daisy asked.

He shook his head, blushing adorably. 'She's studying to be a doctor.'

'Tell Daisy where you met her,' India urged him.

The blushing worsened. 'The homeless shelter in Carlisle.'

Daisy laughed. 'You get sick of living here?'

'I'm volunteering there.'

'OMG,' Daisy sat a little straighter. 'Is this your dare?'

He nodded. 'It's a good one. Charity. I have to help a homeless person change their life. I've found someone whose life I can really make a difference to.'

Daisy sat back, in awe. 'And the girl? It's not her, is it?'

'No. Ross is a nineteen year-old smack-head who's been in care since he was three. He's also a mathematical genius who has no concept of what it's like to have a normal life.'

'Wow. And what's this girl like?'

Sheepishly, he flicked through his phone and passed it to Daisy. 'Her name's Nicole. I asked her out yesterday.'

Daisy blinked, stunned. In between two very smelly-looking men stood... well, Daisy could only describe her as... a plain girl. Average height, mousy-brown hair, not at all the kind of girl she expected Marcus to fall for. Nice figure though, and a sweet smile.

'She's clever, funny, kind... beautiful.' He fought a smile. 'She's kick ass.'

Daisy grinned. Was this how Xander saw her? Did he see everything in herself she couldn't see?

On cue, Marcus' phone rang and, from his blushes and enormous smile, it had to be Nicole. He'd finally found a girl worth waiting for. As he left the room, India sat down, cross-legged, her eyes full of concern.

'Now, what the hell happened between you and Xander? The boys barely tell me anything.'

Comforted by her sympathy, the enormous sofa and a glass of Shiraz, Daisy told her about the events since she'd seen India in October, even the bits that made Daisy look bad.

'Now I know I love him, but he's buggered off. He said we could've been perfect together. God, I hope we still can.'

She glanced at her hands, toying with a lighter. 'Last year at Oscar's, I might have spoken out of turn when I told you not to trust Xander. I doubted his motives, but Marcus told me how Xander feels about you.'

'How he *felt* about me,' Daisy corrected her.

India waved a dismissive hand. 'He's not going to have fallen out of love with you in a fortnight.'

'Can I ask, if you don't mind, but why doesn't Xander like you?'

'You can say *hate*.' She lit a cigarette and slumped back into the sofa. 'Basically, he's never forgiven me for having an affair with Robbie.'

Robbie had an affair? But his unashamed devotion to Vanessa gave Daisy hope that Xander could be equally faithful. If one brother strayed, would the other?

'It was forever ago,' India added hastily. 'He was twenty-one, married and freaking out about becoming a father. I was his chance to escape, but in the end, he chose Vanessa. Xander never forgave me and I don't think Robbie forgave himself, but if Vanessa ever leaves or, heaven forbid, drops dead...' Grinning, she made a mock prayer to God. 'I'll be banging down his door.'

India turned her attention to Marcus as he came back in. 'Darling, have you heard from Xander?'

'Honestly, no. I think he knows I'd tell him to get his arse back to Daisy.'

'Really?' Daisy said, wanting to cry again.

'At the party last year...' He sank onto the sofa beside her. 'I asked Xander who the hell you were and he said, *the most amazing person I've ever met.* He loves you and, in a little brother way, so do I.'

Finally, she'd won Marcus over. It had taken four months, a six hundred pound bottle of wine and lot of humble pie, but she'd done it.

CAROLINE BATTEN

'Now, what the hell does JC stand for?' he asked.

'Jiminy Cricket. You're my bloody conscience.' Giddy with pride, her smile didn't even drop when James walked in, scowling at her.

'Did you see the Facebook page hit ten thousand likes last night?' he asked. 'All thanks to your latest escapades with your ex-husband.'

Daisy knew this would be hard, that James would never give her an easy ride, but she had to rise above it. 'It'll be over soon. We're nobodies. They'll forget us.'

Marcus squeezed her hand, clearly recognising his own words.

'You are all idiots.' India giggled. 'James did me a huge favour by not letting me play. Blackmailed to do dares?'

Marcus threw a cork at her. 'No one could blackmail you anyway. *Heat's* already published everything you've ever done.'

'Xander's convinced you're the one blackmailing us, Indy.' James stared his sister in the eye. 'The poor little rich girl looking for kicks.'

Since when? He never mentioned it to Daisy.

'Oh, pull-ease...' India threw her head back, laughing and turned to Daisy. 'I don't even have a Facebook account. Wouldn't have a clue how to set it all up. I'm a totes luddite these days. Gave up on social media when I was fourteen.'

'I wish I had,' Marcus said.

'What are they blackmailing you with, anyway?' India asked James. 'The schoolboy thing? The money you–'

'Fuck off.'

'Oh, I know...' India laughed, revelling in her brother's discomfort. 'The dodgy housing deal in Windermere?'

'It's not dodgy.'

'But they can't have anything on you though, darling.' She winked at Marcus. 'Far too goody-goody.'

'Don't you believe it.' James smiled, his black eyes glinting. 'Marcus's wine cellar holds a few secrets.'

'James,' Marcus hissed, blushing, 'please... shut up.'

Intrigued as Daisy was, Marcus looked so uncomfortable she had to change the subject.

'When did you talk to Xander?' she asked James.

'When didn't I?'

'Is he okay?'

302

James tapped his fingers against his wine glass. 'Why the fuck would I tell you? You ripped out his heart and fed it to your ex-husband.'

Marcus and India both reprimanded him, but Daisy didn't drop eye contact with James.

'I know,' she said quietly. 'But is he okay?'

James drained his glass. 'He's at Oak Bank.'

'Why didn't you say anything?' Marcus asked.

'Because you'd tell her.'

Then why was he telling her now? Daisy turned to Marcus for reassurance.

'Off you go, *tesoro*,' he said, taking away her half-full glass.

'But–'

India squealed. 'This is *so* romantic.'

'But what if he tells me to piss off?'

'There's always hope,' James muttered.

Daisy tried arguing that she looked hideous, but India dragged her to a bathroom, promising she looked fabulous. Liar. Puffy red eyes from the continual crying could hardly be described as fabulous. And her hair had turned to frizz thanks to roaring fires, central heating and snowy walks with Birkin. Still, these were her sexiest jeans and the black jersey top couldn't be more slinky – the snow boots less so.

With the frizz in a high ponytail, another two coats of mascara and lashings of cherry lip balm, she almost felt ready. A hefty shot of vodka would've finished the job, but she had to drive. The time had come to tell Xander she loved him.

Oh please, please still love me, Xand.

At Oak Bank, Daisy strode past the high-end cars with a forced positivity but really, she wanted to run back to the MX5. As each step took her closer to the hotel's front door, she hoped Xander wouldn't be there. Then she prayed for it.

Sadly, Kate the waitress gave her a polite smile and said he was in the bar. At least Nadia wasn't manning reception. Thank God, for small mercies.

In the hallway of tiny mirrors, Daisy checked her appearance for one final time. She just had to say *I love you*. Or *I'm sorry*. Or she could run away. She couldn't do this. Yes, she could. Taking a confidence boosting deep breath, she pushed back her shoulders and walked into the bar.

And there he was, sitting at the bar, his back to her as he nursed a pint of lager. Oh, please don't be drunk. Or stoned. She needed him to be able to focus on this moment. A black bob blocked her view as Nadia leant against him to whisper in his ear, her hand resting on his thigh.

Daisy stopped.

Why was Nadia's hand on Xander's thigh? She nudged him, nodding in Daisy's direction and he turned, his eyes widening.

But he never pushed the hand away.

Oh God, no.

Daisy clutched the nearest chair, staring at Nadia. Tall, dark and utterly beautiful, a veritable doppelgänger for Vanessa. How had Daisy never noticed? She should run, literally sprint as fast as she could.

But she didn't.

Instead, she strode over to Xander, her fists clenched, suppressing the overwhelming urge to claw out Nadia's subtly made up green eyes.

Xander's jaw twitched and a frown scarred his perfect face — clearly, she still bothered him, but what the hell did that matter when Nadia's hand was on his fucking thigh?

'James told me you were here,' Daisy said, refusing to acknowledge Nadia. 'You need to ring Robbie or you'll lose the Bobbin Mill.'

The hand finally left his leg, but Xander sat there, his expression unchanged. How could she resist the masochistic desire to provoke a reaction from him?

'Why don't you just fuck Vanessa?' she asked before turning to Nadia. 'Surely it'd be better than looking for a second-rate replacement.'

'What?' Xander asked, his frown growing.

Daisy laughed. Had no one pointed his Vanessa-like habit before? With an arrogance that belied her devastation, she stepped closer, pressing her body against his.

'When you get back to Gosthwaite...' She intentionally let her lips brush against his ear. 'Let me know and I'll make sure I'm in the next fucking county while you get your stuff out of my house.'

His aftershave, his scent flooded her head and she turned to flee.

'What the hell…' Xander grasped her arm and lifted the wayward strands from her ponytail. 'You got a tattoo?'

Daisy tried not to shiver as she usually did when he touched her neck and, with her last ounce of bravery, she faced him one final time.

'It means three hundred and eleven,' she said, her voice cracking. 'It's a reminder not to be so fucking stupid in the future.'

Concentrating on the exit, picturing the sanctuary of the MX5, Daisy walked away with dignity and grace.

Dignity, grace and uncontrollable sobbing.

Through a blur of tears, Daisy drove away from Oak Bank, the image of Nadia putting her hand on Xander's leg playing on a loop in her head. How could he be shagging someone else already?

Her hands tightened on the steering wheel.

What if it wasn't *already*? What if it had been going on since the day he started work?

No.

Before she over-thought it, Daisy headed back to Dowson-Jones Manor. She'd bet the rest of her crowdfunding cash that James, the utter bastard, knew the answer.

An unsuspecting housemaid let her in, smiling as she led Daisy to the dining room. Marcus and India sat on one side, James and Tabitha at the other. The table was laden with useless Chinese takeaway cartons, but one of the silver candelabra would put a reasonable dent in James' head.

'You bastard,' Daisy hissed at James.

India hurried over. 'What happened?'

But Daisy never looked away from James' insolent scowl. She didn't care if she looked like a mental case; he had to be given his dressing down. 'You sent me there and you knew.'

Sipping his wine, the bastard actually smiled.

'Is it jealousy,' she asked, 'because he loved me, not you?'

'Pretty much,' Tabitha said, serenely topping up her own glass. 'But I am rather cross though. My money was on you shagging Finn.'

'What?' Daisy asked.

'Well,' Tabitha said, explaining it as if Daisy were seven, 'James said Xander would leave when he saw sense, but I said it would be because you'd fucked Finn. I owe James five hundred pounds.'

'James,' Marcus snapped. 'How could–'

'What?' James sat back in his chair, unrepentant. 'She's made his life a misery. Look what happened with Rousseau the other week.'

'A bet?' Barely able to breathe, Daisy leant on the table. 'You set me up?'

Tabitha rested her elbows on the table, a huge smile lighting up her face. 'I even had a side bet with Finn that you *wouldn't* fuck him. That was for three hundred pounds so all's not lost.'

'But...' She'd planned to buy Tabitha a Chloé handbag for being sweet. 'We're friends.'

Tabitha shrieked with laughter, her tinkly voice causing the wine glasses to sing. 'We're not *friends*.' Her voice dropped its musical edge. 'We never were. He was mine.'

'Xander?' Daisy whispered, but she already knew the answer.

Slowly, Tabitha stood up – the venom in her eyes making Daisy appreciate the vast mahogany table between them. Everything Tabitha had said at James' party, the apologies she'd made at the drunken lunch – all lies. She hated Daisy. She'd always hated Daisy.

'Finn,' Tabitha hissed. 'For four years, he loved me. Four years, then one day, he announces he's met someone else up a fucking mountain.'

'That wasn't my fault,' Daisy said, not knowing what else to say. Finn had been seeing Tabitha for *four* years?

'Of course it was your fault. He was here to see me, and you stole him.'

'And this is your payback, ruining any chance I might've had with Xander?'

'It's a start.' Tabitha flashed a cheery smile.

'And what else did you do?' Daisy asked, anger rising once again. 'The malicious tweets? Are you the Poor Little Rich Girl?'

'What about the game, Tab?' James asked, his voice low. 'Is that you too? Did you threaten us all?'

'No.' She stared down at him, her eyes wide.

'Of course it was you.' Daisy laughed. 'Jesus, I thought it *was* Finn, but it's not him. It's all *about* him.'

'What?' Tabitha blinked repeatedly, the sign of a liar. 'No.'

'Are you like some psycho stalker?' Daisy asked. 'Does he even know?'

'I haven't–'

'You stole his phone, didn't you? When? At the bar in Brighton, or some party?'

'No.'

'You put the sexts on Twitter and you're blackmailing your friends just to make my life hell.'

Tabitha stared at James. 'I didn't—'

'Is it all about him?' James asked, not looking up at her.

'Is it?' Marcus added.

India shook her head. 'Tabitha, for once... tell the truth.'

'No.' Slowly, Tabitha straightened her back, raising her chin. 'This is all about her.'

She fled the room.

'James,' India snapped. 'I want that bitch out of the house, now.'

James nodded, but paused as he reached the door. 'Daisy, I didn't know about Nadia.'

Did it matter what he knew? It wouldn't stop Xander from shagging her.

'Daisy, I'm so sorry,' India said. 'I should have known Tabitha was up to no good.'

'You said I shouldn't trust any of them. You were right.' She had to get out of there. She had to get home.

India glared to where Marcus loitered. 'You swore to me that Xander loved her.'

'He does.' Marcus crossed his arms.

'God, you should see Nadia. She's about five ten with the most perfect black bob. She looks just like Vanessa.' He'd let Nadia put her hand on his thigh. He wanted Daisy to see. God, he must hate her. 'I should ring immigration and get the cow deported.'

India wrinkled her nose. 'Unlikely to happen with the money she has behind her. She makes me look like a pauper.'

'Really?' Daisy asked. 'But she's a receptionist?'

'Nadia's father is the billionaire who owns *Home-from-Home*, that cheap and twee hotel chain. Oak Bank is her toe dip into high-end boutique hotels.' India sighed, downing her wine. 'Xander's always liked rich girls, looking for an easy life.'

'But he does love Daisy,' Marcus argued.

'Clearly, money matters more.' And Daisy had none. 'He's finally got his Vanessa, a rich Vanessa. I need to go home.'

'You're in no fit state,' India argued. 'Stay the night.'

'I've had one glass of wine. I need to go home and curl up in a corner for a week until I'm ready to start living again.' Daisy kissed her cheek. 'Thank you.'

'Daisy, he loves you,' Marcus said. 'You know he does.'

She nodded, heading for the door. 'But he's shagging her so it's irrelevant.'

On the drive home, tears rolled down her cheeks, but she didn't care. Finn had lied and lied and lied. After his birthday, when the gossips speculated he'd been having an affair, he'd denied it. Daisy – the stupid, stupid, stupid cow – had believed him.

She activated her iPhone. 'Siri? Call Finn.'

It went straight to voicemail.

'Why didn't you tell me about Tabitha?' she said, her words little more than a whisper. 'Or were you always planning to keep her on the side?'

She ended the call, tears already flowing. Oh God, she needed Xander, just to talk to him. No matter who he was shagging, he was her best-friend and she needed him.

'Siri?' *Call Xander. Tell him I love him. Tell him I need him. Tell him I'm sorry.*

But after what happened at Oak Bank, he wouldn't bloody answer.

Siri? What the hell do I do now?

Chapter Twenty-Nine

The next day, reality hit hard. The clothes Xander hadn't taken lay scattered around the bedroom and the bathroom still contained half of Clinique men's department. She liberally sprinkled one of his jumpers with Bulgari, inhaling the familiar scent and tears tumbled out. This had to stop. She was being tragic, an absolutely tragic mess. For most of her adult life, she'd never shed a tear over a man, but in the past twelve months, it'd become a dreadful habit. Crying wasn't going to bring Xander back – it only made her self-indulgent and look bloody awful.

Before she talked herself out of it, she pulled on her running gear and plugged in her iPod. She hadn't intended on running for long, but she didn't return for an hour – sixty minutes of mind-numbing jogging along the bridleway. She followed this with two bowls of utterly healthy vegetable soup then poured a deserved glass of Chablis. What next? Should she pick out bathroom suites or get Jack booked in for second fix joinery? Oh God, Xander wasn't coming back. A more realistic plan was to curl up in a corner and die. Bugger it. Taking the rest of the wine and a pack of cigarettes, she curled up in her bed, hugging his aftershave-drenched jumper.

For four days, this was her life. Run, eat, drink, sleep. She hadn't the energy for anything else. On day five, she jogged into the yard with a surprising amount of spring still in her step but stopped dead when she clocked Robbie's Discovery and Clara's Fiesta. This wasn't going to be pretty. With a great deal of reluctance, she walked into the kitchen.

'Daisy, what's going on?' Clara asked, fixing her with the sternest of school teacher glares. 'Jesus, have you been running?'

Daisy busied herself with stretching. 'He got me into it before everything went tits up at Christmas.'

'What happened, Daisy?' Robbie asked, lighting one of her cigarettes. 'You didn't call, so I thought it meant you two were back together, but I got back from Italy to find the contract signed and he'd gone AWOL again.'

Daisy closed her eyes. He'd come back to Gosthwaite but he didn't come to see her, even to pick up the rest of his gear. 'Did he talk to Vanessa?'

Robbie shook his head. 'What did you do?'

Why was it her fault? Shaking her head, cursing under her breath, she took a bottle of wine from the fridge and a glass from the dishwasher.

'Your answer to everything,' Robbie said, his voice dripping with disdain.

'You know me, Rob, always well stocked with wine and vodka.' Daisy raised her chin and sloshed wine into the glass.

Clara raised her eyebrows. 'And I'm sure it's what one fucking does when one's boyfriend fucks off.'

Tears lurked, so Daisy lit a cigarette and slumped against the cooker. 'How the hell did this happen to my life? I came to the Lakes for tranquillity, to escape the drama, but here I am, back in the middle of a broken heart.'

'Daisy,' Clara said to Robbie, 'honestly believes she's really very ordinary but odd things sometimes happen to her. She doesn't realise she's never been ordinary, ever.' Clara took the glass. 'Stop, Daisy. You're using drama to indulge again. Now, what did you do?'

'Why are you both assuming *I've* done something? I know going clubbing and dancing with Finn wasn't ideal but...' She took a long drag on the cigarette. 'I saw Xander a few days ago. He's hiding out at Oak Bank.'

'And?' Clara asked. 'Did you apologise?'

Daisy shook her head. Oh God, she needed to admit it aloud.

'Why the hell not?'

'Because he's shagging *Nadia*. She's tall, utterly beautiful, fabulously rich...' Daisy turned to Robbie. 'And she bears an uncanny resemblance to your lovely wife.'

Robbie closed his eyes, understanding, and Clara put the kettle on, clearly at a loss for wise words or sound advice. For once. Daisy almost smiled. See, it wasn't always her fault.

'It gets better.' Daisy took a long drag on her cigarette. 'About fifteen minutes after I found out that little nugget, I went back to the Dowson-Jones's to murder James. Turns out, Finn lied to me.'

Tears poured down Daisy's cheeks as she told them about

Tabitha's backstabbing antics.

'I left Finn a message,' she said, wiping her eyes. 'But he won't return my calls. Brittany sent me a text, telling me to leave him alone.'

'It's a good job Finn's in a different continent,' Clara said, throwing teabags into mugs, 'because when I get my hands on him, I'll bloody kill him. Why are all men such lying bastards?'

'I'm not,' Robbie said, scowling.

Clara smiled apologetically. 'Of course, you're not.'

Daisy shook her head. 'Oh, he has his moments.'

Robbie narrowed his eyes, but sensibly didn't push the point and Daisy looked longingly at the wine.

'You two made me fall in love with him,' she said. 'What do I do now?'

'Well, you're not going to fall into a vodka bottle again,' Clara said as she poured boiling water into the mugs. 'I'm too pregnant to help and Xander's not here to save you. Renovate another bloody house, go beg for your job back, but you have to find something to do until he comes back.'

'He won't come back,' Daisy said, more miserable than ever. 'Not to me at least. He might come back for the Bobbin Mill.'

'There's another bloody problem.' Robbie groaned. 'Later this week, we'll own it. The builders are ready to start work and I'm meeting the architect on Thursday, but I have no idea what Xander wants to do with the place. He still won't answer my calls.'

'But I know what he wants,' Daisy said, perking up. 'I made him write everything down to stop him from boring me to death.'

In the dresser drawer, exactly where he'd left it, was Xander's A4 notepad containing recipes, clippings and plans for the restaurant.

'You bloody star,' Robbie muttered, flicking through the pages.

'This place will be finished soon. Can I help with the Mill to take my mind off him? Even if it's only to make tea?'

He nodded. 'But no flirting with the builders.'

'Moi?' Daisy feigned innocence for a moment, before taking a mug of tea. 'Are you going to go and see him?'

'Yes. I'll talk sense into him.' Robbie wrapped his arms around her. 'Daze, he's met rich Vanessa lookalikes before. You're different. You're what he needs. Last year, on your lying husband's birthday, he came to see me. He said, *what the fuck has happened to me?* He was terrified, looked physically sick. I did take the piss to begin with, but then I told him to do something about it. He needed to make you feel the same so I told him about the old wagging plan. He loves you and he'll come back. Please make him happy when he does.'

With her heart, soul and a Brownie salute, she promised.

Clara watched Robbie leave with her usual wistful look. 'That man turned up at my house today and for a tiny, dreamy minute, I actually thought he'd come to whisk me away. Then I remembered I'm eight months pregnant and have cankles.'

'The day I walked to Low Wood Farm, he said if you're lucky enough to find true love, you have to be brave enough to fight for it.' Daisy giggled at Clara's *Mills and Boon* gaze of wonder.

'Oh he's so freaking perfect. If only he loved me and I didn't love Scott. I'm sure I could tempt him from his revoltingly beautiful wife.' Clara smiled, for a moment but then serious returned. 'What exactly happened at Oak Bank?'

'You would've been so proud of me.' Daisy rehashed the events in the bar, fully expecting Clara to applaud her actions. Instead, she stared at Daisy, clearly appalled. 'What? I didn't lash out.'

'Yes, you did. You acted like a mentalist because she had her hand on his leg. For crying out loud, Daisy. Did he tell you he was seeing her?'

'No, but he didn't need–'

'You bloody idiot. What if he's not?'

'He didn't come running after me.'

'Would you, after what you did?'

'Tabitha said–'

'She hates you. Are you going to believe her?'

'I don't know what to believe any more.' Daisy rubbed her eyes to stop the tears, the fingernails in palms no longer having any effect. 'Clar, I'm a mess. Finn lied to me and I've lost Xander. I want to talk to him so much I've had to delete his number from my phone. I know it off-by-heart but by the time I press a few digits, I come to my senses and hang up.'

'So what are you going to do? Get drunk and starve yourself to death as usual?'

'I don't know. I've spent a lot of time emptying wine bottles and hiding in bed, but there's no vodka in the house and I'm not buying any. I'm eating real food and I'm running every day. I'm determined to look ace in that bloody bikini. So that's better, isn't it?'

Clara nodded thoughtfully. 'It's time to sober up, grow up and get a proper bloody job. Show Xander you can renovate more than just houses.'

Daisy frowned at her Skank Manor project plan, pinned to the wall. 'I need a To Do List for me.'

On a clean sheet of paper, they planned how to make her life better and an hour later, as Clara drove away, Daisy pinned her list to the fridge, with an I ♥ Gosthwaite fridge magnet. There were ten steps to make her a less horrid person.

1. Absolutely no drugs ever again
2. No Vodka
3. Wine o'clock is 7pm, no earlier
4. No more than 10 cigarettes a day
5. Eat Five a Day
6. Go running every day
7. Get a job
8. Get to a size eight
9. Make the Bobbin Mill everything he planned
10. Make him proud of me

At the Boathouse restaurant, just outside Grasmere, Daisy tried to tackle number seven by smoothing things over with Jennifer Lovelace, the head at St. Nick's. Not because Daisy had any intention of going back there, but a non-devastating reference might be handy.

'Thanks for coming,' Daisy said, standing as Jennifer arrived. 'I wanted to apologise and I figured off school grounds would be... well, less terrifying.'

Since she'd ignored all twelve of Jennifer's calls over the last fortnight, Daisy hardly expected a cheery, worst things happen at sea reception, but to her astonishment, her boss didn't deliver a frosty, eyebrow-knitted scowl either.

'You walk out on me,' Jennifer said, as a waiter laid a thick linen napkin on her lap. 'You won't answer my calls and now you expect to swan back into my life? Did you think afternoon tea at a Michelin-starred restaurant will make everything okay again?'

Daisy stared at her, but no, it was definitely there. Jennifer had a very naughty twinkle in her eye. 'Are you taking the piss?'

'Yes.' Jennifer smiled as the waiter poured a glass of champagne. 'You spared no expense with your sucking up.'

'The crowdfunding project is paying.' Daisy took a deep breath. 'Look, I wanted to say, I'm sorry. I let you down.'

'You did. Ish.' Jennifer glanced around the restaurant. 'Why here?'

This was not going as Daisy had thought. 'It's the nearest classy place to school?'

'And it was a good excuse to see the place that formed a key part of Xander's life?'

Really not going at all as she thought. 'If I admit that I had hoped to see Lucy Errington, would you tell me what you're really thinking?'

Jennifer smiled. 'Yes.'

'I admit I hoped to see Lucy Errington here.'

'I've put you down as being on the sick. Now, I can let a week slide on full pay, but the rest, you'll have to take unpaid. I've smoothed things over with the board.'

'But I walked out.'

'You didn't just walk out. You told the students, and I do believe I'm quoting: *I don't fucking need this.*' Jennifer sat back in her chair. 'But I'm not firing you.'

'The school's over-staffed. You don't need me. I'm not even a good teacher.'

'You add colour. We like that at St. Nick's. We pride ourselves on producing well-rounded students, not simply ones with thirteen A-levels. You help with the rounding.'

'The kids have seen me half-naked on a beach. They're saying *TILF* to my face.'

'Consider yourself lucky. They've never said it even behind my back.'

'I fancy three of the sixth form boys.'

'Let me guess... Travis, Jackson and Logan. Who doesn't?' Jennifer smiled as the waiter delivered the stand of sandwiches and cakes. 'Odd how afternoon tea still goes on. It's such an archaic British tradition.'

Daisy sipped her tea. 'But aren't the parents furious?'

Jennifer pursed her lips for a moment. 'Once upon a time, Daisy, I was an idealistic teacher. My goal was to educate as many kids, especially underprivileged girls, as I could. That goal hasn't changed. For every ten students we have at St. Nick's, there's another bursary grant for a local child. There's a certain breed of parent who sends their child to St. Nick's. They're the India Dowson-Jones' and Fabien Rousseau's. They want colour in their child's education.'

'And I add colour.'

'I'm not promising how long it'll last, but after the Easter holidays, I expect you back in school, with your head held high.'

With a dubious nod, Daisy agreed. 'Xander left me, by the way.'

'I know. I've been following the whole drama on Facebook.' Jennifer picked up a roast beef and horseradish sandwich. 'So have you heard from Finn? Are he and Brittany kaput?'

She might have her job back, but this was the pay off. She'd never escape Finn.

A week later, she met Robbie at the Bobbin Mill. Although nothing more than a building site now the roof had been stripped, potential screamed from every slate inch. Xander would love it, but he'd refused to see Robbie so they had no option but to carry on without him.

'God, it'll be fabulous,' Daisy said.

'Derek, the project manager, says it'll be finished in six months with no major troubles.'

Robbie watched the guy ripping out the wooden panelling surrounding the functional but dull entrance doors. One day, they'd be replaced by two tall French windows – just as Xander had planned. The guy threw a piece of fire-damaged timber onto the scrap pile and noticed her. Jack.

'Daze, thank fuck. Have you come to take me away from all this?' Jack asked, never dropping his cheeky grin. 'How's that sexy ass of yours?'

Robbie's face clouded, but she patted his chest. 'Calm yourself. He's harmless. He's also the reason I found this place.' Daisy grinned back at Jack. 'Can't talk to me like that, sunshine, or I'll sue your sexy ass for sexual harassment.'

'Doesn't sound harmless to me,' Robbie said as they wandered back to the remnants of the kitchen. 'Christ, you're trouble. You promised no flirting with the builders.'

Daisy shrugged. 'Didn't make any promises about joiners, though. So, is this going to be the best restaurant in the world?'

'I bloody hope so.' Robbie leant against the stainless steel worktop. 'It's a massive risk but Xander's a brilliant chef and, even though he's not known for his reliability, since he met you, he's changed. He's grown up, got his head together. I trust him.' He smiled. 'That's the first time I've mentioned him this week and you haven't cried.'

'It's being here...' The Bobbin Mill gave her hope.

'It's an amazing place, isn't it?' Robbie nodded, knowing better than to keep talking about Xander. 'I was sixteen when Dad bought the old magistrates court to turn into Oscar's. I'll never forget the tension in the house. The fear that it might go horrendously wrong mixed with the excitement it might go very, very right. We got the Mill for such a good price, even with all the work it needs, it'll still be worth more when it's finished than we're spending on it. We owe you, Daze.'

'Would you talk to your dad, for advice?'

Robbie's eyes widened. 'Christ, no. You don't get it, do you, how much we don't like him? It was the highlight of my life when they buggered off to the Yorkshire Dales.'

'But...'

'I'd be quite happy if I never saw or spoke to my father again.' Robbie lit a cigarette. 'He really was a bully, telling me I'd failed if I didn't get As. So instead of going to Oxford, which he wanted me to do, I ran Oscar's, bred horses and married a model. If he saw this place, he'd bully us into doing what he thinks we should do. So no, angel, I won't be giving him a call.'

'You married Vanessa to piss your dad off?'

'Of course not, that was just an added bonus.'

'India told me what happened.'

'I guessed. But that was a very long time ago.' He scowled. 'And a very big mistake.'

Daisy mimed locking her lips and throwing away the key. 'But it's nice to know you're not perfect.'

He flicked his ash and laughed. 'Oh, I think you'll find I am. Well, I have been for the last nine years anyway.'

'Come on, I'll make tea and you can show me the plans.' Daisy draped her arm around his waist, realising Robbie smelled as divine as Xander. Was it the same aftershave or the Golding pheromones?

Oh please, come home, Xander.

For the next four weeks, the Bobbin Mill became her obsession. She liked the noise of the radio, the hammering, the swearing – to begin with the guys were fairly restrained in her presence, but they soon got over it.

Every day after a run, she'd cart her laptop to the Mill and research light fittings and window stays. Within a week, she'd decided the project manager and architect, Derek, had drawn up an unrealistic schedule. He didn't seem too worried about sticking to it, so she badgered him on a daily basis, but also created her own, more realistic schedule – one Jack et al were secretly working to. They weren't big fans of Derek's either.

Derek might have wished she buggered off and never came back, but the rest of the team seemed to like her. On top of the endless mugs of tea and coffee she made, every day at two-thirty, she rocked up with brownies, carrot cake and muffins, then they'd sit around the stack of plasterboards having afternoon tea, an archaic but awesome British tradition.

But it was all just a distraction to stop her dwelling on what a stupid cow she'd been. What if she'd had the guts to tell Xander the truth, either the day he left or that day at Oak Bank? What bloody if?

'Hard to believe it's the first day of spring in less than three weeks. It feels more like mid-bloody-winter,' she muttered to Birkin as they jogged back down the bridleway.

With Lum Crag once again covered in snow and ice, running had become her new thinking time – a feat worth praise in itself. She could actually run and think, and not just about how much longer she could run without dying. She planned the work still to do on Skank Manor, wondered if they might have curtains or blinds in the Bobbin Mill, guessed the reds and whites Marcus might pick for the wine list, but she banned herself from thinking about Xander. If she did, she had to run faster until the pain blocked him from her head. She sprinted a lot.

Finally, she made it to the yard gate. To climb or open? Without waiting for her as he usually did, Birkin darted under the gate, dashing off towards the house. What had him so excited to get home? Smoke billowed from the chimney.

She hadn't lit a fire before she left.

With her legs shaking more from nerves than exhaustion, she

opened the gate and tentatively walked into the yard.

Parked up beside her MX5 was a silver Golf.

He was back.

Chapter Thirty

The second Daisy opened the door, Birkin bombarded Xander with yapping, tail wagging and a million dog kisses. Xander ducked down, rubbing Birkin's ears, and Daisy loitered by the door, waiting, wishing she were in Birkin's place, being hugged and kissed by Xander. Birkin, finally exhausted from the run and over-zealous welcome for his best friend, curled up in his basket and Xander straightened, perching on the table with his hands in his pockets. His expressionless face gave nothing away, but Daisy didn't care. She could've stared at him forever. He needed a haircut and a shave but he'd never looked so bloody amazing. He was back. But was he back to pick up his stuff, or where they left off?

'Hi,' she said with the blankest face she could muster.

'I wasn't sure I was in the right house. There's food in the fridge, actual fruit and vegetables, and no white wine open.'

This wasn't exactly the hugs-and-kisses reunion she'd been hoping for, but at least the gap between them was reduced to a few metres – not three valleys and two lakes as it once had been. Should she just say *I love you*? Was this her opportunity? Wasn't it time to be brave? *I love you*. Now say she had to say it out loud. *I love you.*

'I...' *Tell him.* '...need a shower.'

She fled. She couldn't confess everything with a bright red face and sweat patches. Oh, who was she kidding? She'd chickened out. It was the most important conversation in her whole life and she'd chickened out.

Please, please, please. Give me a second, or was it third, chance.

'Daze?'

She wiped conditioner-infused water from her eyes, her hands shaking, and through the glass door, she could make out his blurry figure sitting on the edge of the bath.

I love you.

But again the words sat on her tongue and silence filled the room, drowning out the roar of the shower.

'Talk to me, Fitzgerald...'

Oh God, she'd missed being called that. A strangled sob escaped her throat and Daisy rested her forehead against the glass, letting the water stream over her. It was time to be brave.

'I've rehearsed this a billion times,' she said, 'but I never know which it's more important to start with. Is it how incredibly sorry I am or how stupidly much I love you?'

'Either. Keep going.'

'I'm so sorry, for the stupid behaviour and for just being stupid. Of course I love you. I love you so much it nearly killed me to see you with Nadia, but I honestly didn't realise how I felt until you left. Even then, it took some straight talking from Clara and a photo from Robbie. The silly thing is, I've probably been in love with you since the day we met.' She turned off the shower. 'And I'm sorry about Oak Bank.'

'Me too. I should've come after you. To explain.'

She opened the door, wrapping herself in a towel before stepping out. His fabulous, conker-brown eyes gazed into hers and she stood there for a moment, just relieved he was speaking to her.

'Will you forgive me?' she asked. He nodded. 'Do you... still love me?' He nodded again and although her eyes stung, she wouldn't cry. Not now. 'Do you think you might be able to live with me again?'

He half laughed, half groaned. 'You just don't get it, do you? Come here.'

She didn't need inviting twice. In two strides, she crossed the bathroom and threw herself at him, almost knocking him into the bath. But who gave a crap about playing it cool anymore?

His laugh disappeared into the kiss, his hands holding her face, hers holding his.

This was love.

And she planned to spend the rest of her life proving it.

Dragging her lips away, she gazed at him, resting her forehead against his and pressing her finger over his heart. 'Buried.'

He mirrored her gesture. 'Since the day we met, Fitzgerald.'

In bed, feeling happy, secure and more loved than she'd ever known, Daisy explained what happened in the forty-eight hours after he'd left.

'I did think of ringing you, to talk. Would you have settled for that?'

'Ninety percent of the time I was at Rob's,' he said, smiling as he twirled a curl, 'I would've settled for a text telling me to get my arse back home. But sometimes... if you couldn't have said that you loved me... After three days, I started to believe I'd been fooling myself. You didn't love me and you never would. So I left.' He kissed her shoulder, working his way up her neck. 'Can you get rid of this?'

CCCXI.

'No. It's what I am. Number three hundred and eleven. I hope you haven't miscounted.' He tickled her for her cheek. 'Besides, I can't see it so it doesn't really bother me.'

'I can see it. It bothers me.'

'Good. It can remind you to be a better person.'

'I'm already a better person than you.'

'Did I tell you I love you?' It was about the eightieth time she'd said it but she adored his smile every time she did. 'Way more than I ever did Finn. I get it now.'

Xander's face clouded over. 'I finally talked to Marcus this morning. It's sort of why I... he told me about Tabitha. I'm so sorry, Daze.'

She stared at the ceiling for a second. 'Finn lied. I don't understand why he didn't tell me he was seeing her before he met me. Why wouldn't he? I can't bring myself to ring him, even to yell at him, but it makes me wonder if he was planning to keep her on the side.'

'Can't be helping your trust issues.'

'I promise to trust you.' She took a deep breath. 'But can I ask, I mean it doesn't matter whether you... I mean we were split up, but... what did happen with Nadia?'

'She flirted a lot and it didn't exactly hurt my ego to let her, but that was it.' He rolled onto his front, propped up on his elbows. 'Believe me?'

'I do, though why you'd turn down the second most beautiful woman in the world for a shortarse, frizzy-haired anorexic is beyond me.'

'I didn't turn her down.'

Her heart plummeted. 'What, you came back because she turned you down?'

'No, you idiot. No one turned anyone down because, as Nadia

pointed out, I was very obviously still in love with a shortarse, frizzy-haired anorexic. Actually, she always calls you the Glamorous Blonde.'

Maybe Nadia wasn't all bad.

'Daze, what really happened with Finn when you went clubbing?'

'Nothing. He told me not to ring you, that I should go back to his hotel, but I'd never, ever, have cheated on you.' She looked him in the eye. 'More than that, I knew then, the grass wasn't greener. It's just that I–'

'Didn't trust me.'

'You never did tell me,' she said, unsure if she wanted to hear the answer, 'but why were you glad I was staying at Tabitha's that night?'

'Well, it wasn't because I was shagging Nadia. I was planning a surprise trip to Cornwall to stay with your parents. I thought you'd appreciate a distraction on the fifth of January. It was a lot easier to plan without you in the house.'

Oh dear God, would it be possible for her to be more of a stupid cow?

'I know,' he said, with a cheeky smile. 'You don't deserve me.'

'I really am very sorry for everything I did and I love you.'

'You're totally forgiven and I love you too.'

There was a lot more making up.

She came out of her second shower to find Xander lying on the bed with mugs of tea and, to Daisy's utter horror, he was holding her To Do List.

'How did you get on?' he asked.

'It's private.'

'I'm intrigued.'

She towel dried her hair, avoiding looking at him. 'I've not touched anything illegal, or a drop of vodka.'

'Tesco out of stock?'

She stuck her tongue out. 'There's a strict seven pm rule in this house. Cigarettes are a bit tricky. I go through twenty a day, but I swear your bloody brother and Jack have most of them. You've seen the fridge.'

'The soup in there, who made that?'

'Me,' she said, full of pride. 'I got the recipe from my mum.'

'It's seriously very good. It just needs a little more salt.'

'No, *you* over season.'

His eyes twinkled, full of amusement, but he held up the list. 'Carry on.'

'There are no crisps in the house, although the chocolate Hobnob addiction is still going strong. I don't go running every day but three or four times a week. I start back at work after Easter. And um...' She blushed, busying herself with putting on three layers of mascara.

'You look fantastic.'

'If you dare say I've put on weight, I'll have to kill you.' This had to be the most excruciating conversation she'd ever had, but still she smiled. 'I'm somewhere between six and eight, definitely nearer an eight. I've had to buy new jeans and I feel very fat but I'm trying to get used to it.'

'You look beautiful, almost normal, but sexier than ever.' He put the list down, not asking about the final two points. 'It's funny. I've... When you turned up at Oak Bank and just assumed I was shagging Nadia, I was furious. Nothing had changed. I was angry and you didn't trust me. But eventually, I got it. I knew I wouldn't touch another girl, but why would you ever believe that with twelve grand of guilt presents in your jewellery box?' He fiddled with his mug. 'I'd arrogantly assumed you should just trust me and that's not fair. So, I decided to fix a few things in my life. I got a job at Oak Bank with set hours until the Mill opens. No more random shifts and abandoning you to cover for someone else. And no more weed smoking. I know you hate that.'

'OMG. You had your own To Do List.' She laughed.

'Don't get cocky. I only had three aims. You had so many, you had to write them down.'

'Get up,' she said, 'or we'll be late. What was your third aim?'

'I'll tell you later.' He frowned at her filthy, ripped at the knee jeans. 'Late for what, and why are you dressed like that?'

She'd been saving this bit. 'Late for afternoon tea at your bloody restaurant.'

The Bobbin Mill bore little resemblance to the mess he viewed over Christmas. The evidence of fire and water damage had gone, and the reclaimed slate tiles were up to four courses. Now, he'd be blind not to see the potential.

Robbie leaned against the new door frame, his grin as big as Xander's as they walked in. Her builders already sat around with fresh mugs of tea and, horribly aware Xander watched every move she made, she apologised for being late. Jack bumped fists with her but, thankfully, no one mentioned how she didn't normally wear slinky red tops and perfume with her work boots when she served the bakery's famed chocolate cake. She handed the last piece to Mike the plumber and Xander tipped his head. Time for the guided tour.

He gazed at the new oak roof beams, lovingly touched the window frames Jack had fitted and stared in amazement at the plans. Eventually, in what would be the kitchen in his very own restaurant, Xander wrapped his arms around her and for the first time, stopped smiling.

'Numbers nine and ten on your To Do List?' he said, whispering in her ear.

Nine, the Mill being what he planned and ten, him being proud of her. She rested her forehead against his chest, not daring to look at him.

'It is and I am. More than you'll ever know. The third thing on my list?' He paused waiting for her to look up. 'Marry me?'

'What?' Was he serious?

'You need to know I'm for real, that I'm not going to shag around, and I need to know you know that so you won't.' There was no cheeky smile or glint in his eyes. He was serious. 'Do you want me to get down on one knee?'

'No. So you want to get married so neither of us shag around? That's your romantic proposal?' Still stunned, she couldn't look away from his eyes.

'Christ, you're hard work. Why can't you just say yes, like any other girl I asked would?'

She swatted his arm.

'I want to marry you because it's what people who love each other do. I want what my brother has.'

Daisy wriggled out of his arms. 'Wasn't Nadia a close enough match?'

He raised his eyes, staring at the ceiling. 'So she looks like Vanessa. I don't actually want to run away with my sister-in-law, Fitzgerald.'

'Your brother thinks you do.' She told him what Robbie had

said in September about the Vanessa-likes.

Xander laughed. 'I can't believe he thinks that. Okay, when I was younger I fancied her a bit, maybe a lot, but seriously she's like my mum these days. Why would he think that?' He looked around as if the walls might hold the answers until he frowned at her. 'So does he think all the tall brunettes were me trying to find a Vanessa?'

Daisy nodded.

'It's honestly not true. You usually go for dark hair, right? Well, me too. When in need, look for the nearest tall, dark-haired, pretty girl. Daze, I don't remotely fancy Vanessa and, so you know I'm being honest, Nadia's great. She basically offered me the kitchen at Oak Bank. I wouldn't have to work, but I'd get my own restaurant to play around with. That place should have its first star next year.'

'Is that what you really want?'

'No. I really want, probably more than ever, the things I told you back in September. I want to be a good chef with my own restaurant. And I want you. You're the one who's making my dream come true. Look at everything you've done to this place. I want to be happy with you like Rob is with Van.'

'Happily ever after?'

He nodded. 'Now, will you say, yes?'

'Yes.'

He pulled a red ring box out of his pocket, holding it up for a second. 'And it's not a guilt present. I've worked double shifts for six weeks to pay for this.' He tossed it to her.

Inside sat the most beautiful ring, mounted with a pale blue, square-cut sapphire with smaller, oblong diamonds on either side. OMG, he had good taste in jewellery. She tried, but failed, to stop her ludicrous grin.

'Not being with you made me more miserable than being with you when I thought you were shagging your ex-husband. So, I had to find a way to make us work, whatever it took, and I think this is what it'll take.' He took the ring out of the box and slipped it on her finger. It fit perfectly. 'You know I'm the only person who'll ever make you happy, Fitzgerald?'

'Yes. And I promise I won't make you unhappy again.'

And as her new fiancé kissed her, a slow clapping started from the other end of the Mill. They both laughed, turning to see a grinning Robbie leading the applause.

They were engaged. Now what should she do?

From the shower came Xander's usual humming, this time Bruno Mars' *Marry Me* and Daisy stared down at the foil pill packet in her hand. She hadn't taken it since January 2nd and by some sheer fluke, she'd spotted the packet, peeking from behind her body moisturiser. For the last minute, or maybe ten, she'd mentally debated the morals, ethics and potential outcomes, but still one question rattled around in her head: now what should she do?

It would just take time.

How many doctors had told her that? You're both young, healthy... enjoy life, it'll happen when you're ready. But every negative test had picked a hole in her relationship with Finn until they finally fell apart.

She couldn't let that happen with Xander.

As Xander stepped out of the shower, Daisy blatantly popped the packet back into her make-up bag but surreptitiously dropped the little blue pill down the sink.

If it would just take time, well they may as well start now. She wouldn't stress about it and he wouldn't think her a failure every month; it'd happen when they were ready.

Chapter Thirty-One

Thirty minutes after she became Mrs Golding-To-Be, Daisy rang Clara. Once the squealing subsided and she explained the wedding would be sooner rather than later, Clara declared Will would have to be born before his due date so she wouldn't look like a whale in the photos.

Clearly, she'd given him the schoolteacher death-stare *in utero*, because on March 15th, the day after Daisy's birthday, Will popped out. Xander and Daisy went to visit the next day. Already at home, Clara and Will radiated serenity, but Scott wore odd socks and the bags under his eyes suggested he needed a week's sleep.

'Ah, the alpha male in all his glory,' Daisy said as Scott proudly showed off his son to Xander.

Clara beamed at Xander who was backslapping Scott as they cooed over baby Will. 'Okay Scott, Daisy's turn.'

Scott laid a sleeping Will in Daisy's arms, gazing at his one-day-old son with a dopey smile. 'This is Aunt Daisy, mate. You'll like her. She's nuts.'

Daisy kissed Will's silky forehead, breathing in his Johnson's Baby aroma, but didn't dare look up because *GUILTY* would be written all over her face and she prayed Xander wouldn't notice.

Will opened his eyes and she smiled, pushing the guilt aside. 'You're too cute, mister.'

The cute factor diminished when he started to go red, screwing up his face, ready to cry. Where the hell had Clara and Scott gone? The wail gained volume and she stared at Xander in panic.

'I'll take him,' Xander said. He gently placed Will against his shoulder, laughing at her astonishment. 'What? I have three nieces. You're such an idiot, Fitzgerald.'

The crying stopped as Xander wandered off to the kitchen, chatting quietly to Will and Daisy's guilt eased. He'd be an amazing dad and knowing it had her ovaries popping. When would it happen for them... a year, maybe two?

'Happy Birthday.' Clara flopped down on the sofa, handing her a squishy gift-wrapped parcel. The laziest gift buyer, Clara always gave her fabulous scarves. This one was a cashmere pashmina in an opulent dark plum.

'I heart it and I heart you.' Daisy hugged her.

'Decided on the wedding plans?'

Daisy nodded. 'I spoke to Mum and Dad on my birthday and told them we got engaged. I didn't even get to describe my rock before Mum started banging on about what was I planning *this time*, could I have it in summer *this time*, and I had to invite Uncle Jeff's family *this time* because they've never really forgiven her for not inviting them *last time*.' Daisy mimed stabbing herself in the heart. 'Xander wants to do it soon, super soon, and talking to Mum confirmed what I'm going to do *this time*.'

'You're eloping?'

Daisy nodded, grinning. 'Well, sort of. I suggested Gretna, but Xander wants to have a few special people there. So on April 5th, the absolute earliest I could book the registrar, we're getting married at Haverton Registry Office. There'll be just us, Robbie, Vanessa, the girls, you guys and the three Dowson-Joneses.' Daisy smiled. 'Will you be my witness?'

Clara nodded, tears glinting in her eyes. God, she was emotional these days.

'Is this why you need the bikini?' She handed over a gift bag containing the D&G bikini and the photo. 'Are you there?'

'Nearly, I just need the *ass*-piration bikini to confirm it.'

'When it has, give it back. That bikini and photo are going to be my inspiration too.' She looked at her stomach – shockingly flat considering Will was only thirty-six hours old. 'I'm not letting you get all the hot looks off the men forever, beatch.'

Xander came back with Will still sleeping on his shoulder and Clara giggled. 'OMG, how sexy is your husband-to-be when he's playing Uncle Xander?'

Daisy was thinking more of *Daddy* Xander but very sexy, all the same.

At midday on April 5th, Daisy returned from walking Birkin and frowned at the dodgy latch on the yard gate. Typical it'd jam, today of all days. She'd spent two hours having her hair, nails and make-up done by India's favourite beautician, but now Daisy climbed the rickety wooden gate, praying it wouldn't disintegrate underneath her. As she swung a welly-clad foot over the top, and turned to jump down, there was a cough behind her.

In the yard stood a tall, willowy lady with tidy, dark hair and an equally tall, very dishy guy with silver hair. Their eyes looked anywhere but at Daisy. She glanced down. Oh God. Her dungaree mini-dress wasn't doing a very good job of covering her arse – certainly not good enough for the first time she met Xander's parents. Oh, she'd seen photos of them, but Xander was clearly his father's son. Oscar looked just like Xander, only with grey hair. But what the hell was her name? Had Xander ever told her?

'Hello, we're looking for Alexander.' His mother tried to smile.

'He's in the house,' Daisy said, jumping off the bucket. Bugger, bugger, bugger. She flashed them a quick smile as she dashed into the kitchen to ruin Xander's so far perfect day.

'You have a twig in your scruffy bun thing, Mrs Gee-To-Be.'

For the first time, she didn't pull him up for assuming she'd change her name. 'Your parents are here.' He froze mid-chop of an avocado. 'Do you think they know? Will you tell them?'

'Not if I can help it. Take your ring off?' Xander clutched his knife a little tighter, swearing under his breath. 'Seriously, why did they have to turn up today?'

Daisy stuffed the sapphire rock into her back pocket as they knocked on the doorframe. 'It'll be fine,' she whispered. 'How hideous can they be?'

'Don't leave me alone with them,' he pleaded.

She promised and within thirty seconds of them walking through the kitchen door, she could see why Xander had been worried.

'Mum, Dad, this is Daisy Fitzgerald. Daze, my Dad, Oscar, and my Mum, Andrea.'

Daisy gave her best B-List actor's wife smile and shook their hands as if she'd never flashed her pants at her future father-in-law. They both unsubtly clocked her empty ring finger.

'Well, at least this one's not married,' Oscar said, pacing up and down the kitchen. 'That's the first positive thing I've heard about you today. I received an invoice from the bar. I'll let the odd two hundred pound tab slide, but a thousand pounds of cava?'

For a few minutes, Oscar ranted, oblivious to the rest of them, and Andrea maintained a pained expression. Occasionally, she'd glance sideways at Daisy as if to say, *this is your fault, isn't it?*

'...you've sold your grandfather's house for this money pit,' Oscar waved a disparaging hand. 'You'll never see your money back... lost your job... can't rely on temping for your friends forever... '

He went on and on, ripping apart every aspect of Xander's life, but when he got to Daisy, she did perk up.

'And this one, what is she, a glamour model? You know she's only with you for your money...'

How long would he go on for? Daisy's lips were clamped together to stop her giggles but when poor Xander slumped, dejected, against the cooker, her protective hackles went up.

'...heard you've bought some derelict building you think you can turn into a restaurant, like you're on that *Grand Designs* programme? You've neither the experience or the...'

Daisy leaned in, whispering to Xander. 'I'm really sorry but I can't take any more of this. Please, can I?' He nodded and she gave him a wink before she turned to his dad. 'Oscar?'

He shut up mid rant and frowned at her.

'This is *my* house,' she said, as sweet as sweet could possibly be, 'and I don't appreciate being treated like a child in my own home. Would you like to take a seat?'

She gestured to the kitchen chairs and, as Oscar and Andrea sat down, Xander took hold of her hand.

'I promise I'm not after Xander's money. As far as I'm aware, he hasn't got an awful lot since he bought the Bobbin Mill. By the way, I have every faith he'll make it the best restaurant for miles around. He's so bloody good that Anthony Errington's begging him to work at The Boathouse again and anyway, all he and Robbie are doing is adding value to the site, just like you did with the Magistrates Court.'

God, she hoped Oscar remembered how it felt starting out. The nerves and excitement Robbie described.

'As for this place,' she said, glancing around the kitchen. 'We don't own it. It's a renovation project I'm working on. And actually, it's coming in way under budget. I shop around and it turns out I'm a hell of a haggler. You wouldn't believe what I paid for the granite. I may have fluffy blonde hair but my brain isn't made of the same stuff and although I adore that you think I'm pretty enough to be a glamour model, I'm actually a teacher. I have a First from Northumbria University, but honestly, thank you for saying that.'

Xander's arm draped around her and Daisy smiled at his mum, who sat with her ankles primly crossed. Daisy didn't like the woman – partly because she'd looked down her nose when Birkin tried to say hello, but mostly because she wasn't sticking up for her son.

'The cava is for the Topping Off party at the Bobbin Mill,' Daisy said. 'Sorry the bill ended up on Xander's tab. It was supposed to come to me. Now, I realise you've driven a long way to berate your son and I really ought to offer you tea, but I'm afraid we don't have time. This is very bloody rude, but I'm going to have to ask you to leave. You see, we have a wedding to get to this afternoon and we really can't be late.'

Xander kissed her cheek before smiling, full of confidence, as he ushered them towards the door. 'Mum, Dad, the Topping Off party is three weeks on Saturday. It starts at three and honestly, you're more than welcome to come along.'

Daisy had never seen such stiff upper-lips in her life. She suddenly adored her terribly organic parents and their very relaxed attitude to her life.

Their car disappeared from view and Xander held her hand, smiling. 'Daze, if I ever take you for granted, please remind me of this moment.'

Two hours later, Daisy walked down the aisle, wearing what she liked to think was their relationship. Her white strapless, playsuit bore a strong resemblance to the black number she'd worn to James' party and each accessory told its own story. The pink and tomato red skyscraper heels were from New Year's Eve and, despite clashing with them, Daisy held a posy of peach roses, similar to the ones Xander had once thrown at her feet. She wore the daisy belly button bar and tip money diamond earrings, not caring how he'd earned the money; that was in the past. Her hair was piled in a relaxed up-do, showing off the tattoo on the back of her neck. She'd had *Forever* added underneath the *CCCXI* – her wedding present to Xander.

'You look stupidly beautiful,' Xander whispered.

'So do you.' In a dark grey Armani three-piece suit with a peach rose in his lapel, he looked heavenly. She linked her fingers with his as he took his third deep breath in the fifteen seconds she'd stood there. 'Well, aside from the look of absolute terror you have in your eye. Scared?'

'Only that you'll do a runner.' He managed a brave smile.

'Bit late for that.' This was the right thing to do – she'd never been more sure of anything in her life.

Their minimal guest list watched with pleased smiles and, in Clara's hormonal case, teary eyes, as they were married without drama. Clara and Robbie were their witnesses leaving Tallulah vocally annoyed she didn't get to be a bridesmaid.

After Daisy and Xander skipped out of Haverton Registry Office as Mr and Mrs Golding, they went to the OBB for tapas and ludicrous cocktails. Robbie threatened the manager and the staff with instant dismissal if anyone breathed a word of the occasion to the Golding Seniors, especially after the balls up with the cava invoice. Fortunately, the staff were as in love with Xander and/or Robbie as the women in the wedding party. The barman pressed play on the iPod Daisy had given him and as FUN serenaded them, Daisy handed Xander a shot of vodka.

'Does this mean you'll let me kiss you?' he asked, laughing.

'Maybe in two drinks time.'

They downed the shots then, in the middle of Oscar's Bar and Bistro, they danced. Other bewildered customers looked on but who cared? They'd already sank half a bottle of champagne outside the registry office while Scott tried his best to take photos.

Naively, Daisy had expected their guests to be watching them dance. They weren't. Three week-old babies were little limelight stealers. Vanessa cuddled Will with a gooey smile on her face. Robbie growled at his wife, *no*. Daisy giggled before giving her undivided attention to her fabulous husband who hadn't stopped smiling since she said, *I do*.

'Are we insane?' she asked, already knowing they were. 'We've known each other for less than a year and we haven't a penny between us.'

'We have a dog and the shell of a building.'

'But we'll be happy, right?'

Xander didn't answer; he simply kissed her.

'Put her down. You've done enough of that already.' James dragged Xander off to the bar, scowling at Daisy.

'I wish I had your life,' India said.

Daisy laughed. 'Indy, I'm just an ordinary girl from Cheshire. You're beautiful and beyond fabulous.'

'I'd take your ordinary girl from Cheshire life over mine any day. At least you've found a boyfriend you can trust enough to marry.' With tears in her eyes, India beamed as she took hold of Daisy's left hand. 'That is one perfect sapphire.'

Daisy's inane smile faltered when James glanced her way with utter contempt. She went through the motions of discussing her rings with India but strained to hear the conversation between James and Xander.

'Why the hell did you marry her?' James asked.

'Because I love her.'

'You've never kept that a secret but you didn't have to marry her.'

'This stops now. I love Daisy, so just fucking leave it.' Xander walked away, shaking his head, sending one filthy glare back to his best friend.

James didn't leave it. With a fake smile, he came over and kissed Daisy politely but lingered for a moment with his cheek next to hers. 'There's a very good chance you don't deserve this.'

He walked away, leaving her blinking to compose herself. Couldn't he be nice, just for one day?

'It's official. I hate your new friend,' Clara said, smiling at India's departing backside. 'She has the perfect body.'

And it'd been to bed with Robbie, but Daisy wasn't telling Clara that. 'Like there's anything wrong with your body.'

In a beige mini dress which didn't show the baby sick, black tights and stiletto heeled boots, Clara's silhouette belied she'd ever been pregnant. Daisy took the gift bag containing the ass-piration bikini and photo from behind the bar, offering it to her.

'Need this to prove you're perfect too?'

'You did it?'

Daisy twirled, showing off her outfit. 'This is a size eight and I think you'll agree my tits and arse fill it. Thank you for making me see sense. I feel fat as hell, but Xander keeps telling me how stupidly beautiful I look.'

'He's right.' She downed a massive glug of wine. 'This might be foolish because I'll feel like pants tomorrow, but Scott's offered to do night duty. Although I've got a horrible feeling he's already pissed.' She watched her husband as he danced with Vanessa. 'Ohmigod, where's Will?'

She span round, her eyes wide with panic, but the second she saw her baby son snuggled in the crook of Robbie's arm she feigned a swoon. 'It's like my dreams have all come true.'

'I heard that,' Scott said, pretending to look cross. 'If that boy's eyes go brown, you're in big trouble, Mrs Lancaster.'

Clara blew him a kiss but reclaimed her son, and Daisy took the opportunity to speak to Robbie. He instantly pulled her into his arms and they slow-danced to some romantic twaddle.

'Xander told me what you said to our hideous father. I would've paid to have been there. In fact, if we weren't already married to other people, I'd propose right now.'

'Thank you for making this happen,' she said. 'If you hadn't believed in me, we wouldn't be here.'

'As crazy as you are, I know you'll make my little brother happy.' He leaned down to whisper in Daisy's ear. 'Besides, he fancied my wife for years. It'll be nice to fancy his.'

He kissed her.

It wasn't a long kiss, but it was a real kiss on the lips and turned her face as tomato red as her shoes.

'Welcome to the family, Daisy.'

He twirled her around and Daisy laughed. The Sexiest Man in Town just kissed her. Clara would be devastated.

'Did you have a good day, Daisy G?' Xander asked as they lay in a horribly expensive, five-star hotel over-looking Ullswater, planning two glorious days in bed. This would be followed by a further two obscenely indulgent weeks in bed at home.

'I married you. It was awesome.' She kissed him. 'But I preferred it when you called me *Fitzgerald*.'

'Decided not to change your name then?'

'Do you want me to?'

'I'll love you with either name, but you'll always be Fitzgerald to me.' He kissed her one last time then closed his eyes.

Beep, beep.

Bethany Marshall *has sent a message. Is getting married your dare?*

Xander didn't stir. Daisy bit down on her lip. *No*, she replied.

Bethany Marshall. *He doesn't believe in marriage. So why's he doing it?*

Chapter Thirty-Two

Forfeit Likes: 12,392
@ForfeitHost followers: 15,341
@daisy_fitz followers: 5,197
New hate tweets received: 0

Hanging bunting with her dad while her husband of three weeks knocked together a salad bar for fifty was not Daisy's idea of a honeymoon. The first one, where she and the bastard HMS lolled around on a Maldives beach – that was much nearer the mark. Why the hell hadn't she employed someone to do this? She cursed Xander, her Dad, anyone she could think of. In the midst of her vicious tirade against God, Xander arrived and their honeymoon got a whole lot worse.

At a smack house in Carlisle, Marcus had been robbed, beaten and left for dead. His head injuries were so severe, he was being airlifted to Lancaster. Daisy left her dad finishing the bunting and, as she and Xander hurtled down the M6, they couldn't care less about the party. By some miracle, they made it to the hospital alive – a detail she thanked God for as she climbed out of the car. Xander had taken his driving to a new level of terrifying, and she'd spent much of the journey with her eyes closed, clinging to the door handle. He strode off and she scampered after him as quickly as she could in flip-flops. Before they even reached the hospital doors, he scowled at her.

'Can't you take those stupid things off and just run?'

She pulled her hand from his, stopping and staring at him. Okay, he was bloody upset, but he didn't get to talk to her like that. Ever. He closed his eyes for a second then apologised so she took off the flip-flops and jogged after him, praying her JC was okay.

He wasn't. Marcus lay there, unrecognisable. They'd broken his leg, fractured his jaw, smashed a few ribs, but more worryingly, the severe beating had left swelling on his brain. He lay in a large private room, pale and silent, with James and the Dowson-Jones parents at his bedside.

From her tidy black chignon to her green crocodile skin pumps, Bella Dowson-Jones had the same classy elegance as Xander's mother but, where the latter had a Grace Kelly chill about her, Bella exuded warmth. She leapt off her chair to envelop Xander in a massive hug, kissing his cheeks. She held his face in her hands as she spoke to him in Italian, making him blush. Even Daisy was treated to an excited monologue as Bella kissed her cheeks with the exuberance you surely only get from an Italian mother. Daisy could only assume she was saying complimentary things from Xander's pleased laugh.

A grave Henry Dowson-Jones nodded his hello, but quickly turned back to his son, checking for movement. James gave Daisy his customary glare before dragging Xander off for a chat. It was the first time they'd spoken since the wedding.

'What on earth happened?' Daisy asked Bella.

'The police spoke with Nicole,' she replied, her accent heavy with emotion. 'Ross had called Marcus, saying he wanted a fix too much. The police don't know if this was Ross, or someone else.'

The five of them stayed glued to Marcus' bedside for a couple of hours until an MRI showed the swelling wasn't going down and the doctors decided to induce a coma. With no chance of Marcus waking that day, Bella shooed Daisy and Xander away.

'Go and enjoy your party.'

Xander shook his head. 'I'll cancel it. We can't–'

'It's a Topping Off,' James said. 'It's for your team. You can't cancel.'

The traditional *Topping Off* party, according to Derek the project manager, was held when the roof was on. At the Bobbin Mill, they were a step ahead. As well as a reclaimed slate roof, new oak windows and enormous glass entrance doors, the studding was up, ready for the external wall insulation, and first fix plumbing and electrics were underway.

Xander and Daisy headed back up the M6, wondering if the guests would mind sitting on plasterboard stacks while they ate burgers with no salad and drank warm lager. There was still so much to do and no time to do it. But they arrived at the Mill to find Daisy's dad wiping down tables while Xander's mum arranged chairs she'd appropriated from God knows where. The cava was on ice, the Becks chilled and trestle tables sagged under salads, cheeses and breads. Xander clutched Daisy's hand, but she merely stared.

'Poppet, you're back!' Her mother appeared, holding a vast bowl of pasta. 'Haven't Andrea and your father done a marvellous job with the place? Are you popping home to change or were you planning on greeting the builders in a denim skirt that barely covers your knickers?' She dropped her voice. 'Oscar's pesto isn't a patch on Xander's, but that man could charm snakes with his smile.'

Oh God. Daisy looked up at Xander in horror, but he was already tense as his father, holding a tray of bread rolls, stopped beside him.

'I hear congratulations are in order,' Oscar said, the muscle in his jaw twitching away as he forced a smile at them. 'You could've told us. Lynda from the post office almost burst a blood vessel when she realised we didn't know. Is our relationship really that bad?'

They hadn't told his parents about the wedding; they planned to do it at the party.

'Quite frankly, yes,' Xander said, before swearing. 'Dad, what's going on?'

'Well, whatever else you think of me, you have to admit I know how to throw a party.' Oscar smiled, kindly this time. 'How's Marcus?'

Stunned from the shock of the attack on Marcus and their parents pulling together to put on a party, Daisy watched builders, friends and family wander around the Mill and its gardens, gushing over how fabulous the restaurant would be. Under the blistering April sunshine, she even started to enjoy herself.

'Is it wrong to fancy their dad more than I do Robbie?' Clara asked.

'It's beyond wrong,' Daisy said, admiring Oscar's fit body and dark silver hair. 'That's what Xander will look like in thirty years' time.'

'Lucky cow. *Un renard argenté.* He's not the ogre they think, is he?' Clara tipped her head to the side, checking out his arse as he wandered to the far side of the garden. 'Is he sloping off for a fag?'

'Looks like it.' Daisy smiled as Andrea scowled. 'And my mother-in-law does not approve, but since she's a stuck up cow, she can hate me too.'

Respectably dressed in white linen trousers and a black strapless top, hopefully making up for the dungaree mini-dress spectacle last time she saw them, Daisy strode after Oscar.

'Where are you going?' Xander asked as she passed him.

'To talk to your dad. You wanted me to stop being judgemental so I'm going to make up my own mind about him.' She giggled at Xander's worried frown but headed to the rockery where she found Oscar snipping a cigar. 'Mind if I join you?'

His face broke into a huge smile. 'Please, it'd be a pleasure.'

Clara was right – Oscar was no ogre. 'Sorry for the rant the other week.'

'I'm sorry too.'

'I get a tad protective over Xander.'

'Good.' Oscar lit her cigarette then puffed on his cigar, looking at her with slightly narrowed eyes, clearly wondering *who are you and do I trust you*. 'I haven't seen Xander for over a year. The change is incredible. He doesn't seem twenty-three but then that was always his problem, wanting to grow up before his time. I wanted him to be a kid but he wanted to be Robbie. The arguments it caused.'

Oscar Golding was a sweetie. 'Mr Golding... '

'I think we're a wedding away from that, Daisy. Oscar, please.'

'Sorry for not telling you sooner. Mum and Dad are a bit pissed off too. A lot pissed off.' She took a long drag on her cigarette, wanting to ask questions she knew Xander wouldn't like. Bugger it. 'I know this is a tad nosey, but if you don't mind, why did you leave him and move to Yorkshire? He's quite devastated about the whole episode.'

'He feels we rejected him, but after years devoted to the business, it was our turn to have a life and he didn't need us – he had Robbie and my father.' His jaw twitched, just like Xander's did when he was anxious or cross, but then Oscar scratched his neck. OMG.

'That's not true, is it?' she asked and when Oscar's eyes widened in surprise, she laughed. 'Why did you really leave? Something you don't want Xander and Robbie to know about?' She tipped her head to one side as he scowled again. 'Sorry, I am nosey, but I promise not to tell.'

'You do love him, don't you, Daisy?'

'Utterly and completely. We've had a rather eventful year and I can't live without him.'

'Has he told you everything, even his rather colourful exploits at school? I'm assuming so. He obviously adores you and he's too honest not to.'

Praying no more skeletons lurked, she nodded.

'The Year Eleven Bet?'

Oh God, they knew about that? 'Yes.'

'Xander doesn't know we know and I'd like to keep it that way.'

She mimed locking her lips.

'The girls, some of whom I understand were treated quite appallingly, were daughters of our friends. One girl, Zara, went home and took an overdose of paracetamol. We couldn't avoid the looks and whispers. Henry Dowson-Jones filled me in on the bet. He thought it was bloody hilarious, but I'd never been so ashamed. Andrea stopped going to the WI and I left the Golf Club.'

Daisy closed her eyes for a second. 'You moved to Yorkshire because of what he did, because you couldn't live in the Lakes anymore?'

'Three years later, Zara tried again.'

'She succeeded. He told me. He feels partly responsible.'

'Her mother holds him entirely responsible. She used to be Andrea's closest friend. They still don't speak, you'll understand.'

'But Xander holds it against you. He thinks you're a selfish man who dragged his wife across two counties to get away from him.'

'It's better that way. Xander would be devastated if he knew the truth. I'd rather he hated me than knew he'd broken his mother's heart. You can't tell him.'

'I think you're wrong not to tell him. You said before, he's grown-up. Tell him, make him take responsibility for the things he's done. I do.'

'When you have children, Daisy, you'll understand. I don't want my son to go through any pain he doesn't have to.' His eyes were full of sincerity, but he looked around, changing the subject. 'I hear you made this happen.'

'Do you actually believe they can make it work?'

He lit his cigar again. 'Yes, I do. Xander's a natural chef with an impeccable palate and Robbie can turn his hand to anything. He should've gone to Oxford. He could've been a city banker or captain of industry, instead, he's a glorified holiday rep and breeds horses for peanuts. I wish they'd asked me to help with this place though.'

'But you know why they didn't?' Her mum appeared, brandishing a fresh bottle of cava. 'You're a bit of a bully.'

Daisy giggled, holding out her glass for a refill.

'Ganging up on me?' Oscar smiled. 'I see it as pushing them. They could do so much with their lives but they have no drive. They settle for average.'

'I hope you're not including my daughter in that,' Daisy's mum said, flashing a smile. Oh God, was she flirting?

'No, she's something else entirely.' Oscar laughed. 'With the restaurant, I'd have loaned them the money to buy somewhere better. Xander could get at least one Michelin star if he tried.'

'But this place is fabulous and he's not chasing Michelin stars,' Daisy argued. 'He wants to be a bloody good chef with his own restaurant, that's all.'

'Just like my father. He gave up his London restaurant to move here and live the quiet life. I never understood it.' Oscar sighed. 'I suppose they're more like him.'

'We should swap children,' her mum said. 'Daisy's never understood me.'

Oscar ran his fingers through his thick hair. 'I would like to help the boys.'

'Don't you think it'd be rather marvellous to let them show you what they can do? So you can be proud of them,' her mum said.

Oscar stubbed out his cigar. 'I'm already proud of them.'

'Then you really ought to tell them,' her mum smiled with utter kindness, 'because they haven't a clue.'

Her lavender fragrance lingered as she walked away and Daisy stared at her skinny, organic linen clad back. She'd stuck up for Daisy and she'd stuck up for Xander. Andrea Golding sat drumming her nails while Oscar berated her son. Laura Fitzgerald would never let anyone speak to her daughter like that.

Daisy had never been proud to be her mother's daughter – not until that moment.

She smiled up at Oscar. 'Would you like to come to dinner tomorrow? Xander can show off.' He didn't hide his delighted smile so Daisy did what her mum would do – she hugged him. 'I promise not to tell about the moving to Yorkshire thing. You can tell him in your own time.'

He laughed and dropped a kiss on her head. Ah, so this was where Xander and Robbie picked up the habit. As they returned to the table where Xander sat, Oscar held a chair out for Daisy and she smiled up at him to say thank you.

'Bloody hell,' Robbie said quietly to Xander, 'she really will flirt with anyone.'

Daisy gave him her best Marcus Dowson-Jones patented withering look.

Oh please be okay, JC.

Later, when everyone had left, she lay on the grass beside Xander, staring up at the starlit sky.

'What were you talking to my dad about?' he asked.

'You, me, the Mill.'

'You hugged him. Why?'

'Your dad isn't foul, Xander. He loves you and Robbie. He's a high achiever and doesn't understand why you two aren't, but he's trying to accept it. He said you were a *natural chef with an impeccable talent.*'

Xander's eyebrows were in his hairline. 'He thinks you're bloody marvellous.'

'I am.'

'Before they left, my dad hugged me goodnight. Christ, I don't think that's happened since I was seven. He said, *your wife's a delight. I'm very proud of you.* He actually said that. Marrying you has finally made my dad like me.'

'You idiot.' She kneeled astride his legs. 'Your dad wasn't telling you he was proud of you for bagging an ace wife. He was telling you he was proud of you for being you. Give him a chance.' Xander's hands snuck under her top, pushing it up. 'You do realise anyone walking down the road can see.'

'It's dark,' he said, sitting up, 'but the risk makes it more fun.'

Forfeit Likes: 12,392
@ForfeitHost followers: 15,341
@daisy_fitz followers: 5,197
@jiminy_cricket39 (aka Marcus) followers: 8,730
@dafdjbom: :(Marcus
@beth_marshall_2010: tried to visit him. Wouldn't let me in.
@pixieminxie: GWS, Marcus. And call me.

Two days later, Daisy followed Martin from the ANA Housing

Association around, trying to see errors, mistakes, fuck ups – to see what he was seeing. She couldn't. All she could see were pristine cream walls, satin-soft woodwork, freshly-waxed floor boards and gleaming windows. Skank Manor was gone; the Old Forge stood resplendent in its place.

'It's a long way from the pizza box and porn days,' she said, hoping to make Martin laugh.

Laugh? He'd barely cracked a smile to say hello. She knew why. The quality of her work, the end result would depend on the numbers he wrote on her cheque. Thousands rode on his judgement.

Martin didn't respond to her, he merely ran a hand over the granite work top in the kitchen while peering up at the ceiling. Were there cobwebs, cracks, what?

'Would you like tea?'

'No, thank you.' Finally, he stopped and smiled. 'I've another house to see. A wreck of a place potentially coming up for sale in the valley.'

'Really, where?' Daisy leaned on the breakfast bar, intrigued. *I want it.*

But Martin shook his head. 'Sorry.'

Okay, he was playing hardball. 'So what do I get?'

'The full ten percent.' He fought a smile. 'Plus twenty percent of the remaining budget.'

For all of twenty seconds, Daisy tried not to grin, but then she threw her arms around his neck. Seventeen thousand pounds. 'Thank you, so much.'

Laughing, Martin detangled himself. 'You deserve it. The house is worth three times what it was in September and more importantly, it means we can get a good family out of a hostel. Do you know where you'll go?'

Daisy shook her head.

'We have another couple of properties in Windermere that might suit you.'

Windermere? But she never planned to leave Gosthwaite. Then again, business was business. 'Why don't you email me the details.'

Martin handed over a stack of paperwork, promising the money would be in her account by three that afternoon and Daisy waved him off, determined not to happy dance until he was out of sight.

Birkin ran around, jumping up, barking merrily along with her excited squeals. Seventeen thousand pounds! She ripped open the envelope, wanting to see it in words, in figures.

Blah, blah, blah... *delighted to pay Ms Daisy Fitzgerald... outstanding project management... twenty thousand pounds.* What? Fifteen for completion on schedule and on budget, two for being under budget and three for being ahead of schedule. They'd rounded it up? Holy Mary... *Would like it if you would consider further renovation projects on behalf of the Ana Foundation.* They LOVED her. *Once again, many thanks for your hard work in creating a superb house for the foundation. Yours sincerely...*

Daisy stared at the name at the bottom of the letter. It had to be a joke. There's no way he'd write that letter. But there underneath a beautifully expressive signature, were the words James Dowson-Jones, founder of the Ana Foundation. Ana, not ANA. It was named after his mother, Anastasia.

But James hated her with a passion. So why would he house and employ her? Because Xander asked him, maybe? Okay, she could buy that, but now why would he be putting his name to it after all this time?

Unless he wanted her to know.

She grabbed her car keys and her handbag. Time for her second confrontation with James Dowson-Jones.

The address on the letter took her to the Dowson-Jones furniture factory and showroom. Daisy tentatively wandered in, letting her hand run over a purple silk sofa – it'd look fabulous in the Old Forge. In fact, every bit of furniture would sit perfectly in the Old Forge. One day she'd have her own house and she'd have fabulous furniture.

'Can I help you?' The girl behind the desk smiled up at her.

'I'd like to speak to James, please. James Dowson-Jones.'

'Can I ask what it's regarding?'

Daisy held up the letter.

The girl mouthed *oh*. 'Have to be careful. Poor James has a lot of nutters stalking him because of Forfeit.'

Ground, swallow me now. Daisy smiled. 'Is he in?'

The girl picked up the phone. 'Daisy's here to see you... will do.' She hung up the phone and gestured for Daisy to follow her through the back.

'How do you know my name?'

'It's on the top of the letter.' The girl grinned. 'And I'm a huge fan.'

'Of me? Why?'

'Because Xander's an arsehole.'

'He's also my husband.'

'And he'll break your heart like he broke all our hearts. We have a Facebook support group if you're interested.' She knocked on a half-open door.

'Daisy, come in,' said James' unmistakable drawl. 'Kelly, get us some coffee.'

Hiding behind the door, the receptionist saluted before scurrying away and Daisy, stifling a giggle, stepped inside.

James waved for her to take a seat, frowning from behind his black-framed glasses. Who knew James wore glasses? 'And you would want...'

Daisy refused to be intimidated by James. Instead, she remained standing to take stock of her surroundings. From the front, the building looked like a traditional slate barn – a vast version of the Bobbin Mill – but it was a facade. The opposite side of the building couldn't be more contemporary with its vast glass walls, acres of bare oak beams and cutting edge steel fittings. Plus the whole set up curved around a small tarn.

She could so work here. 'Nice office. Same architect who designed your boathouse?'

'Same *me* who designed my boathouse.'

Oh.

Denied the chance to deliver a sarcastic retort, she glanced away. A huge book case filled the majority of one wall and in the centre, in pride of place stood the Lalique vase she'd given James for his birthday.

'You kept it?' she asked.

'Of course. It's a very nice piece. Thank you.'

'You're welcome.' Finally, she sat down, unable to understand him, even a little bit. She held up the letter. 'Is this a joke?'

'The twenty grand is most likely already in your account.'

'And the rest of what you said?'

'It's just business. As much as I dislike you, you've a good eye for design, a knack for project management, plus more surprisingly, you're a bloody hard-worker. Who saw that coming?' He tossed a sheet of paper across the table. 'We have an internship coming up.'

'You're offering me a job?' Had she woken up in some parallel universe?

'It's working for peanuts, but it'd be a design job, *making* things. You can start in July, after St. Nick's closes for the summer.'

A definite parallel universe. 'But you hate me. Why would you do any of this?'

'Because he asked.'

'He asked?'

'He asked.'

Silence descended as Kelly crept in, delivering the coffee.

'I've found you a house,' he said, pressing the plunger on the cafetiere.

'Martin said there were places in Windermere.'

'No, this is for you to buy.' James handed her a brochure with her coffee. 'You can use your twenty thousand as a deposit.'

Intrigued, Daisy took the auction brochure. Lum Cottage, a rundown, two-up, two-down cottage attached to a barn. In Gosthwaite Mills? She knew this place. It was on the opposite side of the pub to the Old Forge. Guide Price: £200,000.

'As much as I'd love to, it'd still need another hundred grand—'

'I reckon one-fifty to convert the barn as well.' James sipped his coffee. 'Xander loves that cottage. It's where he spent most of his childhood.'

'His parents lived there?'

'Christ, no. They lived at Oakwood Hall. His grandparents lived in Lum Cottage. It's where Xander first learned to cook. He was eleven when they sold it and moved to the farm. What do you think?'

'I love it. He'll love it. But no one's going to give me a mortgage for three hundred and fifty grand.'

'I will.'

Daisy stared at him. 'You'll give me a mortgage?'

'A whacking great one, with very low interest and over an awful lot of years.' He leant forwards. 'But if you screw up in *any* way... default on a payment, fuck your ex-husband, I will do everything in my power to ruin your life.'

'So it's an insurance policy?'

'If you like.'

'I won't fuck up again.'

'Then we have a deal.'

'Does he know you're in love with him?'

Contempt flashed across James' face. 'Probably, but it's not something he'd ever bring up. Only an unthinking cow like you would.'

'Sorry.' She meant it.

'I hate you so much, it's almost irrational.'

'But I love him, he loves me and you need to get over it.'

To her surprise, James nodded. 'That's why I wrote the letter.'

'Thank you.'

'Want a tour?'

Finally, Daisy smiled. 'I'd *love* a tour.'

'Leave your coffee. You'll only spill it on something.'

She trotted behind him. 'You're really going to give me a job?'

'Yes,' he said, fighting a smile. 'But before you get too excited, remember you'll be working for *me*.'

'James!' Kelly the receptionist scurried after them. 'It's your mum... Bella, I mean. She's crying.'

James crumbled, falling against the wall with his eyes closed. As much as Daisy wanted to do anything but, she squeezed James' hand and took the phone from Kelly.

'Hello, Bella? It's Daisy.'

'He's awake, Daisy. Marcus is awake.'

Minutes later, Daisy sat in the passenger seat of James' Aston Martin and they whizzed towards the M6.

'I could throttle Tabitha,' Daisy said. 'Does she even care that her stupid game nearly killed Marcus?'

'I don't think she's behind the game,' James said.

'Why?' Daisy asked, folding her arms.

'She wouldn't do it to me.' He glanced at her. 'I know that sounds... but I know Tab, better than anyone does.'

'So who is behind it?'

'I don't know. I tracked down Uncle Sebastian, the one who sent the game,' James replied. 'I wondered if he knew who was behind the blackmail. To be honest, I wondered if it was him. He was a psychologist, liked messing with people's heads apparently.'

'And?'

'He's pissed up in Thailand these days, shagging some ladyboy and hasn't a clue but he did tell me more about the original game.' James rubbed his temple with the heel of his hand. 'He said her dare... Mum's dare was to get pregnant. She'd always told India that having her ruined her body and she never wanted another baby, but then she went and had one for a dare.'

'Your mum's dare was to get pregnant?' Daisy whispered, her heart thumping in her ears. Did James know it was her dare too?

'My dad's dare was to cheat on his spouse. It was probably just the push he needed to leave my mother.'

'Oh God, James.'

'I don't want Indy or Marcus to know, but this fucking game ruined my family, Daisy. We should never have played. We have no idea what it's going to do to us.'

'Well, it's nearly killed Marcus. All for trying to help someone in the name of a game.'

'No good deed goes unpunished.' James forced a smile. 'But he's going to be okay.'

'Here's an idea. Why don't you use this as a really good excuse to stop being such a twat to him?'

James lost his smile as he determinedly focussed on road in front of them.

'Marcus tore a strip off me last year,' she went on, 'and he was right to. I was selfish, spoiled and horribly judgemental. I know I still am, but if I get petulant, stroppy or sulky, I think of Marcus, my Jiminy Cricket. It's a shame he won't stand up to you. He's a sweetheart and you know it.'

For a millisecond, he smiled at her. 'You know this doesn't change anything. I still dislike you.'

'At least I know why now.' And *dislike* was a massive improvement on *hate*.

In the hospital, they hurried to Marcus' ward, but as they neared and Xander spotted them, James slowed.

'Xander's friendship means everything to me, Daisy. You won't tell him, will you?'

'Not a chance, sweetheart. One day he might decide he likes your ass better than mine and run off with you. I've heard about you public school boys.'

'You're such a bitch.' But he fought a smile.

'You see? You're warming to me already.'

'Tolerating, not warming. And, Daisy?' He paused, ensuring he had her full attention. 'Be careful, because I've a horrible feeling history's repeating itself.'

With a forced smile, she fell into Xander's arms. If she had the same dare as Ana Dowson-Jones, what if Xander had the same dare as Henry? What if his dare was to have an affair?

No.

She dug her nails into her palms and remembered his words at New Year when she asked what his dare was:

Something that'll never happen.

Whatever it was, he simply wasn't doing his dare.

Chapter Thirty-Three

For the fifth day in a row, Daisy woke vowing never to drink again. Ever. She flashed back, mentally tasting the chardonnay she'd drunk the night before, and her stomach churned. She scarpered to the toilet, staring into it for several minutes before finally throwing up. OMG. She rinsed her mouth before flopping back onto the floor, not daring to leave the room. Hangovers sucked.

'How much did I have to drink last night?' she asked Xander as he came in with a mug of tea.

Tea? The clear brown liquid had no milk in and smelled suspiciously like some herbal nonsense. She screwed up her face, but Xander laughed so she relaxed. At least he didn't despise her for getting hammered again. Had she even been hammered though?

She took a sip. 'That's actually really refreshing. What the hell is it?'

Xander sat on the edge of the bath. 'Lemon and ginger tea.'

'God, please stop me if I suggest drinking tonight.'

Although she'd been obeying the seven o'clock rule, the amount of wine consumed after wine o'clock had been excessive of late. Excuses were in abundance: Marcus' recovery, the Mill having running water, dinner for Robbie's birthday and the previous evening, simply because Xander wasn't working the next day.

'Daze... I don't think you're hung-over. You didn't drink that much.' His frown was back. 'I think you might be pregnant.'

She couldn't be, not this quickly, but Xander nodded and his frown grew. Fuck. She ran downstairs to the calendar. When the hell was her last period? She rested her forehead against the calendar, taking deep steady breaths, and thought logically.

She couldn't be pregnant. Hell, she couldn't get pregnant when she used the best bloody ovulation tests known to man for over a year. Xander had only been back for what, six weeks? It simply wasn't possible.

'You're five days late,' Xander said.

'How the hell do you know?' She turned to where he sat on the kitchen table. He didn't look anywhere near as freaked out as she felt.

'You go a bit nuts for a couple of days each month. I pay attention, so I know when to expect it.' He offered her the mug of lemon and ginger tea. 'This is what Vanessa drank to stop feeling sick. You'll have to do a test.'

She put the kettle on. She needed tea, real tea, not that herbal crap. 'No.'

'Don't be childish.'

It's only been six weeks. What if he thought it wasn't his? 'It might be something else. I could have cancer... or some other deadly disease.'

'Or you could be pregnant. Do a test.'

'Can't we just wait?'

'I don't want to spend the whole fucking day wondering, Daisy.'

'The fact that we have lemon and ginger fucking tea in the house suggests you've been wondering about this for a day or two?' He stared at the slate flagstones. 'I haven't and it's a bit of a bloody shock. Just give me an hour or two. Don't you have to go to work?'

'Day off. We were ...'

Going climbing. She nearly laughed. All week she'd been dreaming up wild excuses to avoid potentially plummeting to her death in a Lake District beauty spot – now she had the perfect sick note. Hurrah. She picked up her cigarettes.

'But you're...' Xander's words trailed away under the ferocity of her glare.

'I'm not pregnant yet, sunshine.'

Until she was officially pregnant, she wasn't going to worry about a cigarette or two. Hell, she'd had about twenty the day before, so a few today weren't going to make things a whole lot worse. She headed to the garden, needing the fresh air.

Could she really be pregnant? A surprising smile whipped across her face. God, she hoped so – she honestly really did. She loved Xander, he loved her and they were married. Her parents would be delighted – their first grandchild. And Oscar? She'd love to tell him. Yes, they'd go to Yorkshire to tell him and Andrea, and Cornwall to tell her parents – it was the least they could do after the wedding.

She'd left Xander sitting on the table wondering if he was going to be a daddy or not but, by the end of her first cigarette, she heard his car drive away. Off to the nearest *Boots* no doubt.

Two cups of tea and five cigarettes later, Xander came home with a pregnancy test.

'We need to know,' he said, tossing it to her.

Oh, bugger. She headed for the bathroom with Xander in tow.

'If you think I'm doing this in front of you, think again, baby.' She shut the door on him.

Hold the stick in the stream for five seconds exactly. Once upon a time, she'd panicked about the timing, but a year of pregnancy tests later, her own independent inquiry found that four or ten seconds delivered the same results. Negative. However, for the sake of science and her mental well-being, she held the stick in the stream for as near as she could to five seconds. Then they had to wait for *up to three minutes.*

The silence was palpable as they sat on the sofa, holding hands. *Please, be positive. Please.*

Oh God, if she was pregnant, as happy as that would make her, would Xander be okay with it? She glanced up at him. He had his head back, staring at the ceiling, not looking remotely excited about this. Why the hell would he? He was twenty-three and they'd known each other for less than a year.

Pregnant.

'OMG.' She stared at the little screen.

Christ, there was no ambiguity with digital pregnancy tests. She longed for the cheap, old-school tests, the kind where you triple-checked the instructions to see what a blue line meant. It wasn't a difficult concept, but when you were trying to read the results of a pregnancy test it quickly became rocket science. Was a blue line yes or a blue line no? With this one, it was as clear as her mum's eco-conscience. Daisy was pregnant.

'Oh my God. I guess all those doctors were right.' She took several deep breaths to calm her heart rate, never daring to look at Xander. There wasn't anything wrong with her. She was pregnant. Trying not to smile, she did the sums on her fingers. 'March.'

'It doesn't work like that,' Xander said, finally looking down at her. He had the blankest impression. 'You count from the first day of your last period, so you'll officially be about five weeks pregnant, although in reality you'll have only been pregnant for about two and half, maybe three weeks. I'm guessing, well, I'd like to think it was after the Topping Off party.'

She smiled for a millisecond, remembering the Bobbin Mill garden shagging before the implications of his pregnancy knowledge hit home.

'How the hell do you know all that? Knocked up many girls?' Nausea wafted over her again. Three hundred and eighteen other girls, at least some of them had to go wrong.

'When you're stressed, you can be such a bitch. No, I haven't. You're the first.' He tried looking cross, but the longer he kept eye contact with her, the bigger his cheeky smile became. 'But I... er, am feeling a bit smug. I've succeeded where the HMS failed.'

He kissed her head, hiding his silly grin in her hair, and she swatted him for his Neanderthal man attitude. But really, she adored that he'd made her smile.

'So how are you a pregnancy Yoda?'

'Vanessa's been pregnant a lot. Six times.'

'But there're only...' Three children, which meant three didn't make it. Horrified, Daisy stared at the word *Pregnant* still visible on the little digital screen.

'She had three miscarriages. That's why there's a big gap between Tallulah and Matilda.' Through narrowed eyes, he studied her for a moment, before finally smiling. 'Well, that answers that question. For the first time, I couldn't tell from your face how you felt, but you'd be gutted if you lost this baby, wouldn't you?' She nodded. 'Me too.'

'Aren't you scared?'

He dragged a hand through his hair. 'Christ, yes.'

'It's not exactly ideal timing, is it? We've only been together for ten minutes and there's the restaurant.' Daisy nibbled the skin on her lip.

'No, it's not, Daze, but we'll cope.' He smiled, his eyes twinkling. 'We're having a baby.'

OMG.

'You'll have to stop drinking and smoking.'

OMFG.

'And eat even better than you do now.'

'Oh God, I'll get fat.'

'No, you'll get a bump.'

'Fat,' she said, sulking.

'You'll be pregnant and very, very beautiful.'

Fat. 'Shall we tell Robbie and Van? And Clara?'

He shook his head. 'You generally go public at twelve weeks because after that, the chance of losing it is a lot less.'

'I hate that you know all about this and I don't. Can I Google it?'

He nodded and she left him sat on the bed looking somewhere between terrified and elated – exactly how she felt.

An hour or so later she emerged from Googleland a whole lot better informed and in her element.

'You have no idea how many acronyms get used online,' she said, lacing up her hiking boots, 'especially around pregnancy stuff. Today I had MS, so POAS and got a BFP.'

'You are very, very weird,' Xander replied, picking up Birkin's ball. 'You've just found out you're pregnant and you're excited about a new batch of acronyms. What does that lot mean anyway?'

'I had Morning Sickness, so Pissed On A Stick, that's my favourite, and got a Big Fat Positive.'

'Very weird.' Shaking his head, he hovered in the doorway and held up a key. 'Want to see Lum Cottage?'

She squealed, nodding. 'How–'

'I know the guy who lives next door.' Xander took her hand. 'Did you find out what you're not allowed to eat, drink and do?'

'What, aside from booze and fags? I lost the will to live after that.' Daisy merrily plodded down the road. 'Can't eat offal. No sad loss there. Shellfish, unpasteurised things. Apparently ginger nut biscuits are a good MS repellent, so they might have to become the new Hobnob. Got to be low fat, healthy. It's all fairly pants really, but aside from booze and fags I don't think there's anything I can't live without. Yes, there was. No runny eggs.' Along with his fabulous homemade pizzas, she loved Xander's Eggs Benedict more than she loved him. 'Oh, limited caffeine was a bit of a blow. What the hell do you drink when you can't have wine or tea?'

'Fruit juice? And that clear stuff... water, I think it's called.'

'Sounds awful.' They passed the Miller's Arms and the slate roof of Lum Cottage peeked over the trees to the right. Daisy's pace quickened. 'So honestly, three hundred girls and no little accidents?'

Xander scowled down at her. 'I might've been, as you've so delightfully put it, the school *ho*, but I was a very, very careful school *ho*. Can you say the same?'

Was that the driveway? Deep ruts lay either side of the middle turf track. Xander's Golf would struggle down it, never mind the MX5. She'd have to get a new car.

'No,' Daisy admitted. 'If we ignore my previous married life when I did a test every hellish month, I've done three tests in the past, all negative, which is why I thought it was me. But it has made me wonder...'

'If your ex-husband is firing blanks?' Xander nodded. 'Clearly, it wasn't you. You've managed to get pregnant without even trying.'

In front of them lay the smallest and most dilapidated cottage in the world. Two beds, a kitchen, a bathroom and a living room – the whole thing would fit into half of Skank Manor. And it made Skank Manor look like... well, Gosthwaite Hall.

'How has this happened?' Xander asked.

She'd prepared for the question while he'd gone to Boots. Initially, she'd opted for a flippant, *when a mummy and a daddy really love each other...* retort, but it'd only delay the inevitable. Her plan was to own up – a little bit, at least.

'I've been a bit crap at taking the pill here and there.'

It was almost true. Before Christmas, she must've forgotten to take it at least twice a month and never even had a scare. Considering the amount of shagging that had gone on with Xander, she'd assumed she really was utterly infertile but clearly, she hadn't given the pill the credit it deserved.

'I didn't worry about it because nothing ever happened with the HMS. I'm sorry.'

The last bit was very true.

'It's okay.'

She wanted to cry with relief. Green fields edged all four sides of the house, in the yard there were stables and outbuildings.

'Did you look up the other things you can't do?' he asked, unlocking the front door. 'Christ, I'd forgotten how tiny it is.'

But Daisy could see past the tiny rooms, mentally knocking down partition walls. 'I triple-checked shagging and that's fine.'

'I meant running. You have to keep your heart rate under one-twenty, I think.'

'Really? I have to give up drinking, smoking, looking good *and* being fit? Can't you have this baby inst...' A huge smile took over her face. 'Bugger, I'm having a baby.'

'Finally, it hits her.' In the middle of what may well be their new hallway, Xander hugged her. 'It's not just about being pregnant. It's a baby too. I bet you've been concentrating on the dramatic way you can tell people, haven't you?'

Guilty as charged. 'Are we going to be okay, Xand?'

'Honestly? I'd have preferred to have a few years of just you and me, being happy together, but I love you, we're married and it would've happened at some point. We'll be fine.' He kissed her nose. 'If it's a boy, can we call him Oliver?'

'Of course.'

He could pick all the boys' names he liked, but she knew, just knew this was a girl. She'd have blond curly hair and huge brown eyes, just like Daisy had imagined in January.

'Show me round?' she asked, excitedly heading through the door on their right.

It led to a sitting room, which even devoid of any furniture left little cat swinging room. But Xander gazed around in wonder, running a hand over the yellowing wallpaper.

'It's not changed since Grandma and Grandpa lived here.' Suddenly, his eyes lit up and he darted out of the room, heading across the hallway and into the kitchen.

Daisy found herself in up-cycling heaven. From the white-painted cupboards and pitch-pine worktops, this was serious Lakeland heritage. She'd have to preserve as much as possible when she renovated it.

'Daze?' Xander held out a hand, beckoning her over to the pantry.

Inside were a series of small horizontal lines etched into the wall. Beside each were dates and either an X or an R. The Golding Brothers' growth chart. Daisy pressed her hand to her mouth and she gazed up at him. They absolutely had to buy the house.

Upstairs, the windows were rotten, the floorboards creaking, but Xander's smile simply kept growing and Daisy's brain worked overtime, ripping out false ceilings, knocking through to the barn next door.

'We must be mental.' Xander pushed open the barn doors, frowning at the ancient beams.

'It might be full of hay and cow poo now,' she said, 'but one day, that is going to be your dream kitchen.'

She pointed her finger to the far end of the barn and Xander wandered over, his eyes scanning the space, planning the space. Then it hit her. She'd done her dare. She'd actually done her stupid dare.

In six weeks' time, they had to go to the OBB to reveal their dares but instead of rocking up and admitting she hadn't done hers or making up some new dare, she had every chance of winning twenty-five bloody grand, twenty-five bloody grand she could spend on Lum Cottage.

Of course, since Xander wouldn't be terribly impressed to know she'd stopped taking the pill in January, she'd have to stress it had all happened fortuitously.

Be careful, because I've a horrible feeling history's repeating itself.

Remembering James' words brought back her nausea. What if Xander didn't believe her? He'd forgiven her for so much already, would he trust and forgive her again? It was a risk she wasn't prepared to take. There was only one way out – he couldn't ever know getting pregnant on purpose had even crossed her mind. Oscar said it was better to lie about why they moved to Yorkshire than have Xander know the truth and get hurt.

Surely this was the same.

Chapter Thirty-Four

When Marcus called, on June 28th, Daisy was sitting on a vastly depleted pile of plasterboards, munching a ginger nut biscuit as she ordered slate samples. Robbie wanted cheap from China; Daisy wanted locally sourced. There had to be some kind of compromise. Xander was arguing with Robbie about exactly where the various hobs and ovens should go, so Daisy answered the call.

'Hello, JC. How's the leg?'

He didn't reply.

'Marcus?'

There was a sharp intake of breath. Was he crying or trying really hard not to?

'Marcus, what is it?'

'Tabitha. The Police just came to see me because her parents are away and I'm her listed next of kin. She killed herself, Daisy. Took a cocktail of drugs last night. I haven't spoken to her since February after what she did to you, but now she's dead. I have to go and identify the body, her body this afternoon...'

'Oh God, I'm so sorry, Marcus.' Daisy covered the mouthpiece and darted over to Xander. 'Tabitha's topped herself.'

Leaving him to speak to Marcus, she wandered outside. Tabitha was dead. Dead. And what was her initial reaction? *Hurrah.* The stupid cow had tried to ruin Daisy's life, she'd made them play Forfeit which nearly killed Marcus. What should Daisy do, put on a grieving front and look sad? Lie through her teeth and question why Tabitha would do such a thing? Or should she dance a merry, little jig?

Ding dong, the bitch is dead.

Shame Tabitha had picked such a lovely day to die on? Twenty-three degrees and not a cloud to mar the cyan sky. Daisy had planned to have a picnic in the Bobbin Mill garden – God, it was picturesque, real Ratty and Mole country with the river gently babbling by and the sprawling view of the fells. Hell, there was even a little stone footbridge and a huge willow tree downstream.

For God's sake, she needed to get her head together not daydream of picnics and dangling her feet in the water. Was she supposed to cry? Scowling, she threw a stone in river. She didn't feel like crying. She'd actually told Xander the week before, how she hoped she never saw Tabitha again. Okay, so she wouldn't miss her, but wasn't she a little bit sad the girl was dead?

Quite frankly, no. She wasn't sad.

Tabitha probably only did it for gossip column inches – to get her face in the paper. It'd worked so bloody well for her in January. Bugger it, bugger Tabitha and bugger that Daisy should feel sorry for her.

Thirty minutes after Marcus' call, Daisy peered through a small window in a hospital door at the cold, dead, sheet-covered body of Ms Tabitha Catherine Doyle. Two policemen hovered by the bed and it all felt remarkably like CSI, despite the five star, private hospital setting. Only Tabitha Doyle could top herself and end up in the swankiest morgue in the North West. Daisy had stayed in five-star hotels with lower thread count bedding.

But it was a morgue and that was a dead body, so Daisy refused to go into the room. She'd never seen a corpse before, and she didn't fancy starting with Tabitha. James nodded when she uttered this, seemingly using it as the explanation why he wasn't going in either. But from the tears occasionally trickling down his face – she suspected his reason was quite the opposite.

In the room, Xander and Marcus headed over to the bed, the latter nodding as the older policeman spoke to him. Daisy held her breath as the doctor pulled back the sheet, but chickened out and looked away before she saw anything. The younger policeman smiled. Laughing at her? His eyes creased. Oh God, was he *flirting*? Daisy refused to smile back – even she wouldn't flirt at Tabitha's deathbed – but the guy was serious eye-candy. Actually, the other copper wasn't half bad. Wasn't it typical, that even on her VIP death bed, Tabitha had somehow managed to land fit policemen to watch over her?

'Are you okay?' Daisy asked James as she sat beside him.

He shook his head. Poor guy. Without thinking, she put her arm around him, and to her astonishment, he let her.

'Did she know you loved her?' Daisy asked quietly.

'I doubt it.' James sighed, wiping his eyes. 'Ironic, isn't it? The only two people who've ever vaguely interested me, I have to watch fawn over you and your bastard ex-husband.'

'It's no wonder you hate me.' Daisy stroked his hair. God, how maternal was she becoming?

'Have you told Finn about Tab?'

'No.' She still couldn't bring herself to speak to him. 'He can find out from the papers.'

'The police said it's all being kept hush-hush. No one seems to know about it yet, so they're trying to notify her parents first.'

'Trying? Why, where are they?'

'Middle of nowhere in Sri Lanka,' he said, his voice cracking. 'Opening a school they paid for. No one can get hold of them.'

Her poor parents. They'd be feeling smug and worthy only to be told their darling daughter was lying in a morgue after taking far, far too many recreational drugs. If Tabitha genuinely took the overdose then Daisy felt for her, she really did, but what the hell would make Tabitha so unhappy? Didn't get the Corrie gig? Rather cynically, Daisy's money was still on this being an *attempted* suicide.

'Did she leave a note, you know, explaining?' Daisy asked.

'No, but I don't think this was intentional. It's not like Tab.'

'Who found her?'

'Some guy,' James replied. 'He disappeared after he let the paramedics in. The police are trying to trace him, but all they know is he's an American with dark hair.'

'Todd?' Daisy suggested. The New York DJ fit the bill and he'd done a runner last time Tabitha took too many drugs and keeled over.

'That's my guess.' James leant forwards, putting his head in his hands. 'But what if it wasn't an accident, Daisy? What if she did this on purpose because none of us would speak to her anymore?'

'Then that's the bed she made.' Daisy lifted her chin. 'I will not have her death on my conscience. She did what she did.'

'But I was part of that.' James' voice broke and Daisy hugged him tighter, dropping a reassuring kiss on his head.

If Tabitha weren't dead, she would've throttled the silly cow.

The door opened and Xander wandered from the room, his jaw clenched, his eyes staring resolutely ahead of him. Why wouldn't he just cry? She wanted to dash to comfort him, but James beat her to it.

'That was hideous,' Marcus said, hobbling on his crutches. 'Let's go back to ours. I need a fag and a very large glass of something white.'

How the hell could she get out of drinking and smoking without telling Marcus she was pregnant? Panicked, she glanced at Xander, hoping for an *it'll be fine* wink or supportive nod, but he stalked towards the exit, his jaw tightly clenched. Really, why wouldn't he just cry?

Daisy smiled her thanks to the dreadlocked and bearded porter who held the door open for them. Surprising that such a high-end private hospital didn't insist on smarter staff. Or maybe they were to add *colour*. The porter totally stared at her arse as she walked past, but she tried not to grin. Even pregnant, she could still pull. Hurrah.

'Don't offer Daze any fags,' Xander said as they reached the cars. 'She's finally given up.'

'He nagged me into submission,' she added, crossing her fingers behind her back. Lying to her Jiminy Cricket was the worst.

Marcus fought a smile as he raised his eyebrows. Clearly, he didn't believe a word of it.

'Mum wondered if you two would like to come out to our place in Italy this summer, maybe August?' He glanced across at Daisy. 'We can tour the vineyards, getting hammered.'

Oh, that was too unfair; she'd be four months pregnant. Before she could utter some other lie, Marcus laughed and nudged her with a crutch. He so knew. Mercifully, Xander distracted her, by donning a pair of Wayfarer's James handed him. In just under twelve months, she'd never seen Xander wear sunglasses.

'Why don't you ever wear sunglasses?' she asked him.

Xander took hold of her hand. 'Just because I don't.'

James laughed. 'More like just because his big brother once told him that you shouldn't hide your best pulling tool behind a pair of Oakley's.'

'I preferred it when you two hated each other,' Xander said.

'FYI,' Daisy replied, elbowing him, 'your eyes aren't your best pulling tool.'

'What is?' Even with the sunglasses on, she knew he was looking her over.

'Your well stocked drinks cupboard.'

'You must be the only girl he's had to ply with drink to take to pull. Well done for playing hard to get, *tesoro*.' Marcus high-fived her.

'Want to drive?' James asked her, holding up his car keys to Daisy.

'Are you serious?' she asked, and at his nod, she squealed, snatching the keys. 'This is the *best* day ever.'

The boys all stared at her.

Bugger. 'I didn't mean... well, *this* bit's quite good. And it does mean the stupid game's over. No more blackmailing bitch to worry about.'

'She's dead,' Marcus said, 'and we don't know it was her.'

'Oh, come on. She's the only person who knows enough to blackmail us all. She knows all your dirty little secrets, right?'

Marcus nodded, his frown worsening.

'And what she doesn't know, James fills her in on.' Daisy raised her eyebrows questioning him.

James guiltily looked away. 'And she knew about you, because she stole Finn's phone?'

Daisy nodded, satisfied. 'It was Tabitha, the evil cow.'

'The *only* thing I like about you,' James said, 'is your unfailing honesty. You could've lied through your teeth today, faking concern for the person who fucked your husband. But you? I don't think I've ever met anyone less two-faced.'

'OMG. James, are you aware that was a compliment?' She blew him a kiss and he gave her the finger. But they both smiled.

He was definitely warming to her.

Beep, beep.

Forfeit *has sent you a message.*
I like your new profile picture.

Without hesitation, Daisy clicked on her name, opening the *Daisy – Forfeit Player* page. The narrow, horizontal page header didn't show much, but it was unmistakably a side-on torso shot of a woman lying on a bed. Naked. And the profile shot... God, it only showed her mouth, but it was cropped from the photo on Finn's phone and it suggested everything. Who was doing this if it wasn't Tabitha?

Letting out a banshee wail, Daisy hurled her phone across the room.

This wasn't over.

Finally getting off the phone after an hour long chat to Clara, Daisy found Xander, fresh out of the shower, lying on the bed and staring at the ceiling.

'I hate Clara not knowing,' she said. 'I daren't meet her in person. I feel like I've got *PREGNANT* written across my forehead. Do I look different?'

Xander's eyes lit up with a cheeky glint.

'Stop it,' she said, putting her hands over her stupid, rock-solid nipples. Since she got knocked up, she seemed to be perpetually horny, and Xander sitting there, half-naked only encouraged her rampant hormones. 'It's not my fault.'

'Only you, Fitzgerald.' He winked. 'I know what you mean though. Whenever I see Rob, I'd swear he knows. Look, it's only three weeks to wait and then we can tell everyone about Bean.'

Daisy struggled not to grin. After she'd been to the doctor, passed his test and become officially pregnant, her new hobby was reading about the development of the baby. The week before, she'd discovered their eight week-old unborn child was growing hands and feet and was about the size of a kidney bean. Since then, Xander had taken to calling it Bean – a definite improvement on *It*. She sat next to him, taking hold of his hand.

'Shouldn't you be going for a shower?' he asked.

Yes, but she didn't want to get ready because she didn't want to go out. It was July 1st, the night they were going to the OBB to reveal how they'd completed their dares. She'd done her real dare but got Clara to write: *quit your job and try a different career* on a new piece of card. Despite Clara grilling her for an hour, Daisy refused to divulge the original dare.

'I can't summon the enthusiasm, too tired.'

At least that was the truth. Each week, she'd become increasingly exhausted. She'd yawn throughout the day and barely made it to half-past nine before falling asleep on the sofa, but if Xander sent her to bed she'd be wide awake. He squeezed her hand, frowning with concern.

'I'm fine,' she said. 'Anyway, why are you looking so thoughtful?'

'I've been trying to work out when I fell in love with you.' His fingers linked with hers, his thumb brushing the back of her hand.

'I thought it was on my bastard ex-husband's birthday.'

'No, that's when I realised I was already in love with you. Do you know I stood outside Clara's cottage, staring at you for about five minutes? I kept thinking, oh fuck, no. I'd have been happy to be in love with the Daisy I took to James' party, but the skin and bone mess I saw in August? You were a wreck.' He tipped his head, smiling an apology. 'But I'd never felt like that about anyone before, not even Imogen, and no matter how much I wanted to, I couldn't run away.'

'So when was it, James' party, the morning after out on the deck?'

'No. That's when you realised something had changed.' He brushed a wayward curl off her face. 'I fell in love with you over tea and toast.'

'What, the morning after the one night stand? You're not serious.'

'I'd heard you sneak downstairs and I lay in bed telling myself to let you go, because the last thing you needed was someone like me. But then I thought, what if I needed you?'

'Why on earth did you need *me*?' She'd never understood that bit.

'Because you made me feel twenty-two again.' He looked up at the ceiling, smiling. 'Christ, I could've sat there just talking with you forever, but there was this point, where we looked at each other, smiling. That's when it happened.' He rested his forehead against hers. 'Nothing's changed. I love you, Daisy.'

His honesty broke her heart and tears stung her eyes as she kissed him. There was no way she could lie about her dare. She had to own up or she'd never be able to live with herself. Dragging her lips from his, she pasted on a smile and got ready for a world-rocking night out.

Forfeit Likes: 17,419
@ForfeitHost followers: 17,173
@daisy_fitz followers: 9,301
@polilrichgal: Fugly Ho's going down tonight. #fuglyho
@dafdjbom: did you do the dare?
@beth_marshall_2010: hope you win. #forfeit #hesnoangel
@pixieminxie: someone said Tabitha's dead. Is she?

From the safety of her enormous sunglasses, Daisy stared in horror at the crowd hovering outside Oscar's Bar and Bistro. She'd expected one or two of the cannier Facebook followers to have sussed out the three time and venue changes, but there had to be fifty people sitting in the beer garden alone.

'Come on,' Xander said, kissing her head. 'I love you. Never forget that.'

'I love you too.'

But their conversation was said behind sunglasses, hiding them from the flashes going off around the car. Several looked too professional to be Xander's fangirls. The side door to the bar opened and two doormen stepped out, pushing a gap through the crowd, creating a walkway for Daisy and Xander.

It was now or never.

On the odd occasion she'd attended some red carpet event with Finn, the crowd had yelled and cheered, just because he'd climbed out of the car. But when Xander climbed out, a deathly hush fell over the throng outside the OBB. Daisy took his hand, grasping it to stop hers shaking. What if they booed her, spat at her, threw things at her? Thousands of people hated her, someone had followed her, *@polilrichgal* campaigned tirelessly against her.

Daisy huddled into Xander, adoring the protective arm he wrapped around her.

I will tear down the world...

He'd protect her, she knew that, but she couldn't stop it happening.

'Daisy! We love you.'

'Go, miss.'

She glanced around. Briony and Lola from Year Eight.

'You're the bomb!'

Stunned, she glanced up at Xander, and he nodded to the bar. 'Get inside. The ones who love you, usually hate me.'

'Daisy, Daisy, Daisy...' the crowd chanted.

They loved her. But why didn't that make her happy?

Inside, the tables were filled with chit-chatting customers all pretending it was just another Tuesday in July, but almost every head turned as Daisy and Xander walked through to the side bar where they'd rolled that bloody Teetotum ball on New Year's Eve.

A *Private Party* sign barred their way, but the blonde barmaid refilling the fridge with bottles of Magners waved them in. James and Marcus were already lounging on the vast leather Chesterfield, with their feet propped on the wooden table in front of them.

'Get your shoes off my inheritance,' Xander said, playfully slapping James' foot.

'I got you drinks,' Marcus said, nodding to the pint of lager and the large glass of red on the table.

Oh God, could she pretend to drink it and tip the wine into a plant pot when he wasn't looking? Marcus grinned at her as James and Xander chatted quietly at the other end of the table.

'Try it,' he said, handing her the glass. 'Something we make at mum's vineyard. She hasn't drunk alcohol for years.'

What? The wine looked the part, and as Daisy sipped it, she groaned with pleasure. Okay, it lacked the alcohol burn, but it tasted like the real thing. She had no intention of drinking anything else until Bean popped out.

'I take it Xander knows?' he whispered.

She nodded. 'Please don't say anything.'

'Happy?'

Again, she nodded.

'Congratulations,' he whispered, dropping a kiss on her cheek. 'How's little miss Kick-Ass?'

'Not good.' Marcus ran his hands through his hair, sighing. 'She found out what was going on tonight and that it was why I'd volunteered. She... she basically told me I was a self-indulgent rich kid with too much money and not enough morals. She doesn't want to see me again.'

Oh poor Marcus. 'Don't take any notice. You're not the least bit self-indulgent and your morals are better than anyone I know, even my parents. Prove her wrong. Win her over.'

'I'm going to see her later. When this charade is...' Marcus frowned, looking over her shoulder. 'Ella?'

Ella Andrews sauntered over, a young guy with an SLR camera in tow. 'Marcus, how are you, darling?'

Daisy scowled at Ella. '*You* were behind this?'

Ella shook her head.

'Then why are you here?' James snapped.

'Like I'd miss scoop of the century?' She laughed, flopping into the sofa opposite them. 'Unless you were donating all the money to the National Trust, it's hardly the *Life's* thing, but it'll sell to someone. I'll fill in some *interesting* character profiles.' Slowly, she looked Xander over, and from the glint in her eye, it looked as if she didn't need imagination to fill in the areas his t-shirt and jeans covered. 'How are you, Xand?'

'Fuck off, Ella,' Xander snapped as he moved along the sofa to sit next to Daisy. 'This isn't a scoop.'

'Are you aware,' Ella said, her pencil poised over her old school notepad, 'there are three copycat groups on Facebook alone. They're rolling the dice, necking the shots, doing their made-up dares. It'll make a great state of the nation story.'

Marcus scowled. 'But we're nobodies.'

'You might be, but she isn't.'

'Me?' Daisy laughed. 'I'm hardly—'

'Not you, sweetheart,' Ella said, rolling her eyes. 'Tabitha.'

The silence couldn't scream loudly enough.

It was James that finally spoke. 'Flick... Tabitha's—'

'Ta-da!' The barmaid leapt up behind the bar, her arms raised like a rock diva, before she grabbed her scruffy peroxide up-do, ripping it off her head.

Tabitha.

It really was. She let down her real hair, shaking it out into a tousled auburn bob, then helped herself to a shot of Jack Daniels.

'Am I the greatest fucking actress, or what?'

Daisy wanted to turn to the others, to check out their expressions – to see if any of them were in on it but she couldn't take her eyes off Tabitha. She wasn't dead and that stupid tinkly bloody laugh rang out across the deathly silent bar. The Forfeit stalkers in the main bar, peered through the doorway, speaking in hushed voices, no doubt trying to work out what the hell was going on.

'Have you all done your dares?' Tabitha asked, her elbows resting on the bar behind her. 'Faking my death was mine. *Pride: See who loves you.* Oh, look, you all did.'

'Not all of us,' Daisy mumbled. 'That's why both the policemen were total eye candy. They were actors.'

'Bingo.'

A camera flash distracted Daisy from the clearly insane Ms Doyle.

'Your faces,' Ella said, laughing.

Xander and Marcus still stared at Tabitha, clearly too stunned to move, but James walked straight up to her and slapped her – really, bloody hard, hard enough to leave a huge red mark. Slapping was so underused these days.

'You did it for a dare?' His hands gripped her shoulders – the anger in his face suggesting he might shake her to death, but when she looked up at him, her enormous green eyes filled with tears and he groaned. Disappointingly, instead of murdering her, he hugged her. 'You stupid, stupid...'

'Ding dong, the bitch is un-dead,' Daisy said. 'Try it for real, next time.'

From James' enveloping hug Tabitha glared with venom, but before a cat-fight broke out, he dragged her to the far side of the bar. There, he held her face in his hands, asking if she were crazy, didn't she care what she'd put everyone through... what she'd put *him* through?

From Tabitha's blank stare, clearly no.

'Okay, I'm on your side,' Marcus whispered to Daisy, warily eyeing Ella. 'This has to be part of the Coronation Street master plan. You were right all along.'

'Don't get jaded on me now,' Daisy replied, 'Your trust, honesty and integrity give me hope for the future of the human race.'

When James and Tabitha came back, she sat on the arm of his chair, smiling down at Daisy. Things got worse when she took a mouthful of Daisy's wine and almost spat it straight back out again.

'What the hell is that?' She wrinkled her nose in disgust. 'Sweetie, is that alcohol free wine? What are you, pregnant or something?'

Cue the irritating tinkle. Valiantly, Daisy resisted the almost overwhelming urge to slap Tabitha herself – there were more important things at stake. This was it. The moment Xander would hate her, maybe forever this time.

'Yes.'

'Number Fourteen was my mum's card.' James' brow creased. 'It was in her hand when Indy found her body. You did it?'

It was a close run thing, but Daisy's raised chin won out over tears as she tossed her dare card on the table. 'I did it.'

As she feared, Xander turned to her. She focussed on his eyes, waiting for the disbelief, the horror, the look of hatred. They never came. His face remained emotionless as he kept eye-contact and dropped his dare card on the table. A second item landed on top of it and made her more nauseous than morning sickness ever had.

It was their marriage certificate.

Chapter Thirty-Five

A dare. Xander married her for his dare.

Silence swamped the room and Daisy stared longingly at Marcus' alcoholic wine. Xander had married her for the chance to win twenty-five grand. The ultimate tip money.

What had he done?

What had they *both* done?

The camera flashed again and Tabitha's laugh tinkled next to her.

'We must be mental,' Marcus said, stretching out his recovering leg. 'I read my dare and thought, this is a good challenge. *Kindness: Help a homeless person change their life.*'

'One dare done,' James drawled. 'Ross has a roof over his head. It's a prison roof, but it's still a roof.'

'Wasn't quite my intention and that was Uncle Sebastian's point.' He turned to his brother. 'I talked to mum yesterday.'

James gave a derisory laugh. 'My mother's dead thanks to this fucking game.'

'Bella, the woman who *raised* you?' Marcus said angrily. 'She wrote half the dares, the ones to counteract Sebastian's Sins.'

'She wrote the Holy Virtue dares?' Daisy asked.

Marcus nodded. 'Sebastian's theory was that you give someone a sin and initially they won't do it. Give someone a virtue – they happily will. But give those people a year to think it over, then what happens?'

'We talk ourselves into doing the unthinkable.' Xander leant forwards.

Like marrying me?

'And we get fuck all satisfaction from doing a good deed.' James shook his head. '*Bella* wrote the dares? Pull the other one.'

'She was a psych student with Sebastian,' Marcus explained. 'Dad's brother's girlfriend. Forfeit's where our fucked up family went wrong. And look at us. We've proved Sebastian right.'

'Oh, how's that?' James asked, leaning forwards.

'Tabitha's pride is satiated. She knows we all love her, but do you think she's realised yet that we'll never forgive her?' Marcus shook his head. 'Xander loves Daisy, and he'd have married her anyway, but will she ever believe that? He's risked her trust again, for what? Twenty-five thousand pounds. Doesn't he know that you'd give him fifty grand right now, if you knew it would make him happy? And Daisy–'

'I get it. There's no forgiveness for what she's done.' James shook his head at her. 'I fucking warned you.'

But it was too late and I thought it'd be fine to get pregnant for my own self-indulgent reasons.

Oh God, this was the absolute end of her and Xander.

'Oh, lighten up, James.' Tabitha downed the last mouthful of his wine. 'It was a hoot. What did you do anyway? What was your dare?'

'*Kindness. If someone asks, you say yes.*' He tossed his card on the table. 'It's been hell. And utterly pointless.'

Because he asked.

'My job, the house...' Daisy took a deep breath. 'It was part of your *utterly pointless* dare?'

James nodded. 'He asked. I had to say yes.'

'But you're not actually giving *her* a job?' Tabitha visibly shuddered. 'You hate her.'

'Maybe, maybe not.' James turned to Daisy. 'The job still stands. And the loan.'

Tabitha swore. 'What is it with this *fugly ho*?'

Daisy let out a barely restrained scream. 'You *are* Poor Little Rich Girl.'

'Is Daisy right?' Xander asked, his voice ominously low. 'Are you Poor Little Rich Girl?'

'All those tweets?' Daisy asked. 'They were you?'

'Payback.' Tabitha scowled.

'And the game?' James asked quietly.

'No,' Tabitha said, her eyes filling up with crocodile tears. 'I didn't blackmail any of you. Now will someone get me a fucking drink?'

James poured Tabitha a huge glass of red but as he handed it to her, he shook his head and she stared at the floor, reprimanded and defeated.

But she wasn't the only one. Daisy put her glass on the table and sighed. 'We must be the most immoral bunch of people in the world.'

'Undoubtedly,' Xander said. 'But it's over.'

'It's not over,' James replied. 'One day, she'll have to explain all this to that kid. You'll need this for the therapy bills.' James tossed the fat envelope stuffed with twenty-five grand to Daisy. 'That's the real forfeit, not the money. That's what we've all forfeited.' In turn, he looked at Daisy, Marcus, Tabitha then finally, Xander. 'Trust.'

Daisy watched Xander's impassive face, but he still refused to look at her. She should leave. Run like hell and just drive. She shifted in her seat, about to stand, but Xander held out his hand. Was it an olive branch, to show he would hear her out? Tentatively, she linked her fingers with his. If she expected him to give her a chance to explain, she had to do the same.

'Daisy,' Tabitha said, her eyes narrowing to venomous slits, 'this really isn't over.'

They didn't bother with goodbyes.

During the horrific, death march through the crowded bar, each of Daisy's mental screams of *he married me for a dare* was parried with a *you got pregnant on purpose*, and her tears were only kept at bay by his fingers, clinging to hers. Surely, he would explain. Surely, he could make it all right. Surely, they had a chance.

'Give me the keys,' he said as they stepped into the beer garden.

'I'll drive,' Daisy said. 'You've been drinking.'

'I've had one pint of lager and I'm way too wound up to sit still in a car while you fanny about doing thirty.'

She yanked her hand from his. 'Excuse me?'

Swearing, he crossed the garden, only stopping when he reached the gate leading to the car park. But he didn't go through it. He kicked it. He gave it three anger-ridden, vicious kicks before resting his head against it, his back rising and falling as he took what she could only imagine were deep breaths in some valiant attempt to calm down.

He hates me.

A dark-haired girl sat motionless at a table, the only person not inside watching the finale. She had a glass of something fizzy and white, plus a pack of Marlboro Gold.

He married me for a dare and he now hates me.

Two divorces in two years – her parents would never speak to her again.

Daisy's hands shook as she helped herself to the girl's cigarettes, but the girl didn't object; she smiled sympathetically. She would. Pinned to her chest was a bright purple #*hesnoangel* badge. Where did she fit on the list? Part of the Year Eleven bet, or one of the post-16 masses?

Daisy held a cigarette in one hand, the girl's lighter in the other, ready to face Xander. He'd turned around and for the first time since he'd dropped their marriage certificate on the bloody table, he looked her in the eye.

'What are you doing?' he asked, nodding to the cigarette in her hand.

'You think I can cope with the latest disastrous event in our fatally flawed relationship without my usual crutches of cigarettes and alcohol?' She held the cigarette to her lips. 'Wrong.'

Muttering under his breath, Xander strode over and snatched the unlit cigarette from her fingers. 'That's my baby too.'

A shocked gasp came from the girl.

'Jessica?' he said, flashing a pleasant smile. 'Please, piss off.'

What difference did it make if they had an audience now? Their whole fucked up relationship had been laid bare for Twitter to tweet. But Jessica scampered off, leaving the two of them alone.

Xander perched on a table, running his hands through is hair. 'You did it on purpose? For fuck's sake, Daisy.'

'Don't you dare make me the bad guy when you married me for a dare. Why did you really come back with a ring in March? Nadia say no?'

'You know that's not true.'

'I don't know anything,' she snapped. 'I married you for real.'

'Bullshit. You just wanted a fucking sperm donor because Finn's not up to the job.'

The slap left a red mark on his cheek, but Xander barely flinched.

'I'm going to pretend you didn't do that,' he said quietly.

But she had done it. And it felt good. She couldn't drink, she couldn't smoke, but she needed to vent this rage. It boiled under her skin: rage against him, rage against herself. Her body shook with it. She hit him again, a fist to his shoulder.

Xander blinked, shocked. 'What the hell?'

Then he laughed.

Why was he laughing at her? She hit him again, but he laughed more. She hit him over and over, letting the rage pour out, her fists pummelling his chest, but he simply stood there, laughing. Why couldn't they have a normal life, one where they didn't have a crisis every ten minutes? Why weren't they allowed to just be happy? Why, why, why fucking why?

She screamed through sheer frustration.

'You finished?' Xander asked quietly.

Nodding, she let her arms fall by her sides, her fists relaxing.

'I know you're angry,' he said, his hands resting on her shoulders, 'but you need to calm down. You have to keep your heart rate below one-twenty, remember? For Bean.'

Oh God, she was already the world's worst mother. Taking several deep breaths, she slowly looked up. Xander's big brown eyes stared down at her, his thumbs rubbing her neck.

'Okay?'

'No,' she replied, shaking her head. The pictures were still out there. 'What if Tabitha's right, what if this isn't over?'

The worrying thing, the thing that wiped out her rage and replaced it with horror, was Xander clenching his jaw. He already knew it wasn't over. On cue, his phone beeped.

'Xand, what's going on?'

He didn't answer. He took his phone out of his pocket, swallowing hard before he checked the message. The little twitching muscle in his jaw worked overtime and he swore, several times.

'I have to do something.'

'What?'

'Just get out of here. It won't be... Go to Clara's.'

'But—'

'Please just go to Clara's.' He kissed her forehead. 'I won't be long. Then we'll talk.'

He walked back towards the bar, kicking a chair over on his way.

It wasn't over. Xander was still being blackmailed, pressured to do something. When would Daisy's phone beep, her leverage be applied? When would this ever end?

The abandoned cigarette lay on the floor.

No. She would not give in to her crutches. Not this time.

The game might not be over, but like it or not, she and Xander were going to have a baby. First and foremost, Bean deserved two parents who could communicate with one another. She had to sort her head out before she talked to Xander. But not at Clara's.

Daisy unlocked the MX5. Clara would be all puckered brow and despairing when she said, *pregnant for a dare? What are you twelve?* She'd never let Daisy explain. Okay, she would, but only after she'd made Daisy feel... well, about twelve.

Out the front of Oscar's, a gaggle of #*hesnoangel* badge-wearers pointed at her car, whispering, no doubt appalled with what she'd done.

What if Xander thought the same? What if he didn't forgive her? What if he married her for real, but now hated her for what she'd done?

'Daisy!' India came out of Oscar's jogging towards the car. 'Wait.'

'I need to get out of here, Indy.'

Especially since Freya was heading over too.

'Don't let this rip you two apart,' India said, breathlessly. 'And forget everything I said about not trusting people. You don't want to end up with no one, like me.'

'You have someone, mum.' Freya slipped her arm around India's waist. 'You have me. I didn't do it, miss. I mean, I joined in, but I honestly didn't start it.'

'I know. Tabitha did. *Fugly ho.* You got it from her, like you got *totes* from your mum.' Daisy smiled, apologetically. 'I'm sorry for accusing you, but I never tried it on with Travis.'

'We broke up.' Freya scowled. 'He's been shagging some hideous old witch.'

'Cressida Marshall, by any chance?' Despite everything, Daisy smiled. 'I've got to go.'

It was only twenty-past eight; it wouldn't be dark for hours. She could take Birkin for a walk up Lum Crag and calm down, think things over. *Then we'll talk.* Or she could throw herself off the top. She laughed, wiping away a stray tear. She wouldn't dream of hurting herself; she'd wouldn't dream of hurting Bean.

She wasn't Ana Dowson-Jones.

As she headed back towards Gosthwaite, the rolling green of the hills against the light blue of the summer evening did wonders to lift her spirits and calm her heart rate.

Until her phone lit up – Clara.

'Can I call you back?' Daisy said. 'I'm driving.'

'Which is why they invented speakerphone. *You're pregnant?*'

No answer to that.

'Why the hell do I have to find out via some sobbing sad case on Facebook who's devastated that she's not carrying Xander's baby. He really did a number on those girls.' Clara sighed. 'What the hell are you doing, Daisy? Did you really get pregnant for this stupid game?'

Tears rolled down Daisy's cheeks as she explained it all to Clara. She had to persuade her of her motives, because if she couldn't make her best friend believe her, she hadn't a hope in hell of persuading Xander.

'You really are insane.' Clara sighed. 'But you'll be okay, Daisy Chain-smoker. He gets you. Even more than me.'

'God, I hope you're right.' Daisy wiped at her eyes.

'So why have you left him to deal with it on his own? Some wife you turned out to be.'

Daisy turned down to Gosthwaite Mills. 'Deal with what?'

'Ohmigod, don't you know?' Clara's voice hit an octave higher, buzzing with the excitement of being the one to spill the news. 'He's apologising to the *hesnoangel* girls.'

No wonder he didn't want her to stick around.

'And from the tweets, it's working like a charm. Most of them sound utterly besotted with him still.'

'He's being blackmailed,' Daisy whispered, as much to make herself admit it as explain it to Clara.

'By who? Tabitha's there. Game over.'

'No, she said—'

It really isn't over, Daisy.

'Clar, she knows. Tabitha knows who's behind this. I've got to go.' Daisy ended the call. 'Siri? Call Xander.'

The phone rang. And rang. Voicemail.

'Siri? Call Xander.' Again. Come on, baby. Pick up. Her fingers tapped impatiently on the steering wheel.

'Daze? It's Marcus. Where are you?'

'At home, almost. Where's Xander?'

'Busy.' Marcus paused. 'He's apologising to Bethany Marshall—'

'Marcus, she knows who blackmailed us.'

'Who, Bethany?'

'No. Tabitha.'

'What?'

'Get Xander. Tell him to talk to Tabitha. She knows who's behind all this.'

The call failed. Stupid bloody reception in the stupid bloody countryside. Had Marcus even heard her?

She swung the little MX5 into the Old Forge car park, already unclipping her seat belt as she turned off the engine. Bloody Tabitha. *She's dead,* Marcus had argued. *She wouldn't do it to me,* James had growled. Turns out, Tabitha wasn't and she would. Bitch.

Daisy strode into the house, refusing to let anger take over. Bean's welfare would not be put at risk for Tabitha bloody Doyle. The door was unlocked. Shock horror, Xander hadn't locked the kitchen door. Again. It's Gosthwaite, he always said. It's not 1958, she always replied.

God, and the bloody phone wasn't in its cradle. Daisy stifled a frustrated scream. Why couldn't Xander put anything back where he found it? Birkin trotted over, his tail wagging, instantly calming her.

'What's up with you?' she asked, crouching down to rub his ears. 'You usually go bonkers when I've left you home alone for a couple of hours.'

'I remember that feeling.'

The voice came from behind her and Daisy clutched at Birkin's collar. Finn. She daren't turn around. Last time she saw him, she very nearly shagged him. What if nothing had a changed? No. Everything had changed. She wasn't coked up and several glasses of wine to the wind. She was pregnant and fully aware how much she utterly loved Xander. Where the hell was her KSCP when she needed him? Apologising to his Has-been's thanks to...

She turned her head. Finn leant against doorframe, the hallway providing a dark and moody backdrop. Oh, how could she be so stupid? 'It was you.'

'What was me?'

'Mr Forfeit Host. It's you.'

Aside from a momentary flicker at the corners of his mouth, he gave no real response.

'Of course it was you. You were the only person who knew about Yana. Unless you told someone else?' Daisy narrowed her eyes, studying him, preparing for his next answer. 'Like Tabitha?'

He tipped his head, acknowledging she was right, and Daisy turned away. Anger rose in her again, but she calmly stroked Birkin. She had to or there was a very strong chance she'd stab Finn with one of Xander's super-sharp knives.

'I said it was you at Christmas, but Xander just called me obsessed.'

'Obsessed works for me.' Finn was behind her, his hand on her shoulder. 'I've missed you.'

She closed her eyes, taking slow steady breaths. 'What do you want, Finn?'

'My wife.'

She almost laughed. 'It's a bit late for that.'

His hand brushed her neck. 'Is it?'

Every single cell in her body fizzed with excitement. Bloody pregnancy hormones. Slowly, she stood up, glancing around the room. Her phone was in her bag – still on the floor by the door. And she'd have to hang out of the kitchen porch to get reception. 'Of course it is. You blackmailed me and my friends.'

He leant closer, his lips against her cheek. 'They're his friends, not yours.'

Why was her head tipping, allowing him access to her neck? 'Did you follow me in the car, the silver Range Rover?'

'Yes.'

Seriously, where were the knives? She clenched her fists, fifty percent of her ready to lash out, claw at his eyes, but the other fifty percent yearned to drag her nails through his hair, to have him kiss her neck. 'You bastard.'

'Christ, but you can shift that car.'

Why was she arching her back as his hand slid down it, following the dip of her waist, the curve of her arse? 'All those laps we did at Silverstone weren't wasted. I miss my TT.'

'Is that all you miss?'

'You made your bed when you tied me to one.'

Now why wasn't she knocking his hand away, slapping him and calling him all the names under the sun? Oh God, why wasn't she? Why was she letting him do this to her? Why was she fighting not to press her arse back against him? He'd blackmailed her, threatened her. Jesus, he'd almost run her off the road, so why was she stifling a whimper as his teeth toyed with her ear lobe?

'Stop it, Finn.'

'Is that what you really want?' One hand lifted her hair, letting his lips brush her neck. 'I know you, Daisy. I know what you want. I know how horny you'll be right now. I'm right, aren't I?'

'No,' she lied. 'You bastard.'

Laughing, he flipped her around, pushing her back against the wall, his knee between hers. 'Shall we find out?'

'Don't you–'

His thigh pressed up against her and she closed her eyes. How could he still do this to her? How? His hands slid under her dress, inching slowly up her thighs. Oh dear God.

'You still want me,' he whispered, his lips just to the side of hers. 'Admit it.'

She'd stopped breathing. No, no, no. If he kissed her, she'd be screwed. Literally.

The grass isn't greener.

His body held her against the wall, his leg stopping her ducking away. She couldn't move.

'And I want you, Dee.'

The breath she had in her lungs wouldn't come out.

'I've never stopped wanting you,' he said.

His lips brushed hers, shocking a gasp from her lungs and jump-starting her brain back into gear. She groped behind her... the windowsill. Her hand closed around something hard, something glass. The tequila bottle.

It made an ominous thunk as it made contact with Finn's head.

As did he when he hit the slate flagstones.

The tequila bottle followed, breaking after it fell from her shaking hand, but Daisy daren't move. She stared at Finn, expecting him to jump up and raise holy hell for hitting him. Or was he waiting for her to leave the room and then he'd be gone when she got back, like in some stalker horror film?

Why hadn't he moved?

She nudged his foot with hers. She needed to ring Xander. And the Police. Oh God, why hadn't he moved?

She kicked his foot a little harder and a trickle of blood seeped from under his head.

Bollocks.

What if he were dead?

Chapter Thirty-Six

When Daisy was twelve, she wanted to be India Dowson-Gunn – well, look at her now. Bang in the middle of a social media storm and standing over the lifeless body of her Hollywood movie star ex-husband.

It was a massive lesson in being careful what you wish for.

Finn stirred.

Okay, she might be overreacting, maybe just a tad, but Daisy clutched the neck of the broken tequila bottle.

'What the fuck...' Finn blinked, flinching against the light and trying to move his hands. Good luck with that. She'd tied them behind his head with Birkin's lead.

'Keep still,' she instructed, her foot pinning his shoulder down. 'Not nice being tied up, is it?'

He frowned up at her. 'Did you hit me?'

She nodded, holding up the bottle. 'And don't move, or I might be tempted to take out your pretty face too.'

'You wouldn't dare,' he said, giving a derisory laugh.

'I've been looking through your phone, Finn.' Swiftly, she crouched down, sitting on him. 'There are twelve pictures of me on there. Four of which I don't recall giving you permission to take.'

His mocking smile waned as she held the bottle in his face.

'There are an awful lot of messages on there too, messages I sent. Messages that found their way onto bloody Twitter.' She pressed the longest shard against his cheek. 'You never lost your phone, did you?'

'I was drunk. And angry at you. I'm sorry.' He flashed an easy-going smile, one mean to disarm her, charm her. Not a chance, sunshine.

'You're *sorry*?'

'Christ, they were hot texts.' He shifted beneath her, stiffened beneath her.

'Finn, stop it.'

'It's not my fault. You're sitting on me. Get off.'

No way. She only had control while he was still on the floor with his hands behind his head, but she didn't want his hard on pressing against her either. She wriggled forward onto his abs.

'Oh, because that's helping,' he said, his eyes glittering.

Refusing to blush, Daisy picked up his phone that lay on the floor beside him. 'Yeah well, this might. I've deleted all the photos and sexts. To be honest, I was a little worried there might be other photos of me that that I hadn't seen, so I took the liberty of hitting *Erase All* and wiping everything on your phone and iCloud. Handy that you haven't changed your password all the time I've known you.'

He scowled like a petulant teen whose phone had been confiscated, evidence he didn't have the photos elsewhere. That had been a lingering concern.

'Yeah, I know,' she said, tossing his phone away. 'I'm like a total cow. Still think I won't take out your face?'

He gave a tiny shake of the head.

'Good. We need to talk and we're going to do it on my terms. How's your head?'

'Fucking agony.'

'I've checked your pupils. I don't think you're in imminent danger of a brain haemorrhage, but you have been out for about ten minutes, so I'd say it's safe to assume you have a concussion, most probably from when you hit the deck.'

Finn didn't drop eye contact, or his somewhat bemused expression.

'You were behind the game?'

'Yes,' he admitted, eyeing the bottle warily.

'Explain.'

'I wanted... Christmas Day, I rocked up at Tab's like the ghost of Christmas Past and told her I wanted to make Forfeit The Movie. She'd be the star, but it'd be way better if it were based on a true story so you all needed to keep playing.'

'Did she buy that?'

He laughed. 'Yeah, she totally did, but I might've mentioned my goal was to get back at you for having an affair with the pretty boy.'

'And then you shagged her into submission?'

He glanced away. 'We all have our pressure points. Hers are being famous and... me.'

'Were you always shagging her?'

'No.' He looked her in the eye. 'Never while I was with you.'

'Why didn't you tell me you were seeing her when we met?'

'You were a random girl that I kissed on a mountain. I had no idea if you liked me, or famous me. You really think I'd trust you, just like that?'

'She said you were hers for four years. Did you like her?'

'Until I met you, I thought... yeah.' He let out a long slow breath. 'Four years. Three of them in secret because she was married to Dex and the last because she didn't want to risk her divorce settlement. Four years and then I meet you. That day, I left you at that pub... Jesus Christ, Tab went off–'

'Because she loves you.'

He nodded.

'Do you love her?'

He shook his head.

'Are you shagging her again?'

'Does it bother you?' His face broke into that confident, pant-dropping smile. 'She's a means to an end, that's all, baby.'

For the first time, Daisy actually felt sorry for Tabitha. The poor girl truly loved Finn, but she'd never get to have him – like James could never have Tabitha.

'So Christmas Day, you turn up at hers, telling her you can make her more famous and make my life hell on Facebook.'

'The whole social media thing was her idea. The icing on the cake.'

Daisy closed her eyes, picturing Tabitha shrieking at her across the Dowson-Jones dining table. 'When I rang, asking about the photos, you weren't in New York, were you? It was Tabitha pretending to be Brittany.'

'Yes.'

'God, I'm a stupid cow.'

'You believed what you wanted to believe. You didn't want it to be me, not really.'

'Were you the trustafarian at Tabitha's apartment?'

'Cool disguise, hey?' He laughed. 'I was bored and wanted a night out with you. Tab flipped out when I suggested it and the naughty girl rang you before I'd left.'

'Why?'

'Because that's when she knew I didn't hate you. She nearly ruined everything.'

'Did she really OD that night, or was that part of your whack-job master plan?'

He glanced away, his brow furrowing. 'Totally her doing.'

'No, Finn. *You* gave her the drugs. *You* could've killed her that night. Like you could've killed me the night you followed me.'

The longest of the glass shards on the bottle made a pin prick of blood appear and Finn flinched.

'But ask me why, Dee. Ask me why I did it.'

'I know why. You don't want me to be happy. At Tabitha's birthday, you saw me with Xander and you wanted to ruin it, to make me suffer for leaving you.'

Slowly, Finn shook his head. 'Don't get me wrong, when you filed for divorce, I was angry, but when Tab put those photos online of you and him at James' party, I came up to give you the papers for real. You'd moved on and I'd been offered the New York gig the day before. It seemed like a sign.'

'So why come back and make us play the stupid game?'

'I didn't... not intentionally.' His brow furrowed as he looked her in the eye. 'When I bumped into you at that Christmas Fayre, you were miserable; *he* was making you miserable. I... I couldn't sit back and watch that, Dee. From what India told me, there isn't a thing in the world your pretty boy wouldn't do for money, so I thought the game was the perfect opportunity to show you. What did he do?'

'He... married me, but you're wrong about him.'

'Jesus Christ, Dee. Face reality, he married you for a few zeros on his bank balance.' Finn shook his head. 'Right now, he's apologising to dozens of girls, girls' whose self-esteem he destroyed for a bet. You can't trust him.'

'I can.' *I have to because I need him to trust me.*

'I want you back.'

'Finn...' God, even though he'd done what he'd done – nearly killed her, blackmailed her, tried to ruin her life, she still had to let him down gently. Surely she owed him that. 'I'm sorry, but even if Xander... I can't go back to the life we had.'

'Dee–'

'Do you know why I love it up here? It's because people couldn't care less about the crap that doesn't matter. I can go out walking and I'm just a girl who goes out walking. I can go to a pub in jeans and hiking boots and people aren't judging me for wearing last year's jacket. With you, that's all I am, something to be judged. I can't live like that. It nearly killed me.'

'But it'd be different. We'd be different. No more drugs and clubbing.'

'I'm married to Xander.'

'You can't trust—'

'Finn, I'm pregnant.'

Everything about him tensed – his face, his jaw, his body. 'You're what?'

She looked away, unable to face him any longer. 'I'm preg—'

He whipped up his arms, knocking the bottle from her hand and smacking her to the ground. Her shoulder hit the slate floor, sending an agonising jolt through her body, but she scrabbled to her feet, desperate to get away from him. She had to run. The Miller's Arms would be her safest bet.

Finn grabbed her hair, yanking her back towards him.

'Ow, Finn!'

His fingers knotted tighter in her hair before he slammed her against the wall.

Daisy's mouth opened, but no air went in. Or out. Breathe. She had to breathe. She couldn't. Her mouth was open. It could close, but it wasn't making air move. She stared up at Finn, but he was undoing the rope with his teeth, his gaze avoiding hers.

I can't breathe.

Bean would die if she couldn't breathe.

No.

She looked up at the kitchen shelf where her mobile stood. This would be okay. She just had to stay calm. Instantly, good, sweet air filled her lungs. She could breathe. Bean could breathe. But Finn had hold of her hair again, still pinning to the wall..

Gingerly, she reached up a hand, to touch his arm. 'Finn, you're hurting me.'

'Am I?' His words were barely a whisper and contempt dripped from his snarling face. Roughly, his knee slid up her leg to press against her stomach.

Bean. 'Please, don't—'

'You're right,' he spat. 'We do need to talk, but now we're going to do it on my terms.'

Her heart raced, but again she focussed on her phone and took a deep breath. 'Fuck you.'

'That's not a bad plan.' His knee slipped down, pressing between her legs. 'I am still kinda hard.'

How the hell had she been turned on by him earlier? 'I think the authorities would class that as rape.'

'It's hardly rape when you're begging for it. And you always begged for it in the end.'

'Not a chance.'

'We'll see.' His gaze roved over her, lascivious and mean.

'Scott?' Daisy glanced up at her phone. 'You getting all this?'

From her phone, safe on its vantage point, Scott nodded. Reception might be piss poor inside Skank Manor, but the Wi-Fi rocked. Thank God for Facetime.

'All witnessed and recorded,' Scott said. 'Police are on the way.'

Clara appeared on the little screen. 'Let her go, you bastard.'

'You set that up while I was out cold?' Finn laughed without any humour, his grip lessening on Daisy's hair. 'Clever girl.'

'Thank you. Now. Let. Me. Go.'

He didn't, but his knee dropped. '*Not until I'm thirty*, you said. What changed?'

'You made me play a game of dares.'

'It was your dare?'

Hesitantly, she nodded.

'Jesus Christ…'

Anger again filled his face as he dragged her across the room by her hair. For a second, he let go of her, but his knee rammed into her stomach. Daisy gasped for breath, watching helplessly as Finn knocked her phone off the shelf. Her safety net was gone. All she could do was pray the police arrived before Finn… What would he do? His eyes stared into hers, fury making them burn as he grabbed her hair again.

'So when I ask you to stop taking the pill,' Finn whispered, his lips next to her ear, 'you say no. But for the chance to win twenty-five grand, you're on your back with your legs wide open.'

'It wasn't like that,' she said, her voice breaking with emotion. 'I didn't get pregnant for a dare.'

She closed her eyes, hiding from his malevolent scowl, but instantly, a familiar scent filled her head. Was Xander there?

Oh please, God, let him be there. And if he is, make him listen.

'I read the dare in January and thought, why not?' she said. 'Xander and I were fabulous as friends but an absolute disaster as a couple. But maybe the point of us was to have a kid. We'd have a reason to stay friends forever. Maybe we'd be Parents With Benefits.'

Finn frowned down at her, but if Xander were there, he didn't even make a sound.

'But then he came back and we weren't a disaster.' Daisy sniffed away her looming tears. 'He loved me and I loved him. We were getting married, for God's sake. I didn't need a baby to keep a connection with him and I certainly didn't need my stupid Parents With Benefits plan, but I never took the pill again.'

'Why?'

For the first time, she looked Finn in the eye. 'So Xander wouldn't end up looking at me every month like you did, like I'd failed.'

Finn let go of her hair, his anger visibly ebbing away.

'I did it so I wouldn't be ripped apart by the horrific disappointment that comes from negative test after negative test every bloody month. Not again. I didn't want my fertility issues to destroy what Xander and I have. All those doctors said it would just take time, and I thought it would take years.' Tears loomed but she jammed her nails in her palms. 'I loved you. I would've done anything for you. I know you never believed me, but I really did stop taking the pill when you asked me to.'

The furrows in Finn's forehead deepened. 'But...'

'Clearly, I have no fertility issues, Finn.' *You do.*

'So we'll be a family, Dee. Me, you...' His eyes filled with determination as he glanced down at her stomach. 'And the bun in the oven.'

Was he insane? This needed to end. Now. 'He won't like that.'

Finn laughed. 'Who, the baby?'

'No. It's father,' came Xander's voice.

Sure enough, when Finn looked back, unblocking her line of sight, Xander was standing in the doorway. In a blur he pulled Finn away from Daisy, before landing a punch to Finn's jaw. And another to his stomach. And another. And another.

Jesus Christ.

'Xander, stop it!'

He didn't. He hit Finn square in the face, blood appearing. Holy shit, Xander was going to kill him. Squealing, Daisy grabbed Xander's arm and put herself between him and Finn.

CAROLINE BATTEN

'Get out of the way, Fitzgerald.'

'No. Stop. Please. It's over. Please.'

She glanced back at Finn. He'd backed away, slumping down the wall with his hands cupping his nose. 'Finn?'

'Why are you protecting him?' Xander demanded.

'I'm not.' She pushed Xander back, away from Finn. 'I'm trying to stop you from going to jail.'

Swearing, Xander relaxed and pulled her to him. 'Are you okay? Did he hurt you?'

'No, I'm fine. I was about to knee him in the balls, but you know I love it when my Knight-in-Shining-Cricket-Pads comes to my rescue.' Sheltering in his arms, she let a tear or two fall out – the relief of his presence, the smell of his aftershave overwhelming her. 'Thank you.'

Sirens wailed in the distance and Finn looked up. 'Don't do this, Dee.'

'I'm sorry, but they have to arrest you. Scott said it's the best way to get a restraining order.'

'I should get the fucking restraining order,' Finn said, scowling.

'You'll need one if you ever come near my wife again,' Xander replied with equal hostility.

'This is over, Finn.' Bravely, Daisy left the security of Xander's arms and went over to Finn. 'I will get a restraining order and you will stay away from me, Xander and our baby. And if I ever suspect you're hassling me, the recording Scott made will go public. Your career will be over and you'll go to jail. Get it?'

He nodded. 'But don't you want to know why he stayed at the bar to apologise to those girls, why he sent you home alone? What it was that you didn't want to know about? You played the game because of one last secret. Don't you want to know what it is?'

Daisy glanced across at Xander, hoping he'd laugh off Finn's words. Instead, he perched on the table and appeared to find his trainers fascinating.

'It seems your pretty boy hasn't been entirely honest with you, Dee.' Finn smiled at Xander. 'Ask him why he fucked you last summer.'

'No,' she said, firmly. There were no more bombshells. Xander had told her everything.

'He fucked you because he was paid three thousand pounds to fuck you, Dee.' Finn paused to check his nose in the mirror. 'Jesus,

386

that hurts, but actually, I don't think it is broken.'

Daisy stared at Finn, she daren't look at Xander. 'Who paid him three thousand pounds?'

'Your new boss, James Dowson-Jones. You were supposed to be a challenge, still too hung up on me.' Finn looked her over. 'But you always were an easy lay.'

'And I still have the tequila bottle, you arsehole.'

'But that's not the only thing he forgot to mention. Ever wondered why he worked so fucking hard to worm his way into your life?'

Over and over again. She'd never understood why Xander liked her, but Daisy folded her arms. 'I'm not buying into this bullshit, Finn.'

'It was for one-point-five million pounds.'

She laughed. 'What?'

'The one-point-five million pounds he was told you'd get when you divorced me.'

As far as she was aware, he was worth about three hundred grand at best. 'Whatever.'

'The one-point-five million pounds you gave up when you made me agree to that unreasonable behaviour crap.'

'You had three million?' she asked.

Slowly he nodded, grinning. 'Still worth sacrificing half of everything for a quicky divorce?'

'Hell, yeah,' she said, hoping she didn't sound as dubious as she felt. One-point-five million? She glanced at Xander, but he still stared at his shoes. Surely that wasn't why he wanted to get to know her, for her to move in. But then why wasn't he denying it? And why did the bloody police car have to choose that precise moment to pull up into the yard?

'Is it true?' she asked Xander. 'Did James bet you three grand you couldn't shag me?'

Without looking up, he nodded.

'And did you go out with me, did you marry me, for one and a half million?'

The muscle in his jaw twitched rhythmically, but still he stared at his feet and Daisy had her answer.

Trust. Everything she'd learned... it was all about trust.

A knock at the door prevented any further conversation.

'Dee?' Finn dipped his head, but looked up at her, his eyes

regretful, pleading. 'Come on, baby... You're not going to do this.'

Hesitating, she glanced at the door where PC Andy and another policeman hovered in the open doorway. It was barely for a second, but in that time, Finn's soulful eyes gave way to something more arrogant. Arrogant? Smug more like.

And finally, she understood him. Finally, she saw through him. Like Tabitha, he was a bloody good actor, but how many times had she seen him play the misunderstood guy from the wrong side of the tracks? How many times had she fallen for that bad boy bullshit? How had she fallen for that bad boy bullshit? The truth was, he was a middle class rich kid, who'd had everything handed to him on a plate.

'Andy, thank God you're here,' she said, turning her back on Finn. 'My ex-husband threatened me. He threatened to... rape me.'

'Bitch,' Finn snarled.

'You don't speak to her like that,' Xander said, facing up to Finn again.

PC Andy leapt between them and the subsequent slanging match raged for twenty minutes, ending with Xander being physically restrained by PC Maxwell, and Finn slapped in handcuffs by PC Andy. As the two officers led Finn out, Daisy stood in the kitchen doorway and held up Finn's iPhone.

'Finn,' she called. 'Any message for your followers?'

'Don't you dare...'

It was the perfect shot of him scowling as Andy bundled him into the car. Daisy shared it without a moment's hesitation.

'That,' Clara said from Daisy's iPhone on the floor, 'was better than Eastenders.'

Xander started, clearly freaked by Clara's disembodied voice. 'What the hell?'

Scott saluted him. 'Excellent heroics, Xand.'

'I so wish you'd actually broken his nose though,' Clara said.

Xander examined the broken skin on his knuckles. 'I don't think I've hit anyone that hard since I was sixteen.'

Scott laughed. 'It's all recorded. Come round and see it some time. We'll have popcorn.'

Daisy laughed, picking up the phone, but instead of relief, nausea returned. She didn't want Clara and Scott to go. If they did, she'd be left alone with Xander.

Then we'll talk.

And when they had, where would they be?

'Thank you so much,' she said to her friends, trying not to cry.

Scott waved away her thanks, but Clara elbowed him out of shot. Daisy glanced across to Xander. He'd taken up his place, perched on the table again, his hands shoved in his pockets.

'You okay?' Clara whispered.

Daisy nodded.

'It'll be okay, Daze. Now, go sort it out.'

Daisy blew her a kiss before ending the session and reluctantly facing Xander. He sat with his arms folded, his brow furrowed and dark shadows under his eyes. Why did he look so tired? Surely it wasn't just from that night? But why hadn't she noticed before? Oh God, was the pampered pregnant princess really that wrapped up in herself? Was she back to being that person?

'How long has he been threatening you with telling me about the bet?' she asked quietly.

'Since just after we got married. He had emails I'd sent to James. From Tabitha, I suppose.'

'Would you ever have told me?'

'Honestly?' He shrugged. 'I did think about telling you when I came back in March, but it would've been another reason for you not to trust me and I couldn't take the risk.'

Daisy nodded and sat on the table, close enough to smell Xander's aftershave, far enough not to touch him. 'How's your cheek? I'm sorry I hit you.'

Gingerly, he rubbed it. 'Bethany hits harder.'

'She slapped you?' Bitch.

He nodded, looking up at the ceiling. 'But it was okay actually… a relief.'

'Eased your conscience?'

'Yeah, it did.' He smiled, but no humour reached his eyes. 'Christ, I must be the most self-centred bastard ever.'

'No, you're human.'

Finally, he turned to her, looking her in the eye. 'I never took the money, Daze.'

'Why? You won it, fair and square.'

'I also promised you I wouldn't kiss and tell.'

He'd kept his promise; he always kept his promises. Then again, this was another bombshell. Daisy folded her arms, trying to stay cross.

'What, were you prepared to sacrifice the three grand for the long haul goal of one point five million?'

To her surprise, he laughed. 'Oh come on, it was never about the money and you know it. You told me about the divorce agreement on his birthday remember? It was just before I said *I love you* and just after you'd thrown up.'

'Thanks for reminding me.' But, Daisy couldn't help her grin. Or swatting his arm.

Xander caught her hand, pulling her a little closer. 'When did you stop taking the pill?'

Oh, so he was leaping straight into the fray. 'January the second.'

Slowly, he let out a long breath, his hand clenching around hers. 'Did you know I was there when you were telling him about Bean?'

'Hoped to God, but I didn't know for sure.'

'Was what you said true?'

'Yes.' She hung her head. 'I'm sorry I lied and I'm sorry I stopped taking the pill without telling you, but I'm not sorry I got pregnant.'

His thumb rubbed gently over the back of her hand. 'Me neither.'

'Was the dare why you wanted to get married so soon?'

The thumb stopped. 'Fuck. Okay, if I hadn't wanted the money for the restaurant, I wouldn't have asked in March. I'd have waited to see if we could spend a few months together without driving each other mental. But, I said I'd marry you at Clara's wedding and I meant it. Christ, marrying you seemed like an impossible dream when I read my dare. Best thing we ever did though. Do you think you'll forgive me, one day?'

How could he even ask that? She got up, standing between his legs, her hands holding his face. 'Xand, you've forgiven me for the awful things I've done in the past, of course I'll forgive you. But promise me, no more bombshells, please?'

'No more bombshells. I promise.'

'So can Happily Ever After start here? No more dramas, no more emotional trauma. We'll be the world's most boring couple?'

Xander laughed, wrapping his arms around her. 'With you around, I'm not sure that's even remotely possible. I had a pretty quiet life until you showed up.'

'That'll teach you to knock a girl off her feet.'

He shook his head. 'No regrets. You are without doubt, the most amazing girl I've ever met.'

'And you've met a few,' she said, grinning.

'Exactly.' He brushed her hair back, gazing at her. 'But have you any idea how much I love that you can laugh about it and not get snippy?'

She couldn't resist. 'What else do you love?'

'I love that you're unashamedly vain.' He dropped a quick kiss on her lips. 'That you'll stand up to my dad, and babysit my nieces...' Another kiss, this one on her neck. 'I love that you can tile a bathroom and when you do it, you'll be wearing designer jeans and Chanel No.5.' The next kiss was on her earlobe, making her shiver. 'I love that you're clever and kind and beautiful, but mostly...' His lips rested on hers for a moment. 'I love what you've done to me. You made me believe in myself again.'

Tears stung her eyes, but Daisy responded with a real kiss, one she hoped told him how she felt, because she was incapable of talking. How lucky was she to have someone like him? Not lucky because he was young and stupidly good-looking, but lucky to have someone so willing to see the good in her, someone so willing to forgive her. How lucky was she to have that?

'I love you,' she said, her lips still hovering over his, the odd tear trickling down her cheek.

'But do you trust me?'

Looking him in the eye, she nodded.

'Really?'

'You promised me you'd be faithful. You promised me no more bombshells.' She smiled. 'And if there's one thing you've proved – you don't break your promises.'

His smile said it all as he wiped away her tears. 'I promise I'll never let you or Bean down.'

'I've been thinking,' she said. 'If Bean's a girl, shall we call her Olivia?'

'No.' A grin spread across his fabulous face. 'We're saving Oliver for a boy.'

'But I only ever planned on having one.'

'Well, you planned this one so it's only fair that I get to plan the next one.'

Oh, bugger.

Epilogue

Two weeks later, a week after she and Xander first saw their tiny Bean on an ultrasound scan, Daisy strode as purposefully as possible in flip-flops, swinging a small blue gift bag in one hand and holding an ice lolly in the other. The God who invented cider ice lollies had done so with the pregnant woman in mind.

Up ahead, James lounged against the auction room door, his face crumpled into a disapproving scowl. Okay she was a little late, but the sun hung in a cloudless cyan sky and a gentle breeze kept the heat a few degrees shy of stifling. It couldn't be a more perfect July day for Happily Ever After to begin.

'You're late,' James said, taking out his phone.

'Had to go shopping so I didn't obsess about the auction. Where's Xand?'

'Inside. I said to dress down, not like an Aussie backpacker.'

Daisy glanced over her halter-neck top, denim mini skirt and flip-flop combo. 'I'm running out of clothes that fit.'

'It's your own fault for getting fat.'

'I'm not getting fat.' Not so far at least. Weight gain seemed limited to her expanding waist and boobs, both of which appeared to be growing at an exponential rate. 'I'm pregnant.'

Fat, James mouthed, his eyes twinkling with amusement.

Daisy whipped out the scan picture from her bag. 'Have you seen Bean?'

'Have I been bored to death with: look you can see Bean's little hand in this one, or here's Bean's foot in another? Yes. For at least twenty minutes. Not interested.'

'You'd better be. Xander's going to ask you to be a godparent.'

James looked up at the sky, valiantly attempting to look as if it'd be the worst job ever, but the smile he clearly fought gave the game away. 'Whatever. Get your hands-free set up.'

Daisy saluted him with her ice lolly. 'Yes, sir.'

As a known property developer in the area, James didn't want to be seen with Daisy and Xander in case resentful competitors bidded up Lum Cottage to make them pay more. Sadly, James being James still insisted on being present to stay in control of Daisy's bids.

'Please, don't do anything stupid,' he muttered, slouching once again against the wall. 'And don't forget—'

'No bids unless it stalls before two hundred and a hard two-twenty ceiling. I know, I know.' Daisy wandered inside, shaking her head in despair.

The evening before, she'd endured an hour-long telephone call where James lectured her on starting bids, faux-hesitant bids and when to know it was a lost cause.

Inside the barely filled auction room, her flip flops clattered loudly, causing several people to turn. Xander didn't, but notably, his shoulders sank a little as he relaxed, knowing she'd finally turned up.

'I thought you weren't coming,' he whispered as she took her seat. 'Where've you been?'

'Shopping.' Daisy took the auction brochure from him, gazing at the photo of Lum Cottage, her perfect home – their perfect home.

'Did you see James?' Xander asked.

She nodded distractedly. The uPVC would have to go. Who the hell would put plastic windows and doors in an adorable cottage? 'He's dying to be a godfather.'

'Did he tell you Tab's got the part in Coronation Street?'

Daisy looked up from mentally planning the layout of the bedrooms she'd build upstairs in the barn and found herself smiling. 'Good. She might have been a two-faced cow to me, but after everything Finn's put her through, I think she might deserve a break.'

'Very magnanimous of you.'

'You know me, selfless to the bitter end.'

'She's taking James to Paris this weekend to celebrate. Double date with Marcus and Nicole.'

'Happily ever afters all around?' Daisy glanced across at James.

'You never know,' James said through her ear bud.

The auctioneer climbed up to his little podium, smiling at his congregation over his half-moon glasses.

'Christ, it's about to start.' Xander fidgeted, his feet bouncing up and down. 'Shit, what if we pay too much... or not enough and don't-'

'Xand, if it's meant to be, it's meant to be. Chill, baby.' She handed him the gift bag. 'Here. It's to take your mind off things.'

Daisy sucked on her ice lolly, pretending to listen intently to the auctioneer wittering about deposits and contracts. The reality was she was trying not to giggle as Xander peered inside the bag. Her cheeks were on fire, but she pointedly ignored his raised eyebrows as he frowned at her.

'Shall we get the bidding underway at eighty thousand?'

Silence descended.

'Seventy thousand?'

Daisy itched to raise her hand. What if she could have her dream for seventy grand?

'*Don't even think about it,*' said the control freak in her ear.

So she quietly sat, sucking her lolly as the first bids dribbled sluggishly in.

Seventy... eighty... ninety.

'What's all this for?' Xander whispered, holding up the bag.

'You need me to draw you pictures?' she asked, picking out a Gosthwaite builder and a grey-haired couple as the two bidding parties.

One hundred, one-ten, one-twenty.

But Xander called her bluff, hooking a finger into the bag and lifting out the larger of the items. 'Velvet handcuffs?'

One-thirty, one-forty, one-fifty.

Refusing to give in to mortification, or acknowledge the bloke behind them shifting uncomfortably in his seat, Daisy looked Xander in the eye. 'You weren't meant to let everyone see.'

One-sixty, one-seventy, one-eighty.

'*Are you two taking this seriously,*' James hissed. '*Why the hell have you brought handcuffs to an auction?*'

Mercifully, Xander dropped the handcuffs back in the bag, but as he registered the other toys in the bag, his shoulders shook with repressed laughter.

'Is that a *butt plug*, Fitzgerald?'

Her cheeks were on fire, but she nodded.

'Why have you bought–'

'Read the tag,' she whispered.

One-ninety hung in the air. The bidding had stalled. She glanced across at James.

'*Not yet,*' he said not even looking her way.

Xander lifted the gift tag. *Because I trust you. Implicitly.*

One-eighty-five?

The auctioneer nodded accepting a bid from someone behind her. Oh God, she wanted to look, but James had vetoed any noseying.

'*Game on,*' James said, glancing back at the new bidder.

One-ninety.

'What's this about, Daisy?' Xander asked.

'*Bid.*'

This wasn't in the rules; the bidding hadn't stalled. She glanced over at James, her heart thumping.

'*Now.*'

'I have one eighty-five with the gentleman at the back of the room. Do I have one ninety?'

Quickly, Daisy raised her hand, half-eaten cider ice lolly included. The auctioneer nodded, accepting her bid and Daisy struggled to suppress an excited squeal. She'd just bid in an auction. OM-fucking-G

Two hundred, two-five, two-ten.

Rapid counter bids bounced between Daisy and Gentleman at the Back, but the grey-haired couple faded away.

Two-fifteen?

She nodded without hesitation, but held her breath. This was it. The Gentleman at the Back's next bid would be two-twenty and she'd be out of the game.

Two-twenty?

Silence. People shifted in their seats. Xander bit his thumbnail. Daisy didn't consider breathing.

Two-seventeen?

Please, please, please.

The auctioneer smiled. 'Two hundred and seventeen is bid. Do I have two-twenty?'

Slowly, Daisy nodded. If it was meant to be, it was meant to be.

'Two-twenty-two?'

The auctioneer nodded. The Gentleman at the Back had out bid her. It was over. The auctioneer looked at her, enquiringly, but Daisy shook her head. She'd hit the ceiling. Tears welled in her eyes, but she stuck her nails into her palms. She wouldn't cry here. Later, in Xander's arms, she'd sob her heart out, but not here.

'Do I have an advance on two-twenty two?'

James raised his hand, one finger in the air.

What the fuck? Daisy stared, her mouth open and Xander's feet stopped jiggling.

'I have two-twenty-three with Mr Dowson-Jones.'

Two-twenty-four, twenty-five, twenty-six...

Was this a cruel joke? Had James only wanted Lum Cottage for his foundation all along?

Thirty, thirty-one, thirty-two, thirty-three...

James and the Gentleman at the Back played ping-pong bids, but at two-thirty-eight the latter backed out. Lum Cottage was James' for two hundred and thirty-seven thousand pounds. Daisy's heart was in freefall, her head reeling. On the upside, she'd get to do the work, so she and Xander could live there for six months, a year. Was that better than nothing?

'Do I have two hundred and thirty-seven five hundred?' the auctioneer asked.

Silence.

'It's your turn,' James said, his lips barely moving. *'Like I have hard ceilings where he's concerned. Final bid.'*

Daisy stifled a sob and thrust her lolly in the air.

'We have two hundred and thirty-seven thousand and five hundred pounds with the lady in the middle of the room.' He raised his eyebrows to the previous bidders. 'Going once...'

Everyone please keep quiet.

'Going twice...'

Xander strangled her hand.

'Sold to the lady with the ice lolly.'

Laughter rippled through the crowd, but Daisy could only stare at Xander. They'd done it. They'd actually bought Lum Cottage. Then she was on her feet, her arms around his neck, kissing him, telling him she loved him, grinning as he told her the same thing, over and over.

In a blur, they signed forms, handed over cheques and shook hands with the auctioneer. It was only then, she realised her ear bud had fallen out and she looked for James. He loitered by the exit, his smile more genuine than she'd ever seen.

Thank you, she mouthed putting the ear bud back in.

'Remember, it's an insurance policy, that's all.' He headed for the door. *'Make him happy and... be a better mother than mine was.'*

Xander stood behind her, his arms wrapping around her as they watched his best-friend and benefactor leave. If God really did exist, then he or she, really needed to pull their finger out and give James a break – be it Tabitha or some other person who interested him; James deserved to be happy.

'We did it,' she said.

Xander rested his head on top of hers. 'You were incredible.'

'I lifted a lolly stick.'

'Best lolly stick bidding I've ever seen.'

'But now we're utterly broke. I've got an intern job, getting minimum wage slaving for a tyrannical sociopath and all your wages are getting sucked into Moneypit Mill. It'll be poverty rations for us for years.'

'We can live on tea and toast.'

'Tea and toast? That's your idea of Happily Ever After?'

'With you? Yes.' Xander dropped a kiss on her head. 'If we get desperate, you could always set up another crowd-funding scam, but the restaurant should be able to afford to keep your skinny arse in designer jeans.'

'Ugh, it's not going to be skinny for long.' She looked down at her already solid waistline. 'I'll look like a whale.'

'You're going to look pregnant and very, very beautiful.'

He turned her around and when he kissed her, Daisy had to cling to his t-shirt to stay upright – her legs, as ever, turning to spaghetti.

'You know,' Xander said, his fingers trailing down the bumps of her spine, 'you don't need handcuffs to prove you trust me. I know you trust me.'

Ducking out of his arms, hoping to hide her burning cheeks, Daisy headed for the door, grabbing the gift bag along the way. 'But proving I trust you was only half the reason for my little shopping spree.'

'And the other half?' Xander called, that Colgate smile taking over his face.

She shot him her cheekiest wink and left.

The End

Thank You

There's not an author in the world who doesn't have a shed-load of people to thank, and I'm no different.

I'm starting at Forfeit's beginning. I owe a huge thank you to Claire Purslow for reading the very, very first chapters and not laughing. Your support, PC and printer probably changed everything.

Love and hugs to Sarah McLachlan, Leila Miller and Melissa Hull who were brave enough to read the very first full draft. Again, thanks for not laughing.

Next up are my *authonomy.com* friends. You guys were my mentors, proofers, editors and time wasters. Crikey, we wasted time on that forum. Then again, that's where I learned about comma splices and dangling modifiers... so thanks for laughing. Simon R, a special roll of the eyes for you.

Once Forfeit was half-decently written, it needed an audience. Enter *wattpad.com*. This is where I realised PEOPLE LIKED MY BOOKS. Three million reads is quite an achievement considering neither of my books contain vampires, werewolves, or even a hair from Harry Styles' head. Thank you to Eva Lau, Caitlin O'Hanlon and every single Wattpadder who voted, commented and followed. I heart you guys more than you'll ever know.

Book written, audience building... all I needed was a little inspiration and motivation to publish. Thank you to the amazeballs Jo Millington. She showed me that you can make your own dreams come true.

Big thanks to Laura Kinglsey for her fabulously sarcastic structural editing, and to Alyssa Clarkson and Kirsty Goodall for your proofing.

Thanks to all my May 08 yummy-mummies – for reading, supporting and giving good advice. Chapter Two is for you ladies. :)

Mustn't forget the vanitycasebooks.co.uk girls – Gemma Harris, Janny Peacock, Jo Gardner and Natalie Martin – awesome writers and awesome friends.

Natalie, gets a special thank you. She's been Forfeit's biggest fan since she first read it on holiday back in 2011. She's also been the most patient. She's read rewrite after rewrite and listened to me debate Daisy having a dead or alive husband about a gazillion times. I'm still not sure it was the right thing to do... :)

My biggest thanks has to go the world's greatest cyclist (on certain, small stretches of road), my 90% awesome husband, Stu. Thanks for buying me the laptop - this book's for you.

Finally, to Lissie. Sorry, I've spent a bit too much time on my laptop recently, but now #Forfeit's done we can finish the book we're working on.

Big love
Caroline
x

She's nearly perfect – He's almost the one

Hubble Bubble, the Vet's in Trouble

When Patrick's caught *in flagrante* with a local beauty queen,
his father delivers an ultimatum: one more newspaper scandal and
Patrick will be out on his ear. Desperate not to lose his job at the
family veterinary practice, Patrick needs to avoid trouble
– and girls like Libby.

The Ballerina's Broken

She's a headline waiting to happen and mourning her
short-lived career as a dancer, Libby casts a wiccan spell to
summon a new love: Good-looking, honest, non-brown eyes,
English, good with animals… in a nutshell, she summons Patrick.

And the Old Witch is Dead

But fighting Libby's love spell will be the least of Patrick's
problems when a woman dies from a ketamine overdose
– Ketamine stolen from his surgery.

Witchcraft, Scandal, Murder…
Will anyone find their perfect Somebody?

WWW.CAROLINEBATTEN.CO.UK